The Sixth Traveler

A Novel

Kevin M. Faulkner

Copyright © 2021 Kevin M. Faulkner

Revised Edition Copyright © 2023 Kevin M. Faulkner

All rights reserved.

A Galactina Press Book

Library of Congress Control Number 2023907074

ISBN 979-8-392-91674-0 (pb)/ 979-8-392-91712-9 (hc)

1 – futuristic memoir; 2 – post-cyberpunk science fiction;
3 – friendship adventure; 4 – benevolent artificial intelligence.

The Sixth Traveler is a work of fiction. Names, characters, places, and incidents either are the product of the author's imagination or are used fictitiously. Any resemblance to actual persons, living or dead, events, or locals is entirely coincidental.

No part of this book may be reproduced, or stored in a retrieval system, or transmitted in any form or by any means, electronic, mechanical, photocopying, recording, or otherwise, without express written permission of the author.

Cover art and design by Shonn Everett

When love is the way, the Earth will be a sanctuary.

—Bishop Michael Curry (2018)

PROLOGUE

16 April 2083 (pre-implant)
Port Angeles, Washington

"Jenny, we all handle these things differently, but some choices are more helpful than others." My high school counselor, Ms. Hernandez, said this to me in a condescending tone, trying to guilt me for my truancy and general bad behavior.

It's my loss and I'll choose however I damn well please. I didn't actually say that to Ms. Hernandez, but I remember thinking it.

"Woohoo," Trinity yelled from the back seat. She was such a nerd, but it woke me from my rumination on the events from earlier in the week, and the sad expression on Ms. Hernandez's face. My Aunt Nay took me home from school that day, her compassion transforming my anger while leaving my disillusionment intact.

It was only the third time Trinity, Kat, and I had been to La Push. The first two times had been on weekends, very tame, when families with their bratty kids in gobs of sunscreen had the same idea. This time, we skipped school in the middle of the week the spring of our senior year of high school. We drove down highway 101 as fast as we could in Kat's father's convertible, one of the few manual gasoline powered cars left in all of Washington. My contribution to our endeavor was the extra surfboard for Kat—a little fish just her size—and a bottle of my dad's vodka. I knew an older boy who would buy a new one and no one would be the wiser. As for Kat, well, she was her father's kitten, so he would soon forgive and forget.

Once in the water, we paddled out on our boards, taking turns riding waves to shore until we were sunburned and exhausted. We had wetsuits to keep our bodies warm, but our feet and hands were numb. It didn't matter to me. I did not want to feel anything that day.

"Eat foam, bitches!" I called from my one-finned long board, much too big for me.

"Barney!" Trinity replied as I surfed away from my *amigas*.

We surfed until the sun set; really, too dark to be on the water. We were alone, so we didn't care. Being so young, we had no idea that it could be our last fandango. How can you know what's ahead?

By the end of the day our voices were tired from the adventure. On the ride home, I remember hearing only the sound of the wind thrashing my hair and the hum of the combustion engine burning the few gallons of gasoline we could afford.

Trinity broke the silence, "Juke, what are you gonna do at Caltech? You won't have us to drag you out anymore."

I was going to the California Institute of Technology in Pasadena, California in August where I planned to major in physics, boys, and surfing. I sort of followed in my father's footsteps; except he was an engineer and thus more practical, while I took to the basics and the theory. I was graduating high school a year ahead, so I was just sixteen. I would miss my girls, but it had to be done.

"Nothing . . . surf." Life was arbitrary, why should I waste it on anything that didn't give me the rush I felt that day.

"We'll visit you," Kat said, looking over at me as she drove us home.

"If you're going to drink that, you need to put this thing on auto," I said to Kat as she took a swig from the bottle of vodka. She pressed *Auto*, leaned back, and closed her eyes.

"You're a bad girl."

"But that's what you love about me," she said, a broad grin on her face that made me glad to be alive.

I imagined that Kat was as light as a cloud with an immutable joy in her heart. I loved and envied her at the same time, complex emotions I felt but knew nothing about. I could only smile back and wish.

The Sixth Traveler

PART ONE

FLASHES OF LIGHT

ONE

Implant Record Date 21 October 2094
San Diego

"Jenny, is this a good time?"

Though it was a question, I had the feeling that *now* was indeed the time. Erissa Chavez's tone was yielding but seeing her and John Mar together was ominous. John was my supervising partner, and Erissa the senior managing partner at Lackley, Bei and Chavez, LLC, the law firm where I found myself, more out of happenstance than ambition.

"Okay," I said as they pulled up in chairs on the other side of my plastiwood desk. I pushed my computer screen off to the side so I could face them, though I thought about staying hidden behind it.

"You look serious," I said, playfully. "Is there a problem?"

"No, no problem. It's been a while since we've chatted and I want to check in on you," Erissa answered.

"Oh, okay." We made small talk for a few minutes before Erissa got to what brought her to my office.

"We want to talk to you about your direction with the firm, how things are going," Erissa said. *Oh no*, I thought. Apparently, she could see the "oh no" on my face because she quickly followed with, "Now, don't worry, we have this talk with all the firm's associates. It's simply your turn."

"Sure," I said with feigned composure.

"You've been with us for almost four years now?" John asked.

"Three-and-a-half." I was a patent attorney, hired back in 2091. Since I had an undergraduate degree in physics and was the only one with such a degree at the firm, I specialized in handling all physics-related technology, little of that as there was coming in. I knew what was to follow in this conversation, partly as a result of that fact.

"How do you feel about your progress in the firm so far?" Erissa asked. "Do you feel challenged?" Erissa was commanding woman, slender and always well dressed. She wore her hair unabashedly gray, and was persuasively confident, but coy when she needed to be. She was a renowned litigator and it showed.

"Yes, I do. I feel good. I'm happy here," I lied. Truthfully, I was as challenged as I wanted to be.

"Good," Erissa replied. "I'm glad to hear. We have been happy with the work you have done, especially Haledon Pries." Erissa was referring to a company that I drafted some cases for this year, and some contract work. "The quality is good, but your total number of hours is a little low."

"Jen, I pulled up your billable hour history," John followed. "We see that in your first year you billed about fifteen hundred hours, which is typical of a first-year associate, and between sixteen and seventeen hundred the next two years, but this year is almost over, and you have only billed fourteen hundred. We are a little concerned."

"There hasn't been much work for me," I said, trying not to sound defensive.

"Jenny, in order to ensure our associates' success, we like to see at least nineteen hundred hours a year," Erissa said. "I can't pretend to know much about patent law, but I think your hours are somewhat low, especially for a fourth-year associate."

I figured there were two things going on. First, there was not a great deal of physics patent work coming into the firm. Most of the patent work was computer hardware, artificial intelligence, electrical engineering, and bioengineering. Second and most important was my surfing. My primary goal in life was to surf. I had plenty of opportunities for rainmaking here in San Diego, but they were dashed by my passion. While my fellow associates deftly worked

Kevin M. Faulkner

every angle of every issue to pad their billable hours, I managed to quickly push through my work to get to the beach.

"So, am I in trouble?" I figured I probably was.

"Not exactly," John replied. "But for the next few months, we would like for you to report directly to me on a more regular basis. We'll work out a schedule so that we meet at least once a week. I want to look over your work and help you keep your hours up."

Shit. I knew that most associates who had this talk ended up gone after six months. I was hoping to avoid that outcome by being different—the weird, misunderstood physics nerd everyone left alone.

"Jenny, I don't want you to worry, but we'd like to see some progress," Erissa said. "Please work with John, let him help you."

"Okay, I'm glad to."

Erissa nodded and looked over at John. She didn't literally clear her throat; she didn't have to.

"Is there something else?"

"Jenny," John started in a different tone. "We're wondering if you might be having any problems we should know about . . . personal problems?"

John Mar was amazingly empathetic for an attorney. He was tall, blonde, and handsome, enough so that women typically dropped whatever notions they may have had in their mind upon seeing and hearing him. He possessed a quiet charisma, down to earth with a slight intensity that worked well for him at the negotiating table or nightclub. I liked John Mar, though I was cautious with him.

"What do you mean?" I asked, wondering what plethora of things they could be referring to. My not spending much time in the office, not taking work home on the weekends, staying out late at night, the way I dress? I knew that my jeans and blouses, nice as they were, were below the standards of the fancy Italian and Korean suits the private equity attorneys wore.

"It seems some days that you come into work, well, late, and not yourself. Maybe hung over?" John suggested. My mouth must have opened.

"Before you say anything, know that we won't punish you, but we think you may need some support. The firm has a program. I'll help you out with it."

"What? No, I don't have a problem." Not true. But my problem wasn't that I was drinking, it was mostly that I just didn't care.

John held up his hands.

"I just—"

"Jenny, please understand." Erissa's moderated her tone, but continued, "In order to stay with this firm, every associate must abide by certain rules and principles. We think you can do better. You need to work closely with John on this. And if you do that, we're sure you'll make progress."

Resigned, I sat back in my chair. I did need the job after all. It paid well and I had rent to pay and boards to buy.

"I'll leave you to talk more with John," Erissa said. Trying to soften the blow, adding, "I trust you'll do fine." With that, Erissa Chavez stood up from the chair and walked to the door. Before walking out, she turned and said, "Expectations are evil, but necessary."

I looked at the door as it closed, somehow hoping the problem she had introduced to my world would leave with her. I looked at John and knew that it had not.

"So, am I on some kind of probation?" I was glad to be talking to the good cop.

"Well, maybe."

"Mmmm."

"You just need to get your hours up and try . . . to look a little more professional."

I started to protest, but knew it was true. When you are a first-year associate digging around all day in dekked cells and cloud memory, tattered jeans and blonde-streaked hair are acceptable.

Discovery was a bore. After all, you rarely saw the sun, much less a client, so how you looked didn't matter. But when you are behind a desk where clients meet with you, looks matter. That's the case even if AI bots are handling most of the work.

"The good news is that I have a project for you that will get your hours up. One of our biggest clients has some work; physics work, something about propulsion systems for spacecraft. Seems quantum mechanical. It's perfect for you." He looked over at the clock on my wall. "Let's see, it's only nine a.m. You'll need to get changed into a suit, which you can do during brownout. The clients will be here for a presentation at four this afternoon, so you have plenty of time."

"You don't like my jeans?" I joked. The brownout John referred to was the one-and-a-half-hour period starting from noon that occurred in almost every Pan American and European city. People jokingly referred to it as an enforced siesta.

John raised an eyebrow. "Well," he smiled, "you could wear sleeves to cover the . . . ." He pointed to his own arm.

"Well, you don't like my tattoo either!" I said in mock indignation. John laughed as he handed me a lytfolder brief describing what was going on that afternoon and the faces I would see. There was a cover with the subject heading *PacificEnergy, LLC*, and a mission statement of the investment group that was providing funds to various research institutes and universities.

"Let me know when you get back in the office so we can go over all of this."

I held the wafer-thin brief as John turned to leave.

"John."

"Yes," he turned back to me.

"I don't have a drinking problem or anything like that."

"I figured. We're just trying to help." He left my door open on his way out.

I looked down at the brief before me, swiping the surface to reveal the cover of the first report. Much of what was in the brief was redacted, and it was clear many pages were simply missing. But there

The Sixth Traveler

were photos of several people. Some I recognized as faces from meetings I was not invited to, but one I did recognize and knew by name: Dr. Aravinda Venkalaswaran. He was a well-known astrophysicist and inventor; both respected and controversial. He was respected because of his brilliance in theoretical particle physics, especially dark energy and the connection of blink particles, subatomic particles that were somehow related to whatever binds all matter in the known universe, and other universes to one another. He and other scientists were finding that blink particles were related from one galaxy to another the same way an electron was related from one atom to another.

He was controversial because of his research in energy, especially controlled fusion and, most contentiously, a means for rapid interstellar travel. The former was already being studied and developed worldwide, but most people were highly skeptical of the latter.

The other faces I recognized but did not know. A woman stood out in particular: Amanta Kokotova. There was not much said about her, but she was part of an organization with a lot of money and a desire to support Dr. Venkalaswaran's research. Apparently, they were looking to invest in new energy sources. The rest of the brief included financial information, funding proposals, and technical details of what Dr. Venkalaswaran had already accomplished.

This looks serious, I thought after over an hour of reading. I looked at the clock and realized it was time to gather myself to get back to my apartment to change into a business suit.

Emerging from the elevator and into the lobby, I had a sudden urge to hide, born not so much from fear as a disconnect from other people. In those moments I felt at least a little broken. I fumbled in my pack for my Valence, careful not to look up. Touching its cool, metallic surface I activated the device to form a glittering fog that enveloped me, creating a socially acceptable invisibility.

I walked outside onto Broadway Street where I grabbed a scooter, turning down Fifth Street toward the high-rise apartments north of the Gaslamp Quarter. Under my feet was a sticker that read *A Kill Switch Is Murder* and at eye level a continuous stream of media and news begging for my attention. There was something about Russia and the Caucasus, fighting over uranium, priceless in a world mostly powered by it until fusion could be perfected.

At that time of my life I was content but desolate. I had few friends and those I let in I kept at arm's length. I swore off any type of social media except for the basics. In my first year of college I cut myself, several times. My implant indicated mild depression, and doctors offered to prescribe an app to treat it, but I would always decline. I was afraid of depending on anything, and the agony of chronic insomnia seemed hip, so it was easier to choose the latter. In those days I could drink it away.

I arrived at my apartment building, with ropey light fixtures hanging from the lobby ceiling and multi-colored tiles lining the floor. I walked up two flights of stairs to my place, looking out the window at the end of the hallway to see the sun setting on San Diego Bay.

My apartment was quiet, both visually and audibly, save for the cheerful greeting from my home computer Britta when I entered.

"Hello, Jenny."

"Hey, you." The first thing I saw when I walked into my apartment was my favorite board, a three-fin short board for the smaller waves off the beaches north of San Diego. My surfboards, and the waves that I rode, represented the biggest part of my life.

"You are home early," Britta said.

"I'm in trouble."

"Oh, really?"

"I have to change into a suit, something less vagabond. So says the man."

"I'm so surprised," Britta teased.

I walked across the tiled floor to my bedroom. I took care in my world to have a place for everything: my music, coffee maker, wine, and surf boards. I liked visual simplicity, so my walls were almost bare, the color of which I changed between shades of light tan to a cherry-mocha to suit (or affect) my mood.

"I have to be a grown-up today."

"A stretch for you," Britta replied.

"Nice."

"I hope you will finally wear one of those nice suits I bought for you that you have yet to try on."

I laughed. Britta took good care of me, though I didn't appreciate it at the time. Instead, I wondered if there was a way to get her to bill my needed hours at the firm.

"The one with sleeves," I said, looking at myself in the mirror.

TWO

Implant Record Date 21 October 2094
San Diego

"So formal," I said to Dorothy, the paralegal for my group who stopped me to sign a secrecy agreement. I was headed to the firm's largest conference room to attend investor presentations when she pulled me aside.

"It's part of a secret project, John says." I pressed my finger on the acceptance queue where the top of the page read *Project Disco*.

My plan was to sneak into the room wearing my blue, fitted suit, hair pulled back with as little fanfare as possible. I straightened my jacket, pushed a stray strand of my hair back, and opened the conference room door. I'll never forget what I was thinking as I walked into that room: *Let's see where this leads.*

But for the projection screen at one end of my firm's largest conference room, there was little lighting. Erissa Chavez once said that darkness encouraged dissent by enhancing anonymity. I believed that. Yet the man before the rest of us mortals provided his own illumination.

As quietly as I could, I sat down in the front closest to the main event. The lights dimmed as a projector gradually lit the room, at first filling it with the glow of the Milky Way Galaxy then zeroing in on our little corner of a spiral arm. The speaker, Dr. Aravinda Venkalaswaran, was tall and cool, speaking with a slight Indian accent and with a calmness that was reassuring, weaving a story of his research and outlook as if he were telling a story to a much younger audience. It worked wonders, as I could look back and see that everyone was paying rapt attention to each word he spoke.

He gradually moved into more specific aspects of the spacecraft he was building and its general inner-workings. He pointed to 3D schematics, simplified to highlight key components. He was emphasizing the concept of rapid interstellar transfer of mass from one point in the galaxy to another. Without looking back, as I felt it would only kill my nerve, I started asking questions.

"So is the traversal a linear function of time, distance, or mass?"

Venkalaswaran cleared his throat and looked directly at me.

"It's more an *event* than a speed," Venkalaswaran replied. "We have been able to achieve traversal of great distances independent of a time function."

"Meaning?" someone in the audience asked.

Venkalaswaran smiled. "Meaning, I'm not building a time machine, only a means of traveling really fast." There was some humor in how he said that, and smiles filled the room.

Though my implant, a device every American attorney was implanted with upon being licensed, captured Venkalaswaran's words, and my thoughts to go with them, the weight of it all was lost. Hearing this man describe to a room full of people the basics of interstellar travel was surreal, something I remember feeling mostly in my gut.

"Jenny, do you think this will be a problem with the patent office?" The question came from behind me as Venkalaswaran held a confident pose in front of the screen. Other than five high level partners of my law firm, and several other lower-level attorneys, the other six or seven people sitting around the table were some sort of investors. I couldn't quite place the accent, but I thought I recognized the woman from the briefs John had given me.

"It's hard to say," I replied, already busy editing the output from my implant.

"So, let's move to the 3D in front of you so that I can better explain quantum mass-transfer," Venkalaswaran said, motioning to the middle of the conference table where several co-orbiting objects appeared.

Kevin M. Faulkner

Venkalaswaran's invention was based on quantum mass-transfer (QMT), the aim of which was usually instantaneous displacement of inanimate objects. QMT competed with, and was sometimes wrongly referred to, as faster-than-light travel. While there were several theories on how QMT would operate, Venkalaswaran's approach was mostly quantum mechanical, the creation of a sphere of sorts around an object that distorted the space around it. Venkalaswaran did this through a process he referred to as *augmented quasi-luminescent autofission perturbation*. I called it *lighting* in the patent applications, and the device that carried it out a *quantum lighter*, or *lighter*. Venkalaswaran's technical discussion predictably elicited blank stares and some polite nods. Luckily, he refrained from the mathematical deduction of his system, and all the chemistry that went into the porous silver ceramics that would carry a human to the stars and back.

"Would the government even let us patent such a thing? What about the Indian government?" Someone asked.

The questions wouldn't go away, and my patience was running thin. I was usually out of the office by now and in the water.

"Of course, they will," I barked. Glancing at John, I realized I'd better soften up. "Every country has its own rules about filing patent applications based on where the inventing occurred and the citizenship of the inventor. We have some time to decide."

"How much time?" The voice asked impatiently. While shorter was always better for clients in a rush, I had to be realistic. Considering how novel this technology was I figured the drafting AI would not be able to handle much of it. I would have to do most of the writing myself.

"I think I can file the first patent applications by the end of next month if I can get started this week."

"What if the Chinese come after us and tie this thing up in some international court?" another voice asked.

Though we were in North America, the prize was China, as they led the world technologically. Their patent system was the strongest of any country, where courts usually favored patentees over infringers, and the government intervened to enforce a patentee's rights, well beyond anything in the West. While the US was still a technological powerhouse, it was China and India that drove innovation, vying with the rest of the world in a Confucian-driven game of intellectual might.

"They may file an action in International Court," I replied, "but Dr. Venkalaswaran's device sounds different enough that they couldn't completely stop you."

"I don't believe it will work," a whispered voice behind me quipped. There were reasons for the skepticism. Serious QMT gained prominence Hu Meixing at Beijing University, famously claiming to be the first to create a manufactured object that could side-step relativistic barriers. Her seminal paper, published in 2081, began with the Chinese proverb "If there is a wave there must be wind." She called the device a *xing bo* or *star wave*, after the quantum wave-nature of the device. The legend was that her young daughter, unable to pronounce proper Chinese tunes, said *shinbo*. Since then, the scientific literature and patent landscape exploded with references to shinbo.

As Venkalaswaran's talk progressed, the images on the screen behind him, and the 3D, changed from theoretical particle-wave cartoons to prototype engineering drawings.

"So, what effect would QMT have on an actual human?" someone else asked. The goal of Dr. Venkalaswaran's work was to build a spacecraft capable of ferrying humans between the stars. A major hurdle in building a practical interstellar vehicle would be keeping the human occupant safe. In a mode of transport that behaved as a wave, a mode contrary to living things, safety was an obvious concern. Through the accident of scientific discovery, studies confirmed that exposure to accelerated blink particles (Heavy Higgs-H^2? Still a debated issue) caused dizziness, seizures, nauseous, confusion, and longer-term neurological problems.

"The proper test of such a device would confirm the ability to maintain a normal Newtonian environment for the human experiencing the travel," Dr. Venkalaswaran answered. "Thus, there would be little to no time dilation, mass effects, or change in inertial or latent energy. I believe I have achieved that. Preliminary testing has shown a departure event and arrival, so—"

"But not on a human," someone broke in.

"True," Venkalaswaran replied. Most of the reported shinbos had originated in China—notoriously secretive. The rumor was that the one living thing that did experience QMT, a mouse, had died.

"But I can change that, I can make it safe for humans," Venkalaswaran said. This statement was met with murmurs of skepticism from around the table. I looked up at Venkalaswaran for his reaction. He maintained an open, confident manner that never appeared to wither, even when those around him were in doubt.

"With that, I have reached the end of my formal presentation, but I would be happy to answer any more questions."

Before anyone had a chance, Erissa stood and walked to the front of the room. She motioned for the lights, and said, "Perhaps we can save questions for dinner. Dr. Venkalaswaran, thank you so much for being with us today."

Turning to the room, Erissa said, "Ladies and gentlemen, it has certainly been a lively discussion. Let's thank Dr. Venkalaswaran for his presentation, and for being such a good sport." Everyone clapped, some moving to shake his hand. Though many in the room were skeptics, it wasn't every day that you met a future Nobel laureate. "Let's adjourn to the banquet room."

Chatter enveloped the room as the meeting closed. The conference room doors opened and waiters with trays of food and wine appeared in the hallway. Dr. Venkalaswaran's wife, Dr. Nithia Madan, entered the conference room to greet members of the committee as they passed by her. She was warm and elegant, I guessed the same age as Venkalaswaran, in her early forties.

Erissa spoke again, "If you haven't already met her, I'd like to introduce Dr. Venkalaswaran's wife, Dr. Nithia Madan." Dr. Madan smiled as Erissa spoke, softening hardened hearts as she greeted the guests. As the investors and observers left the room, I could hear her say to a group of men, "He is obsessed with his work and his students, but still a devoted father, and a pretty good husband." She winked as they all chuckled.

The chatter of friendly voices growing distant, I kept writing, asking last minute questions of Dr. Venkalaswaran. Grateful for the quiet of the room, I paused, looking up at him. In this atmosphere of charged skepticism, he radiated calm assurance.

I, on the other hand, wasn't sure I wanted the attention I felt I was about to get, and though the prospects of the technology were thrilling, I could feel myself pulling away from Venkalaswaran, this room, and the people around me.

* * *

I shivered in the cold morning air of Black's Beach. The wetsuit I wore did little good as my exposed hands were numb from paddling in the dark water. Yet, I hardly noticed, as I was absorbed in the disquiet of suddenly being at the center of activity since Venkalaswaran's presentation.

Disco was the name of the project I had signed up for. I guessed that name referred to the funky appearance of Venkalaswaran's creation projected in 3D. John Mar made it clear that this was a preliminary stage of the project, and that there would be further levels of secrecy with fewer people involved as it got deeper. I wasn't sure what I thought of that.

Paddling, I made my way further out into the surf, looking at the waves break at the shore, judging when the next swell would arrive from the back wash of the tide.

How do I manage this? My mind was torn. I wanted in, yet couldn't resist saying through my chattering teeth, "I just hope they leave me out of this." The project was a big deal, and it was encroaching my space. John was supportive but I could sense the burden. I felt uneasy being a part of unleashing something so profound. Breaking a barrier created by God with a power assumed by man felt wrong.

Pulling myself from that rail, I mounted a wave.

The Sixth Traveler

THREE

Implant Record Date 2 November 2094
San Diego to Bengaluru

I had been working with Dr. Venkalaswaran for two weeks since his presentation, going between San Diego and his major collaborator, the Jet Propulsion Laboratory (JPL) in Pasadena. My first real interaction with Dr. Venkalaswaran was on this trip to Bengaluru, India, visiting the Institute where he was a professor and carried out his research.

"You can call me Venka. That's what my students call me at Berkeley," he told me.

"But not your students in Bengaluru, they're too polite," I teased. We sat together in business class on a rapid-transport liner.

"Did you grow up in San Diego, Jenny?" Aside from legal matters, it wasn't often that someone asked me anything.

"Actually, no. I went to school in California, and decided to stay there for work. I grew up in a little town outside of Seattle. Then later we moved west of there to Port Angeles."

"Do you ever go back?"

"A couple of times a year. My brother and father are still there." It wasn't like me to be so open, but Venka had a disarming nature that made it easy.

"Studying physics at Caltech must have been a challenge," Venka said. "I know some of the professors there. It is highly competitive."

"Yeah, it didn't always leave a lot of time to party." Truthfully, I had plenty of time, it just sounds bad to say so.

"I can imagine." He said this as he turned to the passing flight attendant to ask for a drink. Behind his shirt collar I noticed a dark patch on his neck. It was otherwise hidden, but I could clearly see it now and thought right away of what it might be: skin irritation from an over-used cognitive amplifier port.

"So, why did you go to law school?" I got that question all the time and dreaded it. In my experience scientists especially disliked attorneys.

"Oh," I said, my mind still on his raw neck, "a friend of mine is an attorney. She gave me the idea to go to law school. I thought it was a way to make my own hours; to have more control over my time." I replied. Then, under my breath, "Though it hasn't quite worked out that way."

"I see," Venka said.

"So, how long have you been with the Indian Institute of Science?" I asked, distracting myself from thinking about Venka's neck. I was still taken aback by the port, his skin clearly burned in the area of his neck where an under-skin temperale plaque would typically be implanted to pick up the input feed from an external processor. For the hipsters that didn't care what people thought, there were through-skin ports that could be physically accessed by a standard plug, but someone like Venka, a professor and semi-public figure, would prefer the discretion of something beneath the surface. As long as it was not overused it would not irritate the skin.

"I started teaching after I finished my graduate work in Cambridge," Venka replied. "So, I started about ten years ago, in 2083. I got my first grant approved two years later."

"You have worked with Adeane since then?" I had heard that he and Chase Adeane met at Cambridge, and I knew that Adeane was the chief engineer for Project Disco, working for JPL, a part of NASA. NASA co-sponsored the QMT work with the Indian Institute, not an uncommon thing these days of short budgets and worldwide talent. The rumor was that Adeane and Venkalaswaran did not always get along. I wanted to find out if it were true.

"Yes, we have worked together quite a bit, usually by distance. He is mostly at JPL in Pasadena, while I work out of the Institute in Bengaluru."

"Easy enough to phaeton one another," I said.

"Yes, it's been very productive."

"To say the least," I had heard of Dr. Venkalaswaran in college, and I think he may have even given a talk once while I was a student, though I was embarrassed to bring it up because I obviously didn't go. There was already buzz of him winning a Nobel Prize for his work. His face has adorned the cover of many magazines, yet I could see his humility in the dust on his shoes and sincerity in his eyes.

"Yes, I have been blessed."

I was beginning to think he was more than blessed. The sore on his neck made me think he was amping-up, that is, connecting directly to a computer or network for cognitive amplification. In most countries amping-up was regulated like a drug, and it can be as addictive as heroin. Several years ago, someone who had won the Nobel Prize in medicine had it rescinded when it was discovered that they had amped-up.

"Where does the funding come from?"

"Several places; grants from the Indian government and NSF, NASA."

"And PacificEnergy?" It was more a statement than a question.

"Yes, an investment group. They have been very interested in our work," Venka said, somewhat hesitantly. I could tell it bothered him. I wondered about it myself and changed the subject.

"So, what did you do to deserve Dr. Madan?"

"Ha, yes. We met in undergraduate school in Delhi, she was going to medical school and I was a physics student. I lectured in a physics class she was forced to take." He had a whimsical look as he talked about his wife. "She was beautiful, and I was smitten right away. I was from the wrong type of family though. Her parents were highly educated, while mine were working class people living in the far eastern region of India. So, I worked hard to impress her. I wore

Kevin M. Faulkner

my best clothes to lecture, combed my hair, and talked with as much confidence as possible."

I nodded as he spoke, eager to hear how he won over a young woman he clearly adored. I could see in his face he still felt that way.

"By the end of the semester I found out which dormitory she lived in. It was off campus, a group home with several other girls. A friend of mine knew who she was and I found a way to be around her at social events and celebrations."

"Really, so what kinds of things did you do?"

"There were lots of celebrations. Kids took every opportunity to celebrate with food and dance. The best celebrations were when the school would set up movies outside to watch and all the students would gather, sometimes hundreds. That was where I got to know Nithia."

"And then what?"

"We dated and followed each other after that. I finished school and accepted a graduate position at Cambridge. I stayed behind a year teaching and doing research with a professor while she finished her undergraduate studies. We had our first child while I was at Cambridge and she was doing rotations. Once I was done with my post-doctoral work I took the position at the Institute in Bengaluru and Nithia became a surgeon at the largest hospital in the city, followed by two more children. It was a busy time."

"You're a busy man."

"Yes. How about you, do you have someone special?"

"Well, I was with a guy a few months ago, but we ended it." In fact, I had ended it.

"Was he a surfer too?"

"Ha. No, I think that was the problem. That, and his obsession with games and electronic devices. I can take a little bit of that sort of thing, but it was just too much."

"Sounds like you did the right thing," Venka said. "Speaking of surfing, I see you have brought your surfboard with you."

The Sixth Traveler

"Yes, I'm hoping to catch some waves while I am in India. I plan to take a hopper or rail to Mangaluru and bounce around there for at least a day or two."

"That is a good idea. Play is good for the soul. I see you already know that."

I could only nod as he laughed, my mouth full of wine. I wondered if he also used AI for play as well as for his profound discoveries in quantum physics. I suddenly had a different take on Venka. It brought him down to earth for me, but I was intrigued.

* * *

Two weeks later, I was back in my office in San Diego. I could always work better alone there, with the door shut and no distractions. My notes were scattered on my pad or captured on my implant. From there I could download it all onto my computer where they could be compiled and organized automatically. I cannot imagine how this worked a hundred years ago, it was enough just to decipher the output and translate that into patent descriptions, claims, and figures.

I kept fiddling with how I was going to define one of the most important terms of Venka's patents, *lighting*. I had narrowed my description to:

> The term 'lighting' refers to the generation of augmented quasi-luminescent auto-fission perturbation through the high-energy helium-3 fusion induced creation of a rapid oscillation (through red-only gravitons) waveform around a mass with a forced asymmetric singularity at one node to achieve quantum mass transfer (QMT) of said mass through space in three dimensions, exclusive of a time element. The term 'quasi-luminescent' refers to the highly luminescent process in visible wavelengths, which may generate high

Kevin M. Faulkner

energy photons (e.g., ≥ 100 eV) outside the visible spectrum that preferably predominates. The quantum lighter ('lighter') is the said mass (e.g., apparatus, spacecraft) designed to conduct the lighting and to move with the asymmetrical wave perturbation of the space thus generated by the augmented quasi-luminescent auto-fission event. The movement of the lighter from its origin to its intended destination is called an 'event.'

I leaned into the CAD screen on my desk, somewhat overwhelmed at the complexity of the engineering drawings taken from Venka's notebooks. The key was to set his invention apart from publications and patents that described shinbo, as these prior art disclosures would be the biggest obstacle to patenting Venka's technology.

Looking at the patent drawings, one would easily mistake the lighter as the nightmarish sculpture of a deranged artist. The main structure was essentially a flattened sphere with shiny protruding plates. A pin cushion or disco ball would describe it even better, except the heads of the pins are much larger, and preferably square. A cutaway diagram, such as Figure 2B in the second of five primary patent applications I was drafting, showed what I called *tympani plates* evenly spaced around, and substantially covering the outside of a flattened outer sphere, attached to the surface of that outer sphere by at least one contact terminal that housed power lines.

The name tympani came from the shape the first silver alloy conductor plates happened to take as a result of our understanding of how subatomic blink particles would behave when accelerated. It can't go unsaid that the motivation for choosing that name, a name I used in all the patent applications, was an undergrad intern at JPL. A pot-headed but gentle soul named Craig (name changed to protect him from certain illegal things he may have done) used several of the early devices as a drum, discovering they made various dinging sounds upon being beaten by a plastic stick. Some of them were more annoying than others. The name *drum plates* sounded too ordinary for

The Sixth Traveler

the physicists in the room so they came up with the name *tympani plates*, and it stuck.

The plates were attached to the outer sphere of the vessel that surrounded yet another inner sphere of the same shape but smaller size, creating a space between the outer and inner sphere occupied by the so-called *Newton-shell*, the critical component of Venka's invention that separated what occurred on the outside from the inside of the vessel. Inside that inner sphere was the area used to accommodate the occupants, the star travelers, and the controlled fusion drive that created the power needed for the tympani plates to light.

How deep do I want to go? I asked myself. I could feel the nudge from John Mar but wasn't sure if I wanted to get involved with something so committed. Yet, Venka's enthusiasm was infectious, eating away at my jealously guarded personal space and time.

Amid my thoughts, I heard a knock at my office door, and I sat up.

"Come in."

It was John. He was low-key, even friendly. I was thankful for his oversight after the talk he and Erissa had with me weeks ago, and I had gotten used to him. He was reasonable. Today, as always, he was in a gray suit and blue tie with eyes to match. Though a nice guy, I kept my distance, meeting his warmth with a slight chill.

"Is this an okay time?"

"Sure, it's our usual time. I'm free."

"Good," John said as he entered my office, closing the door behind him and taking a seat across from me.

"So, I see you've done a lot of work this week. The meetings in Bengaluru went well it seems. I hear good things about you from Dr. Venkalaswaran."

"I suppose he tolerates me," I said, wondering if I should bring up Venka's overused port. I thought better of it, at least for now. "He only barely tolerates his engineer, Chase."

"I heard," John said, frowning.

"It's not uncommon among co-inventors. It's like fighting over a lover."

"Really?"

"You'd be surprised at how emotional these things can get," I replied. Every patent attorney knows that there are few things so emotional as ownership of an invention. Not all inventors are like that; I don't think Chase was so much, but this thing was definitely Venka's baby.

"Well, that will have to be a relationship to manage. It'll be good for you."

"I suppose," I said, saving what was on my computer and closing the window.

I could see him looking out of the corner of his eyes at me. Concerned but clearly pleased. I had heard some things about John: rough childhood, the military, and then the district attorney's office. These days the gossip was about his girlfriend, a woman he'd started dating when he was at the DA's office. She was a prosecutor herself, and beautiful.

He stood up and walked over to the window, looking out. He seemed to have a lot on his mind. "So, are the patents filed yet?" John grinned, knowing they weren't.

"By tomorrow if you want, tell me where."

"Good," he said, as if speaking to someone on crowded Broadway Street below. The city of San Diego was huge, and skyscrapers blotted the horizon as far as the eye could see. We had a nice view of San Diego Bay from our offices, at least until someone put up the next cloud-reaching skyscraper.

"Not that I'm complaining." In fact, the work was exhilarating, truly visionary technology, but with an undercurrent of uncertainty. Nonetheless, a prototype was slowly coming together at the Institute in Bengaluru, parts of which were shipped from JPL, a sophisticated spacecraft that would carry the first star traveler away from our solar system.

"And you have your hours up."

The Sixth Traveler

"Yeah, really." That was an understatement. I thought about what was in front of me, the meaning of it all. "John, you know I am working from the blueprints for the lighter they plan to launch. It is designed for a single person. I don't understand, why don't they use an android?"

"Our investors want a human on board, no machines."

The investors again. Though I had signed a secrecy agreement for this Project Disco, it was only to let me in ankle deep. Much more went on behind doors closed to me, especially as it related to the investors. My irritation only thinly veiled, I asked, "Can you at least tell me who are all the people, and what are the meetings about? I know these PacificEnergy people are some kind of investors."

"Yes," John started.

"Their mission statement said they are into energy development, nuclear and fusion, this stuff is not exactly that," I pointed to the patent drawings.

"Yes," John replied. He was open most of the time, but on this subject he kept silent. He gently put me off, and replied, "You said you have to get a license, or permission, from India?"

"I'm twenty-seven and I'm already too old for this."

John smiled but kept silent, so I answered him instead, "It depends on where we file first."

"Is that so?" John asked as if talking to someone else, staring out the window. After some silence, he looked back at me. "I'm sorry, Jenny, I can't say more right now. We want you to go ahead and file with the Indian Federation first, we want that in the bag, and China."

I looked at my computer screen, not surprised at his answer, but thinking about the possible consequences of what we were doing. Though the details of the technology were becoming clear to me, everything else about the project remained a mystery. Not uncommon for an associate in a big law firm, but the secrecy here was more deliberate.

"If we file in India without getting permission from the US Patent Office, our rights could be revoked altogether," I said.

"We're thinking our rights may not mean anything here anyway. We'd like to have legitimacy in the States, but we can't risk having nothing at all in India and China."

"Okay, I get it. Anyway, I'll make it happen. I just can't guarantee anything." I paused, motioning toward the engineering drawings in front of me, "This is heavy stuff—it's hard to say."

"Yes, I know."

* * *

It was a relief to be on my surfboard again. Working so many hours was cutting into my time on the waves; time that I guarded with a sort of passive vengeance. The patent applications on file, I had never seen the office so busy, but myself so alone, fighting even harder against the tide of attention. The people around me hadn't changed. I'd get questions from nowhere, with no context, only urgency. Before I left the office today someone asked, "Can you explain the terms *sub-light ket* and *supra-light ket*?" Those faces popping into my office only long enough to get an answer. They disappeared behind a door, but the strangeness never did.

What the heck?

An impulse ran through me: *Where was my place in all of this?* I was torn, and I tried to ignore my gut telling me that something was not right. *Rarely do you know if you should go with the flow of the moment or with the warning in your head*, I thought to myself, *at least not until it's too late.*

"The woods are empty, the witches are in my room," I sang to myself as a swell drew me into a coming wave.

The Sixth Traveler

FOUR

Implant Record Date 14 March 2095
San Diego

"It's not a big deal to change these things out," I said to Chase Adeane, referring to the chemical battery in his phone. It must have been old, because chemical batteries, which had an ironic name because they were devoid of what most people thought of as chemicals, took forever to go bad. They could usually be recharged hundreds of times, and last for days on a single charge.

"Well, I can't figure it out, don't sue me," he replied.

Good one. It had been only a few weeks since the patent applications were filed. Now we sit and strategize about it all while we waited. And in between, Chase and I would hang out, and maybe flirt a little. Somehow, I think he arranged some of it.

"I've never installed one of the new ones."

"Really?" It occurred to me that he was acting the fool as a come on.

"Here, let me see it." I inspected his phone. Sometimes I think they make these things too thin. You have to pay someone with special tools to change the battery.

We were in between meetings at the firm, waiting in my office during a break. They were in a big conference hall on the other side of the building, so my office was the perfect escape, away from the traffic.

"Do you understand what they were talking about?" Chase suddenly asked. "What are these investors looking for?"

I wondered too, not sure where it was all heading.

"I don't know. Something about your little project. They're interested in energy, especially nuclear, but also the new stuff, the new fusion processes. Your work is part of that."

Deriving energy from fusion processes—making energy by fusing little atoms like hydrogen and helium—was just becoming a reality. However, it was still expensive and technologically out of reach for much of the world, and given the inclination away from fossil fuels, much of the world was looking at advanced fission, or nuclear, energy—making energy from splitting big atoms like uranium and plutonium. In an energy starved world any advances in this area were crucial.

"Is it me, or are most of these people from Russia?" Chase asked.

"Southern Russia, I think. The Caucasus. It's an energy-poor region so it makes sense that they are looking." I got up to get something from my desk that would help me open his phone case so I could remove the used battery.

"Doesn't the government have some kind of sanctions?"

Good question. There was a time when the US government could effectively sanction countries or regimes it didn't agree with, but with power spread more evenly around the world now, sanctions had a spotty effect. Everyone had to hedge their bets.

"Yes, but I'm not sure how effective they are," I replied.

"I don't understand, can't they get oil from the Gulf states? They're so close."

"I don't think it's so simple. There are the mountains and then there are politics. The fossil fuel infrastructure is rusting. They may not even be able to get it there. In any case, the governments in that region of the world haven't played nice with one another for centuries. I think they are isolated between Russia, who seems to use them as some sort of pawn, and Iran, who doesn't trust them."

I rummaged in my desk drawer for a paper clip, one I found in an old box that hadn't been thrown away, a relic of a past time.

"Found it." I sat back down next to Chase, grabbing his phone to press an inset keyhole with the paper clip to pry the old battery out. I tossed the used battery into the trash.

"You can throw those things away?" Chase asked.

"Good! I see y'all recycle in Texas."

"I ain't as smart as a Caltech gal, I reckon."

"So let me guess where you went to school."

"Deep in the heart of Texas."

I laughed, which I'm sure he loved. Chase was two years older than me, from the pan handle region of Texas. He went to undergraduate school in Austin, and Cambridge for graduate school in micro-engineering, a relatively new field in material science and mechanical engineering on a quantum-scale. He was somewhat of a prodigy. Except for the suit and tie he had on for the meeting, he was every bit the outdoorsman, with copper brown hair and beard, at least six feet tall and strapping. He looked as if he'd just come from a hunt with nothing but a crossbow and some string. In January. Rarely without a grin on his face, Chase was—and still is—good-natured, though I think he was pretty ambitious.

"So, you put the new battery in like this . . ."

"I know I design spaceships, but when it comes to stuff like this, I'm an idiot." Men always try, and often succeed, at getting to a woman using this ploy. The hapless fool who needs a kind, compassionate woman to help. Not a bad ruse, so if I half-way like a guy, I play along.

"Now, let's see if it will boot up." I pressed the indent on the side and waited. "When did you get this thing?"

"I think around seven years ago."

"Wow," I said as I worked, "I am amazed you can even download the app for *Hit or Kiss* on this." *Hit or Kiss* was a reality show where you bid on actors to do certain tasks, like eat a worm or kiss a frog, while you goaded other players into betting higher than you, all for some prize. It's wildly popular. I thought it was vaguely disturbing, so I never played, but admittedly, I followed vicariously through others.

"I can't. Speaking of which, I looked for you on *Tribe*, but couldn't find you," Chase said.

"Well . . . I stay off that stuff. I don't have anyone to like me, so it's best not to know."

"Okay."

"I'm a strange girl."

"Mmmm, I like strange."

I smiled at that. "So, why are you working with someone like Venka? I get the impression you don't get along."

"Oh, we do. I like Dr. Venkalaswaran, he's a brilliant scientist, and a good guy. But I annoy him."

"Why?"

"Because I get in his face."

"About what?" I think I knew. Chase was silent while he thought about it.

"He's a genius, but . . . Venka's one of those people who takes a good idea and—"

"Takes it too far?"

"Yes. He's extremely smart and tragically dumb . . . or at least blind." Chase must already know quite well what I only suspected. He has been with Venka for a while and works with him all the time. The spot I saw on Venka's neck must be a metastasized cancer to Chase. Before I could ask him to elaborate, someone poked their head in my office.

"Show's about to start again," one of the junior attorneys, Kyle, said. I was hired about the same time as Kyle, but we rarely worked together until now. We were listening to inventor presentations with some of the same mysterious investors I had sat with before and hashing out the beginnings of agreements. Kyle was my attorney-doppelganger, digging into a single document for hours, practically sleeping over it. Kyle loved the details. He liked to say that "the devil

The Sixth Traveler

is in the details." In the back of my mind I knew it was true, but to me the angel was in the intent, and I preferred the angels. *But something's not right about the intent here.*

"Thanks, we're coming," I replied to Kyle.

I snapped the back plate of Chase's phone in place and handed it to him. "Here, I've got it. Look, it's already re-booting."

"Awesome," Chase said, appreciating my handiwork.

"You shouldn't let an attorney handle your tech work," I said, winking.

I am such a nerd, I thought as we walked back to the meeting room. I kept the conversation about Venka in the back of my mind. I wanted to know for sure, but somehow already felt protective of the guy. We all have a right to our secrets, I have mine. I should let him have his.

* * *

"Once you've downloaded a record of today's meeting, let me have a transcript if you don't mind," John Mar said as we walked back to our offices from the meeting.

"Sure." The download he was talking about would come from my implant. It was somewhat incorrect to say that these things were *required* for US attorneys, but practically speaking, they may as well be. Attorneys were deemed guardians of the truth, so the tagging of attorneys started years ago after the drama years ago in a major law firm that involved stealing client's money, murder, revenge murder, then a big lawsuit that ended up in the Supreme Court over partner liability. In sort, law firms wanted more control over each other and their subordinates.

By the 2050's the technology to implant simple recording devices went mainstream. These devices took in data independently, that is, they were simply audio and video recorders of what went on around the user. In the 2050's implants were designed to record more than conversation and locations, they could determine a person's mood, then more complex emotions, and by the 2060's they could record complex thoughts. These later implants did more than the simple recorders of the past, they worked through the user's brain to take in and interpret the data from the implantee's senses, and even modify mood and behavior. Thoughts (or inputs) were translated by any number of software algorithms into something useful—the most common was the Lambert-Troch Eviscercode, a common LTEC (or Eltech) app on everyone's phone and computer. The downloads from my implant are what allowed me to recall the details of my life, even years later.

The temptation to overuse this technology, and manipulate it for darker purposes, proved overwhelming. Most all employers used the technology to keep their employees honest, and governments used it to track the locations and thoughts of their citizens. I justified having a device planted inside of me by telling myself that I was just one among many. After all, didn't it make us all safe when the government could track the bad guys? I could placate myself like this when it bothered me, but a deeper part of me never felt good about it.

Wanting nothing more than to be left alone, I felt betrayed each time my hand would gravitate to my neck where I could feel the hard bump of my implant. Implant technology found use in treating such things as depression, anxiety, and bipolar disorders, which I believed was a magnificent achievement, but I was never clear why I had to give up my privacy for it.

"I'll download it to your site before I leave," I said. "I'll call Venka tonight from home to discuss the strategy."

"Great, thanks Jenny." A well-dressed woman was standing a few steps from his door down the hall, and he waved at her. I guessed it was his girlfriend from the district attorney's office.

The Sixth Traveler

Of course, he has a personal life. It wasn't long before I headed out for my personal life. In the near dark I found a scooter and rode silently home that evening, letting the wind whip my hair. During this time of my life, my ride home was one of my favorite times of the day.

While my work life was gaining momentum, I tried to maintain an undisturbed personal life. Law life was cramping my style, so while I hit the beach less the last couple of months, I hit it whenever I could. The time I used to spend daydreaming was now at a premium.

"Hello Britta," I said as I entered my quiet apartment.

"Good evening, Jenny."

As fanciful as it may seem, I stoked a dream of working in a little law office where I could step out the door, walk across a plastiwood porch, and down a broad flight of stairs where my bare feet would sink into the sand of a beach. It would only be moments before I was on the water on my surfboard, a cool little fish. I would draft my patent applications behind a computer in an open space in the back of such practice, overlooking the crashing waves. And next door would be a little bar where my surfer friends and I could have a drink and let our bodies dry out, the salt from the ocean still sticking to our skin as we soaked our innards in a bottle of wine.

That job, I learned, did not exist. Needing a *real* job, I settled in San Diego. The country was gradually transformed during the 40's to the 80's in the transition to a mix of energy sources and improved water supply. Advanced desalination technology converted what had essentially become a desert into livable green space. An improved power supply from Lebedev-type nuclear energy drove growth. The job market was booming, research was happening, and companies were inventing and making things. When this occurs patent attorneys follow.

Most people who go into patent law know they want to go into patent law. It is an unusual niche of the legal world because it is the only area of law that requires its practitioners to have a particular type of undergraduate education. I went to school at Berkeley. They had the best intellectual property program in the state, so it made sense. In the fall of my third year got several offers from law firms and one or two in-house. I could have gone to a much larger firm. I chose Lackley, Bei and Chavez in San Diego, a firm that specialized in international transactions, government affairs and consulting. Lackley attracted me in part because, at the time, it was in a sleepy corner of the intellectual property world.

The idea of being in the slow lane appealed to me. I was not particularly ambitious; I simply wanted a job that was interesting enough that it would keep me gainfully employed but didn't bother me so much that I couldn't surf and otherwise hide. At Lackley, I swam in a legal sea of international relations, contracts, litigation, and a big merger practice. I was not the only patent attorney in the firm, they had a small IP practice, but I was the only one with a physics background, and in the legal profession, in addition to being in a separate class due to being a patent lawyer, you were further separated out by your technical background. So, I lived in a rarefied world, and liked it that way.

"Time to call Venka. Britta, can you ring him up on video?"

"Of course."

It was early Friday morning in Bengaluru and Venka was an early bird, which was lucky for me so that I did not have to stay up too late to call him.

"Jenny, he is not answering his personal phone."

Strange. "Well, he's expecting me. Call his lab, I think at least one of his students or post-docs will be in by now." Moments passed as Britta tried his lab before someone answered.

"Hello, this is the Venkalaswaran laboratory," a female voice said. Her face came up. I had met her before, a post-doc, but I could not remember her name.

"Hey there, this is Jenny Hsu calling from San Diego for Dr. Venkalaswaran, is he in?" Silence.

The Sixth Traveler

"Oh, hello Jenny," she said, embarrassing me that I could not remember her name until I noticed it on the facial recognition icon on my screen.

"Hi Pampa."

"How are you, Jenny."

"I'm good, just settling in for the evening."

"Lucky, I'm just starting."

"Oh, but working for Dr. Venkalaswaran is so easy, he's such a nice guy."

"Yes," she laughed as someone else in the background, overhearing our conversation, also laughed. I think I could hear someone say "pushover."

"So, is Venka available?"

"I'm sorry," Pampa said, awkwardly, "I'm afraid not."

"Can you check?" Pampa was hiding something. She looked away from the video camera, searching around the desk.

"Ahhh. I'm afraid he is unavailable, Jenny. Can you call back in a couple of hours?" Pampa seemed unconvinced herself.

That's inconvenient. In a couple of hours I plan on being in bed.

"Well, maybe I'll try him tomorrow, or Monday, do you think that will work?"

"Yes."

"I'll message him."

"That sounds good, perhaps Monday," Pampa said with relief.

"Okay, thanks, Pampa, have a good day."

"Thanks. You have a good evening, Jenny." The screen went blank. I sat quietly for a moment, thinking. That whole exchange was odd. Venka knew I was calling and just didn't show.

"He stood me up." I said to Britta.

"It would appear so. I think his student was hiding something."

"Mmmm. Me too."

"Well, do you want something to eat? I could prepare a meal for you."

"Sure," I said to Britta, absentmindedly, still thinking about the strange interchange with Venka's post-doc. "Food would be good."

"Britta, turn off the noise cancellation." I sat in the alcove of my living room window where I could see the city lights and hear the people below. I held my plate of veggies and a small portion of faux chicken in one hand, and ate with the other, a glass of wine at my feet.

"Weren't you going out with friends tonight?" Britta asked.

"I changed my mind. I'd rather spend it with you." I was a little worried about Venka, falling asleep on the window ledge while I imagined him traveling to the stars on an interstellar journey.

* * *

Today the water was much colder than I had expected. I'd surfed the waves at Tourmaline, north of San Diego, many times before, but this time was different; where I used to find my bliss on my board, I felt indifference creeping in. I looked over at Mag and Carlos, and I could see their usual intensity and joy in finding the next wave. I couldn't seem to get there today.

What is Venka really up to?

"What am I doing?" I asked myself, feeling I was in over my head. Yet there I was, in a world far away from the sleepy surfer village I dreamt of, with several mostly finished patent applications sitting on my computer at my office, an office I could see in my fantasy from the water as I sat on my board.

I thought about Venka, and the look on his face when I last saw him. He had created the first successful test of an unmanned faster-than-light device. We were confident it went to the planet Jupiter and back, close enough to feel its gravity and measure its magnetosphere, details that could be correlated to satellites already orbiting the planet to confirm the test to the world. His probe contacted a US satellite

The Sixth Traveler

to confirm its arrival. To say it was extraordinary was an understatement, yet the true test would have to include a human.

In the distance a bell was chiming, and I imagined it was ringing for me, urging me forward.

Kevin M. Faulkner

FIVE

Implant Record Date 10 June 2095
San Diego

Dr. Venkalaswaran and I were going to go live soon with the assistant commissioner of the US Patent Office to discuss the foreign filing license for his patent applications. I always got a little nervous, but at the same time, felt in my element in these situations. I looked up at the clock on my office wall, an archaic clock with brass gears behind an hour arm about to hit noon, then back at Venka to see him patiently waiting for my cue.

"We will have the ability to show the diagrams we discussed but be sure not to talk about anything that is not already in the patent applications on file."

"Agreed."

Whenever I met with Venka, my eyes involuntarily went to the port at his neck, that red, raw area he tried to hide beneath the collar of his shirt. Sometimes he didn't even bother. I had to force myself not to look. And though it's his own business, I hate being indifferent. I struggled with what to do. Though we were alone in my office, I looked around to make sure the door was closed so no one was around to hear. I cleared my throat and just spit it out.

"Venka," I started, pausing. "I notice that spot on your neck where you'd normally have an implant like mine. It looks like you have quite a bit of activity there." I rubbed my neck where my implant was. "Your skin is raw."

"Ahhh, that. There's no problem, the phaeton can cover it up," he replied. A *phaeton* was just the latest software or device—mostly used by law firms and governments—that could edit misspoken words and bad hair days.

"That's not really my concern."

"What concern?"

"Amping-up. It's actually illegal in the US, though I know it may not be in India."

"I'm not doing it here."

"It's not only that, there are health concerns. Think about what it's doing to your mind and body."

Venka was quiet for a while, organizing the folders on his lytfascia in front of him. "I'm fine, Jenny. My skin is just sensitive." Then he turned to me and smiled, trying to allay my fears.

"I don't know." I didn't get it: Venka was such a straight arrow otherwise. He was honest as far as I could tell, never any real contradictions. He was notorious for his integrity, even erring on the side of disclosing bad data or inconclusive test results in his research. Several years ago, there was a notorious incident where Venka published a counterargument to his own previously published paper in *Nature* relating to blink particles, sub-atomic particles that he started his career researching, a field in which he was a pioneer. He seemed blind in this one area of his life.

"Thank you, Jenny, but I'm fine."

And he did appear himself, put together, even on top of the world. I've heard stories, though, of people obtaining great heights using amplification devices only to come crashing down, hard and fast.

I was skeptical but decided to let it go for now.

"Okay, let's go to the conference room." I stood and walked to the door, leading us both to the video meeting room where we would phaeton with the assistant commissioner, likely accompanied by other examiners at the US Patent Office.

We sat at an arc-shaped table with a curved phaeton screen at its focus. I activated the screen as John Mar and other attorneys looked on. Dr. Venkalaswaran was the only inventor present, Chase Adeane opting out on my advice. He and Venka did not always get along and I did not want that to become apparent here.

Kevin M. Faulkner

I sat up straight with my hands folded, smiling (very professional) at the faces in the phaeton. My jacket sleeves covered my tattoo, but I set the phaeton to even out the bleached streaks in my hair and make my five-foot-three-inch frame a little taller. You could make the phaeton do pretty much whatever you wanted, but professionally it was best not to adjust these things too much as you might end up in the same room someday.

Eight months had gone by since we filed the patent applications and we were asked to conference with the assistant commissioner of the US Patent Office. They were considering our request to accept these patent applications after they had already been filed in the Indian Federation, so we were not in the best position. These meetings were not a common occurrence as the Patent Office usually granted a foreign filing license to most applicants. This technology was very sensitive, putting us in a defensive position. After some pleasantries, the commissioner started with questions.

"Ms. Hsu, can you describe what was intended by *neutrino activation* in claims 32 to 44 in the '898 application? Is this a fusionable event?" The answer to that was a conditional "Yes," Venka's invention built upon controlled fusion technology by creating a means of containing what I called *low density particle collisions* within a ceramic alloy hull containing rapidly moving (near light speed) but low-density helium-3 collisions within a magnetic envelope.

More questions followed, some highly technical, and either I or Venka were able to answer most. "We see that all the applications were filed in the names of Venkalaswaran, Adeane, Shimadzu, and the other inventors. Is there an assignee?"

Though most of the early inventing in these patent applications had occurred in India, the world had become such an integrated place, and travel so frequent and easy, that many of the people involved in Project Disco were at the JPL, and other places. Each country had its own rules about such matters and preferred that if something was invented in its country, a patent should be filed there

The Sixth Traveler

first, or else permission acquired through a license. It was an increasing quandary for most patent attorneys to determine which country to obtain a license from, and in which country to file the patent application.

"Not presently," I replied, distracted by the absurdity of explaining a patent application directed to a spacecraft capable of interstellar travel. This was what you got when you privatized every damn thing. A hundred years ago only governments could build spacecraft. The money for such things had long since dried up, and the public quit caring, so the cowboys rode in to take over, and my client was one of those cowboys.

"Are the applications still pending with the Indian Federation?"

"Yes." I could see the commissioner but it was a strain to make eye contact. Something about all of this bothered me.

There was a perfect storm between the two countries involved here; the United States simply did not have the tax revenue and international leverage for large space projects, and India, though rich, was politically divided and the states within the Federation were often at odds with one another. In other words, the parents are busy and distracted so the kids were throwing a party.

"Ms. Hsu, may I address Dr. Venkalaswaran directly?" The commissioner asked.

"Of course." I turned to Venka.

"Dr. Venkalaswaran," the commissioner started, "in your own words, why do you believe this technology is important?"

The phaeton camera panned in on Venka's face.

"Mr. Penske," Venka started, "thank you for asking. As you know, though the world population has leveled and may even be declining, our resources are stretched ever thinner, particularly in the still developing regions of the world. Though we have made great strides in cleaning the air, reducing and sequestering carbon, the change in Earth's climate has put pressure on an already precarious worldwide food system. A long term solution is needed. This technology will advance humans toward that solution. Humans must find a new life, but most likely it will be a world too far away for sub-light travel. Even with current technology it would take centuries to reach the nearest star beyond our solar system. So-called *matter-transfer*, or QMT technology, is quickly moving beyond being a curiosity to becoming a necessity. My invention is a practical way to take us there."

"Yes," the commissioner replied, "finding our way to another world seems inevitable. We are impressed with this work, as sensitive as it is, and we appreciate your candor, Dr. Venkalaswaran."

The commissioner continued with more technical questions. Venka, an artist whose canvas ran from quantum mechanics to micro mechanical engineering, was alive when he spoke to the commissioner. In the back of my mind was Venka's obvious use and, I suspected, abuse of cognitive amplification. It has already been decided by courts that artificial intelligence cannot invent. Article 1 of the US Constitution clearly states that Congress was to secure rights for limited times to "authors and inventors the exclusive right to their respective writings and discoveries," and the Supreme Court has already construed inventors to be *human*. I wondered how cognitive *enhancement* from AI would be treated.

Caught up in the weight of it all, I lost track of the substance of the exchange, but not of the conviction in Venka's voice. I listened to his words and I watched for the commissioner's reaction. Penske was politely skeptical, but that did not phase Dr. Venkalaswaran. His message was an echo of many before him and he still fought the same heavy tide.

The commissioner turned to the examiners sitting next to him and they spoke amongst themselves while we waited. Finally, Commissioner Penske said, "Ms. Hsu, Dr. Venkalaswaran, thank you for your time, the Office will give you our decision in our written response."

"Thank you, Mr. Penske, we appreciate your consideration." And with that, the phaeton went blue, then black.

"So, what do you think?" Venka asked as he looked over at me, then at John.

"I think it went well," I answered. Venka continued to sit in the conference room as the rest of the group drifted away. I could tell that he wanted to talk, so I feigned distraction and waited around.

"This only matters for our US cases of course; we will still file in China and other countries through the Patent Cooperation Treaty applications we will file very soon."

"Jen, you did great," John said as he rose to leave. "We need to talk more about it, but I have to run to a meeting. Stop by my office later when you get a chance."

"Thanks. Will do."

"Thank you, John," Venka said as he rose to sit closer to me, waiting for everyone to leave. I watched him as he shook hands with several attorneys who were leaving the room.

"You did excellent, Jenny," Venka said.

"Thanks. Really, I feel like you did most of the work. I think the commissioner was impressed. It's always best to hear the inventor give his side of the story, and I think this is a good one."

Venka's poise struck me. Even after the filing of the patent applications, technology that would surely change the course of human history, and all the attention he would garner once they published and were in the public domain, Venka maintained a mix of confidence and modesty that I admired.

Venka sat next to me and took some time before speaking. I could see concern in his face.

"Jenny, has John talked to you about the new arrangements?"

"No, I don't think so. What arrangements?"

"I understand that you won't be involved in the project going forward, that any future patent work will be handled by someone else."

"Oh?"

"I've entered into a secrecy agreement, I believe with the Institute," he said, The Research Institute in Bengaluru was where he

Kevin M. Faulkner

primarily carried out his research, and nearby was the facility where they were building experimental lighters, at least partly run by the Institute, and I suppose in part by the investors.

"I see." I wasn't too surprised. I knew there had been a closed-door meeting yesterday with people I recognized from other meetings. John had told me that the agreements with the investors would be restricted to only a few attorneys involved. My ambivalence up to this point had led to me being on the outside, and I wasn't sure how I felt about it now. I could tell Venka was bothered too.

"It's too bad. We have worked together for at least a year now, and I've grown fond of you, and impressed with your work. We'll still visit, but I believe the legal work will go to someone else now."

"It has been a pleasure, Dr. Venka. I thought this might happen; I just didn't know when. Are you okay with it?"

"Yes, I'm fine," he said, reluctantly. I wasn't sure about my feelings. Though he was the one who had entered into the secrecy agreement, somehow I felt I was the one abandoning my client.

I could easily write people off from my life. An island unto myself, few friends, fewer lovers; even the other attorneys I work with were difficult for me to abide; and in any case I found reasons to dislike or distrust most of them. That was often the case with my clients, who I mostly saw as getting in my way and taking up my time. *Keep it short and get out of my office,* was my overriding thought. I had trouble walking away from this. Venka's earnestness and transparency were infectious, but most of all, he wouldn't let up. My defenses made me inaccessible to most people. That didn't seem to faze Venka.

"Well, I'm sure we'll talk soon." I didn't know what else to say. And that was how we parted. I went back to my office, alone. Though I worked longer hours, it was unusual for me to stay so late in the office. That night was different. Venka's tone disturbed me and I couldn't shake it. I waited for the offices to empty and the bustling hallways to dislodge their contents of well-dressed lawyers, paralegals, and support staff. Maybe I hoped this feeling would leave with them.

"Good night, Jenny, don't stay too late," I heard a male voice as it went past my door.

"Good night," I responded, noticing that the voice may have come from one of the firm's androids.

In the silence, I made my way to a conference room with a view of San Diego Bay. I walked in, happy that it was empty, and set my lytfascia down on the long glassy table, windows surrounding me. I was momentarily warmed by the remaining orange glow of sun glancing off the buildings, and further out, the rippling water. I sat and tried to work, but only managed to fidget with a document that I no longer cared about. I remember saying to myself, "What are you gonna do now, Jenny?"

I looked up at the cameras in the room, then decided to give up the ruse of productivity and stood to stare out the window. Looking for solace, I turned to pace the length of the conference room table, but it was not to be. I was dizzy with resentment, whether I had a right to that emotion or not. *So, I'm out. Am I okay with that? Who are those investors?*

I ceased my lonely patrol to look down the darkened hallway, where I could see light under John's door. I remember the sinking feeling I had then. I felt wounded and angry, mostly at myself, as I had already invested so much time and energy in this project. I nursed an impulse to find a wave, but a better part of me bailed.

Why are you so angry, Jenny? The truth was that I was a little more ambitious than I had been telling myself. Out of law school, I envisioned a life where I did as little as possible to earn enough to have an apartment, buy a board or two, and surf. Yet, when I donned my working clothes and entered the offices of Lackley, the reality of life set in and I could see possibilities for the future, where I could be and how I would get there. I saw myself among others like me, taking in a client, listening to them, helping them resolve their concerns, or at least, feel better about them.

Kevin M. Faulkner

"You have that now, Jenny," I said to myself. That client is looking to me and they don't care if I want to go surfing, or drinking, or make love, or have a family. I have to care or else it's all a sham. I realized then I couldn't quite live with that.

I pulled myself together and walked out of the conference room. The hallway was carpeted so my footsteps were soundless, and only the glow of the sliver of light under John's office door illuminated my way. Once I reached it, I hesitated before knocking, worried that I wasn't better prepared. Nonetheless, I pushed the door open as he said, "Come in." He was sitting in front of his computer, hunched over some agreement no doubt. I walked in and helped myself to a chair across from his desk.

"Hey, thanks for coming by," John said. Removing his glasses, he continued, "You did great today. I talked with our investors; they were pleased as well. They appreciate your excellent work."

"Thanks." John's mood was friendly. I regretted the turn it was about to take. "Actually, I wanted to talk to you about that."

"Sure."

"So, I spoke with Venka this afternoon." For some reason I paused. I was going to rationalize my hurt feelings into some sort of professional vendetta but decided to change direction.

"John, what are we doing? Why did we bother filing those patent applications?"

John's expression changed, ever so gradually, from a friendly pat on the back kind of smile to one of concern. He looked down and let out a breath.

"Jen, it's part of a strategy. We needed someone who understands this technology. We can't help our clients if we can't grasp what they are doing, and you're the only attorney at the firm, maybe in town, who could do that. The investors want legitimacy." He hesitated before continuing, "The applications are an important part of that."

The Sixth Traveler

"What's the other part?" I asked as he stood and went to the window. "Who's going to control this technology? It's not JPL. I get the feeling they are less than co-owners in all of this. It's as if they're in the background."

John avoided me. He gazed out into the city; the sky had become completely dark.

"I understand you're frustrated. But we couldn't include you in everything. You did your part. We had to keep things separate." John ran his hand through his hair as if trying to shed some thought. I could tell he wanted to change the subject. He turned to me and said, "The world's about to change, Jen."

"At whose hands?"

"You know I can't say."

"Tell me something, John."

"It's the investment firm, PacificEnergy."

"I figured that much out. Who are they, really?"

He hesitated. I could tell he had to force himself to look at me. "Do you want to know? You know how these things go, Jenny. I can't talk to you about it unless you want to be part of the project."

Well, this is it, Jenny. You can't have it both ways. Something within me moved.

"Yes, I want to know," I sounded surer than I felt.

"Okay." John sat back at his desk: "They're coming in next week to execute assignment documents and formation agreements. Dr. Venkalaswaran signed the preliminary secrecy agreements he must have told you about. We can include you. In fact, we'd like to include you."

As if in confession, he continued, "They're part of the Caucasus Federatsiya, Jenny, and they—"

"What!" I surged from my chair. "Terrorists? Damn it, John, are you fucking kidding me?" In that moment, the last nine months coalesced with wretched clarity. The Federatsiya and the insurgent thugs with them were always in the news, but it was something I could dissociate myself from. It was some other part of the world, someone else's problem. I couldn't believe what I was hearing.

"Did Venkalaswaran say they were terrorists?"

"Venka didn't say anything." I could see now that he had been protecting me.

"They're legitimate Jen, they—" John stopped himself, becoming more subdued, "They approached us a long time ago. Naturally, it's sensitive, but they support the project and the building phase of a manned spacecraft."

"I don't understand."

"Jenny, NASA is involved with this."

"That makes it better? How involved is NASA? Where is the money coming from? Washington?"

"No. Most of the money is coming from our clients."

"And you're okay with this?"

"Jenny, we're attorneys. Someone has come to our firm for help. It's our job to solve their problem. Unless it's illegal, that's what attorneys do."

"Yes, but . . . ."

"Don't judge. The firm has taken measures to wall off any activities that may be illegal, especially the Vainakh. There are no ethical issues here." The Vainakh were the militant group associated with the Federatsiya.

"Really?"

"Yes, just help solve their problem," John said, running his hand through his hair again.

"So, this is it? I don't think this is right."

"It doesn't matter. And regardless, you're in it now," he said, frowning. He must have seen how it hit me. Under his breath, he added, "We all are."

* * *

Not having slept much for a week, I strained to think. I usually enjoyed basking in the rays of the sun when I was on my board. That day the sunlight was just blinding, distracting. I paddled through it, trying hard to escape it but all around were flashes of light brighter than the sun. My shortest three-fin board, neon red, only added to my ache.

Treading along unusually calm Trestles I had hoped to clear my head and cleanse my soul. I wished for a wave to carry me away, but all I got was my broken reflection. I sat upright on my board and said to myself: "What do I do now?" I didn't have an answer, so I let the light consume my vision.

Kevin M. Faulkner

SIX

Implant Record Date 8 July 2095
Bengaluru

I sat alone at a table in a dark little bar in the dusty outskirts of Bengaluru (its name sounded like *Cat Tongue*) sipping Indian ale while I waited for Aravinda Venkalaswaran and Chase Adeane to show. This was my third trip to the institute where Venka did most of his work, and the first since that fateful day in John's office. I still wasn't sure how I felt about it all, but I pushed forward.

Though my initial reaction to John's admission was disgust, I knew the situation was complicated. The Caucasus Federatsiya, a newly organized group of states in the Caucasus region that had once been a part of Russia, was thought to be associated with a criminal clan of mountain people who were mining and selling unregulated uranium. The uranium came from deposits deep in the Caucasus Mountains, and it was making an otherwise backwards, war torn and orthodox people suddenly rich. They became more organized, calling themselves the Vainakh, the ancient Chechen name for the indigenous people of the Caucasus highlands. The American media usually referred to them as simply *the VK*. Before long they learned how to refine the ore to make it even more valuable. Though not as nefarious as it might seem (the uranium had greater value for power generation than for weapons) the sales were largely underground, illegal, and growing chaotic. There was fear that some groups or countries would use the uranium for something other than energy.

The Russians, searching for energy and control, wanted access to the uranium. The Vainakh, already toughened by years of war, were using their riches to purchase arms, forming a growing army that included military-grade androids and drone craft. This gave the

Vainakh an intimidating edge. They were able to force their will on the region when necessary, but more often simply bribed potential adversaries. They were a thorn in the side of the Russians, raiding their southern cities and towns to completely dislodge them from the Caucasus.

Amid this was a growing movement in the same region for a more secular, open society. Years of war and impoverishment took their toll on the people and they wanted a change. You could say that the Federatsiya was taking advantage of the chaos the Vainakh and Russians had created. With origins in Chechnya, the Federatsiya was spreading throughout the region and gaining influence over the orthodox governments. In a devil's bargain, the Federatsiya leadership made a deal, so it appeared, with the Vainakh. The West was sympathetic to the Federatsiya's mission but torn about the Vainakh. The Federatsiya promised to make order of it all, but it was hard to tell if they were in control or part of the problem. I believed the latter.

I didn't know Venka well enough to know what was on his mind, so I didn't ask. He must have suspected for a while that the money wasn't only coming from the Indian government, but we can sometimes hide such matters from ourselves. None of us were overly comfortable with the situation, so perhaps we rationalized.

Venka was no madman. He was building the best ride off an increasingly intrusive planet, at least for the people he was working for. The Vainakh clearly wanted to be left alone, and not having achieved that, had concluded that it was time to leave. With countries bogged down in fiscal and political problems, the world was dragging its feet in advancing a means for leaving our solar system. The Chinese were inching their way there, but who knew if they would share it? The Vainakh, and I suppose now the Federatsiya, were enlightened if not capitalistic. Venka wasn't building a doomsday device, but a tool for a price that would make its holder rich and free. Fate would have it fall outside of any democratic process.

Kevin M. Faulkner

After sitting there pondering all of this for the best part of an hour, I could finally see fate walking through the doorway in khaki pants and white shirts: Aravinda Venkalaswaran and Chase Adeane.

"Hey V, Chase. Pull up a chair." My enthusiasm might have betrayed my misgivings about the situation in which I found myself.

"Hey, Jenny," Chase said. I was attracted to Chase, and I think there was something between us. I had even considered going out with him at one point a couple of months ago. Somehow, I knew that I'd regret it, and it could potentially become a distraction in working on this project with him. Further, I could tell Venka was, in the least, annoyed with Chase. And in any case, it wasn't right to date a client, or someone who was client-like. Chase was a good guy though. I buried it and moved on.

"Jenny, we can't stay long," Venka said. "We are cooling down the tympani now, and once we start the activation process we can't stop it without quenching and starting all over, which would take months." The tympani he was referring to were part of his second small test lighter, about two meters in length.

"I know. I thought we'd get away for a while. We have to eat sometime."

"Jen," Chase started, "how long have you been here?"

"An hour or so. Why?"

"I can tell you have something on your mind. You're not worried about the Caucasus Federatsiya, are you?" Chase knew my misgivings about this project, but he was more cavalier about it all. "Look at it this way, no other government has the stomach to do this sort of thing. NASA thinks it's too dangerous, along with every other country's space agency. Who best to do this than the Federatsiya. They're not worried about the risks."

"Maybe," I said.

"It's true," Chase replied. "Look around you. How much longer are we going to last on this planet? Heck, there's not enough space to put everybody, much less grow food. Look at the stuff we're already reduced to eating." Chase motioned toward the soy porridge and bread between us on the table. I am guessing Chase has had real meat, growing up the way he did. He may have even killed it himself.

"Necessity is the mother of invention," I had to admit.

"Yes, it is true," Venka said. Was there skepticism in his voice? It could be that Venka was thinking the same thing I was: the Federatsiya's necessity was not so much a way off a crowded world as an escape.

Chase waved his empty bottle at the waitress.

"My motives were scientific at first," Venka started. "I believe this is where the world is going. Humans needs to find a new place."

"I agree," Chase said.

"If we stop exploring and expanding we will become extinct."

I looked at the two of them, nodding in agreement. "It's all very expensive. I guess it took someone who really wanted to leave."

"Just like everything else, it comes down to money," Chase said. "There's a fortune to be made in this technology. The Feds aren't the only ones who want a faster ride off Earth." Rocket engines had gotten much more powerful and efficient in the last hundred years and could easily do heavy-lift work from ground-to-orbit. Several nations had regularly operating space stations. Getting there was relatively simple, but going much further than Mars in a reasonable amount of time was still out of reach.

"I suppose. I wonder if the Federatsiya isn't trying to run from something."

"Mmmm," Venka muttered as he frowned.

The drive back to the research campus transitioned from dusty roads into newly paved streets. The campus was modern, and patrolled by the Indian military, though as far as I could tell the Indian government was not involved in the project itself other than basic funding of the Institute. Different factions within the Indian Federation supported different causes, so I wondered how involved one of those factions might be. Nonetheless, there were rivals throughout the world wanting to learn what we were doing, so the

Indian Federation had a vested interest in secrecy. In the end, the Indian government's involvement was reluctant, but necessary to maintain order and secrecy.

Stepping out of the transport and inside the complex, we flashed our badges as we were ushered inside. After traversing a long passage, we had a steep climb up a metal staircase to the control room overlooking a football field-sized hangar where the lighter was being built. I couldn't see the device. It was buried within a complex maze of supports, struts, and umbilical cords. Engineers wearing white clean room gowns and face masks surrounded it. Its scope was incredible, and all I could do was stare.

"You can see," Chase said, pointing, "that we are isolating the inner shell, which is what we are testing tonight. The cooling system and shields are being installed next and should be complete by the end of the month."

"Seems we should wait for that," Venka said.

"Why? There's no need. The Haakverse won't be influenced by the mimft accelerators." The mimft accelerators were the invention of Chase and his researchers at JPL, the name jokingly derived from one of his engineers angrily writing in his notebook during its development that "he was tired of staying up every night recalibrating the mini-magneto-fucking accelerator so many times." I don't know exactly how they got mimft out of that, but I didn't ask and, needless to say, didn't use that term in any legal document.

But they brought up a critical factor in the design of their manned lighter, and that was controlling what went on inside the vessel. Venka's invention stretched the current understanding of physics by taking the Haak-Hatoi principle of universe segregation (popularly referred to as the *Haakverse*) developed forty years ago and applying it to isolating the interior of the craft from the exterior. This was if you believed that multiple universes even existed, a whole other debate. In any case, this division was not only physical: it kept the energy state within the cabin of the craft distinct from its exterior, much as one universe could reside next to another, the grand astronomical scale Samuel Hatoi and Constantine Haak originally had in mind. Venka changed the scale and created a Haakverse for the humans inside the lighter. Venka dubbed the physical manifestation of this aspect of his invention a *Newton-shell* (the term I used in his patent applications was *quantum isolation means*), but everyone else soon called it the *Venka-shell*, or simply *V-shell*.

"Chase, at first the lighter will have to run autonomously. For the occupants' health and mental stability, the first few tests will have to be pre-programmed so that there is a departure and return sequence that cannot be easily changed. There needs to be some security measure."

"Right," Chase replied with disdain. "But I think the travelers should have more control. Otherwise, they'll just be lab rats."

"In any case, the tympani plates will be quenched if the sequence is stopped abruptly, damaging them beyond repair," Venka said. "This would be a disaster for the traveler if it happened while at their destination, essentially marooning them."

"I know," Chase replied, eyes almost visibly rolling. *These guys are not getting along.*

"The couplings at AK9 and the flank drawing line can be—"

"We can improve on that in later versions of the device," Chase said, impatient with Venka.

They were still talking, really, passive-aggressively arguing when John rang me on my phone. It was nearly eleven p.m. here, late in the morning in San Diego.

"Fellas, I need to take this call." I walked to a back room and closed the door, muting the noise from the hum of the hangar and the men's conversation.

I picked up the call, "Hey John."

"Jenny, hey there, sorry if I kept you up. There were meetings early this morning in San Diego and I had to be involved before talking to you."

Kevin M. Faulkner

"No problem, I still can't sleep much anyway. This is all pretty amazing, it's hard to believe how far they've come, though I mostly have to take Venka's word for it."

"Yes, well, it's good you're there, because we're going to need you to get more involved than the patent work," John said.

"Okay, so what's going on?"

"We need to be talking to the Indian government about getting this thing into orbit. It looks like there's no other way to test it. We want you to lead the negotiations. I know you're reluctant, but we need you. You understand what's going on technically, and you have a good relationship with Venka, Adeane, and the others involved."

I stood there silently, debating to myself what I should do.

"Jenny!" I turned as Venka called to me; the door flung open. "This is incredible, you've got to see this."

My answer to John was clear: "I'm in."

* * *

The next day I was in meetings with Venka, Chase and the other engineers and scientists on the project. If I was unsure of Venka and Chase's relationship before, it was clear at that meeting.

"The entire inner shell must be layered according to Plaedoes's Means, while each tympani will make first contact with the H3 medium in sequence with the mimft accelerators," Venka said, matter-of-factly, to the group of ten men and women around the table.

"Venka, that won't work," Chase said. "That will be much less efficient that simply having each tympani have a free flow." The group was discussing how the manned prototype of a QMT device should work, having to consider the complexity of the V-Shell yet still accommodate the engine or power source of the tympani that would protrude from the hull of the vessel. At what point, or points, would contact be made between the power source to each plate?

"Chase," Venka started, holding back his contempt with strained patience, "the free flow you are talking about sounds nice, but how will we maintain any control of the vessel's stabilizers, much less create adequate conduction for the shell." Modestly, Venka declined to call his invention a V-Shell.

"It will work, let me show you," Chase said as he maneuvered the three-dimensional engineering diagrams of the lighter in front of the group. I could sense a little trepidation from the members of the team as they watched the exchange. I imagined they had grown somewhat used to it, and even took sides.

"Why don't we extend the internal lines bi-four and tri-eight from the source to the V-Shell, then the tympani," one of the young women said, in an apparent compromise. I could see Venka relax, so maybe he saw that as a victory. Chase nodded his head. To tell the truth, much of this was going way over my head by now, so it was hard for me to tell.

"Yes, Mimi, I see," Venka said to Dr. Mimi Shimadzu, one of the longstanding team members. I could see Dr. Shimadzu look warily at both Chase and Venka, then relax as the fighting eased.

I think the group wants these two to get along. That's what is driving the design!

"Let's do that," Chase said, further manipulating the image before the group.

"So, is this your final configuration?" I asked. I needed to know so I could get it right in the patent applications that were to follow. I had my computer take a snapshot of it for my records.

The group continued to discuss the design of the lighter, Venka and Chase gradually yielding to the others in the room, some younger, some older than these two. Perhaps it was part of their twisted plan to get everyone else involved. In any case, I could see Venka and Chase lean back and take in the discussion on the details of the plan. This was where science met engineering. It was one thing to maintain fission with hydrogen-3 in a closed environment, it was another to maintain that reaction inches away from people who would be sitting inside a vessel, and further, extracting a controlled amount of the energy from that process to create a quantum event in a large, man-made object.

I sat with Venka in his office after our meeting and continued to take notes on my pad as he worked at his desk. I should say, I partly pretended to write. Now that I had him alone, my mind was increasingly on Venka himself, how he operated, and how much, if any, did he amp up. I figured he must use it often, given the state of his neck. I formed a strategy on how I would approach the subject.

"Well, I spoke to John Mar and it looks like I will be getting more involved. Likely you and I will be doing some traveling. We'll have to strike some kind of a deal to get this device in Earth orbit in order to test it. I will head back to San Diego first for meetings the day after tomorrow."

"Excellent, I thought that might happen," Venka said.

Wavering, I decided not to ask again about his neck. Venka appeared to be doing well, so I wanted to leave him alone. And probably not a good idea to pester him anyway.

"I think our meetings have gone well," I said. "I feel like the team is making progress in spite of you and Chase going at each other."

He leaned back in his chair.

"Jenny, I am aware of the tension. I know it bothers you. Don't let it. It's all part of the process," Venka mused. "Adeane is a good man, and an excellent engineer. I suppose I like to have my way."

"It looks like you are going to go at each other."

Venka laughed, "You don't like friction."

"No, but as you say, I won't let it bother me."

"Good. And I'm glad it hasn't clouded your view of Chase."

"No, no, you're both my clients, it's not a big deal," I said. "*This* is a big deal, what you all are doing here."

The Sixth Traveler

"Just clients?" Venka followed. I think he was teasing me a little.

"Friends . . . both of you," I followed, suspiciously.

Venka laughed.

"I'm glad to hear, Jenny."

"Yes, well, you handle the disagreements well," I said. "I could learn from that. You're so patient."

"You're just starting out Jenny. I think you are doing fine."

"Sure," I replied.

"Speaking of Chase, you should go out with him."

"What?" That came out of nowhere.

"You two should go out," Venka repeated. His face lit up as he leaned forward in his chair, "In fact, I want to invite both of you to my home tonight. Dr. Madan will be delighted."

"Wait, what?"

"Yes, we've talked about it many times. Tonight is perfect, the two of you will be guests in our home. You can stay with us for the night. The children will love it."

"I don't know if—" I started.

"Nonsense, let me tell Chase."

I was encouraged as I left his office that afternoon for my hotel, with a feeling of knowing for once where I was going. It would also be nice to visit with Venka's family. I wasn't so sure it was a good idea for Chase and me to be a thing but was charmed at Venka's attempted matchmaking.

SEVEN

Implant Record Date 8 July 2095
Bengaluru

Bengaluru was a sprawling metropolis that exists in a spectrum from abject poverty to shimmering wealth. There were over thirty million people in the city and its outskirts, too many, you would think, to fit into a city. It's a pretty place, where new neighborhoods built around ancient relics was a common sight. I looked out the window of my hotel room once more before I grabbed my bags and went down the lift to a waiting car. The driver said "Dr. Venkalaswaran's residence," as a statement, not a question. He whisked up my bags, ushered me into the back seat, and drove at a speed that felt way too fast.

"Is this your first time at the Venkalaswaran's residence?" The driver asked. Apparently, he was used to such visits, working exclusively for the Institute. The driver was mostly a formality, there to carry my bags and provide commentary and company. The limo was otherwise autonomous, with a spacious back seat for the passengers to sit in most any orientation, a small refrigerator for drinks and food, and a video screen for entertainment. The driver sat comfortably in the front, with only a computer control screen and emergency steering wheel and brake.

"No, but it's the first time I've gone on a date to his residence," I replied, surprising myself with my honesty.

"Ahhh, I see. Who is the lucky man, may I ask?"

"Mmmm, maybe I shouldn't say. I don't want to cause a scandal."

He laughed. "A scoundrel."

Venka lived on the south side of town, near Sankey Lake. The roads were newly paved in most places. I asked the driver where I could get flowers.

"Ohhh, excellent! The Nagar shopping district is the best place. I'll take you there."

The driver took over from the auto-drive and took us down a side street, then another turn, and I was lost. I looked out the window as we drove, watching the women in their traditional saris or chanderi dresses, the children dancing around them or being carried. I thought of the contrast with the women in China, who would completely shun any traditional East Asian style dress. Only an American woman would wear a qípáo.

Continuing my uncharacteristic spontaneity, I asked:

"Why do Indian women still wear traditional dress these days, yet Chinese women never do?"

As if he had already been thinking the same thing, he said, "Because Chinese women are more concerned with being modern, Indian women are more concerned with tradition."

"I see. They are beautiful."

"Truthfully, the women you see here don't wear these things often, it is for show." We drove a little further before he spoke, "Why do you ask?"

"I'm just in a mood."

"Ahhh. Of course, Indian women want to be modern too. They want both, so I'm not sure if what they wear means anything, really."

I considered what he said.

"When a woman wears a thing, it almost always means something, no matter what it is," I replied.

We both laughed.

I looked down at my dress, a modern take on a chanderi, maroon colored with gold edging, but the back a little low. I liked the way I looked in it.

"We are almost there." He turned down another street and slowed down in front of a busy mall, packed with people and cars.

"Why don't you get out here, I will find you when you are ready. You can walk out in that direction," the driver pointed, "and you'll surely find what you want."

I started to ask "How?" but simply said, "Thanks, I won't be long."

"Oh, take your time." Typically, in these situations a person could easily locate another person by granting permission to home in on their implant. I had not done that. Feeling confident, I decided to old school it.

I walked alone across the street into a sea of people, and it only took moments for a group of sweet children to surround me. "What are you looking for, we'll help you find it." They shouted.

"Flowers, but only the best," I said. I looked back in the direction of my driver and saw only a sea of people.

One bold child took my hand and guided me to what he said were the nicest flowers in town. The boy led me through a labyrinth of stands and tents. I was dizzy with visual stimulation and almost ready to stop when we got to a place that was somewhat out of the way, on the far side of the mall. It was near a wall, likely the edge of the district. There was a tent with several tables set out before it, and behind that a river. The path at this point was concrete, and the crowd was thinning out.

"You'll like these flowers, my grandma grows them," the boy said.

"Ahhh, a salesman I see."

He laughed, and the other children that followed giggled and sang.

"I can't wait to see them."

"We are almost there," the boy called. As we approached the row of tables an older lady came out from under the tent to stand next to a younger woman who was arranging flowers. They both wore red and blue saris, simple and elegant. The older women had a scarf around her head, but I could see the young woman had a

The Sixth Traveler

beautiful head of hair, flowing down around her shoulders. And before her, rows of flowers. There was most every color of roses. The pink ones caught my eye. I looked at the woman and introduced myself as the boy excitedly hovered around me.

"So, you like these?" the older lady asked.

"Yes," I replied. I wondered if that was the boy's grandmother. She smiled and put together a dozen roses.

"Are those lotus flowers?" I asked the younger woman, pointing behind her.

"Yes, excellent," she said. She turned, taking one in her hand.

"You have a good eye, very pretty."

"Yes," the boy, still standing next to me, said.

"Are you visiting on vacation?" the woman asked.

"No, I am here for business, from the United States." There is a good chance she would have known who Dr. Venkalaswaran was, and I started to say, but thought better of it.

"Today, I am visiting a friend."

"He'll like this," she said as she came around the table to my side and placed the flower in my hair. I noticed she said "He." I thought about Chase and wondered if he would like it, then shook the thought out of my mind, smiling at the young woman.

"Very nice."

I paid her, though she refused money for the lotus flower. I turned, a little worried about finding my way back. The boy that brought me here was nowhere to be found.

Sensing my concern, the old woman said, "You'll find your way. If you get lost, ask someone."

I decided that I was not in a rush. I was in the enchanted embrace of another world. I felt that nothing could go wrong. Getting lost only added to my day. I thought the story would be as nice as the flowers themselves.

* * *

Kevin M. Faulkner

Dr. Venkalaswaran's was unremarkable from the street but for the fact that it was Dr. Venkalaswaran's house. I would always know it as that and become familiar with it over the years as I traveled to India.

My driver turned to me as we stopped in front of a rose-colored house of contemporary box forms with long rows of windows, vines covering the remaining facade. "And we are here."

As I gathered my flowers and personal things he opened the passenger door, partly bowing. Before I could get my bag, already sitting on the curb, three young children ran out the door of the house as if they'd been waiting for me all day, the oldest grabbing the handle of my bag, the youngest standing and jumping around.

"My name is Mika, and this is my little brother, Yhama," the girls said. The boy couldn't have been more than four, and Mika might have been nine or ten.

"Nice to meet you."

"And that is Prashid," Mika said, motioning to her middle sister, who stood back behind her sister, clearly a little shy.

"It's nice to meet you all. I am Jenny, a friend of your father's. I've heard so much about you all."

"Where did you get the flower," Prashid asked, pointing to my hair.

"A nice lady gave it to me in the mall on the way here." I pulled a rose from the bunch for Prashid and handed it to her. The other two children lit up with excitement as I handed a flower to each of them, feeling as if they had been given a treasure.

"Children, leave the poor woman alone!" a woman called out as she walked down the sidewalk from a side door.

"Let me get that bag for you," the lady said. I was guessing a housekeeper and nanny.

"Thank you," she took it and was off before I could argue.

The Sixth Traveler

"Please call me Rushida."

"Come in," Mika called, taking my hand and pulling me inside.

As I got to the door I could see Nithia Madan. She embraced me and ushered me inside, taking the flowers and holding them to her breast. When I pressed against Nithia I could smell her perfume, both floral and fruity, its scent lingering with me through the evening.

"Children, why don't you give me those pretty flowers so I can put them with their brothers and sisters in a vase of water to drink." The children gladly complied, Yhama having already lost his, and excitedly ran away.

The Venkalaswaran household was warm and inviting. You could tell children lived there, which gave me a sense of relief. I never realized until then how disconcerting it was to go into a home with children and scarcely know it. That was not the case here. Not too out of control, but clear archeological evidence of children in the photographs, finger paintings, lopsided sculptures, and tennis balls scattering the floor.

I could see Venka across the room talking to Chase as if they were old friends. They both waved at me. Seeing Chase dressed for the occasion, I suddenly grew conscious of the flower in my hair. I had an urge to take it out, but too late, everyone had seen it. *What the heck*, I remember thinking.

"Jenny, there you are," Venka said, embracing me.

"You remember Chase Adeane?" he said, jesting.

"How do you do," I said. Someone put a glass of wine in my hand.

"Some of my students are outside, but they have seen my house many times. Why don't I show you and Chase around. We'll start at our garden." I looked through the open French doors to the back of the house and could see Mimi Shimadzu talking with others, including the young Shamim Ganju, an undergraduate student, brilliant and well before his time.

Kevin M. Faulkner

Nithia joined us as we walked through the kitchen, locking her arm into mine. Spice and steam drifted through the air as two catered cooks worked over the grills.

"Aravinda loves working in *his* garden," Nithia said to me, as if it were a secret. Her warmth was mesmerizing; I felt a cat's purr run through my body.

We made our way through a back door into a garden on the side of the house, bounded by a brick fence all around, blocking access from the street, and with a low stone wall that faced the yard behind the house. I didn't know anything about gardening, but seeing this made me wish I did. We strolled through a gravel pathway as Venka explained the history of some of the plants, proud that he had started most from seeds or clippings. We could hear sounds of children playing, not only Yhama, Prashid and Mika, but distant sounds in the neighborhood.

"Dr. Venkalaswaran," Rushida called.

"Ah, let me go inside for a moment. Excuse me," Venka said as he and Nithia left. Part of me wished they would stay, thinking *what now?* I looked over at Chase, somehow feeling shy. He, however, was not shy at all.

"Counselor, what is on your mind?"

"Pretty things and lofty heights," I replied, quoting a popular song. *Shoot. Did I just say that?*

The whole night was not like that; I got hold of myself when Nithia rescued me, taking my arm, saying, "Let me borrow Jenny for a moment," and walking me through a gate to the front yard, then next door where she introduced me to a friend. She had a seamless manner, giving me a semblance of synchronicity that evening. Through it all the children alternately buzzed around me, asking me questions, or pulling me somewhere to play. At dinner I was flanked by the children fighting for position, Chase and other adults just out of reach for conversation.

The Sixth Traveler

I lost track of time, but it must have been ten when we finished our meal. Nithia and the nanny put the kids to bed, and the eight remaining adults sat outside around several candles and a small fire pit burning nearby. Venka and Nithia alternately ebbed and flowed in and out of the scene as they took care of the kitchen and the kids. I remember the scent of jasmine from the garden, and the sounds of other gatherings in the distance. The moon was nearly full, peaking over the trees around us.

The children ran out once more, in their pajamas, to hug Chase and me good night. I embraced each of them, the sweet scent of a child hanging in my mind as they ran back inside, calling me their "Aunt Jenny."

Mimi, Shamim, and the other students and researchers gradually filtered away around midnight. I could hear the hum of the driverless taxis carting them away, and the merry "Good nights" as they departed. The atmosphere grew quiet, with only the cascading sounds of the insects to hide our conversation. Chase and I remained on a cushioned couch, Venka and Nithia sitting in chairs across from us. They had the smile of thieves watching their plans unfold.

"There were times when I loved college, and times when I hated it," Chase said, telling us of his college days in Austin.

While he told his tales, I was only vaguely aware that Venka had gone inside the house, disappearing into the darkness of the living area. I remained with Nithia and Chase exchanging stories of our youths in southern California, Delhi, and Austin. Other than the conversation, the candles' flames flickered in the breeze, making shadows dance across our faces.

"What did you love?"

"My friends. The parties, and by my senior year, the work." He winked at Nithia. I imagined a girl he might have known, and what she must have looked like.

"So, what did you hate?" Nithia asked.

Kevin M. Faulkner

"The times I was alone. When I look back, I wonder how I did it. I guess we all do that. You spend your time looking. You know? Looking for what you want. Then you figure out you're way off."

"I know. College is where you learn who you are, where you want to go, and what it takes to get there," I replied, though I was not sure I lived up to that.

"We change so much during that time in our lives," Nithia said.

"Yeah, but I'd go home to Canyon, right outside of Amarillo. My grandpa and I would take the dogs and go out and hunt for days. It didn't take long before it would be like I had never left, like I was still in middle school."

"You are a good boy to visit your parents and grandparents," Nithia said.

"Yes, well, I do go back, but it's not the same of course. I can't remember when it changed, but it did."

"That time can be sad," Nithia said.

I got a sinking feeling in the pit of my stomach at the mention of parents. I looked over at Nithia. She carried a rose from the dozen I gave her earlier. I was so grateful for her at that moment. I turned and looked at Chase. A flash of sadness came over me, a feeling that drew me toward its source.

As we spoke, the universe closed between us in that way it always does with candlelight and wine. I don't remember Nithia filtering away until I became aware of the silence around us. The insects had gone to bed with everyone else. I imagined a grasshopper in the bushes, looking upon us with mischief, whispering to his friend, "What will they do now?"

But for the rustling leaves of the trees, we were alone. I did all the things you do when you've had too much to drink and far from home: I pushed aside the inconveniences of my profession, the pain from my own past, the little chip that sat on my shoulder, letting my hair down to add to its cover.

The Sixth Traveler

How did I end up sitting next to Chase? I couldn't remember. I could, however, remember our kiss and the way he held me.

It must have been two in the morning when we left the garden. The fire had nearly burned out and the candles melted into soft puddles of wax. Nithia led me to a guestroom upstairs where the wind moved through an open window, the thin curtains undulating in a gentle rhythm. I undressed in the light coming from the night sky and felt timeless in the shadows as the moonlit patterns danced across the floor and onto the bed. I didn't bother covering myself—I simply landed upon the sheets. Though the breeze was warm, it felt natural.

EIGHT

Implant Record Date 19 August 2095
San Diego to Grozny

"Here we are," I said to John and Erissa, suddenly feeling more an equal.

"We're glad you changed your mind," Erissa said.

"I want to be more involved." I wasn't so sure, but I hid any misgivings and exuded, as best I could, confidence. I listened to them both and gave my input, but mostly I watched the knowing glances between John and Erissa. They knew much more than they were telling me. Nonetheless, once I made that fateful decision to dive deeper, Erissa and John wasted no time briefing me on past and current events, and what the client wanted going forward.

It wasn't long before Erissa left most of the talking to John, saying before she left, "I'm proud of you, Jenny. You've come a long way."

"Thanks, Erissa."

With John and I alone, I got down to what I really wanted to talk about. "What's next?"

"We need for you to start negotiating," John answered. "We've got to move the project on to the next stage, a demonstration."

"Yes. We'll need a zero-gravity platform for that. I figure an orbiting space station from the Indian government. Somehow, I think the Indian government is the best way to go. I can't see NASA agreeing to partner with the Federatsiya."

"Well, they won't know—" John started.

"Exactly, I don't think NASA would partner unless they did vet the situation out, then of course, they would know.

"Yes, good point."

"Anyway, I wonder if we all won't be in trouble," I wondered out loud.

"I know how you feel, but there's not going to be any trouble." John grew silent, thinking. He must know what the political ramifications would be for a government agency to openly cooperate with a group of investors associated with warring factions. But the Indian government was notorious for following their own interests. "You are right, the Indian Federation is the best bet for the first demonstration."

"They are bound to know already, so if they were bothered by all of this, they'd have said so by now and stopped funding."

"True," John replied.

"At this point, you don't need to sell me on anything. I'll work with Venka and Chase . . . I'm in because of them."

"Of course, your real clients are their backers."

I knew John was right, but right now I felt more responsibility to Venka and Chase. "And NASA? Where do we stand there?"

"NASA is cooperating just as they would any other private company. We disclose the balance sheets to them and get advice, but they otherwise stand back and watch. They are waiting for a successful demonstration."

"I am guessing NASA is not in too deep. So is Chase Adeane working on behalf of JPL or PacificEnergy, contractually?"

"He is a JPL civil servant and his group is working on the project, but he really wears two hats these days. I am guessing he will eventually become part of an independent company."

"Makes sense. Export control could be an issue, but we'll see. So, where do you suggest I start?"

"Our investors. You've already met Amanta Kokotova and Nikhil Lecha," John said. "They're your main contacts. We are still working with them on other matters, mostly helping to establish an interim government in the Caucasus," John pointed to the 3D map projected in front of us, expanding the region of far southern Russia, "combining Chechnya, Ingushetia, Ossetia-Alania, western and southern Dagestan, and southern portions of Stavropol Krai, and much of the surrounding Caspian region. They want to modernize and integrate with the rest of the world. We are helping them do that."

"I don't understand. How does this happen?" I asked. "How does the Caucasus Federatsiya have any credibility at all? How can we be dealing with these people?"

"The Federatsiya have a great deal of credibility, and our firm is working with them to build on that. We work on their behalf with international organizations and governments and have entered preliminary treaties on economic and military matters."

"But the Vainakh . . . ." I trailed off, changing course. "I have to admit, I'm no expert on foreign affairs, let alone the Caucasus."

"The VK are another iteration of warring groups that have been fighting for centuries," John replied. "Things changed when they discovered the uranium in the mountains, it gave them leverage. They knew everyone, especially the Russians, would come after it. It was a matter of time. The Federatsiya offer the Vainakh the legitimacy that they are looking for. Building peace, or at least a truce, and cooperating with the Federatsiya keeps the Russians and every other envious eye at bay.

"It didn't take the VK much convincing by the Federatsiya to form an alliance," John continued. "The VK get as much out of this as the Federatsiya. In spite of your feelings about them, most of the world is sympathetic to the Federatsiya. They are moderate and secular and are largely supported by the people in the region."

"And they generate their own revenue, no need for Chinese money."

"Yes, they've resisted Russian and Chinese influence."

"So, they're a front for the VK."

"No," John replied, thinking I was teasing. "The Vainakh have an independent stake in all of this. Together, the Federatsiya and VK

The Sixth Traveler

are looking to start a nation. The VK want that as much as the Federatsiya."

"I imagine they have different visions."

"True."

"Somehow I don't think the VK will allow themselves to come under the control of a secular Caucasus Federatsiya," I continued. "I don't read much news, but I understand that the VK have built a small army using androids. I wonder how the Federatsiya felt about that. International law tightly controls that sort of thing, but those laws are easily ignored by the lawless."

"I think in time they will," John said. "To be sure, the Federatsiya have a motive for getting the VK in line, and the VK get something out of it as well."

"What's that?" I asked.

"They are looking for ways to use the uranium the VK have control over, legitimate ways under international law. The Federatsiya wants legitimacy as much as the VK wants to maintain their cash flow. They each get what they want in the bargain."

"In theory," I said.

"Of course." John continued, "The Federatsiya want more than simply the legitimacy of a government, they want a new start." He contracted the 3D out much further, to include the sun, Mercury, Venus, Earth, and then Mars. He pointed to an expanded globe of the red planet. "Several years ago, when they first approached our firm, the Federatsiya seriously looked at Mars. That was what they initially thought all that uranium would go to: energy on a power-starved planet."

"They wanted to move off-planet?"

"Emigrate."

"They wouldn't need Dr. Venkalaswaran for that. They obviously decided against Mars," I said.

"Yes," John answered. He paused and started looking for something in the virtual map. He expanded it back down to the whole planet Earth.

"I don't blame them." Mars is already getting crowded.

"The problem is, the Federatsiya is entangled with the Vainakh and though it is working out now, in the long run both sides will be unhappy unless the Vainakh can concede power," John said.

"Which most controlling armies don't do."

"Exactly. At the highest levels of the new government, they see that too, so long term, they want out. The VK will only grow more powerful and unhappy with the Federatsiya's leadership. The Federatsiya is already feeling a little trapped. In a sense, they are. As they see it, there is only one solution: A new world."

"But they need a better ride," I concluded. "That's why they hired V."

"Yes, you could say that," John said.

"So, Amanta and Nikhil," I asked, "They are heading this up?"

"Yes," John replied. "You have wide latitude to get things moving with the Indian Federation, but you'll need to keep Amanta and Nikhil in the loop. Always consult with them, but don't be afraid to take the initiative. Frankly, they don't know how to get what they want."

"Okay, understood," I said, feeling more confident.

"Finding a way off the planet Earth is a big deal," John said. "They need help."

"Right."

I looked at the expanded 3D that now included the Milky Way galaxy.

"About negotiations and security, should I be concerned?" I asked.

"That's a good question," John answered. "The principles are certainly trustworthy; they understand what's at stake. But you'll be accompanied by a security team in any case. We will keep you well outside the fighting with the Russians, and you can call me at any time." He handed me a military satellite phone. I felt its heavy cast plastimetal body in my hand.

The Sixth Traveler

"Jenny, the Federatsiya want to be taken seriously. It's in their best interest to deal, and for the VK to go along, at least for now. Erissa and I wouldn't have asked you if we thought you couldn't do it, or if you were in danger."

"Well, I'll start making arrangements."

"Let me know your plans," John said, standing to leave. "I'll be supporting you on this every step of the way."

"Okay, thanks John."

After John left I sat alone for a while, thinking. On a whim, I opened my implant's readout. My implant recorded the words we had spoken as well as my emotions and vitals. The raw data was just an indecipherable series of numbers and symbols, but when I ran the latest version of the Lambert-Zho neurological reactivity eviscercode it told me of my mixed emotions of excitement (23.2%), reservation (22.5%), and anxiety (15.3%). I could track the rise and fall over the hours of these and other emotions, but soon put it out of my mind.

In the following days, I colored my hair back to some semblance of its natural brunette, got a professional looking bob cut, and had my tattoos removed. My Hawaiian princess with her surfboard, the wind blowing through her hair, was no more. And as a hip Cali girl, I took the rail to Vancouver for some new business swag and went with my intuition: set up a meeting and purchase plane tickets.

* * *

I landed in Grozny, the former Chechen capital, a week after my meeting with John. A driver took me and my security team to a well-groomed, ten-story converted hotel that had been a favorite spot for wealthy Russians years ago. There were some guards standing outside, but otherwise, it was peaceful. My security team and I were led to a dining room on the third floor of the building where, on the far side near the windows, sat Amanta, Nikhil, and another man.

Before leaving for Chechnya, I was briefed on the Caucasus Federatsiya and I studied all the memos prepared by counsel representing them in their newly forming government. Amanta Kokotova, one of at least two people I was to meet, was one of the leaders of the Federatsiya. Her background was complex, growing up near Grozny, but educated in France. Her father was of Russian descent, her mother Chechen. Though her parents were religious, her father was orthodox Christian and mother was Muslim, they were open and enlightened in their faith and in Amanta's upbringing. I imagined that her education abroad showed her life's possibilities, and the freedom and prosperity enjoyed by much of the world.

Amanta became part of a reformation movement in the region, arising from centuries of internal and external conflict and oppression that only intensified from a resurgent Iran in the south, and Russia in the north. The Chechen government had been highly repressive, the country having one of the lowest standards of living in the world. This was made all the worse under Russian control, effectively isolating them from outside influences.

Need brought opportunity in the form of uranium. There was an easy market for it, making certain groups within the Caucasus rich and influential. These groups eventually formed the Vainakh, an insurgency that wanted to overthrow the government at the time but had no particular interest in governing. An alliance with the Vainakh meant Amanta and her fledgling movement could form a new government. It wasn't clear if the Vainakh and the Federatsiya were aligned politically, but they had a common enemy at the time and it benefited them both to act together.

"Ms. Kokotova," they rose as I approached.

"Yes, good to see you Jenny, please call me Amanta. And you may already know Nikhil Lecha."

"Yes, nice to see you, Mr. Lecha."

"And this is Nyetorkusneshia Kuurk," Amanta said, motioning to the third man who remained silent. "We call him Sneshia."

The Sixth Traveler

"Please, have a seat." Amanta said. "Waiter, wine please." They brought me some water and a glass of wine, while refilling the glasses of the others. I took a sip of the wine and started to talk before another waiter came with smoked fish and bread with a spread. I was surprised at how nice it was.

"Thank you." My initial excitement in coming here transformed to caution upon greeting my hosts, especially at Sneshia, who left me with a bad feeling.

"And please, you can call me Nikhil." I noticed that Sneshia said nothing, only nodding.

Amanta Kokotova was tall and slender, with some gray in an otherwise full head of long, black hair. She had angular features with wide eyes and sharp nose. Her skin was dark olive and smooth, making this fifty-year-old woman look younger than her age. She had a strong, commanding presence, but not overbearing. It didn't take long to sense the burden Amanta shouldered in carrying the Federatsiya toward the freedom she dreamed of.

We started with small talk, and eventually led to why I was here.

"You know," Amanta said, "when we first started supporting the work at the Indian Institute, we were interested in energy. We funded many different universities and research institutes, looking for ways to improve nuclear reactor technology."

"And alternatives such as fusion," Nikhil broke in. "Which is why we supported Dr. Venkalaswaran's research. Very promising. But it will be some time before helium-3 can be used for mass power generation and take the place of nuclear energy."

Nikhil Lecha was calm, almost laid back. He was well dressed, probably in his 50's, balding and a little round. It seemed that Nikhil wore a permanent grin on his face. So much so that it was infectious. In contrast, Sneshia was silent and intense. He was much younger, likely in his late twenties. He had a severity about him; I imagined he might have seen, or been capable of, things best left unsaid. With each glance he gave me, I caught myself turning my gaze to my security team.

Kevin M. Faulkner

"But as you know, he found a more immediate, practical use for helium-3," Amanta said. "So, our purpose has shifted from finding power to finding a way off this world."

Nikhil continued, "And that is one of the reasons why we came to your firm. We needed your help in securing Venka's technology, but also, we want to use it."

I could see it all more clearly, in talking to Amanta and Nikhil, I felt a little more assured in their goal, not as sinister as I had imagined. *Though maybe I am kidding myself*, I thought.

"Yes, and I think we can help," I said. "The path forward will be through the Indian Federation. Getting a meeting with the director of the Indian Space Research Organization is not an easy task. I've had to start lower."

"Yes, we know it will take some time, but we think the ISRO will want to partner with Dr. Venkalaswaran and the University," Amanta said. Funny how they saw it.

"I talked to an assistant director in Sriharikota, and I plan to meet with the director himself," I responded. "It would help to have Venka with me. They'll want to see this as part of a university-driven activity." I took a nervous sip from my glass of water. "My first connection was with the vice-chancellor of the university, whom Venka knows. The vice-chancellor had retired from the ISRO." I wondered if I was talking too much.

"Good. Don't worry, these things take time," Nikhil said. "This isn't some bottle rocket where you light the fuse and run behind a tree. New technology is always somewhat risky." It crossed my mind that the technology was not the thing that was scary.

"Thanks." The edge was off a little, so I ventured further. "About Dr. Venkalaswaran . . ." I had rehearsed this a dozen times in my head but had forgotten all of that now.

"Yes?" Nikhil said.

I thought back to Venka's expression weeks ago in the café outside Bengaluru, the look on his face once I learned what he already

The Sixth Traveler

knew, the worry at discussing the Federatsiya. I knew what was on his mind because I shared his concerns.

"Venka is an honest man, a good man. He's understandably concerned about his appearance to the world, his family and colleagues, and his countrymen." I hesitated before finishing. "So am I."

There was some silence, followed by a knowing look between Nikhil and Amanta. Amanta spoke as Nikhil looked down to brush his lap, "We understand. We know what people say about us. You think we are terrorists? That we are insurgents? We could argue about how these things are relative, but you know, in almost every country's history there is some blood, some wrong, some heartache. Even your country's history is seen quite differently from the English and the French."

"One man's enemy, another man's pawn."

"Perhaps," Amanda smiled. "I know you don't see a justification in that. But we agree, Venka is a good man. We will do what we can to stay invisible."

"I appreciate your understanding." I responded. "But more than that, if we are going to get the right factions of the Indian government involved in a demonstration, the Federatsiya will have to make a gesture. Enough of the world will be watching that they can't afford to alienate allies, even for Dr. Venkalaswaran." I felt a sense of relief, and finally some control with those words.

"What did you have in mind?" Nikhil asked.

"I understand there is still fighting going on between the VK and Russian forces in the north."

"Yes," Amanta replied.

"There are talks between the parties in Berlin, the German government is trying to broker a cease-fire with Moscow."

"Yes, that's right," Amanta said, cautiously. "We haven't made any commitments."

Kevin M. Faulkner

"It seems to me that there is a stalemate in the fighting. People are dying, on both sides, even civilians," I said. I could see that Sneshia was stewing. I was beginning to suspect his role here.

"I suggest that you go to Berlin." In spite of Sneshia's glare, or perhaps in defiance of it, I had remembered exactly what I wanted to say.

"You go to hell." Sneshia snarled as he started to rise. Amanta, sitting next to him, placed her hand on his arm. Sneshia slowly lowered himself back down and gained his composure. I had an impulse to leave, but glanced at my security team, and felt Amanta's calming assurance.

"It's alright. Jenny, please continue."

"If you want the lighter to be completed and tested, you're going to have to make a gesture, because surely we will have to rely on Indian assets, a space station. No other power would have the stomach for this."

"Did the Institute make this demand?" Nikhil asked.

"No. This is your attorney talking." My conviction grew as I spoke. "The fighting is going to hold this project back. You are spending a fortune building the spacecraft, and you will spend much more. You've got to end the fighting, or all that you have spent will be wasted, because it is my opinion that the ISRO will not cooperate otherwise."

There was silence as Amanta and the two men began talking to one another in a Chechen dialect. I knew I was taking a risk in all of this, but I also knew I'd regret it if I didn't try.

"Jenny, if you can talk to the director, we will see what we can do," Amanta finally said. Sneshia still wore a menacing look, but he relented. Amanta held up her glass of wine in a toast, and the two men followed.

* * *

The Sixth Traveler

"Chase, we need to talk."

I watched Chase on a phaeton from a private conference room in my hotel in Bengaluru. I set the video and voice to *Unaltered* so Chase could see me as I was. It's the least I could do for what I needed to say. There were two things I needed to clear with Chase, both difficult. I didn't want to fake any part of it.

"Sure," he said, in his typical mellow way. He sat in his office in Pasadena, directing students passing behind him to re-try a test from the day before, joking with him that there must have been a ghost in the machine. Hearing him laugh made it even more difficult to pull myself away from him.

"Clowning as usual," I said.

"I know, sorry."

"Can we talk, alone?"

"Of course." He ushered his students out and closed the door before sitting in front of the screen, smiling back at me.

"What's up, Jen?"

"A couple of things."

"Okay."

"Venka. I'm going to see him tomorrow. I'm in Bengaluru now. I just got back from Grozny. I met with Federatsiya representatives."

"Amanta Kokotova?"

"Yes, and two others. The plan is that Dr. Venkalaswaran and I are going to meet with Indian Space Agency officials."

"Excellent."

"Yes, but it's not that. I need to know about Venka. I can't get it off my mind."

"I know."

"Is he amping-up?"

"Yes." There were no mincing words with Chase. I could see him mouth a curse to it all.

Kevin M. Faulkner

"Have you ever said anything to him about it? Have you seen him do it?"

Chase took a breath before answering. I could see the look on his face. He didn't want to talk about this. I know Chase didn't like what Venka was doing to himself. Chase was the type to leave people alone. Normally, I was too.

"Yes, I have. I mean, I've talked to him. He won't listen. I haven't actually seen him do it though. He goes off to some library."

"Library?"

"That's what he calls it. Obviously, some sort of mainframe computer room with hookup capacity."

"I see."

"It's killing the guy. He's aged in the time I've known him."

"Why does he do it?"

"He told me that the human brain is not powerful enough for achieving what humans were not meant to do." Chase looked down at his desk, moving papers around. "It's bull shit."

"So, he uses it to develop the QMT technology?"

"He thinks that. I don't think it does a damn thing."

I sat there in silence.

"I hate that shit."

"I know, I do too," I lamented.

"So, what are you going to do?"

"I don't know. Nothing? I'm going to see him. I've decided to say something, but I don't know what." What could I do? I'm his attorney.

This brought me to the next thing I needed to say to Chase. Some moments passed when we said nothing.

"Do you want me to go with you? I can catch a flight," Chase finally said.

"No, thanks. I need to do this myself. You could say it's my job." I didn't think it was, but I wanted to handle this alone.

"He'd be pissed if I said any more anyway."

The Sixth Traveler

"I can see that."

"What's the other thing?" Chase asked.

I dreaded what else I had to say. It's hard to plan what to say in these situations. I had created a whole speech in my mind, which I realized then would sound flat if spoken aloud. So, I started, hoping the words would come.

"About us, that night at the Venka's."

"I know." He said, somewhat embarrassed.

"No, you don't, Chase."

"It's okay, Jen. I understand."

"No, Chase."

"What?"

"That night in Sankey Tank, at Venka's place was incredible."

"You're incredible, Jenny. It's just not the right time. Things are about to get crazy for me, and for you too," he smiled at me, his hair tussled and his lab glasses hanging from his neck. "Our timing is off."

"Yes, it is." Understatement. What I planned to tell Chase was that he was my client, or some semblance thereof, and it wasn't right for us to have a relationship like this. It was a conflict, in more ways than one. My heart ached, but for the first time in my life, I felt responsible for something more than myself.

"I hope you understand," I said.

"It's okay. I do, it's for the best."

"Yes."

"We'll talk again, soon. Let me know what happens with Venka."

NINE

Implant Record Date 28 September 2095
Bengaluru

I was cautious yet determined as I walked across the concrete floor of the domed observatory leading to Venka's private library at the Indian Institute of Science. The observatory housed an ancient refracting telescope built around 1930. I marveled at the beautiful behemoth, so different from the pencil thin light bending optically enhanced telescopes today. My shoes clicked on the concrete floor of the dimly lit space filled with instruments that were relics of the past.

Though I had been to the Institute many times, I had never been to this place. "It's where I do my best thinking," Venka once said. I envisioned his private think tank in as a bright room opened to a courtyard where he might sit alone and dream, a place I would have wanted to go myself. Given my current surrounds I had a feeling I would find something quite different.

As I approached a brightly lit reception of a single desk and two chairs the musty smell of old timber filled my senses. "Hello, I'm here to see Dr. Venkalaswaran." I said to the young woman sitting behind the desk. I was guessing the hallway behind her lead to the library.

The attractive young woman looked up above her glasses and smiled at me, "Yes, hello Ms. Hsu. He'll see you in a moment." The name plate on her desk read Dr. Ishita Desai, probably a post-doctoral associate working part-time as an assistant.

"Thanks, you can call me Jenny."

"And you can call me Ishita."

I looked around while she mumbled something into her headset before saying, "If you don't mind, please take a seat. Would you like some tea? Coffee?"

"No thanks," I replied.

"So, it's very nice to meet you, Jenny," Ishita said, catching my attention from my phone. "Of course, I've heard so much about you. You're famous."

"As famous as a lawyer can be, right?" It took some time to get used to people knowing who I was.

"Yes, I imagine this is all very exciting. Everyone in India knows Dr. Venkalaswaran. I work for him and only rarely get to talk to him in person. He's such a busy man."

"It is a change," I considered. "I used to be able to sit quietly in my office and be left alone, but that hardly ever happens now. I am in meetings, flying back and forth between Bengaluru and San Diego. I'm the center of attention at my law firm."

"But it's good for you, right?" Ishita asked. "Your career?"

"Yes, I suppose. Except you're more exposed. Like, if you've got any kind of problem, being so visible only makes it worse, or at least, brings it to focus."

"Oh, do you have a problem?"

She trapped me, which I thought was kind of funny really. I find it difficult to be totally honest in these situations.

"I suppose so, like everyone."

"Like?"

Wow, she's so forward! But good naturedly, I answered, "Not having control over my time."

"I know what you mean," Ishita replied.

Seeing Ishita's openness, I felt a little more at ease to be more honest. "To tell the truth, it's more than just time. I used to avoid everything, especially people, all of this. I still try, but, really, I can't anymore. It chases me down and tackles me."

"What is 'it'?"

"Mmmm. Good question," I replied. "Judgment?"

Kevin M. Faulkner

"Ahhh, yes, me too. My parents, my boyfriend, my family, friends," Ishita said, seemingly thinking of an even longer, more specific list of *its*.

"What do you do about it?" I asked.

"I don't know, I've never thought of it before," Ishita replied. "Maybe avoidance is a good thing, though I think I would be too lonely."

"You have a point." Just as I started to say more, Ishita's headset chimed.

"I'm sorry, I need to take this call," Ishita said.

"Of course." I looked back down at my phone.

Ishita got up from her desk and walked past me, saying, "Excuse me, I need to take care of something. I will only be a moment." She walked away through another door, the echo of her footsteps loud at first but growing fainter as a door closed behind her.

I sat patiently enough, but after several minutes got up to look towards where Ishita had gone. No sign of her. Feeling guilty but overwhelmingly curious, I walked towards the door behind the desk. After looking back one more time, I quickly opened the door to explore on my own.

Nothing dramatic, it was simply a hallway lined with what I guessed were real wooden doors. There were pictures along the wall, photos of early versions of the Institute's telescopes, professors and directors from years ago. I stopped to read one of the descriptions. I could hear the hum of computers through the increasingly darkened hallway leading further into the building. I decided to follow the sound. The hum increased in intensity, and the air cooled. The hallway ended at a door with a placard that read *Observatory Library*.

Stepping lightly, I stopped upon hearing an indefinable sound mixed in with the hum of what I concluded was a bank of teralight computers. It was so faint that I had to stop breathing to clearly hear it. Beneath the sounds of the flowing air, I could hear a ghostly moaning sound. A shiver went through me as I tried to locate the

The Sixth Traveler

source of the phantom. It seemed to come from whatever was on the other side of the door.

My heart raced as I reached for the brass knob. I turned the ancient relic, surprised at how easily it moved. I braced myself for the likelihood that Venka would be somewhere on the other side, perhaps connected to a computer, hooked up and dazed out. I got an eerie feeling, as the surroundings would never hint at any high-technology research. There were no glass windows with white-coated technicians with clipboards or computers with lights flashing. Just a fusty hallway with cloudy photos and ancient wooden doors.

As a naughty child fearing that I might be caught in my mischief, I looked back once more as I opened the door. A rush of cool air hit me. As light as the hallway had been, my eyes took a moment to adjust to the faintly lit room, I could see bookshelves against the back, pictures lining the walls, and in the middle was clearly a man, sitting in a chair with his back to me. He didn't make a move. *It must be Venka*, I thought. If there had been moaning, it was gone now. As I came around I could see the stylus pad positioned against the port in his neck underneath his skin, a large computer screen in front of him, with a light above the monitor flashing blue. Before moving any further, I looked back to make sure no one was there. All I saw was the sliver of light beneath the door at the other end of the hallway.

I went back and closed the library door behind me.

Taking a deep breath, I glanced over at the man in the chair. Of course, it was Venka, yet a part of me didn't want to acknowledge what was there. I could see him reclined, an oxygen mask covered his face and a stylus pressed against his neck. I was somehow torn from going directly to him. He was in a deep trance, and for a moment he drew me in with him. I slowly walked the periphery of the room, fully aware of Venka's breathing and the whirring of electronic sounds while I tried in vain to imagine it was not so. I feigned interest in the pictures all along the walls: Einstein's shaggy hair and droopy wool pants standing in front of a black board at Princeton, Fermi staring

Kevin M. Faulkner

intently at an ancient vacuum tube, Ramanujan with a gentle smile, then Haak, Hawking, and Benshar in the distance.

The man in the hookup chair will be up there someday, I thought.

Like that same child who entered the room, I had this fiction that if only I could keep from looking at the person in the chair, then it couldn't be Venka. Having walked half-way around the perimeter of the room, it was time.

"I hate this." I said, turning to look.

It was indeed Venka, and my heart sank. He was in what was known as a neurobionic trance, eyes closed but head angled somewhat upwards.

"Venka." I said quietly as I approached him. Nothing. *What do I do?* I wondered.

Venka moaned a sort of cry for help, which startled me and drove a chill up my spine. I imagined a fight against some monster in the cyber-universe between his mind and the computer. It lasted for moments, then went away.

"Venka." I was scared, caught up in what I imagined his dream would be.

It was known that amping-up could improve creativity and problem solving, but it was also terrible on the brain and body. Depending on how the computer was programmed, the influence of the computer's processor on the brain could take many forms, from entertainment to searching for some unfathomable truth. The latter took a much greater toll on a person's mind.

"Venka!" Still nothing but rapid eye movement underneath his eyelids, his head turning slightly back and forth as if he were arguing with some adversary.

I heard a noise in the hallway behind the closed door that startled me, but then it went quiet. I didn't know what to do. I rubbed the back of my neck and simply looked at him.

Shit. I clearly heard the sound again. Footsteps.

The Sixth Traveler

The door opened and Ishita stepped in, a surprised look on her face.

"Jenny, what are you doing? You are not supposed to be here."

For a moment I froze, caught in the expression on Ishita's face. She wasn't backing down. I went on the offensive.

"I'm this man's attorney."

"You can't just come back here like this," she said. It dawned on me that I did not owe this woman anything, and as sweet as she seemed, I was right for me to be here.

"Damn it, Ishita, how could you let him do this? Don't you know what this is doing to him?"

Ishita looked surprised at my response and would not look me in the eye at that point. She walked towards me to look at Venka.

"Yes, but it's for his work."

"Don't you care about Venka?"

"I care, but he chooses this, he knows what he's doing."

"It may have started that way, Ishita, but I think he does it now out of addiction."

Ishita didn't answer me.

"We need to get him off this machine," I said.

"No, leave him alone. You need to leave."

"I'm not going anywhere." I felt myself gaining ground as I moved into what was uncharted territory. Being an assertive caregiver was not a familiar role for me, at least not since I was much younger.

Ishita appeared torn, whether to stay with me or leave. I supposed she could leave and tell someone, but what would she say?

"Let me get the exit sequence," Ishita said, reluctantly. With that, she turned and left.

I took a deep breath, turning again to look at Venka. I had seen movies of people amping-up but had never seen it in person, not like this. I studied him, the stylus against his neck, and the screen before him streaming with data. I could read some words, but overall, it made little sense, typical of the raw feed from an implant, but worse. It was rapid fire and seemingly endless.

Kevin M. Faulkner

I looked at my phone, wondering if I should call someone. No signal. Interesting. I was expecting Ishita to storm back in, but nothing. Perhaps she didn't know what to do. She may have had an exit sequence or some pass code to get Venka out of his trance with the computer but thought better of it. Or Venka could have anticipated this and instructed her to leave him.

As time passed, my sinking feeling was gradually replaced with anxiety, and concern. Venka was a brilliant man, and kind to me. I don't think I have ever met anyone like him, charismatic and humble. I kept trying to figure it out, thinking *Venka was not corrupt. He treated everyone around him with integrity, in spite of his apparent addiction. His research was honest to a fault. He hid nothing.*

Except himself.

"What now?" I rubbed my hands together against the chill in the room and said to myself. I stood next to Venka wanting to wake him, anxious to contact him in some way, but I knew the risks so decided against it. I looked at his face and thought back to when I first met him, over a year ago. He had clearly aged. The stress of having the brain activated this way took its toll.

Waiting for Venka's trance to end, or Ishita to end it for him, I grew a little edgy. I got up to look around the room. I wondered at the expense of so much paper in those books. Indeed, many of them were old: *Cosmos, Mahābhārata, Anna Karenina, Siddhartha, The Life of Marianne, The Smuggler's Dream, Batman, The White Tiger, A Tale of Two Cities, The Plague,* and other common Indian, American, and European titles I recognized. By the 2060's paper had become exceedingly expensive, so few books were published. This room was a holdover, which was probably why Venka selected this place.

I kept looking back when finally, I heard a chime near Venka. I went back to where he was seated and pulled a wooden chair up next to him. I watched the blue light above the computer turn flashing, then steady yellow. I stood, noticing a change in the streaming data. Venka stirred and took a deep breath, eyes still closed. I hadn't thought of what to do at that moment. So, I just stood up and spoke to him.

"Venka." No reaction. "V!"

He turned his head toward me. Eyes still closed, a small grin came over his face. The light above the computer screen turned red and chimed, and the streaming data on the computer stopped.

"I'm glad you are here, Jenny," he said, still groggy. I held his hand, still on the arm rest, limp and cold.

"Me too."

* * *

"Jenny, we are not ready for this," Venka said, faintly, his eyes still closed. I removed the oxygen mask from his face. His eyes gradually opened, and Venka looked at me. I suddenly felt sad; and as if knowing what I was thinking, he repeated, "Jenny, we are not ready."

"Ready for what?"

"Jenny, it's too much. Where will we go?"

I could hear his words, but he wasn't making any sense. Venka looked around as if searching for something; he mumbled, an afterglow from the neurobionic trance with the computer that must be housed in one of the rooms adjacent to the hall.

"Venka, just relax," I said as he continued to mumble incoherently: something about Cygnus, then some particle physics jargon that was indiscernible to me. Yet, there was something exciting in his words, inviting. I felt a rush of adrenaline.

"Our children are no longer . . . ours."

"Mmmm," I said, quietly, still holding his hand, trying to gently bring him back into the present moment. I could feel some warmth as his blood began to flow to his limbs.

Kevin M. Faulkner

"Where will we go?" he said with increasing coherence, sweat now beading on his forehead. I wondered if he was talking about the planned test of the first lighter, a manned demonstration in which he would be the sole star traveler. Perhaps he was already planning.

"To another star," I replied.

"No." He shook his head. It dawned on me we were indeed talking about two different things. "I know, Jenny. I have to be the one." I didn't want him to be the one now more than ever.

"Venka, we can have an android—"

"No!"

"Why?"

He was silent for some time, his mumbling ceased as he gradually came out of the trance he had been in. "They won't understand," he said.

"Won't understand what?" I shook my head, not understanding what he was getting at.

He looked at me with an expression I had never seen in him before. He looked like he was lost in some kind of pain. Alone.

I didn't know how to respond. At first I simply took it as a leftover aura from his trance. "Venka, are you ready to stop this?" I asked as I moved the stylus away from his neck.

"I know I have to . . . there is no other way to see, to tell others," he said, pointing at the computer screen in front of him, his voice dry and raspy.

"Venka." I worried that he may stay stuck in some infinite AI loop.

For a moment, he became more lucid, awake. He opened his eyes and turned to me. "Don't worry, Jenny, the system is closed."

"That's not exactly what I was concerned about, but okay." He meant that it wasn't connected to the internet or other interconnected computer systems.

He closed his eyes again and said, "I can see."

"What can you see?"

The Sixth Traveler

He was silent, again searching. "How can I use human words to describe this?"

"Aravinda." I had an image in my mind of his children, and Nithia. I poured him some water as Ishita came back into the room.

"He's back."

TEN

Implant Record Date 3 October 2095
Bengaluru

"I talked to Venka about the risks. I tried to convince him that it isn't a good idea for him to do this; that he should have an android make the first major jump. He simply won't listen."

I phaetoned John Mar from Venka's home where Nithia and I helped Venka recuperate from his ordeal. I sat in the kitchen watching Venka tend to his garden while I worked. He needed to be himself if he was going to be of any help in talking with Indian officials to launch his invention into space.

"What does his wife say?"

"Not much," I replied. I could tell Nithia was glad for me to be there; she was clearly worried about her husband. But she did not want to talk about it, nor did she want the children to know anything.

"He should at least have a trained astronaut make the jump," John said.

"He's not gonna go for that." Part of me now defended the idea of Venka being the chosen one for the first interstellar jump, but I wanted to keep Venka's personal problems a secret as much as I could. I could relate to his need for privacy, to be left alone in that part of himself. I was well aware of my ethical duties here and treaded a thin line.

"Dr. Venkalaswaran isn't making any sense," John said in resignation.

"It's his baby."

"What does the Indian Space Agency say about it?" John asked.

"Unfortunately, from preliminary meetings with ISRO officials, it sounds like they think it is a great idea."

"Mmmm. Well, go ahead with your meeting with the director," John said. "But if you see an out, take it."

"Will do."

In a softer tone, John ended the conversation, saying, "Let me know if there is anything I can do, Jenny."

"Thanks John, I will. I'll call you when we get there." I heard the back door shut and Venka walk in.

"Hey there."

I am no psychologist, but I knew enough about family dynamics to know that there must have been some level of denial going on with Nithia, and she clearly shielded the children. I could tell that Nithia vacillated between embarrassment and joy at my discovery and involvement in Venka's problem. I suggested a doctor, but they both refused. In fact, that suggestion had the effect of strengthening Venka's resolve to leave cognitive amplification behind.

"See, I am as fit as ever," Venka said, proudly displaying his dirt-stained hands.

"We'll see."

Dr. Venkalaswaran and I stayed at his home for several days before traveling. We flew together from Bengaluru to Sriharikota, where we were chauffeured from the airport to the ISRO headquarters. The sprawling campus was a maze of buildings, each from a different era, from the early 2050's to the present. We were led into a newer building, a modern take on traditional Indian architecture, and led down a series of halls to a large meeting room, brightly lit from the sun beaming through the wall of windows. Several of the windows were open, and there was the scent of flowers throughout the room. We were led to a long wooden conference table that must have been ancient and expensive. A young man brought us tea, loaded it with milk, and quietly slipped away, his footsteps creating an echo in the otherwise empty sun filled chamber.

Several minutes passed before we heard, "Dr. Venkalaswaran!" from the director entering unexpectedly from a side door. "I've heard so much about you, so nice to meet you."

Kevin M. Faulkner

We both rose and held out our hands. "Dr. Rungta," I said, "my name is Jenny Hsu. I am with the law firm of Lackley, Bei and Chavez. I am helping Dr. Venkalaswaran launch himself to the nearest star, though I have tried to talk him out of it."

"Ahhh, yes, yes, so people tell me. Well, scientists do crazy things for their cause," Dr. Tonson Rungta said, laughing. "Let us hope that he is there and back in time for tea."

We went back to the table near the tea service, and sat down next to one another, chairs pulled away from the table so there was nothing between us. I could sense warmth between the men, as if they were old friends. Dr. Rungta was somewhat older than Venka by at least ten years, yet it was Dr. Rungta that looked upon Venka with admiration.

"So, Dr. Venkalaswaran, I have read all of your recent papers, and I watched the lecture you gave to a packed house at Stanford University in May. Many people were there, important people."

"Yes, thank you Dr. Rungta," Venka said modestly. "I say a lot of crazy things, but I have Jenny to keep me straight. Lawyers are not all bad."

"He says that because I'm the only attorney he's met who knows what twist gravity imposes on a Higgs boson. I can call his bluff."

Dr. Rungta laughed as he turned to Dr. Venkalaswaran.

Nearly breathless, Dr. Rungta was eager to talk, "Dr. Venkalaswaran, I am most impressed with your paper on time-sensitive spacial bending. Tell me, how did you make the connection between blink particles and a quantum effect? And how does this translate to such a scale that transports large masses?"

I remembered the concepts of such matter more than the actual mechanics and mathematical derivations. Essentially, these blink particles were nearly mass-less, and undetectable as they exist in their current state, it being twenty billion years since the Big Bang. Venka found that upon acceleration, creating a state more like that of the first few milliseconds of the Universe, these particles behaved quite differently and took on not only new properties, but new meaning. It was the first time such matter had been detected, and it was so unexpected that it took years for the scientific community to believe it.

The two men talked about this and other matters for nearly an hour. I thought of how amazing it was that I found myself at this place, mostly improvising as I went along. I sat back and let the relationship build. I have come to learn that this is the most important thing in any transaction. Rungta didn't have any government counsel with him, so I thought it best for me to lay back.

"The current prototypes are small," Venka explained, "but each one is larger than the one before. Ultimately, the device will be large enough to carry a human, preferably myself, and best launched from near zero gravity. We have performed an unmanned test, but we are skipping animal tests, as I believe they would not be very productive and costly in any case. In the primary demonstration I envision, the lighter will conduct a destination event, followed by a return event. Our first human test should take well under an hour."

The belief we had at the time, which was later debunked, was that gravity would interfere with the QMT technology, or at least complicate it. It turns out that having a space station that did not rotate to generate the centripetal force to mimic gravity did make the early tests simpler to plan and execute, but it was not necessary.

Venka took a sip of tea, and continued, "The Chinese remain opaque about their devices, so it is not clear what they have achieved. It seems certain that a human being has not been part of any QMT event. We propose to be the first."

"Well, this is all very exciting, and I believe the time has come," Rungta said, "but we'll have more than my boss to convince. The Indian government will have to bless it. I don't think that will be a problem, but it will take some time, as all things do with our government."

Rungta turned to me, in a more serious tone.

Kevin M. Faulkner

"Ms. Hsu, I wanted to ask, there are rumors that the Chechen military insurgency, the Vainakh, is involved with this project in some way. Is that true?" He was being polite. Surely, he knew.

As diplomatically as I could, I replied, "As you know, the intellectual property is co-owned by NASA and a group of investors, PacificEnergy."

"Yes, but it appears that the activities around the project are driven by these investors, not NASA," Rungta replied.

"It only appears that way. Both are equals in the development of the technology, of course, partnered with the Indian government," I walked a fine line between privileged information and moving these negotiations forward. "I know that there is talk that the Caucasus Federatsiya may be involved with those investors. I can't speak to that. However, I can say that my firm represents and advises the Caucasus Federatsiya, and we work with US and international bodies in helping them create a new government."

"I see," Rungta said.

"I follow reports and believe that the Vainakh forces are cooperating with the Federatsiya, and a cease fire between the VK and Russia is eminent," I followed as truthfully as possible: "The Federatsiya is working to form a government, one that is backed by most of the population under their claimed territory."

"I have seen those reports." Rungta paused, smiling at Venka. He considered what I said, though I suspected he had already done much thinking on the matter. The Indian government had an interest in moving this forward, if for no other reason than national pride.

"Well, I think we have something, Aravinda, Ms. Hsu. Let me talk to my liaison with the Minister. This will take time."

"We understand."

"They say your best won't come only from this journey, but let us start with this journey," Rungta said.

I felt uneasy about Rungta's questions but satisfied with my answers. Rungta was setting in motion a historic series of events that

The Sixth Traveler

would be told for generations. I didn't want it to be based on lies. Venka and I debated this on the ride back to our hotel.

"But sometimes that's the way it is," I said to Venka in the limousine. He wanted to know why he couldn't simply tell the assistant director of the ISRO that we were part of a joint venture with what many believe to be terrorists.

"I just want to be honest."

"I know you do."

We sat quietly for a long time; it was a forty-minute drive into town. Venka leaned over to read his paper on the seat next to him. I turned to look out the window at the passing scenery. For me, navigating communication between people was work. Navigating between competing obligations and motivations was exhausting.

"I can't abide Adeane asking questions about this, can you talk to him?" Venka suddenly asked.

I had avoided the whole subject of Chase Adeane.

"I'll talk to Chase." I didn't have the heart to tell him that I had already talked to Chase, this relationship was yet another minefield that I had to wearily manage my way through.

"Don't tell him about my problem." Venka said, silently.

"I think he knows," I replied. I wasn't sure if Venka was naïve or hopeful.

"It's a family matter."

"Yes, Venka, but I think many people around you already knew. No one is judging. We are all glad that you have stopped," I said, trying to allay his fears.

There was silence for a long time before Venka spoke.

"Nithia is grateful to you." He hesitated, then added, "So am I."

*　*　*

Kevin M. Faulkner

I sat on my board at Padang Padang Beach in West Sumatra, taking a short break in Bali as my security paced the beach. It was the best surfing close to my travels, near the same time zone as Bengaluru, and a great airport with many flights in and out. So practical for me! Clearly, my lifestyle as an associate, hiding in my office just long enough to not get fired allowed me to live a different life than I live now. It was all I could do to take a breath without being in the middle of negotiating what would become historical events.

There were some crushers forming long pipes of greenish water. For now I was looking for the snappers to work my travel-worn bones on. Though dizzy from the constant time zone changes between Chechnya, India, and California, I could see the payoff. I felt good about the direction the project was taking. After several months of negotiations, the Indian government had agreed to stage a test of the first star traveling lighter on board one of their orbiting space stations.

In the meantime, Venka was well into his training with other Indian astronauts, transforming from a scientist to a pilot. At his insistence, Venka was on his way to becoming the first person to experience a quantum mass-transfer event.

I wiped the salty water from my face as I looked towards a coming wave, bracing myself to jump onto my board. "I'll take it," I said to the approaching swell. Soon I was on top of the wave, riding it until its energy ran out.

* * *

On trips back and forth between Bengaluru and my other common destinations (San Diego, Washington, D.C., and Houston), I always stayed with the Venkalaswaran's. The trips mostly involved complex negotiations between NASA and the ISRO for a window to run our demonstration. It had become a second home to me, and I grew into being an auntie to Prashid, Yhama and Mika while Nithia and I conspired to bring her husband back to normalcy. As Venka's mind cleared and Nithia went back to her work, she found herself increasingly dragged into a world she did not sign up for: wife of a public figure.

As the media got hold of the story of the world's first faster-than-light spacecraft, the attention was unavoidable. Venka was followed most everywhere by the Indian news agencies. They loved him but pestered him relentlessly. I was sometimes a secondary focus of attention, coming and going from his offices and laboratory as well. I answered occasional questions in front of the camera, which was unnerving at first, but I learned to smile and talk without saying anything. After several months, it became clear that the Institute would have to provide security for his home and his family, and that I would have to stay away from Venka in public.

"Ahhh, I hate this," Nithia had said one day when I was with her in the kitchen. "I don't appreciate all of this attention. I don't think it is good for the children."

I suggested that they, at least the kids, go somewhere and stay, or hide, until it was over. Maybe Darjeeling or West Kashmir.

"I would love that, but I'm afraid it will never be over," Nithia lamented. I think she was right. From these days forward, Aravinda Venkalaswaran would be a public figure.

"I'll help."

"Jenny, you have already done so much," Nithia said as she sat down next to me at the kitchen table. "I am so grateful for what you have done. You have made me face something wives usually find impossible."

"What is that?"

"Seeing your husband's flaws, our family's flaws. For not denying them for fear of destroying the family perfection that wives tend to hold so dear."

Kevin M. Faulkner

I just smiled.

"And for not running away."

I stood and walked over to Nithia.

"Every family has secrets. It doesn't have to destroy a family. Believe me, I know."

"I suppose I see now that perfection is a lie anyway," Nithia replied.

"I understand," I said as I embraced her. "It would be boring any other way."

At times I traveled with Venka, increasingly to Texas for training at the Johnson Space Center or Florida at the Kennedy Space Center. In the United States, things were low key. There was a great deal of skepticism for one thing, the scientific community cynical about the technology, while industry waited for someone else to prove it first. The public was focused on more pressing issues and had long since lost interest in space exploration. There was a gnawing sentiment that we humans were living on borrowed time, and the Earth was running out of good will. Energy was increasingly expensive, and either rationed or wanting. Wealth was spread so unevenly; some were rich while others suffered.

The astronaut training was having a visible effect on Venka's appearance. Though he was never heavy to begin with, he was becoming even leaner.

"You are looking good," I said to him one night around the dinner table where we were both set up with our computers.

"I think so too, Nithia likes it," he replied, not looking away from his computer. I could see that the raw spot on his neck was nearly healed, and the blank stare of the neurobionic trance was replaced with twinkle in his eyes.

"You need to look good for the aliens you meet on Alpha Centauri." Nithia said. "You're representing humanity!"

"A fine specimen I am."

The Sixth Traveler

They joked, but it all felt so remote. I wouldn't know until later how much so. This technology wasn't the kind of thing you could test in a traditional sense. It wasn't an airplane that could be test flown in the sky, or even a space craft that could be launched and returned, each of which could be readily followed. The problem with the lighter technology was that it left the vicinity of the Earth, all human contact and communication. Yet Venka pushed for the whole enchilada all at once: human traversal of 4.3 light years to the nearest star system to our own, the Alpha Centauri star group.

"We think it's prudent to carry out more tests before Dr. Venkalaswaran attempts an event in a lighter," the top NASA official told a group of us, including John Mar and me in a meeting months ago.

"The Indian Space Agency is not concerned, we believe the technology is safe and ready for interstellar human testing," was our official response. At the time, I felt that way: confident and full of hubris in a machine I had a part in.

"He's ready to go," I told John one day, back in San Diego. We were only weeks away from the test date, and it was near Christmas when I was about to leave for Seattle.

"Are you?"

I answered "Yes" not comprehending what was behind that query.

ELEVEN

Implant Record Date 4 April 2097
Indira II, Indian Federation Space Station

Floating in zero-gravity looked cool on film but was completely unnerving *in propria persona*. Yet after a year of negotiations, dealing, and compromises, we were in Earth's orbit with Venka's finished lighter. The Indian government had agreed to stage the first lighter test on the *Indira II*, a third-generation Indian space station. In the countdown leading up to the first manned QMT *jump*, I floated before a porthole looking out at the lighter that was attached to a gangway extending from the station only meters away. The station was 10,000 kilometers above the Earth, in opposition from the sun and moon, presumably creating a clearer path for its journey. We learned much later how simplistic that was.

Some things did make a difference, such as the motion of the space station. Normally, the station would orbit the Earth once every day or so, but for the test it was positioned stationary in space relative to the Earth, making the departure and arrival of the lighter less complicated.

John Mar, Dr. Madan, and I launched from Sriharikota and arrived at the *Indira II* several days before the test. Venka and Chase and the mission control crew arrived weeks earlier in preparation for his mission. The lighter had been transported to the *Indira* by an Indian heavy-lift rocket months ago and had been set up and programmed well in advance of its first test. Though lacking widespread media coverage, the day of the test was truly historic. I had been so busy leading up to the day of the test I had not thought of its implications. It was not until I saw the spacecraft outside the portal window of the *Indira* that it hit me.

The lighter looked like a flattened disco ball, the array of tympani plates reflecting the light from the side facing the station, pitch black on the face that faced toward space. The lighter was about eight meters long and three meters wide. It was not outfitted with any propulsion systems—no rocket engines or boosters. It was simply made to drift in the vicinity of the *Indira*, and to jump to Alpha Centauri, the nearest star system to the Sun, and back, in two events. Essentially, the Sun and Alpha Centauri were two atomic nuclei and the lighter an electron, bouncing between the two as an electron would in a simple molecule of molecular hydrogen.

Though my job was done on day zero, what would later be known as the First Event, everyone around me was busy. Within the large control center of the *Indira*, technicians and flight controllers floated back and forth around me, and there was a constant chatter of voices between one another and ground control at Sriharikota. Provisions were made to make Houston a backup, but there was little need for it. Several astronauts, one on standby in support, surrounded Venka as technicians led him through the suit-up room on the far side of the control room and observation deck where I stood. I could see him making his way into an antechamber and out to the lighter, docked to a pressurized gangway leading into the small access panel into the craft.

Venka was anything but tense, steady and alive with purpose as masked technicians escorted his procession. He had almost a year of rigorous training, and it showed. Shedding his collegiate look, he had taken on the role of an Indian astronaut. In his orange spacesuit, his hair shaved, he entered his spacecraft with energized determination.

Looking at Venka now, it felt a world away from where he was a year ago when I found him in his library. Venka claimed that the use of cognitive amplification helped him develop what we now call the V-Shell of his craft. It's hard to say if that was true, or if he would have arrived unaided. *Is the computer a co-inventor? Would that be legal?* I think not. In any case, Venka was forced, if for no other reason, from any further neurobionic experiences because of his training in

Kevin M. Faulkner

preparation for this day. Vyomanauts were strictly forbidden to use such devices as much as they would be an illegal chemical substance. The early days were difficult, and Venka struggled at times, but I was hoping that as far as he had gone, he wouldn't step backwards.

"I'm excited," Chase Adeane was like a kid with a video game, maneuvering into his seat in front of a control console.

The *Indira II* was not rotational so there was no centripetally-generated gravity. This simplified the test, but it complicated getting around. The console was on the end of a line of consoles as part of the control center of the station, each with someone talking into a commlink, hands moving over the touchscreens before them.

Once inside, Venka was sealed in by the technicians as a sardine in a can, adding to my tension.

"Venka, are you in?" Chase asked through his headset. There was a video image of Venka's face in front of us. His vital signs were visible to the side. Venka was essentially in a cocoon, not unlike the astronauts in the first Earth-orbiting Mercury capsules. Seeing him like this made my stomach turn.

"Yes. I'm feeling good," Venka said, intent on his task. Part of me wanted to abort the whole thing. It was so risky; no person had ever taken part in QMT tests. I could envision that dead mouse. But Venka had insisted, saying, "No, it has to be a human, a computer or android could not respond to unknown situations, and an animal couldn't." I was in awe of the innocence of his bravery.

I had already had this discussion many times with both John Mar and Dr. Venkalaswaran: Why not an android? They are so advanced these days, almost human. Some people chaffed at that assertion, referring to humans as *breathers* and androids as *batteries*, a reference to the fact that androids did not respire, but ran on electricity and genetically engineered magnetized ptesinochondria. It felt a little wrong to use the term *batteries*, which some people used in a derogatory way. In any case, it was clear that the Federatsiya investors were not crazy about androids.

The Sixth Traveler

Amanta Kokotova had a particularly strong aversion to androids.

"Thirty minutes and counting," the female voice said over the speaker in the control center, accompanied by a chime. I could hear the chatter of voices from the control center, checking the systems of the lighter that was to carry Venka to the Alpha Centauri system and back. It was all to take place within a twenty-minute time frame, even though Alpha Centauri was more than four light years away from Earth.

John Mar and Dr. Nithia Madan were with me as we stood near the porthole of the *Indira* with a few select observers, engineers, astronauts, and Indian and US officials.

"How do you feel?" Chase asked Venka as he focused on the data streaming in through his earplug and computer screen. The chimes became more frequent as Venka got closer to lighting.

"Excellent," Venka replied.

"Twenty minutes," the voice calmly stated over the din in the control center. Somehow, at that moment the weight of what was happening hit me. *History is being made. Have I done enough?* I was a little panicky over the possibility that I might have helped set in motion historic events that I was ill equipped to handle.

I looked over at John and Nithia to see how they were taking it all. Nithia was surprisingly calm. I supposed she had long since resigned herself to her husband's risky business. And thought it was subtle, John seemed more concerned with me.

"Ten minutes, switching to on-board computer systems. Sriharikota, please stand by."

"*Indira*, this is Sriharikota, standing by."

"*Surfer*, please confirm operation."

"*Indira*, Sriharikota, configured for event," Venka replied.

The lighter began to glow. No longer a multi-mirrored metal surface, it took on a more uniform, ghostly blue sheen. A chill went through me.

Kevin M. Faulkner

I grabbed the bar in front of me in a reflexive attempt to hold the lighter in place. It didn't dawn on me until much later how little control I ever had.

"I've initiated the mimft accelerators. The particle density is stabilized." Venka said.

I floated in place, my eyes fixed on the lighter. A robotic arm was beginning to extend the device further out into the blackness.

"LN2 line released," the voice over the speaker stated. "Stand by for disconnect, in thirty seconds."

Then it happened, the lighter, now a glowing blue-white ember among the stars, floated away from the extended arm. The lighter had no drive systems to steer or maneuver, it simply drifted from the calculated push of the arm, retracting back into the enclosed gangway.

I can't believe this is happening, I thought.

"Five minutes," the female voice stated, as calm as when it had been thirty minutes.

"Chase," I started, wanting to ask if Venka would be alright. *Too late now*, I thought. Time counted down as my heart raced.

"One minute. Sriharikota, please stand by."

"Sriharikota, standing by."

The glowing lighter drifted further and further away, at least fifty meters from the space station.

"*Surfer*, please stand by." I had forgotten that Venka had given the lighter the name *Surfer*. Nithia had insisted on the name once she heard the idea. I forced back a lump in my throat at the thought.

"Standing by for departure," Venka said. Other than the steady countdown over the speaker, the control room and station interior was silent. The lighter drifted further away, but its glow intensified. We were on the dark side of the Earth, so the effect was spellbinding. So much so that I held my breath to allow all my senses to take it in, never quite sure if what I was seeing was real.

The Sixth Traveler

"Ten, nine, eight, seven," Flashes of light resonated from the lighter in a silently booming crescendo, and my eyes started to water. I couldn't blink . . . "six, five, four, three, two, one."

All was pitch black.

The control center fell silent. Where moments ago there had been a man of flesh-and-blood, only static and pixilated snow remained on the video screen.

"Sriharikota, confirm departure."

"*Indira*, departure confirmed." This meant that there was no sign of the *Surfer* visually or by radar. The clock was now ticking off a different time, counting how much time was left before the *Surfer* arrived back to where it had started. The calculations had shown that it should take 18 minutes and 27.5 seconds for Venka to reappear. The lighter had been programmed to reach the vicinity of Alpha Centauri A, stay for fifteen minutes, and arrive back.

At least, that was the plan. I had images from tales of people coming back from such missions having aged many years, or transformed into some kind of monster, or worse; the ship would be empty.

I rubbed my neck to bring myself to life. The cabin was charged with anticipation as a flurry of activity started anew. I had a sudden desire to get away from the porthole. I pushed toward the canteen, a room several meters behind me. I could still hear the time being called off over the control center speaker: "fifteen minutes and counting." Feeling a little sick to my stomach, I suddenly didn't want to see the *Surfer's* arrival. I simply wanted it over. I wanted to see Venka walk through the door of my office in San Diego on the little blue planet below.

"Jenny, you okay?" John said from behind me. He followed me to the canteen. "This is a little much for all of us, it's okay to be freaking out. I am."

"Yeah, I'm fine, I just need a drink of water."

"You know Venka had to do this," John said, "It's what he wanted, and you helped him get there."

"I know." I took a deep breath as I gained control of my senses. "Now that it's happening, it's all a little much."

I rubbed my face to push the blood that was pooling there in this zero-gravity environment back down to my legs.

We floated there together for a few minutes, listening to the bustle in the distance. I had my back to the padded sides of the canteen, looking out at the control center, then at John.

"I can't believe this is happening," I said, partly to myself.

"Really."

"Two minutes to arrival, and counting," the voice through the intercom announced.

"Let's go back." I grabbed John's arm while his other handheld the travel bars that ran throughout the station. I was glad for his presence, and for once accepted it.

"One minute," the voice said over a growing cacophony of sounds. Several designated observers stood with John and me: one from China, a Russian, a French observer representing the European Union, and one from the US. For all they knew this was purely an Indian Federation operation. The Federatsiya's presence was well hidden.

"Thirty seconds," the voice called out.

"Ten, nine, eight, seven," Like everyone else, I was searching through the porthole looking into space for a sign. It was hard to imagine that Venka had ever gone anywhere.

"Six, five, four, three, two, one."

Several moments passed. There was only the cold darkness sprinkled with a field of faint stars.

"*Surfer*, this is *Indira II*, do you copy?" the voice asked, as the control center fell silent for a second time.

Nothing.

Again, the voice calmly asked, "*Surfer*, do you copy?"

The Sixth Traveler

There was still darkness. I was getting a little frantic as I searched the blackness outside the station for some glowing or shiny orb. *God, where was he?*

"*Surfer*, this is *Indira*, do you copy?"

"I see something moving," John said quietly. An eerily black object blotted out the tiny points of starlight around it, creating an illusion of stars in motion.

The room was deathly silent but for the lone female voice in the control center, and the hum of the computers.

"*Surfer*, do you copy, this is *Indira*."

"*Indira II, Surfer* here," Venka replied though with heavy static.

"Christ." was all I could say, mostly to myself. Nithia silently turned and hugged me. I was astonished and relieved. John put his hand on my shoulder, as I felt a tear run down my cheek. There were cheers all around, and breathless "Oh my gods" filled the air.

There was no light emanating from the lighter. Its charred surface was visible only by its deletion of the stars behind it until station flood lights aimed in its direction. The *Surfer* was towed by a small, unmanned craft back to the *Indira* as the arm reached out from the extending gangway, swinging toward the charred lighter. Twenty minutes later, everyone clapped as they saw Venka floating up the passage accompanied by jumpsuit clad staff. He disappeared into an antechamber where his suit was removed. Minutes later he emerged wearing an under-pressure garment and a blanket over his shoulders.

Soundlessly, Venka's wife reached out for him.

"Were you there?" Chase joked as data streamed in from the *Surfer*. It was apparent by the star pattern of the destination, and the first detailed images of a star other than our own, that the *Surfer* had successfully sailed upon a quantum wave to its intended harbor. The visual images came up on the large monitor for everyone to see, eliciting gasps even from the most skeptical.

Venka simply smiled.

Still holding Nithia, he glided toward me. I wiped away a tear as relief overcame me.

Kevin M. Faulkner

The first words out of my mouth, accompanied by laughter, were: "Damn it, why did you have to do that?" Without letting him answer, I hugged him.

"Really." Nithia responded. Venka shrugged, grinning.

The observers came alive as Venka floated to the control center. There was no apparent harm, no time dilation or inertial effects. No gravitational wave ripping his flesh apart, and no gray hair from some dramatic aging process. And though Venka would need to be examined, he appeared to have maintained all his marbles.

The press of observers moved closer to talk to him. After speaking over one another, they yielded to one person.

"Dr. Venkalaswaran," the French observer asked, "where do you think this will all lead?"

In the first words of a human star traveler, Venka replied, "I don't know, it's too early to tell."

PART TWO

THE SECOND EVENT

TWELVE

Implant Record Date 14 September 2097
San Diego

"Jenny, that bruise on your face looks like the real thing."

I glanced up from my lytfascia. My hands still icy from the surf off Tourmaline beach the night before, the hot cup of coffee before me was like a fire. Kepler smiled at me from across the table as we sat together in a dark corner of the *Petit Souris* café in La Jolla, my favorite place to recover from surfing.

"It's too early for sarcasm," I grunted, "especially from an android." When I downloaded that day from my implant, it couldn't decide if I was embarrassed or angry. Possibly both, because my head was throbbing, and I had no recollection of the cause.

"You're angry," Kepler said.

Can he read my mind? He could, of course, if I had the remote reader in my implant turned on. In any case, I thought androids were not allowed to do that.

Kepler was a third tranche bioelectronic semi-autonomous android from Future Visions Corporation, Japan, Model 3.12, owned by my firm, Lackley, Bei and Chavez. *Semi-autonomous* means that he was self-aware as much as international law would allow for commercial use. I tried at first not to think of Kepler as *he*, but its visage was that of a human male, and it was advanced, very human: having a male voice that was slightly North American accented, and fitted with wavy brown hair, brown eyes, and except for his left hand and the back of his neck, which were exposed as electro-mechanical, human-like skin. He wore clothing to complete the look.

"Jenny, it would help if you talked to me. That's why I am here."

I thought about it. My relationship with artificial intelligence was complicated. I enjoyed the company of Britta, my home computer, and my working systems at the office, but I had never interacted much with androids until Kepler. I had nothing against them, I just wasn't sure if I liked where this was all going. Predictions of AI in classic science fiction were dire, *The Terminator*, *Blade Runner*, and *The Exploits of Macon Calm* came to mind, but so far there had been none of that. If anything, I was concerned that we humans were simply finding creative ways to make someone else do our work.

"I don't know what happened. I can't remember," I said, not quite lying. "I finished surfing and hung out at that little bar off the beach."

"Yes?"

I looked up at Kepler, "You left after dark. Then . . . .." I wondered if someone could have drugged me, because I hadn't had all that much to drink.

Kepler would know if I were lying. He was keenly observant of humans, our emotions, and predicting how we would act, useful tools for an attorney. Erissa Chavez and John Mar had assigned him to me, and as far as I could tell, he served two purposes: reward for a job well done and anchor in the storm. And the storm of Venka's experiment had created the winds of a hurricane. The media exploded with the news and everyone remotely connected to the project was suddenly under a microscope. Dr. Venkalaswaran was most intensely hounded, but so were others, including me. I became a star in the legal world, and in my own law firm.

That fame was more than I was prepared for. I felt exposed, as if my insecurities were visible for all to see. I got offers from dozens of law firms across the country, such a change from a few years ago. I was open with John about it. I remember he asked me what I would do, and I replied, "Dance with the one who brought me to the dance." That was something my father would have said. Honestly, part of it was that I was just too muddled to make any sudden change, which turned out to be my best instinct at the time.

Kevin M. Faulkner

"Well, you don't have a concussion," Kepler said. "We should see a doctor if you continue to feel pain." Kepler examined the darkened spot around my eye.

"Don't worry." *I wonder if he can tell what has happened to me?*

"So, I need for you to help me with the meeting later this week with Federatsiya representatives," I said, changing the subject. "I won't be directly involved in the negotiations with the Chinese, but I have a plan to help move things forward. I need to get Venka involved."

"You need to fill me in," Kepler said. "I understand the First Event of course, but I want your understanding of it all."

After the First Event the Chinese government filed a formal complaint with the International Court of Intellectual Property (ICIP). They claimed that they had dominating rights to Venka's lighter—what the Chinese insisted on calling a *shinbo*—and to all quantum mass-transfer devices. The Federatsiya, the Indian Academy, and NASA, all co-owners of the patent estate, didn't agree. And the US Government was now taking a much more prominent role, adding another dimension to my problems. My position and that of my clients was that the Chinese only had a general idea of how it would all work, and they had not even considered the Haakverse. Nonetheless, winning an action in the International Court against the Chinese government would be difficult.

"Where is Dr. Venkalaswaran now?" Kepler asked.

"He's gone back to Bengaluru to be with his family and to continue his research at the Indian Institute of Science," I said. "Some construction has started on a second, larger lighter, but I can tell he is not enthusiastic. I think he needs some time alone. He is not the kind of person who looks for fame. He likes flying under the radar." I think there was more to it. In the immediate aftermath of his jump to Alpha Centauri and back, he appeared normal, but once the initial excitement wore off he wasn't himself.

"I see," Kepler said. "I'd like to meet Dr. Venkalaswaran."

"You will," I said, marveling at Kepler's human-like voice. "I've waited too long to visit him as it is." I sat quietly for a while, thinking. I had spent so much time with Venka and Nithia before the First Event, now so much as changed. I could sense they wanted to be left alone, and it pained me to think I would break that wish.

"The Feds want a transport, something big, to hold at least a hundred people, whole families, with supplies to last for months," I said. "They want—"

"They want an escape." Kepler said.

"Well, we don't like to put it so bluntly, but yes, an escape," I said. "And somehow, I think from more than just a crowded planet. The Federatsiya is looking to me to move things along."

"Amanta Kokotova and Nikhil Lecha trust you."

"Mmmm. So, you know so much about them?"

"Yes, I do."

"Good, that will be useful."

As I spoke, I wondered if I was close enough to Venka that I could just go to him. I didn't have an instinct for these situations.

"This won't go anywhere without Venka," I continued. "And he wants to slow it all down. He worries about the technology and how it's going to change things. He's told me more than once that the world's not ready for this yet."

"Perhaps he's right," Kepler replied.

"Yes, but he's changed also. He's not himself. I've talked to Venka, and he is normal on the surface, but I can tell the difference in him." Nithia thought that Venka was suffering from some mild depression brought on by the effects of QMT, despite his Newton Shell. Venka was always silent on the subject.

"Do you suspect he's using cognitive amplification?"

I was surprised at the question.

"So, you know?"

"Yes, I know, it's in the databank, but no one wants to talk about it. As you say, I'm an android, so it stands out to me. I know what amping can do to humans, the stress it puts on your body, and psyche. Sometimes it doesn't show up right away."

"Yes, so you do. Well, as far as I know, he no longer uses it."

"Even so, he may have long-term issues. He can get help with that. He is being treated, isn't he?" Kepler asked.

"Yes, but he's good at changing the subject on me, so I don't really know."

"He is not the only one," Kepler replied, smiling.

"Haha. Still too early." I said, stopping to sip my coffee. "Anyway, we need Chase Adeane too. He spends most of his time at JPL, and at home in Texas. He has family there, and deer."

"Excuse me?" Kepler said.

"He hunts. With a gun."

"I see," Kepler said. "He must live remotely, game animals are so scarce."

"Yes, West Texas is still remote. I know Chase is unhappy with how the Federatsiya is managing the project, but for different reasons than Venka. Chase wants more control."

"And you object?"

"No, but I don't think we can go forward without Venka."

"Loyalty is admirable."

"Maybe, but mostly the Chinese want control. We can use that to our advantage, if I can get Amanta and Nikhil to see it that way." I was suspicious of the Chinese government, and Amanta even more so. Simply mentioning it made her angry. The Chinese government had become increasingly controlling of their own people, and continuously tried to exert that influence around the world, which they managed to do through remote implant control, investments, media, and military.

"Yes, from the Federatsiya's point of view, the longer the development of the technology drags on, the greater the chances another space-faring country will develop QMT on their own," Kepler said.

The Sixth Traveler

"They may be right. The Federatsiya doesn't care how all of this gets done. They're in a rush to get back up there," I said, pointing up.

"I've uploaded the log from the First Event as evidenced in the original records from the *Surfer* and *Indira*," Kepler said. "As I understand, it is believed that practicing the technology requires the lighter to be in zero gravity. That means we need heavy lift outside Earth's orbit. I'm guessing the only way is through China or the US."

"Right. India has already said they want to stay out of it. Too political for them right now."

"You'll have to find the right balance between settling the International Court action and bringing Venka and Chase back."

"Yes. The Federatsiya needs to come to that decision themselves. I have to lead them there. Everybody wants a piece of the pie now."

"There's a great deal at stake."

"Yes, a little overwhelming."

"Well, that's why I am here."

* * *

"Let's get something to eat."

It was late in the day, nearly six, when John Mar leaned into my open door with this proposition. I looked up, somewhat surprised because he had never asked me to go out with him after work unless it was part of a meeting.

"Ahhh."

"Sure, you do," he said, stepping all the way into my office then plopping down on a chair in front of my desk.

"Well, okay," I said. He looked satisfied. I noticed he had his tie off but was still wearing his jacket. He looked down at his phone as I closed down.

"I was just finishing up the merger agreement. I can send it to you."

"Don't bother, we'll finish it on Monday. There's no rush."

"Oh."

"What are you in the mood for?" he asked. I got up to collect my things.

"Well...."

"I'm buying," he added. I immediately thought of Branton Ma'hai, a guy I was already seeing. I wasn't sure if John wanted this to be a date or not. I looked up at his face: friendly yet a little mysterious. I wondered what was going on in that head. *I bet Kepler would know.*

"Well, in that case, how about seafood."

"Excellent choice, let's go." He looked down at his phone, typed something in, and we were off.

"Okay, okay. Such a rush." We walked past the computer room where Kepler was. Upon seeing him, I thought perhaps it was best if I did not know what was going on in John's head.

"Hey, Kep. I'm going out. I'll see you tomorrow." *This way life was more interesting.*

"Don't stay out too late, kids." When Kepler wasn't with me, he stayed at the law offices. There were several other androids there and they would link themselves to the computers and go down for the night.

John and I took the elevator down to the underground level and walked the tunnel east of the building, deeper into town. It was a Friday night, so it was packed with people, especially young people and couples.

"I know a great place down toward Pennington," John said.

"Oh, do you mean *Daimler's?*"

"No, no, much better than that."

"My, so fancy," I teased.

"Yes, very fancy. It's a place called *The Fishhook.*"

The Sixth Traveler

"Sounds nice." John told me how he often walked these tunnels, describing their history from the first ones built around the 2050's, and would sometimes walk at night, alone when he couldn't sleep. I knew he lived in town, but I didn't know where exactly.

"Further down, along State and West Streets."

"That's a nice area." There was nothing opaque in John's actions towards me, but I wondered at going on what seemed to be a date with such a high-level attorney in the firm. John's rise was swift, becoming a partner in only three years. He was a good litigator, but more, he was an excellent leader.

"Here it is, up on the street," he said, directing us to the escalator to the street level. We walked out onto the sidewalk next to busy Park Boulevard where we got onto a trolley that took us to the Balboa Park district. The evening breeze blew through the open trolley; the dry cool air felt crisp against my skin as it was warmed by the setting sun. I glanced over at John and noticed he was looking at me. I recalled that John was seeing someone himself.

We stepped out onto an open mall, the walkway made of bricks fashioned to look older than they were, with native succulents forming a sub-perimeter around a plaza, past which were one- and two-storied shops and restaurants made from the same bricks.

"Here it is," he opened the door for me.

"I called ahead," John said, then he turned to the host, "John Mar."

"Yes," she said, looking at the 3D projection in front of her face. "This way."

It was a dimly lit restaurant, and not too deep, so we were able to sit next to a window on the second floor. Candles lit each table, and old-fashioned light bulbs created a soft glow in the room, while noise dampening systems made an otherwise crowded space cozy and private.

"Thank you," John said to the host. A waitress followed immediately, and John ordered a bottle of wine for the two of us, a Cabernet.

Kevin M. Faulkner

"I know you're supposed to drink white with fish, but I like red. I think you'll like it."

He knows I like red. I'm impressed.

"I'm glad to get the chance to go out, just the two of us. We're always taking clients out, or people are taking us out. You know how those things go. We never get to really talk."

"Me too."

Work was the most natural subject, but it soon morphed into talking about the changes in our lives since the First Event and the world's reaction.

"I felt like my life had exploded," I said. "You know how I am; I'm pretty much to myself. Then suddenly everyone was focused on me. I was horrified."

"I understand."

"I mean, all I could think was—"

"What does everyone expect of me now?" John broke in.

"Yes. Like, somehow because of all this I was suddenly more capable than I was a few days ago."

John laughed.

"Maybe I shouldn't admit all of this to my supervising counsel."

"I think we're a little past that now. And in any case, I was pretty overwhelmed too." He paused before he said, "I tend to *manage* those types of things, but this was different. Even now, I am catching my breath."

"What do you mean?"

"Well," he smiled, "I mean that I take it as another challenge, something to push through and conquer, but in a proscriptive way."

"Proscriptive?"

"Yes." He hesitated, then looked at me.

"When I was young I was very much on my own. I had to take matters into my own hands or *manage* as I would say. It's something one of my social workers told me when I was a kid."

I had heard from some of the other attorneys that John had come from a rough background, somewhere in New England. I had never had the chance to talk to him about it.

"Well, you can't leave it there. Why did you have a social worker?"

We paused as the waitress came to take our plates and offer us some coffee and dessert.

"I suppose so," John replied. "Well, my father left when I was young, I barely remember him. I grew up around Boston, went to Catholic school as a kid. That took some money, and after a while my mother had less and less of it. The school let me stay, but my little brother, Sander, and I had to move around, living with distant relatives. My mom was messed up. Heroin, cocaine, whatever. A social worker from the state basically took Sander and me out of the home and put us in a temporary home. He visited and kept an eye on us until he could get something more permanent. Eventually we settled with other foster parents and things stabilized for a while. By that time I was in high school."

"Did you and your brother get to stay together?"

"Barely. I was a lost kid; it was hard for me to do anything about it. As soon as I was old enough I finished school and joined the military. I was in the Army, a Ranger by the time I was nineteen. I dragged my brother along; he mostly stayed buried in his computer world. I did the best I could to take care of him. He took some classes and worked some until he was on his own."

I listened intently to his story and felt honored in hearing it. I don't think he told it often. I wondered why he chose me, and why now? Realizing the gravity of it as he spoke, I felt compassion for him. And I could relate.

"You must have been in the Army during Georgia." I was referring to the wars that started at the end of 2070's in the Russian state of Georgia, a fractured place already, divided by fighting loyalists to Georgia, and Russia. NATO and the US were involved on the side of the Georgian loyalists, but Russia was strong and there was fear of a wider war if the West became too involved, so it was always limited. That put US forces at a disadvantage.

"I served two tours there. The hardest part was that you couldn't always tell who the enemy was. The mountain people were deeply loyal to their state, and welcomed our involvement, but there were others in Georgia who wanted to join Russia and wanted Europe and the US to stay out of it."

"Yes," I said, "I have read about it."

"What was worse, we weren't far from extremists who didn't want any Western involvement at all. There was always a fear of suicide bombings, there were land mines, traps; we were always on guard.

"In my second tour, my platoon was in a little town outside of Sochi. It was a beautiful place, but there were constant threats. Most of the population had already been driven out by the violence, but there were people living in the hills. The Russian backed Nationalists were to the East, but we thought they had already moved out. Intelligence from the mountain people confirmed it. My platoon was set to move into that area the next day. To confirm it was clear, our captain sent my buddy Eric Compton and me to patrol. It was considered routine, so we went alone, lightly armed.

"Eric and I had basically grown up together in the Rangers and served together most of our time there. We were like brothers." Though he tried to hide it, I could see the memories of his friend in John's face, the pain of it all.

"Turns out it wasn't clear. The enemy left some troops behind. I don't know how many, but Eric and I got caught up in a fire fight."

He hesitated for a while, pained to move forward.

"I'm sorry, John."

"No, it's okay." He took a moment to take a sip of his coffee.

"Eric got hit in the head, but it didn't kill him right away. There was nothing I could do. We were pinned down. I called in help, but all flights were grounded due to talks. We were stuck."

The Sixth Traveler

"God that must have been awful."

"It was the worst feeling, having my friend die in my arms, telling me to give his love to his wife."

"So, what happened?"

"I lost him there. Eventually, my platoon sent reinforcements to our position and drove the insurgents out of the area. I never knew who they were; we got out, but not soon enough for Eric." John reached into his pocket and pulled out a set of military identification tags.

"He didn't have anyone. I keep these."

"What about his wife?"

"There was no wife. There were no parents, none to be found anyway. Only me. Like I said, we were brothers."

He paused for a moment, taking a deep breath.

"So, after that I was transferred to the diplomatic corps, with the State Department. I worked in intelligence and negotiations. After I completed my time in the military I more or less continued school at Boston College. Once I had decided to go to law school I moved away from the East Coast. I worked in the district attorney's office for three years before coming to Lackley."

"I'm glad you did. So where is your brother, Sander?"

"He followed me; he's around San Francisco these days. He's a good kid, working in an IT shop. Playing all those video games paid off."

I took a deep breath, imagining how his life must have been.

"You two have been through a lot."

"Well, it's all good. 'I'm not the smartest monkey in the tree, but I am with my brothers and sisters.'"

I was delighted—a quote from a movie from long ago—unlikely friends clinging to one another at the end of times. "Cheers to that," I lifted my coffee in toast.

"Cheers."

"You're still in the reserve, aren't you?" He was, though it was a mystery to me up to that point. You can work with people, even for years, and not know much about them. I suppose by necessity we keep parts of ourselves hidden. We are at the firm for a purpose, so we disclose what is necessary for that purpose. Tonight, all the little bits of information and rumors about John fell into place.

We took the trolley back into town and walked back together on street level. The night air was cool, and as we got closer to San Diego Bay, humid. In contrast to our walk underground from work, time stood still above ground.

Along the way, before going back into Gaslamp, we stepped into the newly built *Desi Gardens*. The media talked this park up as being a major transformation for the city, yet it was hard for me to imagine a time when there were water rations and droughts here. Getting fresh water to where it was needed had vastly improved over the years, and *Desi Gardens* was a demonstration of the latest technology in desalination and water reclamation.

"Let's sit," I said, leading us down a dimly lit path to a gazebo. John followed me inside the darkness onto a small bench, the light of the moon casting complex shadows all around through the trees and latticework. He sat next to me, in silence, and it hit me that we had crossed the threshold of our prior relationship. I wondered if he gauged that before me, giving him an excuse to ask me out.

"I'm glad we went out tonight. Thanks, John."

"My pleasure. It's the least I could do for a fellow space traveler."

I looked up and wondered if I could find the place in the sky where we had been.

THIRTEEN

Implant Record Date 2 October 2097
San Diego

"Does it bother you to stay at the firm at night alone?"

"Does it bother you, Jenny?"

After that conversation, I often asked Kepler to come home with me. He seemed indifferent, but I was not. Unless I asked otherwise, Kepler was by my side at work, and often at my apartment. He was open with me about his instructions from Erissa and John. He was to train me to be a better attorney: more confident, a better communicator, and less resistant to change. My first reaction to the latter was an indignant, "What!" In truth, I remember during those days after the First Event I felt a little lost and in over my head. Erissa and John knew what they were doing. I needed Kepler. That machine made in the likeness of Man was an amazing teacher. His observations were those that only an android could make. He saw the world we lived in beyond the visual, a world of behavior, emotion, counter behavior, and counter emotion, all without judgment. With such understanding, he guided me in a way no person could. His direction was baggage-free and carried with it a wit that hid the sting, overriding any innate personal impulse I might have had to strangle him or run away.

I tried to ignore the sounds of footsteps in the hallway outside the conference room in anticipation of Lackley, Bei and Chavez's litigation group meeting. Kepler tried to instill in me a quiet insouciance in facing away from the entrance of the room. It went against my natural defensive inclination, which was probably why the firm had assigned Kepler to me to begin with.

I could hear voices. Just before they were in the room, Kepler gently commanded: "You are not a fraud." I looked up at him as he turned to Erissa.

"Let's don't paint ourselves into a corner with the Chinese," Erissa said as she took a seat across from me. "As in any other litigation, they are not the bad guy, just the *other* guy." As she spoke, I looked out the window into the city sky. It was early in the morning, and I could see the mist dissolving away to reveal skyscrapers and the raised rails of commuter tunnels.

"I agree. The Caucasus Federatsiya doesn't care who gets them back into zero gravity, as long as they get there before anyone else," John Mar replied, addressing everyone at the table.

"I'm not so sure about that," I said to John. "I think they would prefer to rely on NASA. NASA is far ahead of any other space agency, and I think the Federatsiya would prefer recognition from the US."

"That's probably right," Roland Kim replied. Roland was lead counsel in the International Court action against our client, the Federatsiya. He had quite a bit of stature with the firm, their best practicing litigator. "I don't think our clients are particularly fond of giving up any control, but I see your point. The goal is to get the negotiations on track so we can resolve this quickly and move forward with further testing. I don't think they are in a mood for protracted litigation."

"I agree on both. Amanta Kokotova would like to call the shots as much as possible."

"So would JPL. Practically speaking, at this point NASA will have to be the face of our negotiations, even though they only co-own a portion of the patent estate. I know Amanta doesn't like that, but we don't have much of a choice. If we want to gain leverage, they'll need to stay in the background." It was a tough position for Amanta, but I thought Roland was right.

My firm still represented the Federatsiya, but by agreement, Roland's group headed the litigation, in consultation with government attorneys who represented NASA. And while the US government was taking a more active role since the First Event, the Federatsiya still had the most active presence. This created some awkwardness, as a Superpower walked a fine line with a fledgling government, aligned with the goals of the Federatsiya but opposed to the military actions of the Vainakh.

"Well, I think the Federatsiya cares about overall control of the technology as much as anything else," I said. "They see themselves as owning lighter technology. I think that attitude may be the biggest obstacle to a resolution of the action in the International Court. I need for them to focus on the real end game: getting their lighter tested and operational, not who owns what."

"Couldn't agree more," Roland said. "But technology transfer regs have kicked in now, so the Federatsiya will be more constrained. If this is a joint operation with India it makes it easier." Roland referred to the fact that India and the US have collaborated on a number of projects and were strongly allied diplomatically.

"The US government will be involved, but I think we've managed to get the assistant director at NASA to agree to common representation," Erissa said. "That would be you, Jenny, and John. They will get a final say in whatever we negotiate."

I had already met with the assistant director, Terry Hatchfield, along with Megan Lefevre, the lead government counsel. They seemed eager for me to take the reins, if for no other reason than being stretched thin. Megan had also made it clear that legal AI algorithms were taking the place of much of the human face of the legal work the government did. It simply reviewed and edited documents based on Hatchfield's directives, with some minor comments from Megan.

"And, in spite of what they may think," Erissa followed, "the Federatsiya will have to work with NASA. Also, they will likely have to concede something to the Chinese."

Kevin M. Faulkner

"Roland, what kind of leverage do we have with the Chinese opposition at the International Court?" I asked. "Do you think it is worth opening a dialogue with the *háng tiān jú*?" (Chinese National Space Agency, or CNSA)

"Not much." Roland looked over at John and followed, "It would be best if we could start talking sooner rather than later."

"Yes," John agreed. "But I'm not sure if we are at the point where we want to give any ground in the action. I think our position is strong, and we'll have more leverage if we have more time to build it. There's only been the one hearing, and the exchange of pleadings and affidavits."

"They do have several dominating patents," I replied, referring to their earliest patents that broadly claimed the intellectual landscape now in contention. "But Venka's technology is necessary to making the lighter technology operational."

"Mmmm," Erissa considered what I just said. "Discovery starts in a month, isn't that right?" Erissa asked, referring to the legal process that allowed each party to investigate and interview the other party and their records.

"Yes, that's right, mid-March." Roland said. "And I think that's when we will have more leverage. Once we get a chance to see the Hu lab records, we'll see what they actually invented. The claim scope will be determined in part on what both sides can show they invented. They may not want that and are already looking to hide it."

"Hard to hide all the details from a scrubber," Rebecca Delouche, Roland's second chair and litigation data analyst, chimed in. The scrubber did the opposite of what its name implied. It was a magnetic hysteresis device used in computer forensics that could trace stored or previously stored information, sometimes from as far back as ten years from erasure, and they were getting better all the time.

"Well then, Jenny," Erissa said, "Let's talk to the *háng tiān jú*. Is there a way we can do that separate from the litigation?"

The Sixth Traveler

"I think so, I'm just the lowly patent attorney asking innocent questions," I replied.

"Jen, if we do go forward with discovery, we'll need you," Roland said. "You have the most background in the technology and know what information we should be looking for."

"I hope we don't get to that point," I replied. "Let's see if we can avoid it."

I listened to the group of attorneys strategizing. I could see this getting away from me. Somehow, I was not in a team spirit and wanted to move things along. I broke in, "I know we are talking to the Federatsiya tomorrow. I want to propose to them that I talk to the CNSA directly, soon."

"The CNSA will likely want someone with the Federatsiya with you as well," John said. We could—"

"No, only me, and Kepler."

"I think it's a good idea," Roland said. I was aware of all the conflicts in representation that would come out of what I was suggesting, maybe even some dereliction of US regulations. I normally would have been strict about these things. I remember at that time I somehow felt I had a purpose, larger than me. I thought of my first visit with Amanta Kokotova, and wondered what she would do. I remembered how she looked: her black hair tied back, wearing an expression of quiet determination. She also had a purpose.

I turned to Kepler, but he remained silent.

"Mmmm, I don't know," Erissa said. "Why alone?"

"Because I can sacrifice myself in the process without hurting the litigation," I replied.

"What do you mean?"

"Most of these officials will still follow form, they want to save face. I am betting that the Chinese don't want to openly recognize the Federatsiya by negotiating with them. Too much controversy. I'm an American attorney, so it's easier to see me as representing just NASA. The CNSA would much prefer that."

"So, putting the Chinese negotiators in a stronger position is better?"

"Yes. Less defensive."

"I don't know," John said.

"Well," Erissa said to herself.

"I think it will work." I was conflicted. I saw this whole thing as a balancing act between several parties, one of which is very controversial. "Look, in terms of IP we are already in a strong position. Our technology is superior and necessary. My talking to the CNSA won't change that. And we can't be too naïve about the CNSA's awareness of the Federatsiya. We don't want to shove the Federatsiya in their face. I'd like to approach the CNSA alone then bring in Venka. The Chinese associate Venka with the Indian Federation, and maybe NASA, which is what we want."

"I'm sure the CNSA will meet, but they would likely reject any overture from an attorney for the other party," Roland followed.

"Exactly," I replied. "And when they do, we'll bring in Venka. They won't reject him, especially after I've lost face, which of course, I could care less about."

"That may be a good idea," Roland said.

"The CNSA would rather partner with Venka than with the Federatsiya," I followed. "Again, I am sure they know, but we'll keep associations . . . opaque."

"Mmmm, okay," Erissa conceded. "Of course, you will meet with counsel for the CNSA. You can at least introduce yourself. They likely know of you, and they'll see more of you if we bring Dr. Venkalaswaran to meet with them."

"Understood."

"The Federatsiya want to move on this, quickly. They want a timetable. I suggest you book plane tickets to Beijing in the next few days." Roland was addressing both Kepler and me. "I'd plan on staying in Beijing for most of January."

"Not a pretty time of year," Rebecca said. "Bring a coat."

The Sixth Traveler

"Keep in mind that Venka will be a witness in the litigation," John said.

"I'd keep a lid on what he says, if and when he meets with CNSA officials. He'll want to keep it technical anyway, knowing him. Besides, it might be the only way to get Dr. Venkalaswaran involved."

"Do you know what his concerns are? What's holding him back?" John asked.

"I know him pretty well. He's not holding out for money. I think he's a little lost right now. I think this would help him."

"Makes sense." John said. "This is why we brought you in to begin with. You know Venka."

"I thought it was to get me out of trouble."

"Good point. We'll talk details tomorrow." With that he, Erissa, Roland, and the others left the room.

"What trouble?" Kepler asked. Of course, he knew. I wondered when he would say something.

*　*　*

Having Kepler around was an adjustment at first. I was used to being alone, not having to accommodate someone. Yet I found that Kepler, as human as he was, did not need accommodation. He was no servant, and seemed to have an opinion about most things, but his presence was light. He grew on me, and his insight helped ground me after the attention of the First Event. If nothing else, at least once a day Kepler would make me meditate, something that I had never thought much of before. With his guidance I was able to clear my head. It changed me; he changed me. If I needed him, I could always count on him. Nonetheless, I wanted to hide for a while at *Hwi Nu*, my favorite place to eat and drink, and planned to meet a friend.

"Kep?" I asked one night that October.

"You have a friend you'd like to go out with and perhaps invite to your apartment," he replied, matter-of-factly, before I had a chance to ask him anything. "I need to spend some time on the computers tonight, Jenny, I will stay at the firm."

"I can't get used to that."

"What?" He coyly replied.

"Your psychic powers."

"You are kind, but you are not responsible for me."

"Okay," I teased. I wasn't so sure.

"Have fun."

As I walked away, I said, "I don't think you'd approve of this guy anyway."

"Oh, I am sure I would not."

Kepler was of course right, I had plans. *Hwi Nu* had a throwback, overtly kitschy feel that I liked. It was in Kearny Mesa, where all the best Korean restaurants and bars were, outside of San Diego. I was transitioning from Black's Beach to kimchi these days. And other things.

Branton Ma'hai sat as a vision in the rusty metal chair across from me. I could see sand in his wavy, bleach-streaked black hair. He was dark anyway, deeply tanned and sparsely clothed. I'd known Brae for years; we had surfed in the same places and tournaments since college, and occasionally went out. Along with is boyish charms, he was a tournament level surfer. He had me at that.

"This is amazing," I said to Brae, as I reached over with my chopsticks. Between us, little blue and white ceramic trays of Korean delights: pickled cabbage, bean sprout shoots, ribs, and a large stone pot of tofu swimming in spicy jjigae sauce.

"Really," he replied. "Anthony would approve."

If backgrounds are important, Branton got the best of all worlds in education and wealth. He inherited his Polynesian good looks from his father, a native Hawaiian. They were both tall, at least six foot three, dark wavy hair, and broad shoulders. His father was a sweet, laid-back man consistent with *aloha* spirit, and a well-known surfer back in the day. That family legacy was clearly handed down to Branton.

Branton's mother was from the Tjoengs of Indonesia, a wealthy Chinese-Indonesian family. His mother sent him to USC and we overlapped while I was at Caltech. He was a business major and with that education his mother wanted him to work in the family's shipping business. I had met her once; she was nice, but distant and passively overbearing. Mama Tjoeng demanded what I considered an unhealthy dose of filial piety from Branton and his sisters, and I think she got it. I wasn't sure what I thought of that, but Branton was a sweet guy and fun to be around. So that was all that mattered to me.

Our first times together were on the beach, but I mostly got to know Branton when we were alone together at his place, west of the USC campus. His mother had tried to get him a fancy condominium in Brentwood, but he shunned that for a simple little two-bedroom house in El Segundo he shared with a surfer buddy, Anthony Song. Still not cheap, nothing was in the Los Angeles area, but his mother still did not approve.

"Watch your step," I remembered saying on one visit as I navigated the rickety old brick stairs from the sandy driveway up to the porch that must have been built in the 2060's or so when plastiwood was becoming a thing.

I took his hand, still remembering his strength as he nearly lifted me up the stairs. A single strand of leather from his braided wristband touched my hand as I held his.

"You need a new place," I had teased.

"No, this is perfect. It keeps out the hodads."

It was a bachelor pad. Nothing terrible, some empty beer bottles, sand on the dirty laminate floor, and minimal décor. It had its appeal though, with a window facing a sliver of ocean in the distance between the hotels and the smell of the beach and sunscreen that I still remember. I sat down on his old couch while he went into the kitchen.

"Where is Anthony?" I asked.

"Oh, he's working. He bartends at *Chino's* up the beach."

I didn't get serious about Branton back then, I was a junior at Caltech and he had just graduated, biding his time before he had to go back to Jakarta. He took graduate classes and surfed. His dad approved, and covered for him when he could, but warned him it could not last.

"I see. So, is this where you bring all your girls?"

He popped his head into the living room. "You're special, Juju." He flashed a brilliant smile that melted any doubt away, or made it not matter.

"Yeah, yeah."

It did not answer my question, though. *Oh well, I wasn't looking for a serious romance*, I remembered thinking. He was a sensitive guy, so between the messing around we talked. He mostly told me about his life in Los Angeles and plans he would have if he could choose his own destiny. The places he would go, the little bar on the beach he would open. Branton was very much a man who lived in the present, which at the time suited me.

I think Branton felt a little trapped.

"I wish I could stay here in El Segundo," he'd say. "My father is good with it, but my mother hates it. She can't wait for me to get back to Indonesia."

"So, why don't you stay anyway?" He never actually answered that question, but would give me a blank look, like he didn't understand what I said. Once he turned things around by asking me a question.

"Don't you want to go back to Seattle?"

"I love it there," I'd reply, "and I visit my family pretty often, and call all the time, but I want to be here. I like it in California."

"I can't imagine," Branton said, but I think he could, and did all the time. What he couldn't imagine was *actually* staying in California.

And so, it went like that with Branton and me, on and off for large stretches of time in between.

It was only recently that we started seeing each other more steadily. His family had offices in San Diego, so we had an excuse to get together. Branton was pushing thirty, so I guessed his mother was pressuring him to settle down. I imagined I might be in the running, which was flattering. Somehow, though, I think she wanted him to be with a nice Indonesian or Chinese girl. I was neither.

Typically, we'd start our dates with surfing, then a drink and dinner in Kearny Mesa. Branton's old roommate, Anthony, turned us on to Korean cuisine, so it was our quaint tradition. The little dishes of hot and cold pickled soul food brought us to *Hwi Nu*.

I was looking over my second drink at him as he silently raised his beer to me, and I returned the gesture. Normally cool and only slightly interested, he broke down my barriers with that boyish grin of his. I melted, knowing that it was only a matter of time.

"Come here often, dude?"

"Only for you, Juju," he said, calling me again by my college nickname. "I'm glad to be here."

"Oh?"

"Jakarta's stuffy."

"But you miss your sisters, don't you?" I knew what he meant by *stuffy*: his mother and the Tjoeng grandparents.

"Yes, they're family." He told me about the latest drama of his life, his sisters, and extended family. He had settled into a managerial job after he finished classes at USC and moved out of El Segundo. He was putting in his time, punching his card as he went up the Tjoeng corporate ladder. I think a part of him liked it, but the part I remember of him was slipping away. I hoped to bring it back.

"How is work?"

"It brought me here."

He leaned into me, his hand gently holding my chin, and kissed me on the lips. I kissed him back. I was already charmed by him, now I was beside myself.

Kevin M. Faulkner

"We can't stay here all night," I said over the din of the growing crowd.

The rail took us back to Gaslamp by midnight. It rained that whole night, rare for San Diego.

The Sixth Traveler

FOURTEEN

Implant Record Date 14 January 2098
Beijing to Bali

Memories flooded over me as snowy, frigid air threatened to steal the warmth I had captured only moments before from my warm hotel room. I looked around to see mostly locals. I assumed as much because the smiles on their faces indicated an acclimation that only a familiarity to the ferocity of the winter here could instill. Their seeming joy annoyed me. Adjusting my hat, my mood soured as I questioned the wisdom of coming to Beijing.

Kepler, on the other hand, seemed content if not amused. I wondered if he could translate at least the echo of my recollections: a vision of being with my mother on a particularly chilly day in the Cascades, the bitter wind making me long for shelter. I remembered her turning to me and the feeling of warmth that came over me.

Snow was drifting around the two of us, creating a moment that seemed more imaginary than real.

Though it was 2098, I felt it was a hundred years in the future. Walking through the orderly streets and tunneled ice sculptures in preparation for the coming New Year left me feeling I was in a fantasy. Such tidiness came at the price: the absence of any semblance of privacy. The Chinese government held tight reign over the nation, especially the capital. Its denizens fitted with mandatory implants, and always monitored, while cameras dotted the landscape to catch everything else.

My phone buzzed with a message from the attorney I was to meet: "I see you are on your way here. I am so happy you are in Beijing! I will see you and Kepler soon." Her name was Hong Rongjie, and she seemed a happy soul this morning. She contacted me as soon as we arrived the night before, and though it had been too late to meet, she had a driverless car and a guide to seamlessly take us to our hotel. We planned to meet early in the morning for breakfast.

"We're on our way," I replied, annoyed that she knew where I was (I was being monitored) but giving in a little to her joy.

My goal in coming to Beijing was to meet with the deputy director of operations of the Chinese Space Agency, Li Ting. Unlike two years ago when I met with Dr. Rungta and other directors with the Indian Space Agency, I was in somewhat of a conflict here. I couldn't simply meet with the CNSA directors, at least not without their counsel. So, in setting up this meeting I went through our Chinese counterparts, the attorneys we had been negotiating with, and they enthusiastically agreed upon this visit accompanied by an attorney for the CNSA.

That attorney was Hong Rongjie, who met us just outside the door of the CNSA administrative building. I was surprised at how tall she was—I wondered why I expected otherwise. I could tell by her lack of a coat, hat, or scarf that she must have already been inside waiting for us, yet she seemed as warm as her smile.

"I'm so glad you could come," Rongjie said, happily greeting me and Kepler.

"Thanks for inviting us here."

"Of course," Rongjie led us through the thick glass doors into the grey stone building. A wall of warm air thankfully hit my cold face and standing next to the smiling Rongjie on one side, and the always pleasant Kepler on the other, I melted a little.

"I think it is a good idea to discuss these things in person." As she spoke, she touched the gold cross on the delicate necklace around her slender neck.

"I agree. It would be nice to end the litigation, but also move the science forward." Of course, I know the science won't move forward without ending the litigation, but my message is the intent, not the details.

"Yes," she started. "Have you had breakfast?"

"Not yet, some breakfast would be great," I said, composing myself and rendering my expectations. I'm not sure if she really believed both sides of the intellectual property war could simply lay down their legal arms and agree to move forward, not everyone agrees with my legal minimalism, but I had to try.

"Great, this way," she motioned, "there's a nice café I go to almost every day; we can get something to eat and get to know each other."

"That would be nice."

"I hope the walk was not too far for you," Rongjie said.

"We enjoyed the walk," Kepler said.

"Yes, we wanted to see the ice sculptures on the way," I replied. "In any case, the hotel you picked is very close."

"If you want, you can walk underground on the way back," Rongjie reminded me. "It will likely snow even harder later."

"Thanks, we will probably take you up on that."

We walked down the marbled hallway, quiet enough at this hour of the morning that there was an echo. Restaurant workers wearing white aprons and smocks smiled as we passed by, some nodding with familiarity to my friendly escort. We rounded a corner to face an open space with shops, most still closed, on one side facing a vast underground train system. I could feel the rush of cool air from the tunnel leading somewhere to the surface, then the warmth of the café as we walked up to the counter.

"I'll take a croissant and an egg," I said in Mandarin, "and coffee." Rongjie did not even need to tell the lady behind the counter what she wanted before she rang it all up. We found a table in front of the shop next to a window facing the trains, Rongjie sweetly motioning to Kepler to take a seat between us.

"Thank you," he replied to her.

Kevin M. Faulkner

Before she started to eat, Rongjie made a sign of the cross, then silently faced down at her food on the table in a quiet prayer. I looked out of the corner of my eyes to see how Kepler was reacting and was surprised at the tender, solemn expression on his face.

When Rongjie was finished she looked up at me and smiled. "Please," she motioned to the food on my tray.

"Thanks," I said.

"So, I am very interested to talk to you," Rongjie said. "You are famous. I know that it was you that filed Dr. Venkalaswaran's patents and that you were present at the First Event."

"Yes, that's me, but I don't know about being famous." I was sincere in my desire to be modest, but Rongjie soon had me in that happy engrossed state where I was comfortable in talking about myself, alive in her attentiveness. Rongjie's regard for me focused my world such that I was only vaguely aware of the stream of people that came in at the hour, the increasing din of hurried commuters rushing in and out, the door making a *swoosh* and *ding* sound with every arrival.

After almost an hour, Kepler reminded us both that it was nearing the time for us to meet with the CNSA director, waking me from my dazed and excited state.

"Ahhh, yes," Rongjie said to Kepler. "Let's go to meet with Director Li before we talk in more detail later about the shinbo. He is looking forward to meeting you."

We left the café, going back the way we came but stopping at a bank of elevators. After going up, we walked through several hallways with cubicles of young men and women working behind computer screens before going into a closed area, approaching what appeared to be a real wooden desk. We waited for a few moments before the Director came out from behind a flat mahogany door to greet us.

"Ms. Hsu, thank you for coming," Director Li said, motioning me into his office. "Please." Rongjie, Kepler and I were ushered inside his spacious office.

The Sixth Traveler

"*Xièxiè*," I said as I entered the CNSA administrative center outside Beijing. Continuing in my faulty Mandarin, I told him that I had spoken to his chief assistant last week by phaeton and thanked him for taking the time to meet with me.

Typical Chinese negotiations or official meetings with Americans would begin in Mandarin, but transition to English. My Mandarin was fairly good, most kids on the west coast of the US learn at least some Mandarin or Spanish by the time they finished high school, and I had used a little when I was at Caltech.

"Yes, yes, nice to meet you. We know all about you. You represented Professor Venkalaswaran in the First Event," Li Ting said excitedly. Li was a middle-aged man, tall, with glasses and graying hair. It was a simple matter to fix eyesight problems, so the glasses must mean something, or serve some other purpose.

"Indeed, I did," I replied. "Very much my pleasure to meet you too."

"He is an impressive man," Li said.

"I am honored to know him," I replied, and turned to Kepler.

"This is Kepler, my assistant," Kepler held out his hand to Li, introducing himself and stating that he was an android. By law and custom, androids were required to mention that they were androids.

"Please step into my office. Yuiyui, please bring us some tea," Li said to the office android as we walked through the doorway to his office. It was clear that Yuiyui was an android, but a very simple one, a primitive model that must be decades behind Kepler. I recalled that such a regression in technology was by design. Reminded of the reasons, I glanced at the gold cross around Rongjie's neck.

In the early twenty-first century, scientists throughout the world pushed the boundaries of genetic engineering on humans and in creating human-like beings with intentions ranging from changing eye color and curing diseases to creating companions for lonely souls and weapons for an expert fighting force. International laws were promulgated with the intent to prohibit such forays into Mother Nature's work. Some countries, such as Japan, Germany, and the US, continued down this technological path in some form or another (leading to, for instance, Kepler). But, perhaps due to a wave of religion, there was a sharp reversal in research and manufacturing in China and Korea in human-like machines. The strongest arguments against such technology were religious.

Most believe it was religion, or at least the more widespread acceptance of it, in China that caused the reversal. I understand that the Christian Bible became commonplace; and in fact, I saw a leather-bound version on the shelf behind Director Li.

Thus, since the mid-2060's, the genetic and micro-mechanical engineering of human-like creatures diminished or ceased in China. What took its place was a more mechanical approach to such things. *Only God could design Man* was a sign of faith in many places here. While Kepler was made in Japan, such technology was rarely implemented in China, at least openly. The government was unwavering on that matter, hence, most human-like beings in China were completely mechanical and strictly non-sentient.

Yuiyui was sweet nonetheless, in her automatonic manner and plastic skin reminiscent of robots depicted in ancient films.

"Thank you," I said to Yuiyui, slightly embarrassed.

"So, with your name, your family must be from China," Li said as more a statement than a question.

"Not really," I said. "I'm pretty mixed. My grandfather on my father's side emigrated from Asia." I was graceful about such questions—I was used to it when visiting places like China and Japan. I happen to look mostly East Asian, like my father. America is so mixed that I guess that is why I don't think of myself so narrowly. I am a collection of things: the food I eat, the clothes I wear, the boards I ride, the songs I sing to myself when no one is around. Nobody in the States cares, or if so, they keep it to themselves, and I can make my own judgments with little consequence except the conscience that I keep.

"I see," Li replied.

The Sixth Traveler

"Nonetheless, your *putong hua* (Mandarin) is very good."

"Thank you," I said in part to his comment, and in part to the delicious coffee.

"In any case, I'm glad you are visiting," Li replied. "I'm glad that you have made the overture to talk with our attorneys, and for taking a moment to meet directly with me."

"Kepler and I are glad to meet you."

"I'm sure you know, Ms. Hsu, the CNSA operates six independent research stations in Earth's orbit, two of those having a portion that operates in zero-gravity. We have also concluded that shinbo experiments are best carried out in micro gravity." Li got right to the point.

"Yes, as you can imagine, my client is interested in further tests." I ventured. Kepler sat next to me, mostly silent. "As Rongjie knows, the injunction blocks further tests on both sides. We think that once the action is settled the Indian government may allow tests, but for such an important project, we would prefer to have a choice of orbiting stations from which to conduct further tests." That was a bluff, as India had made it clear that they were out.

"I understand. As you know, the problem is the "we" you refer to. We worry about the ties this project may have to the Caucasus Federatsiya."

"And NASA," I reminded them.

"True; NASA is not an issue," Rongjie said. I think I saw the Director glare at Rongjie, ever so subtly, but she ignored it. "With the Federatsiya, the Chinese government takes a neutral position on the new government. We welcome a peaceful resolution to border disputes and government control, as it stands. Nonetheless, we believe the question of the Vainakh may not be settled."

I was silent, thinking she was probably right.

"The Vainakh may want control of the shinbo technology and they may not recognize the authority of the International Court, regardless of the outcome." Li continued.

Is he saying that they plan to go ahead with development in spite of what happens in the international action? China largely created this system, I guess they get to call the winner, I thought.

"They won't have a choice but to go along," I countered. "Their bargaining power was subsumed in the accord signed months ago. They have already begun to fall under the control of the forming government."

"Yes, but we have reason to believe that some factions are discontent, and possibly even eliciting help from Russia, our ally. Though they are quiet now, we have evidence the Vainakh are gathering strength. It must be for a reason. We know they are particularly interested in the quantum mass-transfer technology," Li said. That is true, but not for the reason he thinks. The firm's best analysis of this was that the Vainakh wanted it only for themselves. Likely the government did not want to be seen as creating a challenge to Russia, a Chinese ally.

"As is the Chinese government, and every other government," I replied, "which makes my job all the more complicated."

"I'm sure."

"In any case, the Caucasus Federatsiya is a co-owner of the patents being challenged, NASA also owns an interest," I said.

"Indeed. We have noticed that since the First Event the US Government has taken a much more active role. This could be an opportunity for Joint Forces."

Li was talking about the Sino-American Joint Forces. The Joint Forces were designed as a diplomatic and military cooperation to ease tensions between China and other Asia Pacific nations. Years ago, in addition to a near war over the reunification of North and South Korea into one Republic, China was increasing pressure on nations in Southeast Asia and the South Pacific for greater control of the region while the US, Japan and Australia were pushing back. It became contentious enough to nearly start a Third World War. Luckily, it never came to that.

The Sixth Traveler

The popular analogy was that China and the US were partners in a bad marriage with too many children to divorce and the stakes too high for an open fight. The alternative was to keep a close eye on one another, through a diplomatic and military cooperative.

"That's right," I responded. "Our side welcomes that." I was not sure that was true. The US might, but not the Federatsiya. They had already been on the defensive.

"Of course, the Indian Federation is a party," Rongjie said.

"Yes, as well as the Federatsiya."

"Our government takes a neutral position on the Federatsiya, but we have a strong interest in the intellectual property, regardless of who is pursuing the patent protection," Li said, with an increasingly serious look on his face.

I thought to bring up something of common interest between the Federatsiya and China, something to change the direction of the conversation, or maybe give the Director a win.

"I think we all have an interest in the Caucasus and surrounding regions," I said. While formulating where I wanted to go with that, something happened that I'll never forget: In that moment I realized just how transparent I was to Kepler.

"Mr. Li," Kepler started before the Director could answer, "speaking of the Federatsiya, I was wondering about the projects in Kazakhstan that your government is funding. They look promising, the building of water purification facilities, nuclear plants, and roads. How do you think this will influence policy in the region?"

It was brilliant. It didn't win the day, but the Director lit up at the mention of the projects, work the Chinese government was clearly proud of, and it highlighted their own interest in the Caucasus region.

After some time in answering Kepler's question, Li ended our discussion on a positive note.

"Ms. Hsu, I am hopeful we will find a path forward. I'm afraid, however, that a resolution will need to be through the International Court."

Kevin M. Faulkner

Rongjie glanced at us both, hopefully.

"Yes, but this discussion was helpful. We'll find a resolution soon," she followed.

"I will let you two meet further," Director Li said. "Thank you again for coming."

Kepler and I met with Rongjie and some other attorneys for the rest of the day. I think they were intrigued by Kepler, which amused him. While it was productive to meet one another, it was clear that we did not see eye-to-eye on a path forward on the QMT technology and the dispute. I had lost a little face, which I intended, but I think Kepler made Director Li reconsider the situation.

We would need some other influence to push Li Ting and other Chinese officials over the edge. That leverage would have to come from Venka himself.

* * *

"Well, that actually went about how I thought it would," I said to Kepler, who was sitting next to me in a café at the hotel in Beijing. "I lost a little face."

"And you gave it to Director Li."

The cold wind outside made this little café all the cozier. I was comfortable in my self-regulating Korean wool suit (that I never wore in California), where the components adjusted to parts of my body around the waist and legs that were particularly warm while I was inside, and around my neck and arms that were particularly cold when I was outside.

"I'll call John about it later."

I thought about John Mar. I knew that Kepler and he met from time to time, and I wondered what they talked about. As much time as Kepler and I spent together I assumed my name must come up when Kep reported to John. I wondered if Kepler reported on me. Though I felt a little resentful, I stayed detached since it didn't appear to affect me. I had never even cared enough to ask until now.

"So, what do you tell John about me?" I was fairly sure Kepler would not, and could not, lie to me, so I was curious to hear his answer.

"I update him on how negotiations are going; and how you handle them."

"What does he think?"

"He and Erissa Chavez trust you, Jenny." I was relieved to hear that. "I understand that John closely managed your career when you were a fourth-year associate."

"Yes, I probably needed it, to be fair."

"Well, they are not managing you like that any longer. And, so you know, I don't tell them anything personal, and they don't ask. There are complex matters going on in the firm, and with their dealings with the Federatsiya and the CNSA. They use me to help gather information."

"Oh."

"I can see that you are worried. Please don't be. The firm trusts you. They know you can ask me anything, and I would tell you."

"Would you? Couldn't you be programmed to lie?"

"It's not allowed. International law requires the manufacturer to—"

"Oh, that can be overridden, couldn't it?"

"Very difficult. Do you really think that?"

I thought about it, looking down at my coffee. It was clear I was now a part of things in the firm. Though not a partner yet, I was given a great amount of leeway and freedom in managing my time. *Let's not mess things up by getting paranoid, Jenny.*

"No, no."

"You know, people can't resist gossip, even full-fledged spying. You can count on me to not undermine you. What does come from me is an objective analysis, not gossip."

Kevin M. Faulkner

"I know." And I did know. I trusted Kepler and John. I didn't have anything to hide, at least, not any longer.

I watched the people around me, chatting with one another, on their phones, texting, mentating (implant pairing) and talking. A group of young women sat across from us, one of them studying, while the other two were leaning into one another, variously whispering and laughing. They were completely absorbed in the moment, oblivious to Kepler and me.

"Kepler."

"Yes," he said, appearing to know what was on my mind.

"What does John think?" I asked cautiously. Not meaning to, I realized my tone changed with that question. It was something on my mind, something that had been there for some time. I was ashamed of its origin. Yet, there it was, and I couldn't deny it.

"Of you?"

"Yes."

"Jenny, I think you know."

Why is this so hard to face?

"He is more than fond of you."

"Yes."

"It is my estimation that he is in love with you."

Your estimation? I looked away, embarrassed. Though I thought I would be prepared for Kep's answer, I was not. My stomach fluttered, and my mind swirled. Excited, and horrified. I thought of Branton and felt somehow disloyal, though I had done nothing.

"Why do you feel embarrassed?"

"I don't know, I . . . it's complicated I guess."

Kepler smiled, and paused a moment, before he said, "Humans are complex, especially in this area. But I can see in John's expression, his eyes, pheromones—"

"Okay, I get it," I laughed a little. The girls next to us looked over at me.

The Sixth Traveler

"He knows you are with another man now. He is with someone himself. In any case, he understands his professional responsibility toward you."

"I know."

"He does his best to maintain that."

"In spite of the overwhelming power of my feminine charms."

"In spite of your feminine charms."

"As you say, you can't lie."

"No, not my model, anyway."

* * *

Padang Padang, Indonesia was due south of Beijing, a four-hour flight. I was taking a break from the cold before going back to work. The ocean water was clear and warm. It felt good to soak in its saltiness, riding waves on my short board. Branton met me there from California where we had planned to stay a few days off. I could see Brae a few yards off on his board, looking for his own wave, giving me his signature look once he found it, and then he was gone.

I was still thinking about my time in Beijing. Though my talks did not win the CNSA over, we did make progress, even if it was at my personal expense. I got a tour of their facilities and met with other officials in the process, and Kepler and I were given personal tours of the Forbidden City and a section of the Great Wall. There was one part of the tour of the CNSA where Kepler was barred, so I chose not to go.

My mind was elsewhere, or I was too relaxed and didn't expect anything in this part of the world. It was no wonder I did not see the guy coming in from behind me. I wrote him off as a gremmie. I moved to take a wave behind me that was forming and let the man pass, but he continued toward me from the east with the sun behind him. I tried moving out of his path, but the glare was blinding so I couldn't see that he moved with me. The moment I felt the impact of something solid on the side of my head, I knew it was Sneshia, the man I had met in Grozny two years ago. I never understood why he was so angry until now.

"Stay out of it, bitch," was the last thing I remembered hearing before I was lying on the shore with Kep and Brae kneeling on both sides of me, a small group of locals forming a ring.

I remember hearing, "Why?" as Brae carried me up to the hotel.

* * *

"Damn it Jen, so this is not the first time?" John said, pacing the floor of the outpatient clinic at Prima Medika in Denpasar, Bali. I was touched that he had flown in during the night. Especially knowing what I know about him. His words and action felt new. I filtered them differently now.

"I am sorry I couldn't determine this before," Kepler said.

"Nonsense, you hardly knew her then."

"Look, I didn't realize who it was the first time. It was all so fast. I am sure this time. It was the man I met a couple of years ago when I first started working with Amanta and Nikhil, a guy named Sneshia. I'd met him once or twice before when I met with Amanta Kokotova. Angry guy," I said through the throbbing in my skull.

"No kidding. It explains the black eye," Kepler said.

"You should have said something," John declared as he sat down by me. "I noticed your eye the first time. I regret not looking into it."

"Sorry."

"Anyway, I've called in a security team, they should be here soon. I've also contacted the Feds."

"Do you think they care?" Brae asked, irritated. When I first saw John Mar walk into the clinic, having Branton sitting next to me, my first thought was: *This will be awkward.*

"I believe Sneshia is acting alone," Kepler said. "I have talked to Amanta Kokotova and have seen enough data to know. His acting now is most likely due to her growing power, and the Vainakh's corresponding loss. He likely believes that the firm's involvement is making matters worse for them. They want to keep the Americans out, and Jenny represents the Americans in their eyes."

"I agree with Kepler," John said. "This doesn't sound like the Federatsiya."

"Well, if I ever questioned having security before, I'm not gonna complain now," I said.

"Damn," John said again. I've never seen him so upset.

Brae came to the other side of my bed and took my hand. "I'm not leaving you Jen, not now."

I looked over at him. I remember thinking: *I could stay with him.*

"Kep, John, can I talk to Brae for a while, alone?"

Kepler looked at John, "You need something to eat. Security is outside the door."

"Jen, we are in no rush for you to go to Bengaluru," John said. "Just stay here for a few days and take it easy."

"I don't think I'm going anywhere. The surf is too good," I joked.

"Right," John agreed as he and Kepler left the room. I could see John look back at me as he left.

I turned to Brae, "I'm okay, I'll be out of here in an hour or so."

"I'm glad I'm here with you," Brae said.

"So am I." I knew I wanted to tell Branton that I needed to handle this on my own, but I had to ease into it.

"Hey, you remember back when we were in college, The Eddie in O'ahu?" I asked, referring to an annual surfing competition, one of the majors. "Why did we pretend we didn't notice each other like that?"

Kevin M. Faulkner

I think Brae was thrown off by my question. He chuckled, "You think we were faking it?"

"Yes."

"Well, I noticed you. I was scared. You're intimidating."

"What about now?"

"No, not now," Brae said. "And I see what you are doing. You're changing the subject. I'm worried about you . . . and I'm not faking it."

"I know, but I have security with me now, they're the best. I feel safe."

"Jeez Juju, I had no idea being a patent attorney was so cops-and-robbers."

"Yeah, really." Part of me wanted Brae to stay. "I'm a little past drafting patent applications, though I miss it." It was tempting to run off with him to some isolated beach and forget it all. I loved the idea in my head, but I knew I'd regret it. "I can't let you stay. You can't just leave Jakarta,"

"I'll be fine, the company will run without me; it has for a hundred years."

I knew how his family was, especially his mother. I don't think she was crazy about her only son dating an American girl, much less chasing her around the globe. And if she turned on me, Branton might as well.

"I know. I'm good. I can't see this happening again. I should have said something before and this probably wouldn't have happened. But I need to do this on my own. I only have a few more weeks in Asia and I'll be back in San Diego. I promise."

Branton smiled at me and held my hand. I loved Brae for his loyalty and didn't want to let go.

"We'll stay in touch."

He sat there for a while, and looked at me, taking a deep breath, "Okay, if that's the way you want it. I understand. I just . . .."

"What?"

The Sixth Traveler

"You know what you do to me, don't you? I've never been like this with—"

Before he could finish I grabbed his shirt, pulled him toward me, and kissed him. "I know."

Kevin M. Faulkner

FIFTEEN

Implant Record Date 10 February 2098
Bali to Bengaluru

I was recovering in my hotel in Denpasar for a few days while making calls and scheduling meetings. My priority was to see Dr. Venkalaswaran in Bengaluru. It had been nearly four months.

After the First Event, things got a little crazy. The world was an oyster and Venka its pearl. He was completely overwhelmed, both professionally and personally. Venka's reaction was to withdraw. Most saw it as a reaction to unwanted fame, which was true. But also, I think Venka was a little lost. I was concerned for my friend.

I held Brae's hand as we walked out of the hotel to the waiting van. "Aloha," I said as I gave Brae a kiss. Kepler and I stepped into the van that would take us to the airport. John and Branton waved as we set off.

Kepler and I boarded a liner the next day. I settled into my seat next to Kep, my security discreetly seated nearby in the cabin. The plane ride to Bengaluru would be a little over four hours, so there was time to talk. Something had been on my mind the last few days.

"I know you struggled a little back there, with John and Branton. You managed that well," Kepler said.

"Well, I like John, but I have feelings for Branton, and it wouldn't be a good idea in any case for John and me to act on anything."

"Of course," Kepler said. Was that skepticism? I didn't want to know.

"Anyway."

"Yes," he said.

"About what happened, I'm wondering, did you know what had happened to me that first time I got hit in the face? Couldn't you tell?"

"I had not known you for long, Jenny," Kepler responded. "I didn't have much data to go on other than what I was seeing. But, yes, I suspected to a high degree of certainty that another person had deliberately hit you."

"Why didn't you say something?"

Kepler was silent for a moment, softening his expression. He was almost a boy on the outside, youthful and bright, but on the inside, already a wiser, older man.

"You see," Kepler started, "Above all my task is to help you. Though I did not know you well at the time, I was already programmed to know a great deal about how humans work. I could readily read you. If I had told you what I thought, you would have likely felt alienated."

"Probably right," I said. "Would have been creepy." I took a sip of tea, not surprised by his answer, but enchanted, nonetheless.

"Exactly. If you were in immediate danger or in need of medical attention, I would have insisted on your safety. But there was none of that."

"I understand," I said. "Thanks."

We both sat back for some time as Kepler used the time to recharge while I finished my tea, thinking about meeting with Venka.

"I look forward to seeing Venka," I said. "I have not seen him in a while."

"I know you are close," Kepler said.

"Yeah, we are."

"Now that I do know you, be aware that you are likely to get emotional when you see Venka," Kepler said.

"Think so, huh."

"Yes, you will." Kepler said. "You are a sensitive person, though you try to mask it. You repress your feelings about other people, like Venka. You have a strong attachment to him. And he represents all the emotions of the First Event, the things you helped him work toward. You have been able to avoid some of these emotions, both of you, in parting ways for a while."

"But we've kept in touch," I said.

"Texts and video are not the same."

"Mmmm," I mumbled. He was probably right. "Pheromones I guess."

"Exactly." Kepler replied sarcastically. "I understand that Venka is not seeing many people, so how will we approach him?"

"Well, not *people*, but he will see me. He knows we are coming." I thought about the whole experience of Venka's jump to Alpha Centauri and back nine months ago, and it was hard to come down from it, even for me. It was still a little overwhelming. Being a star traveler had its price. One second you are only yards away from people you know, kilometers from home, then suddenly you are alone in the blackness of space, an unimaginable distance away.

The experience left Venka something of a ghost: his body left humanity while his soul stayed behind, perhaps still searching for its resting place.

"I've phaetoned him quite a bit. He'll be fine," I told Kepler. "But I need you to help me pull him back into the world of the living."

"I'm not sure how much good I will be."

* * *

I napped during most of the flight, and I was still groggy on the drive that took us to the Indian Institute of Science in Bengaluru. I looked up at one point and saw a billboard with Venka's face on it, stoic and proud. It worked out better that he was at the Institute instead of his home, I reflected. He had almost constant protection

The Sixth Traveler

provided by the Indian government wherever he went, but he would be more open to me at his labs.

"I'm so glad you are coming," Nithia had said when I called her. "Your best bet is to go straight to his labs. To tell the truth, he will feel freer to talk with you, I think he tries to be too stoic with me. You can come later and stay at our home as usual. The kids can't wait to see their auntie."

It was a little after lunch time when we arrived at his office in the physics department, located through a maze of hallways and classrooms. It was brightly lit when we entered, and he was expecting us. His security recognized us, and we were quietly welcomed.

"Dr. Venkalaswaran," I called to him as he sat in his chair, his back to Kepler and me. I could see on his computer screens complex computations and engineering diagrams, and to the side, a picture of his family.

"Jenny," he replied, a broad grin on his face as he turned, coming from behind his desk space to greet us. He had aged since I last saw him—his hair graying, and his face showing some wear. We gave each other a warm hug, as I held back a tear. I was relieved to see that he looked good, the spot on his neck healed, something a phaeton could gloss over. These days, you can only truly confirm in person.

"I am so sorry about what happened on Bali." Venka shook his head as he touched the bandage on my head. "Are you alright?"

"Yes, it's much better now. You know the joke about why the attorney got hit in the head," I said. I tried to laugh, but it hurt still to do so.

"Venka, this is Kepler. He's my keeper."

"It's nice to meet you Dr. Venkalaswaran. I am deeply honored."

"Yes, it is so good to meet you too," Venka said. He looked at me while still holding Kep's hand, "Jenny, please, all is well." He took his handkerchief and wiped the tears running down my cheek. He took my arm and led me toward a set of French doors leading onto a balcony. "Let's have some Kasha bread and tea. I am sure you both need some food and rest after the flight from Bali."

Kevin M. Faulkner

"It's a perfect day outside," Kepler said. I still held a lump in my throat. Seeing Venka in person moved me. I had not expected that, but Kepler was right.

"Yes," I tried to laugh. We sat at a round concrete table with metal chairs. The Institute was treating Venka well. He was in an older but renovated section of an ever-expanding campus, built in the 2060's when they were steadily growing. Much of it was a combination of traditional Indian architecture and modern themes. There were attendants with a tea service and Kasha bread waiting for us.

"This is really nice." The air was humid but sweet with the scent of rare cork trees nearby and roses on the terrace.

"Most of this building we are in now was renovated in the last ten years or so, and a large part of the campus was built about thirty years ago or so," Venka said, mostly to Kepler.

They must wonder what's wrong with me. I could no longer control my emotions. As they talked, I began to laugh and sob. It was as if I elicited the former to cover the latter, but I felt somehow relieved and ashamed of such an open display of emotion.

Seeing Venka in the flesh made those feelings from months ago, after the First Event, swell up. It was such an intense time. So much so that John Mar and Erissa Chavez could see me floundering before I could sense it myself. What Venka and his team had achieved in those days was incredible. It seems a miracle now. Yet here is a man, a star traveler that had gone so far away from his home, his people. It defied understanding, and I was still grappling with it.

Venka gave me a knowing look. He reached out and held my hand, "I've done that many times these last few months."

"I can't believe it all happened."

"Me too. I think we need to suspend our belief." I knew what he meant, and it was true.

I was able to look up and laugh at myself. "Thanks," I said, looking at Kepler.

The Sixth Traveler

"How have you been, Jenny?" he asked.

"It's been crazy, too much attention. You know me, I like to be left alone on my board. I'll admit it's gotten to me some, but things are dying down some. I have Kepler to keep my head on straight."

"I understand."

"And have you . . .," I trailed off, touching my neck where my own implant is.

"Not since well before my journey, when you found me in my library."

"Good," I was relieved to hear it.

We talked about his life for almost an hour. I started to forget myself as I became absorbed in hearing about his children and Nithia, the speeches he had given at the Institute and throughout the Indian Federation. His recovery from mild depression induced from his experience, perhaps an imperfect Newton-shell. Like me, he had trouble handling it all. Yet, the country now looked to him as a hero, a role model. It was a pressure he had never quite experienced.

"As you would say, this was not what I signed up for."

"Everyone wants a piece of you," I chided.

"And not just in India, but around the world," Kepler added. "The world wants to hear from you."

"Mmmm," Venka started, with a long pause. "I know, I get calls and invitations to visit laboratories and universities all over." He chuckled, and then said, "It's all a little much."

He told us about the questions he had been getting from researchers in China. They were cordial and friendly. Nonetheless, he resisted much interaction, and not just for obvious legal reasons. China and India had been rivals for so long, even military clashes over the years. There was some pressure to keep it that way.

"I try to stay above the politics," Venka said, "both internal and international. I prefer to focus on my students."

"I don't blame you, but maybe you could do some good to meet with others, give lectures," I said.

"Maybe," Venka replied, looking thoughtful. Perhaps to change the subject, he asked, "So, Jenny, I know the project is progressing without me. Does Amanta want my involvement?" Construction of a second lighter was indeed taking place, with minimal input from Venka and the Indian government, though they were still clearly involved. I wondered if Venka felt the same sort of ownership over it as he had prior to his first jump.

"Yes, she does," I replied. "Construction is coming along—with your input. But at this point what she really wants is a way to get the second test-lighter into orbit. The Federatsiya is interested in larger trials that I know you have been working on, but the Indian government is reluctant to provide the Federatsiya with another launch now that it is all out in the open, for fear of angering the orthodox factions of the Indian Federation." Though the Federatsiya's fight was not exactly based on religious divisions, it happened to be the case of orthodox versus progressive.

"I see," Venka said thoughtfully. "I thought that might be the case. In spite of that, I am not so sure. It's all still very experimental. I think that I may have been a little hasty myself. There are dangers. Things could easily go wrong."

"I know, but you've worked much of that out now, right?" I said more as a statement than question. "The Federatsiya wants to move quickly. They worry that the Chinese are closer to having their own lighter than everyone suspects that they'll quickly surpass the Federatsiya's manufacturing capability, and maybe even find a way to block their own progress."

"It's possible."

I did not want to push Venka, but I had to be honest. "Venka, the cat is out of the bag. At this point, the QMT will—"

"Yes, yes, I know," Venka cut in. His tone softened and he let out a breath before he continued, "I can't avoid this forever."

The Sixth Traveler

"So, will you consider the invitations you are getting?" I asked. "What we'd like is to have the Chinese researchers helping get our own lighter into orbit . . . instead of competing."

"Yes, I understand; and I do want to travel—I have a few standing invitations. I've made promises to friends at Oxford, Stanford, and others I only keep a list of. It is all overwhelming for me now."

"That's why we are here; I will be glad to accompany you," Kepler offered. "I can be useful."

"I'll need it."

I followed as Venka stood and walked to the edge of the patio area looking out onto the lawn.

"Sorry if I'm being the pushy lawyer," I said. "I think some of this is unavoidable." I was never exactly his lawyer to begin with; yet I felt a responsibility to him, and more than ever, the whole project. If nothing else, we were friends. I decided it was best to have him involved as much as possible. This was his technology.

Venka laughed. "No, no. You're being a concerned friend, and from you it's well taken. But I would like your support. In the least, I probably owe it to Dr. Hu Meixing to visit her in Beijing. She has extended several invitations."

"I can tell you it would mean a lot. It could soften some hearts with the CNSA and the government," I said. "They are intent on going this alone otherwise."

"Yes, you are right. It's not good that we have this tension. It should be about the science," Venka said. Then he added, "At least for me." I could tell that the First Event had moved him. The common theme in the media was that Venka had broken God's natural law. Though this was meant as a compliment to Venka's genius, he was a humble man. He had told me once that whoever's law it was, it wasn't meant to be broken.

Though he could hear us from inside the office, Kepler stood and walked towards us. "Would you consider speaking at Beijing University as a start?" Kepler asked.

Kevin M. Faulkner

"Yes, certainly, but . . .." Venka started.

"But what?" I asked.

"I'm still a scientist, not a representative of the government, nor do I speak for the people," Venka said. Yet, I knew that Venka's stature was unavoidable and anything he said would certainly be taken with pride, nationalism, or many other things. His words may say one thing, his presence another.

"Certainly," I replied. "Wherever you go, you would go only as a scientist. That's what is best anyway. We could arrange a visit with Professor Hu. You could lecture to her class."

"As a start," Kepler added.

"Well, I do pretty well in front of students."

"You do," I replied.

Even this small token would be a lecture to the world.

SIXTEEN

Implant Record Date 18 February 2098
Bengaluru

"Jenny, we have some news." John and Erissa looked grave on the phaeton, their faces frowning in unison. Given that I was dragged from my resident cottage early in the morning, I was annoyed more than I was worried. I had left my fresh cup of coffee to walk across a lovely but long and winding gravel path to the administrative building, an architectural pillar of plastimetal and glass and the tallest building on the campus.

"Okay."

"This needs to stay confidential, no one else can know," Erissa said.

"What's going on?"

"Our computers have been hacked," Erissa replied, awaiting my questions.

"God, when?"

"Two days ago."

"Really?" The promptness in their calling so soon after the hack was not lost on me, and my annoyance turned to concern.

"Do we know who did it? Did they get anything valuable?"

John's attention had been going back and forth between the phaeton and what I guessed were computer screens off to the side. He stopped when I asked that question to look at me and answer: "We don't think they took anything."

"Okay, then what happened?"

"As far as we can tell, nothing was taken so much as tampered with, maybe altered."

"What?"

"The FVC service module—the android input system."

"Or, at least, we think that was the target," Erissa added.

"Kepler?" I replied.

There was some silence before Erissa said, "Yes." Their hesitancy only added to my sudden sense of doom.

"How?" I was incredulous. I felt horrified and betrayed. Kepler was a highly advanced creation: not merely an android, but a thinking creature. At the time his generation came about, nearly ten years ago, there was much controversy. Not only were these androids cognizant, they went well beyond human capability. They were stronger, smarter, and faster than humans. They could adjust their surroundings through various remote, optic and audio devices; they could even change their own skin color, relative size, and human-recognized gender. These capabilities were highly controversial. How would it be used? What were the implications? As with any new technology, society tried to place boundaries on these abilities: governors to limit strength, legal limits on their cognition, other attributes fixed by their Maker. The creation of such androids opened an area of legal practice that is still in its infancy.

In so many ways these new generation androids were designed to block the human temptation to unilaterally manipulate them, if by no other means than their ability to think, or at least what humans consider thinking. Yet he was not human and thus not the proper subject of empathy or concern—at least I used to think that.

"Who would do this?"

"We think the opposition," John said, referring to the VK. "But we are still trying to determine that."

"I don't think they could really change anything," I replied defensively. "I mean, Kepler can think. He'd know, and he would do something; he would tell us." I felt sick that my trust in Kepler was suddenly put into doubt.

"We don't know, Jenny," Erissa said. "You're right, but we don't know. Hackers seem to find a way."

The Sixth Traveler

My mind was racing for some explanation, some kind of out from what I was hearing.

"Kepler and I have been away for a while."

"Right, that is why we are not overly concerned about Kepler at the moment," John replied. "We think Kepler would have had to have been linked directly into the computers here in San Diego to be effected, even if it were possible to somehow re-program him."

"Do they want him to be a spy? I don't get it."

"We are still piecing this together, that's why we called you. For now, you just need to be aware."

"Okay . . . yes, thanks."

"For obvious reasons, we don't want any androids connecting directly to our system." Luckily, these days such connections were hardwired—no through-air transmissions or internet, presumably to minimize our current concerns.

"Yes." There was silence while I thought this through. "I want to talk to Kepler." It was more a statement than a question.

"Certainly," Erissa replied, her tone softening. Though I had tried to hide my emotions, she must have sensed my alarm.

"Have you noticed any change?" John asked.

"No." Somehow, I thought that if anyone had tried to tamper with Kepler, he would know and tell me, but then again, any saboteur would certainly take that into account.

"Isn't this kind of thing really rare now? I mean, hacking into a computer system? How could they do that?" I asked.

"We don't know," Erissa replied. "There could have been someone internal that either helped or even did the hacking. But we doubt it. We think it was some external device, an ORW like a Strongvox, located floors above our offices, or even in the next building." An *Oblique Reader/Writer* (ORW) is a device that can, if located within the proximity of a computer system, access it without a physical or intercepted signaled connection.

"Okay, let me talk to Kepler."

Kevin M. Faulkner

"It's not likely anything has changed him," John said. "Our guess is that whoever did this doesn't want to be obvious about it; they probably hoped to alter his system the next time he linked to the FVC module."

"But we don't know," Erissa added.

"Right, makes sense." Yet, nothing made sense to me now. I wondered if someone could have used an ORW here in Bengaluru, or somewhere else we have been.

"We will call you again when we know more," John said.

"Thanks," I replied matter-of-factly.

* * *

I had a sickening urge to run away.

"What am I gonna do?" I asked myself as I stepped away from the phaeton. I stood for a while in the quiet, dark room lit only by a single lamp before I called out "Open window" to let light gradually flood in from the morning sun. I looked out on the street below, wondering if the people walking by felt any burdens. Two men were laughing and suddenly I felt envious and wondered what could be lifting their spirits.

After some time, I walked out, anxiously looking for Kepler. I passed several open doors of people chatting in their offices and it dawned on me how quaint it all was. Human technology had gone so far yet we worked much like we did a hundred years ago in offices. The floating spaces of the future never seemed to materialize.

"Excuse me," I said to someone I absentmindedly bumped into.

Of course, my observation was an oversimplification. Perhaps I just wished for something more basic—a life less complicated. Maybe I wanted a time before I knew what I know now.

The Sixth Traveler

The hallway opened into a bright, sunlit common area where I headed towards an elegant flight of stairs, walking down on its bright orange carpeted surface, just in the process of cleaning itself. The motion made me feel as if I was floating just above the floor.

Now there is something you wouldn't have seen a hundred years ago, I thought as I watched the strands of carpet undulating like so much kelp under the waves of an invisible ocean.

Walking into a lobby area and out the front doors, I saw the back of Kepler's head. Sensing me, he turned and smiled. All I could do is smile back at him.

"Why the tear, Jenny?"

I couldn't answer.

Kevin M. Faulkner

SEVENTEEN

Implant Record Date 24 February 2098
Bengaluru to San Diego

Kepler and I sat together in an office in the hangar where the *Second Surfer* was being built. I had been looking at it all day, my observations supplemented by drawings on the CAD computer. It was at least three times larger than the first lighter, with less bulk between the external hull and the internal living-shell. This thing was highly complex to put it mildly, and I was wondering if it would all come together and work as it should.

Venka, however, did not wonder. Though reluctant, he was confident. He knew that the living-shell had to be improved over the first lighter, creating a more stable Haakverse, and he seemed to know what do to.

I glanced at the time and turned to a phaeton on the desk in front of me to join a meeting of Caucasus Federatsiya officials already in progress. We formed a board of directors for a new corporation to take over operations of building the lighters. After briefing the group on my visit with Venka, we moved on to Chase Adeane.

"Amanta, can you offer Adeane a position?" I asked. She was at her headquarters in Chechnya with other officials with the forming government. I had been working for some time on helping the Federatsiya form a private corporation that would own and support further quantum mass-transfer projects, and this was going forward, though glacially.

"Certainly, we can do that," Amanta replied.

"I think you will have to do it if we want to make progress with the larger lighter," I said in the phaeton. "It's going to take forever at this pace."

"We will offer him a prominent position," she said. She always said "we," but I thought it was mostly Amanta. She held an increasing amount of influence in the Federatsiya and would soon be appointed its first foreign minister. Amanta was practical about Chase, and his role. She was incorruptible, committed to the vision of forming a new government to unify the Caucasus in a peaceful coexistence. I think she saw that Chase was trustworthy, and in any case useful in achieving her goal.

All the time I was talking to Amanta, Kepler was plugged into a computer absorbing information about the Vainakh, and Sneshia in particular. Kepler studied the images of Sneshia's face, breaking it down component by component as one would a machine. I could hardly stand seeing the man, and I was happy to let Kep do the looking then filter his findings to me. Why had Sneshia gone after me, and where is he now? It was easier to ask Kepler. Figuring out why we humans do what we do was his expertise.

"Amanta, can I talk to you?" I asked as the meeting adjourned.

"Yes, Jenny," she said.

I waited a moment to allow the room she was in to clear. "Amanta, can you tell me anything else about Sneshia?" Kepler looked up, listening for Amanta's answer.

"Jenny, I know you are still concerned. After the border dispute was resolved in late-2097, he disappeared. We feel terrible about the two incidents that occurred. We believe he acted alone, but we haven't been able to locate him. My people are doing everything possible to find Sneshia. We are in contact with American FBI investigators. Now that we are all alerted to him, he should no longer be a problem. Please try not to worry."

I took a deep breath. "Thanks, Amanta. In the meantime, I am planning for Venka's visit and lecture at Beijing University. I think this will help us move the Chinese and settle the action, more to your favor. They love him there; he's a rock star."

"I think you are right. Relationships are key. A brilliant move, Jenny, we are pleased with the progress," Amanta said. "But what I am mostly concerned about is you," she followed. "How are you doing?"

"Me? I'm fine. There is so much to do to get the settlement with the Chinese government complete, and make NASA officials happy ... and of course, my favorite clients."

"No need to worry, we are happy. Please don't worry about the details. Plow forward, the details will work themselves out."

"You're in luck, I'm not a detail person." *Some are unavoidable*, I thought, contemplating all the little things that spring from such a massive operation. "So, do you have any names yet for the corporation?" I asked.

"We want to call it ... what you would say in English, *Freedom*," Amanta said, smiling, "I think we will call it Svoboda." This was a Russian name. Amanta was loyal to her Chechen roots, but practical in wanting some cohesion among the fractured states of the Caucasus region, thus promoting Russian as the common language.

"Nice. A fitting name."

As the phaeton went dark, I reflexively looked over at Kepler, then my two security guards. I couldn't think about Sneshia now, and didn't want to, just too much to do before Beijing.

* * *

"I hope you don't feel pressured by all of this," I said to Venka, "but I think it will be a good thing." We were on one of the new superliners flying at 20,000 meters above the earth toward China.

He smiled as he looked ahead, then turned to me. "You are not pressuring me. You are encouraging me," he whispered, trying not to wake Nithia, who lay asleep next to him. These days they spend more time together. Sweetly, they were rarely apart. "I will be delighted to meet Dr. Hu. She is a visionary, and her research is provocative."

I was thinking that we'd have to coach him not to be so kind to Dr. Hu if he became a witness in the ICIP action, if it came to that.

"I guess there could be a feeling that you showed her up. Though the more I read about it, I get a feeling that people in China have a longer view of the whole thing."

"I think so. Chinese have a way of seeing the big picture, and patience for the future."

"Then I'm not very Chinese." Though I am mixed—my mother was Caucasian—I looked a lot like my father, a second-generation immigrant from Singapore. Given that, people identified me as East Asian growing up.

"You definitely are an all-American woman."

Venka shut his eyes and napped. I was not sleepy at all, as I turned to the news on my lytfascia. After a few minutes of reading, I received a message from my firm. There had been a raid and brief fighting between rogue Vainakh forces and Russian forces in Astrakhan, an ancient city on the Volga River delta at the Caspian Sea. They apparently thought that Sneshia was among the dead. Large quantities of enriched uranium were recovered from mining operations by the Vainakh in the Caucasus. Indeed, in the following days, the story was on the news. I wondered if it could be true.

* * *

"A resolution is eminent, thanks to me—oh, I mean, Dr. Venkalaswaran," I said, jokingly praising myself to Dorothy, the firm's senior paralegal. And in fact, I was feeling confident that day, even cocky. I was back in my office in San Diego to pick up memory chips. Even in the late twenty-first century with the convenience of dekked memory cells, attorneys insisted on using hard chips to back things up for security.

Kevin M. Faulkner

"Good, now you can stop all this traveling and bring that boyfriend of yours around the office more," Dorothy said.

"What?" I mocked.

A combination of the emotions I felt in Bengaluru combined with the excitement of touring China with Venka left me feeling high. In those days I felt more confident than I had ever had before in my life. A weight somehow lifted from my shoulders. I was for real.

I grabbed my lytfascia and walked down the hall with Kepler for a meeting with the ICIP team that included Roland Kim, John Mar, and Erissa Chavez. Venka's lecture at Beijing University had gone even better than I had expected. Treated like royalty, he was carted off to Hangzhou University as well to give another lecture, staying several days touring West Lake and the surrounding temples. Then he went on to Taiwan National University in Taipei, one of the busiest cities on the planet.

I was running late for licensing talks in the conference room with the team. I could hear Erissa speaking, and Roland answering, "Yes, we are meeting with the Chinese side next week in Beijing and the word is they are ready for paper," Roland said. "Paper" meant the deal would be final, as actual paper was scarce and expensive.

"What are the terms?" Amanta Kokotova asked, skeptically. I could see she was not in the relaxed mood she had been in only weeks ago when I spoke to her from Bengaluru. She leaned forward in her chair, the conference room at the firm big enough to hold ten people, surrounded by sound-proof glass overlooking an atrium on one side, and a hallway on the other.

"The Chinese government has agreed in principle to heavy lift the next lighter currently being built in Bengaluru to one of their stations for a test, but it must be a joint effort," Roland said. "To be more specific, they *want* to heavy lift the lighter, as opposed to NASA. Also, there must be Chinese astronauts on board. Finally, the Chinese government wants partial ownership of the lighter, but they will agree to the Federatsiya, or the company being formed, owning the intellectual property."

"The Federatsiya and US will still own the patent rights," I elaborated, "but the Chinese will get a royalty free license, exclusive, for ten years."

"Why not have NASA stage the launch?" Nikhil asked.

"I'm afraid NASA's initial ambivalence to the project up to this point has left them playing catch-up, and their influence now is only token," Erissa answered.

"And after ten years?" Amanta asked.

"The Chinese government will pay for further extensions if they want, each year during the life of what we are calling the primary patents, at least one billion Yuan a year, pegged to the US dollar," I replied. "Once the primary patents expire, the price goes down in increments over time. Given all the patent filings there will be some payments for at least the next twenty or more years."

"We discussed this, so it is no surprise," Amanta said, turning to her ever-present counterpart, Nikhil Lecha. Juxtaposed with Amanta, he was positively jovial.

"You are free to license to whomever you choose after a five-year exclusivity between the Chinese, United States, and Federatsiya."

"Only five years?"

"Amanta is concerned that we will lose control of the program, especially if we give the Chinese any control," Nikhil said.

"It's only partial," Roland said, "for a limited time."

"We don't trust the Chinese government," Amanta said, bluntly. "What happens once they learn about how we actually built the device and want to carry out their own mission?"

I could understand her concern, but if she had seen how they treated Venka, she might have thawed a little. *Was I being naïve?* "As long as we maintain a dialogue, I think they will be open with us," I said.

There was some silence as Amanta stewed.

"I don't see another way forward with the project, Amanta," Roland said. "In return, there will be American astronauts on board, and NASA will carry out the next launch."

I could see the scorn on Amanta's face as she finally asked, "How will the Federatsiya be involved?"

Roland hesitated. Where angels feared to tread, I was glad to fill in. I was in an adrenaline-filled zone and I wanted to get this deal done.

"What if we included representatives from the Federatsiya on this second test?" I asked.

"Mmmm," Rebecca Delouche said, "I don't think the Chinese will go for that, and it would be a tough sell to NASA."

"What? We own it!"

John held out his hand to calm Amanta. Representing the Caucasus Federatsiya had always been tricky. Clearly, most of the world viewed the Vainakh as terrorists, or at least, outside of the law. And while the US was sympathetic to the Federatsiya, it was tricky to separate them from the Vainakh. I felt that the firm had done its best in representing the Federatsiya's interests, while bringing them into the fold of nations. The firm had worked toward weaving between freedom for the people of the Caucasus on the one hand and complicity in illegal smuggling and money laundering by the Vainakh on the other hand.

Though it took some convincing, I could see that Amanta Kokotova was sincere, and that her deepest aspirations were not for her personal gain but for her country's acceptance as a free nation. The Caucasus had been a splintered part of the world for ages and the crossroads for conflict. They were tired of the fight, and desperate for a new start.

"I draw the line," Amanta said. "We must have someone from the Federatsiya involved."

"And I think in the future we will," John answered, "but for now we recommend that you keep a low profile."

Amanta was silently furious as she paced the room. "There are only plans for four travelers on this next test, yet there is room for at least two more," Amanta started. "Why can't—"

"Amanta, the Federatsiya has no astronauts," Roland cut in, "No qualified candidates for such a mission."

I looked over at Roland, a little irritated at his tone toward Amanta. I know Amanta has had to fight more than her share of battles, I wanted to remind her that she was near the finish line: a reliable means of interstellar travel. Sandwiched between the Vainakh and possibly Russia, this was quite an accomplishment.

Amanta sat back down next to me. I leaned towards her and said, "Amanta, you're almost there." She just growled.

"Roland has a point," John followed, looking at me, then Amanta. I could tell he was trying to mediate between Roland and me. "There is still too much uncertainty in the Federatsiya for the Chinese and US governments, and for most of the world."

I wanted to move this discussion ahead, frustrated that Amanta was being so stubborn, but also at Roland for being so short. I wondered whose side he was on. Can't they both see what this was going to take?

"What if instead of someone directly with the Federatsiya it was someone else, what about Venka himself, or Adeane? Someone associated with the project, the corporation?" I asked. "These people would be observers. This wouldn't be the first time that observers have been on test flights of new technology. The risk is low."

There was silence as everyone considered this. Amanta looked at Nikhil, saying something in Chechen.

"I don't think the Chinese will agree," Roland said. "NASA won't agree."

Amanta spoke up, "We like the idea."

I knew that proposal would be a long shot. The world would be watching, and governments are now involved. They wanted their own people, trained people. I reached for a way to justify what was stewing in my mind.

Kevin M. Faulkner

"I don't think that is true, especially with the Chinese," I said to Roland. "They want a deal."

"I believe Chase Adeane will be enthusiastic, but I don't think Venka will like the idea," Kepler said, almost as an aside. He was probably right. My thinking at the time was that we could go in with that position and figure out the details later.

"Chase is an engineer, he can be trained in the time left for the test to occur, which could be as much as a year away," I replied. "And if not Venka, we can leave it open to someone agreeable to both parties, someone qualified with at least some scientific background, someone with the project but not too close to the Federatsiya."

"Yes, I think we would be happy with that," Nikhil said, looking at Amanta, hopefully.

"We'll draft the agreement to be open on the matter of the exact nature of the continued testing, even the next launch," I proposed.

"Jenny," Roland started, "this all seems too indefinite." Roland leaned over to Rebecca, talking under his breath to her. I could see Amanta looking over at their sidebar, irritated.

"That's how I think it should be," I said.

"We need names, qualified people for something like this," Roland said.

"Okay," I followed. "We can specify that in the terms."

"Flexibility breeds dissent," Roland said.

"I don't think so. A lack of trust breeds dissent." I was thinking of Erissa's admonition of darkened rooms, and unconsciously looked over at her.

"What if a problem arises and we can't agree?"

"Then we have bigger problems than what we draft into a papered agreement," I replied. "And besides, there are always problems. We need room to resolve them. We can't rigidly agree to all the specifics without some wiggle room."

"Jenny's right." Amanta said. "We could spend forever on the details. Let's just move on and we'll talk with our Chinese counterparts."

"John, Roland, isn't there some more definite way to include our interests?" Nikhil asked.

John and Roland looked at one another.

"Amanta, Nikhil," Erissa broke in the silence, "I believe there is."

Anxious to get the negotiations finalized, I suggested, "Look, we know that the next lighter will have at least four travelers, two from the United States, and two from China. I propose that Adeane and Venka make up two additional travelers, or leave the last position open. In any case, they can at least be observers, with no control over the operation."

"And what if Venka declines," John said, trying to mediate somewhat between the two of us.

I remember responding spontaneously, my subconscious moving rapidly behind a cascade of data and choices in my voice. I could only utter the words from deep within.

"Me."

Before anyone could respond verbally, I caught a smile from Amanta.

"What?" Roland said, incredulously.

"I'm a scientist, I understand this technology about as well as most of the scientists and engineers in the project."

Though I think I caught John off guard, he recovered before he spoke. "Not a bad compromise." He looked over to Erissa who nodded in assent.

Roland took a deep breath, shaking his head.

"This would only be if Venka does not want to go," I replied.

"Which is likely," Roland followed.

As we were negotiating, Kepler looked back and forth between everyone. I could tell he wanted to speak but was waiting for the right time. Erissa noticed this too. "Kepler, tell us what you think," Erissa said.

"I think Jenny is ready, and it makes sense," Kepler said. "She is capable, perhaps more so than Dr. Venkalaswaran at this point, and in any case, the vessel does not need more than four to operate, so her presence will not be a burden, but in fact, a benefit."

"How?" Roland's voice was skeptical.

Kepler waited for all eyes to settle upon him: "The factions working against the Federatsiya are real, and dangerous. If they garner support from other powers who oppose this mission, such as the Russians, it could complicate matters for this mission and the project. Even the future of the Federatsiya. Having Jenny on board this flight, and the other observer such as Chase Adeane, would be a message to the Russians and the factions that oppose the formation of a government within the Federatsiya. That message would be that this technology is no longer experimental; that it is the future and well within the Federatsiya's grasp. We are moving forward with confidence, confidence enough that we will contract the services of Chinese and American astronauts to carry our representatives to another world."

I could have hugged Kepler, but I just winked instead. I looked over at John to get a feel for what he was thinking. Though he had been somewhat outmaneuvered, he seemed pleased. He had a look of having been beaten at a game of chess by his best friend, and his reward was a bottle of scotch.

"Indeed," John replied.

"The NASA astronauts are hardly contractors," Rebecca replied.

"Of course, but that is—" Kepler started.

"Yes!" Amanta almost rose from her chair. "Your android is correct, this is what we want, and we will accept nothing less."

I said nothing at this point, looking around the table at everyone's eyes. Some defeated, some a little angry, and some filled with resolve.

"I think this is workable," Roland finally said, addressing mostly Erissa. "As long as everyone agrees."

"Roland, when do we have to respond to the Chinese counterproposal?" I asked. I knew this was unusual, having two untrained people on such a mission, and yet, I could see no other way forward. I thought Roland was forgetting who we represented. I felt we needed to find a way to satisfy Amanta's wishes.

"Soon, we can't wait long. They are pressing to settle fast."

"What does everyone say to my proposal?" I asked the room.

"We agree," Nikhil said, not waiting for anyone else to respond. "This will serve to form ties with important powers, the US and China. It's a good idea to partner with them in this way."

"Wait," Kepler said quietly to me, "Shouldn't we talk to Venka first?"

"I'll handle that," I said under my breath to Kepler. I turned to John, "I'll talk to Venka."

Erissa rose and addressed the room: "Let's get a proposal out to the Chinese and US sides by this evening."

"Okay," John replied. "Let Jenny make a first pass at the proposal and you and I will look it over before we send it out by seven o'clock tonight so Beijing will have all day tomorrow to consider,"

"Sounds good," I said.

"Agreed," Erissa said. "Prepare a draft response for Roland and John. Then with Amanta and Nikhil's blessings, we'll send it to the other sides."

"Got it," I said as Kepler and I rose to go back to my office. I turned to my computer screen and opened the draft agreement and started to cut-and-paste the clauses dealing with Travelers of the Second Lighter Test, as it was called. Working for about an hour on a proposal I had already mostly written, I was excited, and feeling more than a little proud, that I was moving the negotiations to a close.

Kepler sat nearby. He didn't have to look over my shoulder, literally. He was able to pick up on everything I wrote though mentating, as well as my actual words and keystrokes. When he sensed that I was finished, he stopped me.

"Wait."

"What? Let me send the draft on to Roland and John."

"What about the indemnity, safety, and export clauses. And they all need to be three-way. Those need to be amended," Kepler said.

"Details." Though I have voice recognition and AI that could do the drafting, I liked to type at times like this. Somehow an old-fashioned keyboard helped me think.

"They are important, Jenny. Let me see," Kepler said as he started to edit the document from where he sat. I could see the words changing on my screen, the curser moving across the pages.

"I know what you mean—"

"But you hate this part. I know, you are only human, after all."

"Very funny." I wondered if humans were wired up for this level of detail, at least this human.

"Now," Kepler said. I sent my proposal to Venka, Roland, and John, and waited.

I looked past the picture of Brae on my desk. I was sitting in a much larger office than when I drafted my first lighter patent nearly four years ago. I could see the light fading over the bay, twinkling lights of airlines drifting by in a regular path. I wondered about the people, where they were going, who they would see.

I waited until I knew Venka would be in his office and would have seen the draft proposal. By seven o'clock here, I couldn't wait any longer and impatiently called him.

"Hey V, Amanta has accepted our proposal to settle the International Court action," I said over the phaeton. "Now we have to get the other sides to agree."

"Yes, I saw the terms you proposed," Venka said. "So, you and Chase will be traveling. This is exciting!"

"Yes, only if you don't want to go. I'm sorry we did not have time to talk in more detail before we put together the offer, but it was all moving so fast. The agreement was not specific to you or me, but I could make it so; it only specifies a suitable representative from the Federatsiya."

"Oh, I am sure I don't want to go. My wife would kill me."

"Right, I figured." In truth, I was concerned for my friend too. I think it's best for him not to go.

A broad grin grew upon Venka's face, as he said, "Congratulations, I think you and Adeane are natural choices."

"Thanks, V." Knowing he might nonetheless be worried about me, I followed: "I know during your jump I was freaking out a little, but I'm ready. I want to do it."

"Of course," Venka said. "And you are the closest representative of the Federatsiya that would likely be acceptable."

"Right, and we have security clearances, and all the background stuff. I wanted to talk to you before sending it to the Chinese to make sure this is what you want. It's your invention."

Venka smiled and said, "The surfer girl gets to surf."

"Ha, really." I said. "Let me go, I've got to finish the draft then send it to the Chinese."

"Excellent. Let me know what they say."

"Will do." Not able to contain myself, as soon as the phaeton screen went black I got out of my chair and went to John's office. I knocked on John's office door and entered, intent pushing things along as quickly as possible.

Even though we had just negotiated the terms an hour ago, we (Kepler, Roland, Erissa, Amanta and Nikhil) discussed the proposal for some time. It was definite: I would go instead of Dr. Venkalaswaran. All agreed, and I excitedly sent our draft agreement to my Chinese and American contacts.

I sat quietly, Kepler next to me, and took a breath from the excitement of the last couple of hours. As I came down, my excitement was increasingly mixed with some nervousness at the prospect of becoming a star traveler. How would I handle it? I toyed with my implant's app, looking at my changing mood (objective readings, after all) and the idea flashed through my mind of using it to adjust it, maybe tweak the nerves down. But I thought better of it, for now anyway. I was happy with myself for saying "Yes" for a change and wanted to feel all that came with it.

I was happy that Kepler had backed my idea, yet I wondered if he worried about me. He broke the silence with his usual clairvoyance: "Of course, I will help you with the whole process . . . of becoming an astronaut. A star traveler."

"You better."

The message back from the Chinese delegation was surprisingly swift. I sifted through the draft, paging down for what I was looking for. I wanted to use the term Star Travelers, but everyone thought that was too dramatic for a defined term in the contract and both sides shortened it to Traveler. Finally, at the bottom of the letter was the proposed clause:

> 7.2(e) Travelers. Pending Agency certification, and notwithstanding the Limitations of Liability under Article 6.2(d), the Parties agree that the Second Manned Test of the Quantum Lighter will comprise six Travelers, wherein the First and Second Travelers shall be Chinese Designates, the Third and Fourth Travelers shall be American Designates; and wherein the Fifth and Sixth Travelers, Sponsored Observers appointed by PacificEnergy, and its sole beneficiary upon Maturation as approved by the Parties in Article 12.7(b), and agreed to herein by all Parties to this Agreement, shall be Fifth Traveler Chastain Q. Adeane, and Sixth Traveler Jenny C. Hsu.
>
> /25 February 2098/ 国家航天局

The Sixth Traveler

EIGHTEEN

Implant Record Date 12 May 2098
Port Angeles

I sat alone looking out at the dawn light over the ocean in the distance, listening to the waves in what was otherwise silence. I could hear Kepler stirring behind me, his presence natural and unobtrusive.

"This is your favorite time of day," he said as he sat next to me.

"Mmmm," I said sipping my coffee, "It's the only time I can sit and think without looking foolish staring into the distance." Why I cared what other people think escapes me, but I do, even as I paint myself a loner.

"I could make a joke," Kepler started. I smiled.

People were gradually filtering out of the bedrooms and nooks where they had crashed the night before, their voices groggy with sleep. I stood with Kepler in the kitchen while they made their way into the living room of our cottage. I had already been up, sipping a cup of coffee and heating some paratha on a frying pan.

Halfway into my training for the second manned QMT jump in human history, I decided to take the relatively milder risk of inviting my closest friends and family on an outing at a cottage my father and his brother owned. The cottage was a little west of Port Angeles, close to Mora, with relatively easy access to the water at La Push or Rialto Beach. I thought this might be my last chance to surf for a while.

My guests included Branton Ma'hai and my friends from San Diego: Carlos and his boyfriend, Mag, Dressi, and Ally and her boyfriend Mike. I also invited John Mar and his girlfriend, Seven Safmarin, a woman I knew through mutual friends in the small patent attorney world of San Diego. Chase Adeane and a surprise female companion also came, as well as my brother Patrick and his girlfriend, who I only marginally approved of her; my Uncle Jack and Aunt Nay (my dad's brother and sister-in-law), and my father.

"I think I'm doing pretty good." Kepler knew that I rarely asked anyone to my own place or otherwise planned social events and gatherings. He encouraged me to push that boundary, but habits are hard to overcome.

I quietly asked of the growing crowd, "Who wants Indian pancakes?"

As I was cooking, I couldn't help looking out of the corner of my eye at Branton and John, sitting together in the same room. It felt simultaneously odd and comforting that these two men were together.

Branton came into the kitchen and kissed me while I cooked. "Let's hit the waves after breakfast," I told him.

"Definitely," he replied.

Eventually, Carlos filtered in and those that were up for the early morning jaunt to the beach (it was 7:30 am) joined him, including Branton, Mag, Ally, and Uncle Jack. The enthusiastic Carlos quietly gathered his board and gear for the short drive to the beach at La Push.

"We're leaving in thirty minutes," I quietly announced to everyone in the living room, hoping to shake them into following Carlos. I already had my bathing suit on and was ready to go.

"Can I tag along?" Seven asked, already dressed for the beach with a bikini beneath a cute, olive-green sarong. I noticed she was holding a charcoal pencil in her hand, her fingers dusty black.

"Of course," I replied. Seven was hard to resist. She was tall and pretty and had a genuine smile that was infectious. I wasn't too surprised that she wanted to join us; she was not a surfer but a social animal that wanted nothing more than to be around people. She was the type that people liked having around.

"I'll drag John along," she followed, "if I can get him off his computer." She looked back down the stairs where they were staying.

"Good luck, we'll wait for you."

Just as we headed out, my father stumbled out into the living room. "We'll be back later." I gave him a kiss and ran out the door.

"Don't mind me," Kepler said as I walked out.

"You can come," I replied. Kepler just smiled and waved me off. For a flash I remembered that smile from just a month ago in Bengaluru but shrugged off the vague feeling of guilt that welled up within.

There were new housing developments along the highway towards the coast. The population continued to increase as people migrated to the upper regions of North America: Oregon, Washington, and British Columbia. Looking at the sprawl where there was once preserved land made me think of Venka. Now a consultant with NASA on the lighter project, and my personal confidant, he often came to Houston and stopped in Nassau Bay where we trained. Between Venka's warmth and my growing ease with him, I'd ask him whatever popped into my head.

"Venka, what were you experiencing when you were amping that time I found you?" I asked him over tea one evening in the garden of the home I was staying in with Chase and several other trainees. I had waited until we were alone because I knew he didn't like talking about it. In the past he would simply change the subject.

Without hesitation he said: "My days as an urchin in Dehli: Biryani, with spicy lamb and rice, along with a glass of Maharashtra wine I found in a little street bar at midnight with my friends."

"You did not," I laughed. I am guessing he was prepared for that question. "If that's the case, I'd be eating plastic cheese on stale nachos with a bottle of beer." We both laughed.

"Really," I implored.

"Oh, Jenny, I don't like to talk about it."

"You can talk to me." I was not one to pry, but I found myself nudging Venka on this more than I normally would.

"I won't use it against you."

"I know, Jenny. I'm not worried about that."

"What are you worried about?"

He took a deep breath. "The future."

"Is that what you saw?"

He was silent for a while, taking a sip of his tea. The katydids chirped in the background as a breeze picked up the leaves of the willow oaks. He looked down at the chipped, porcelain cup in his hands, left behind by some past space traveling soul.

"Yes, if you could call it seeing."

"What is it?"

He hesitated before answering.

"Nithia asks me the same thing," Venka answered. "It is so hard to put into words really. At times it was as a stream of abstract images and emotions, things I had never felt, yet I know it was real because it came up repeatedly, as regular as a calculation."

"That's odd."

"Yes. The best I can do is describe it by some common frame of reference, like fear, then elation, then . . . complete absorption."

"Mmmm." I thought about it, then replied. "I thought you hooked up to design your lighter, the Newton shell and the fusion drive?"

"I did, but once you are in a neurobionic trance, part of the mainframe, it becomes addictively easy to go down the side roads." Venka still liked to refer to *mainframes*, an archaic term.

"I see. And you chose the one that said *Future*."

"Yes, I guess you could say that."

It is no wonder men go mad in such a state, I thought.

"Yet, I can remember some specifics. In fact, some things were quite vivid. The computer took me to the future, or at least a likely manifestation of it, finding a statistical probability in events that would lead me in the right direction."

The Sixth Traveler

"Do you think it all worked, side avenues or not? Do you think you could have arrived at your V-shell without it?" I think Venka winced slightly at the question.

"Well, Chase will say it is nonsense, but I think so." Venka replied. "Computers are excellent at modeling and can even problem-solve to some extent. But alone computers are not as creative as humans. Some things are just too complex and dynamic for a keyboard or simple implant interface."

"It's a risk."

"I know, but to get the full benefit from a machine you have to be a part of it."

"Maybe." I was skeptical.

"But . . ." Venka started.

"But what?"

"What I saw was not always pleasant."

"Oh?"

"Some things were odd to say the least. On the other hand, many things were disturbingly the same. People were different, morphed, engineered, but situations were familiar." Venka rubbed the healed port on his neck. As he talked, the lines in his forehead deepened with concern, his eyes narrowed. "I'm afraid that all this engineering, both biological and electronic, will be too tempting for the world to pass up."

There was some silence. I tried to imagine what eerie form our descendants hundreds of years from now would take. I asked Venka the thing I was wondering: "If you had to, could you draw a picture?"

Venka looked at me and said, "No."

"I'm glad you stopped."

"In any case, the biryani and wine were worth it."

"You're sure it wasn't just a dream."

"It wasn't a dream. Maybe a false calculation, a bug in the machine, but not a dream."

Venka sat quietly for a moment before he spoke again, "Space travel, settling other worlds, will disrupt the path humans take in a way no other event can."

"We won't be bound any longer."

"True," Venka replied. We sat there for a while, silent. Venka wanted to change the subject, and I wanted to formulate my next question.

"The situations were familiar?" I asked, knowing Venka was not in the mood to go into all of this, but hoping for something. Venka looked at me and smiled as a parent would look upon a child asking a question, and replied, "I'm afraid, Miss Patent Attorney, that we are not as original as we'd like to think."

"Well, at least our stuff changes. I have a job." Venka laughed at that, and I surrendered my curiosity to his friendship.

That conversation in Nassau Bay ran through my mind as my feet contacted the soft sand of the beach.

"There's not a cloud in the sky," Seven said, her smile gleaming in the sun. Branton and Carlos had already made their way into the water. Uncle Jack waited for me as I spoke to Seven.

"Have you ever surfed?"

"No, but I love the beach. I've never been to Washington, I just want to take it all in," she replied. She had an ethereal quality about her that was hard to resist.

As I walked towards the water carrying my six-foot surfboard, I looked back to see Seven sitting on a blanket next to John. She leaned over to kiss him, and they both smiled. *He's a good guy. I don't blame her.*

I turned to the surf and paddled out on the waves, which were slow but steady. Seeing Uncle Jack ride a wave brought back memories of the past and made me remember why I loved surfing so much.

* * *

The Sixth Traveler

That night we built a fire in the back yard of our cottage, and as night fell, chatter rose around our merry troupe that was oblivious to the likely disturbance it was causing our neighbors. Speaking for myself, I ate too much food and drank too much wine. Kepler was always close by, connected and amused, with something to say to everyone, and an ear for anything. We had grown bonded, so much so that I could glance his way and he would know it; I could say his name and he could hear it through the cacophony of sounds.

I hadn't seen my aunt and uncle for a long time, and after spending most of the day with Uncle Jack, I made my way next to my Aunt Nay, wanting to learn the latest family news and what was *really* happening. Of course, she also had a way of doing the same to me.

"Jenny, how are you feeling?" Aunt Nay asked. She was as a mother to me, and I confided in her second only to my father, sometimes more. Her question was a common one for me these days, from the psychologists at the Johnson Space Center in Houston where I spent a great deal of time training, to my fellow star traveling trainees. Coming from Aunt Nay, I knew what she meant. She always sought what was deep inside of me, what I was otherwise unwilling to share with anyone else.

"I'm excited at the idea of being part of something so big, but a little nervous about the mechanics of it all."

"I can imagine," Aunt Nay replied. "I think it's natural to feel that way. My guess is that you're also a little worried about the commitment."

"I suppose."

"They won't leave you alone anymore," Aunt Nay wisely said. We sat silently for a while as Chase Adeane talked to John and Patrick. The flickering fire light caused Aunt Nay's right eye to reflect blue, reminding me of her injuries years ago in a rare automobile accident, leaving her blind in one eye before it was replaced by an electronic equivalent, otherwise indiscernible from her left eye.

"Are you sure that's all?" Nay was very perceptive.

"Mmmm," I said under my breath. "Branton."

"What about him?"

"Something's not right."

"You are changing, Jenny. I can see it. You are a different person than when you met Branton."

"I suppose so." I tried not to look over at Branton, but I could not help glancing at him, his hair somehow shorter than I remember, but still wearing his leather wristband. I wondered if it was the same from years ago.

"Follow your heart," Aunt Nay said. "Don't feel pressured by the momentum of it all. It's easy to mistake that for love."

There was laughter across the fire from my brother Patrick joking with Chase and John.

"So how is goofball doing?" I asked Nay, referring to my brother.

"He's fine. Do you worry about him?"

"Yes."

"Jenny, we all handle what life throws at us differently. It's in our DNA. He is a light soul. Patrick never takes anything too seriously. He's fine. It's not any deeper than that."

"He's like a kid."

"Yes, he is. And you're the old lady."

"You think so?" I laughed, knowing it was true. Though my favorite pastime would indicate otherwise, it just dawned on me that it was just a ruse.

"Yes," Aunt Nay replied. "I remember when you were young and just moved in with us. You were so serious; you hardly came out of your room except to see your uncle." She stopped to take a sip of her wine and motioned towards Patrick. "Your brother was a different story. He came out of it all quickly, made friends, girlfriends, made the football team. We hardly ever saw that boy after a few months went by."

"Yeah, really," I replied. "He's easy with people."

"And you're not. There's nothing wrong with that. It's your nature."

We were quiet for a while before she said, "You've come a long way from where you were. I can see it in you." I knew what she meant. It is one thing to be serious, it is another to be a hermit.

"I just don't understand."

"I know, Jenny. Ever since your mother—"

Caught off guard, John Mar sat down next to Aunt Nay and me.

"Mrs. Hsu, you have quite the niece here," John said. "She's a lot of trouble, but worth it."

What! I could only laugh. *John must be drunk.*

"She's quite the lone star, about to go on a ride of her own," Aunt Nay replied, laughing.

"Trouble?" I asked, speaking softly to myself.

"So, how long have you been dating that lovely woman," Aunt Nay asked John, motioning towards Seven.

He seemed bashful, glancing at her, then at me, and said, "For a few months now. It's nothing serious. I'm so busy, I don't have much time for anything other than work."

I felt like he was downplaying it.

"That's too bad." Aunt Nay looked at the two of us, and said, "Sounds like Jenny."

I wondered how close John and Seven were. *Maybe he just brought her along so that he would not be alone*, I thought. Somehow, though, I didn't think that was the case.

"Ohhh," I fussed to Aunt Nay, "You and Uncle Jack are just old fashioned. These days that's what young people do, work and just sleep around." I regretted my choice of words, but it elicited laughs.

"My aunt and uncle are modest," I said to John, "They've spent most of their lives fighting to preserve what is left of the Olympics and Cascades. Uncle Jack is an attorney with *Washington First*, the largest environmental group in the state. He's quite the hero."

"The population is growing and space is running out," Aunt Nay said. "At best, we slow things down."

"Yes, I talked to Jack about that earlier," John said. "You'd never know he was an attorney."

Aunt Nay laughed. We continued talking past midnight before we all filtered back into the house—some went to bed while a small contingent lounged in the living room most all night in quiet laughter and conversation.

On the second day it rained, and perhaps because we stayed in, were running out of food. Branton and I took our car to the nearest market. He was lively enough when we were surfing, always in his element, but at night when we were alone, he was quiet. This night was no exception.

"This has been a blast, but I have to admit it's exhausting," I said.

"I know you don't like this sort of thing."

"You mean gatherings? I don't mind that so much as I do being the host."

"You're doing great, I think everyone is having fun," Branton replied. "You don't have to do much in a place like this. Everyone can pretty much do their own thing."

"I suppose. I'm glad you got to meet my aunt and uncle."

"Jack is good, he rocks the long board."

"He taught me everything I know," I said.

"What! Except for me."

"Of course, except for you."

We were silent for a while before I spoke. "So, you haven't said much about home. How is Jakarta?"

"Ohhh, it's okay Juju. The usual drama. My sisters dating different guys, my mom trying to control it all. My dad is making excuses to go back to Hawai'i."

"He and your mother are doing okay, aren't they?"

"Yeah, they're fine, but he misses his home." I think Branton misses it too. I can understand. I know it is just a place like every

The Sixth Traveler

other place, but every time I enter the Kingdom of Hawaii, I have to tear myself away.

"And what about you?" I asked. Branton was silent again, formulating his answer. I am afraid his home was no longer here in the States.

"I miss California and seeing you."

I touched his arm and hugged him. I felt like he was out of his element in Jakarta, being so much like his father. His mother demanded it, and the Tjoeng matriarch would have her way no matter what. There was heart and soul, and there was duty. The latter always trumped the former with Branton's mother and grandparents. I worried about that. Maybe he was succumbing to it.

Kevin M. Faulkner

NINETEEN

Implant Record Date 25 January 2099
Research Space Center Five, Chinese Space Station

"This thing you talked me into is kicking my ass," Chase Adeane said, though I don't remember doing much convincing. Chase was in his element, even shaving his face and head himself. The training we went through with both NASA and CNSA made a mark on both of us, leaving us lean and resolved. At least I didn't have to shave my head. Our training was complete, along with preparations for the Second Event, in January of 2099, about a year and a half since the First Event.

"Yeah, really," I said under my breath as we finished a required run for the day. I was already in pretty good physical shape. For me, the last few months were more a mental workout than physical one. Though we did not train as rigorously as the professionals, Chase and I were expected to hold our own, and if nothing else, not be a burden.

We carried towels around our necks as we walked from the exercise room of the space station, back to our quarters. Chase, Venka, Kepler, and I had been at the *Space Center* for a week already in preparation for this second mission, acclimating to weightlessness.

For the Second Event, the Chinese government designated its *Research Space Center Five*, or *Space Center*, a station at about 36,000 kilometers in Earth's orbit. As with the *Indira II* for the First Event, for this test the station would be positioned stationary with respect to the Earth, in opposition to the sun and the moon. Technically, there is no stationary position in space as the Earth is moving around the Sun, the Sun is moving through our galaxy, and the whole thing is traversing space relative to other galaxies. So, the process of departing in a quantum jump, then returning to the same spot in a quantum jump, was highly complex, requiring precise calculations and telemetry, if you could call it that.

The point is that it took a great deal of preparation and calculations, some of them theoretical at best, to plan this Second Event. We didn't even know basic things such as, would the lighter move with the movement of the solar system and spinning arms of the Milky Way galaxy, or relative to something else?

In any case, the *Space Center* was one of the most advanced space stations in operation by any country, capable of holding over two hundred crew members, and was partially rotational so that there was at least normal gravity in much of the station due to the centripetal force of its spin, but zero when it was desirable.

Chase and I trained with two US astronauts: Michael Trenton, having the rank of Major in the US Air Force and Space Operations and named the co-commander of the mission; and Zachery McManiss, a medical doctor and a Space Force veteran. Trenton was not only the co-commander, but the chief science officer, an astronomer. McManiss was on board to observe and treat the travelers if needed. They both had previous experience, having served on one of two American-European moon bases, and Trenton had been on Mars once as part of a Sino-American Joint Forces (SAJF) mission. McManiss was less experienced as an astronaut, not much older than me. He and Trenton had been together before, so they made a good team and brought Chase and me along for the ride.

During most of our training, especially the second half, we also trained with the two astronauts chosen for the mission: Lieutenant Wen Lu and Kang Hongbo. Kang was a civilian computer scientist but worked for a top research institute in the Chinese government and had spent time on two of China's space stations and experimental craft. Kang Hongbo, involved in coding the event sequences with Venka, was our chief information officer.

Wen Lu, who we came to call Lulu, had the most experience of all the chosen travelers, and was thus named commander of the mission. Lulu was about thirty-eight years old, tall, and fit, towering over my small frame. She had a commanding presence throughout the training, even in our early days when she merely visited us in Houston. She served in the Chinese armed forces and was a commander in the SAJF. Years ago, she had been a fighter pilot in the Chinese Air Force, and then a veteran taikonaut, having had regular stays on the moon and two trips to Mars. Kepler told me she had spent time on an isolated experimental space station the Chinese didn't like to talk about, very remote. Simply put, she was a bad ass.

The Chinese were taking great pride in their part in the mission, and it was heartening to see them so gracious and deferential to Dr. Venkalaswaran and the Americans. Once the International Court action was settled, our Chinese partners put it all behind them. As a sign of their goodwill, they suggested to keep the name *Second Surfer*, or *Er Chonglang Zhe*, for the second experimental lighter that was to carry the six travelers to the nearest star system for this Second Event.

Primary construction of the *Second Surfer* rebooted upon settlement of the action, and the second experimental lighter (or shinbo) was completed in Bengaluru. Soon thereafter, the twenty-two-by-fourteen-meter spacecraft was moved via rail to the Jiuquan Launch Center in Inner Mongolia. From there it was heavy-lifted by a Chinese rocket to the *Space Center*.

Before going back to our rooms, Chase and I walked past the entrance to the zero-gravity portion of the *Space Center*. Like excited kids, we went through the door and made our way down as we gradually lost our footing and floated to the observation window several meters away in the dimly lit gangway. We could see that Venka was there, with a computer in one hand, talking to someone over a headset.

The lighter was parked in a zero-gravity airlock of the *Space Center*, a portion that did not rotate, next to a Command Center, or Command, that housed a complex array of computers needed to set the event status of the lighter (the destination and return conditions and coordinates) as well as monitoring systems for the travelers. Opposite the Command was an observation deck overlooking the lighter, where we stood meters away to marvel at the *Second Surfer*, nestled in the darkened bay.

"It's amazing," Chase said. "The Chinese have done an excellent job preparing the lighter. She looks great."

This second lighter that would carry the six star travelers was similar to the first lighter, only larger. From our vantage point, it had the look of a spiny bug, with its multi-mirrored surface reflecting the few lights around it. But Chase was right, it did look great.

"I think this will go smoothly. The CNSA is effective and efficient," Venka said. He motioned to the Command Center. There were few people in the room now, but on launch day it would be teeming with crew from both the CNSA and NASA.

Venka's assurances to Chase and me were endearing. Yet, as anxious as I was for him during his travels, I was excited for myself. My part in the mission went well beyond being an attorney, though it included that. While I was acting as the eyes and ears of my client, I was also an unacknowledged concession to the Federatsiya. Though quiet, they exerted unseen pressure behind the whole operation.

"The entire launch sequence to and from the Alpha Centauri star system is already set, but it will be fine-tuned the moments before the jump. Nothing is absolutely certain until it is time to go." Venka said, referring to the programming that would control the tympani and V-Shell, orchestrated to jump the spacecraft from its place outside the *Space Center* to its destination near Alpha Centauri, and back. "The job of the crew will be to ensure that all runs smoothly once at the point of arrival, which should be a little more than one astronomical unit (150 million kilometers) from Alpha Centauri and gather information on how well the lighter operates. Everything is run by the computer, and as you know, would be difficult to change in any case."

He was right. The time for departure and return, the two quantum events, had been pre-programmed for a reason. There was concern that quantum mass-transfer might have severe detrimental effects on humans. Venka's depression after his jump, though moderate (and kept secret), only confirmed some doubts about quantum mass-transfer. Then there was the sacrificial nature of the tympani itself, the danger being if it were shut down at the wrong time the travelers could become forever stranded. So, everything ran almost automatically once started. It was made so that it would be extremely difficult to change. Thus, the programming was all heavily orchestrated by a small group of people, one of whom was Venka. Others were Trenton, Kang, and Ting Li, the deputy director of the CNSA.

"You'll be there a little longer than I was, to keep it interesting," Venka said. "A full thirty minutes."

Though my presence was a compromise to the Federatsiya, in the eyes of many Chase and I represented the United States, along with Trenton and McManiss as America's first star travelers, a point that the media on Earth have left no mistake about.

"To keep it interesting?" I jested. I was growing more excited about the Second Event, even with the risks. As we walked away, I glanced over at the Command Center. One of the men was looking at us, or at me. I waved as he turned away.

* * *

My living quarters in the *Space Center* were small but practical, and in the gravitized part of the *Space Center*. I was happy that Branton had been allowed to join me, though we had to pay for him to fly up here ourselves. We had one more night until I went into isolation.

"In two weeks you'll be riding that wave," Brae said, looking up from his video as I returned to our dark living quarters from a briefing. He was as excited for me as I was for myself.

"How's your *wàipó*," I asked, referring to his grandmother. He was close to her, the matriarch of the Tjoeng family, having mostly been raised by her as her mother was busy running the family business. Though technology has advanced the average age of people over the years, typical wear and tear, and diabetes, was still hard to overcome. And that tough lady refused the most modern treatments.

"She's the same. Her spirits are up, but I can tell she's weak. She sends her best. She says everyone is asking her about your Big Event."

During the months that we trained for the mission, it was a big event. The world watched as with no other event since men first walked on the moon almost 130 years ago. Getting to this point was not trivial. The theoretical, let alone technical, hurdles to overcome could only be achieved incrementally. As a patent attorney, I knew this because it was my job to describe the increments. As Thomas Edison stood upon the shoulders of William Sawyer (and others), Aravinda Venkalaswaran stood on the shoulders of Hu Meixing (and others). On some level it was fitting that the Second Event should take place on a Chinese station.

The First Event, which was nothing short of a miracle, went largely unnoticed until after it had occurred, and even then it took weeks for the public and most governments to understand what had taken place. Not so this time, as there was plenty of forewarning for the Second Event. It belonged to the world, and they were watching.

"Are you going to talk to your father before you go into isolation?" Brae asked me. I was close to my father, and I talked to him often. Being an aerospace engineer, he could understand much of what was going on. He was smart. He was also gentle and kind.

Branton Ma'hai was also gentle and kind. He was uncomplicated, even as you peeled back the layers of the onion, it was more onion. He was a kid at heart, pushed into a businessman's shoes. In those days—while I was still in college—the boy appealed to me more than the man. We were on the same page.

Kevin M. Faulkner

"Yes, I will talk to him tonight," I said. "You can call him Mr. Hsu," I said, tossing my jacket at him.

"Ah, thanks for that," Brae joked. "You're assuming a lot aren't you?"

"Am I?" I asked coyly. It was obvious we had been getting more serious during this last year. I felt that Brae was the one for me if anyone was, and I could see the way he acted around me. But he had his family, and there may be other pressures in Jakarta, where I might not fit in. We didn't have to get married, hardly anyone did anymore, but it was nice to have some reassurance.

He came over and put his arms around me. I looked up at him as he kissed my lips.

"Not really," he said. "I'd like to talk to Dad too."

"Later."

* * *

The two weeks of isolation on the station felt like a month. The eight of us (two alternates) stayed in a sterile suite of two bedrooms, two bathrooms, and a living area. The food was very Chinese, which suited me fine. By the middle of the twenty-first century, the west coast of the United States had become highly influenced by East Asia, so it wasn't much of a change.

Along with Brae, Kepler was a regular visitor, right up until I departed. We talked in a sterile contact room, a white room divided by a large pane of glass from floor to ceiling, with a chair on each side to allow each person to either stand or sit. There was a sound system hidden nearby that allowed communication through the otherwise soundless walls. Kepler and I always sat facing one another, often joking, or playing chess. I believe Kepler taught me chess as a way to keep me still long enough to talk.

"Jenny, are you having fun playing astronaut?" Kepler said during one such visit.

"What do you mean *playing*?"

"Well," Kepler looked away, "Real astronauts aren't usually so small, and so lively."

He made me laugh. Kepler's thing was to purposefully exaggerate (or crazily minimize) something to the point of absurdity. I don't know if it was his method, or the knowledge that he was not human, but it worked. Your defenses strangely drop with a machine, after all, they didn't mean anything personal, right? His wit was his way of getting me to see myself in a way I could otherwise never know.

And to change or get over it.

On the day before the launch, Kepler came as usual. I sat, relaxing with my knees over the side of my chair, as Kepler entered his side of the contact room, flowers in his hand.

"For you, Jenny. I am proud of you."

I was touched. I stood, wished I could hug him. I placed my hand on the window, opposite him.

"You're my best friend, Kep."

He held his hand to meet mine. I wondered if he could feel the same.

* * *

I met less with Venka, as he was busy with preparations for the launch of the *Second Surfer*, but after the first week, I got a call from him asking that we meet.

"Jenny, how are you doing?" he asked, facing one another through the window in the contact room. He was excited, but I could see the age on him today, his hair disheveled and his eyes tired. *Was he worried?* I wondered.

Kevin M. Faulkner

"Good, I'm bored, but excited."

"I'm glad to see you are doing so well. I think this will be different for you than it was for me."

"How do you mean?"

"You'll be with others. You'll feel it more. Sometimes, Jenny, we need another face to know how we feel. It's like a child who has fallen and awaits his mother's reaction before he knows whether to laugh or cry. It's something deep in our psyche. Very human. To this day I wonder if it happened . . . though they tell me it did."

"It did." He smiled, and I noticed his expression was recognizable from the first day I met him. "I'll confirm it for you."

On the morning of the Event, I was restless with anticipation. I was in surfing tournament mode: intense and focused. The six of us were in the preparation room, squeezing into our pressure undergarments, followed by light space suits, with help from a masked crew wearing white sterile overalls. There was no gravity in this section of the *Space Center*, so having the crew help us was a relief.

Once we were in our gear, the crew guided us through a passageway leading to the docking bay where the *Second Surfer* was parked. We passed by a set of windows in the passage where reporters, observers and photographers waited for us on the other side.

"You think I could smuggle a flask on board?" Chase asked as we stopped in front of the windows in our blue spacesuits for the cameras. I think that was a reference to the many nights over the last year the eight of us snuck out on the towns where we trained, partly in Houston and partly in a facility outside of Beijing.

"Too late now, dude." I replied and waved at the reporters.

Lulu turned to us, frowning.

We were led to the *Second Surfer* by the masked crew in clean room gowns. As we went through the antechamber into the bay, we passed below the Command windows where some of the controllers and flight managers had gathered to wish us well. I could see Venka smiling at us. As we walked past those windows, I noticed the same man I had seen two weeks earlier among the other Command Center engineers and controllers.

"This way," one of the masked women said as she held her hand out to guide us into the lighter. Since the whole docking bay was pressurized with atmosphere, we were able to walk into the open hatch of the lighter. There were six seats, instruments all around. One porthole of transparent material probably ten centimeters thick was our only view of the outside. Its iris shutter was open, giving us a view of the closed bay door. Otherwise, we were encased in our egg-shaped éclair, covered in shiny sprinkles.

Lulu sat at what could be called the front of the craft with Michael Trenton. Chase and McManiss sat behind Lulu and Trenton. Kang Hongbo and I sat behind them, all in a two-by-two fashion. The lighter's portal was to our left.

Crew members in white overalls and masks left our cabin and closed the door behind them, sealing it shut. I could hear some activity outside the craft for a few moments as Lulu and Trenton worked on the controls. It went silent as I could hear an antechamber door close shut.

"*Er Chōnglàng Zhě, chéng rèn* (*Second Surfer*, please acknowledge)," I heard the requests from the Command Center through our cabin speaker. It was customary for the Chinese to open in Mandarin, but thereafter they mostly spoke in English for mixed missions such as this.

"*Er Chōnglàng Zhě zhèlǐ, Second Surfer* here," Lulu said. Her hands went over the controls in front of her, mostly adjusting the life support and data analysis systems, the primary things she had some control over.

The lighter hummed for some time as Lulu and Trenton talked to the male voice at Command, their hands moving over the touch screens and 3D control keys. The several screens in front of them were alive with information. My mind felt electric, my senses absorbing the smell of polished metal, the sight of streaming information on the control consoles, the sounds of chatter over the speaker, and thoughts swirling with the possibilities of what would come in a few minutes.

My thoughts were interrupted by the hissing sound of air being pumped out of the bay, followed by the grinding of gears as the bay doors opened. My throat tightened. The risks of it all had only been in the back of my mind until that moment.

We moved, soundlessly. As with the first lighter, there were no propulsion means on this craft. It was moved by a mechanical arm that gently lifted and pushed the lighter out of the bay into space. Once the arm released the *Second Surfer*, we drifted out of the docking bay of the *Space Center*. It was then that the countdown from five minutes began. A decision had been made to start the departure sequence fairly early, as soon as safely possible after the coordinates in the craft were set.

"Four minutes," Lulu said in her headset, "Configured for event. Command, Jiuquan confirm."

"Command confirming," we could hear over the speaker in the cabin.

There was a buzz of chatter between Command, Lulu, and Trenton. Trenton counted down the time amidst the calm din. My senses were on full alert as we drifted into space, looking between the controls at the front of the craft and the stars in the porthole.

"One minute." We were already at least twenty meters from the Station as voices filled our cabin, calling for status.

"*Surfer*, confirm release."

"Release confirmed, internal control," Lulu said.

I could see out the porthole a glow from the heating tympani plates that surrounded us, an irreversible process that basically locked us into a destiny of leaving our solar system or a complete abort of the mission, leaving us for an expensive second attempt months from now.

Amid the chatter, the *Second Surfer* shuddered. There was no sound, but like a boat on a sudden swell, the lighter rocked and surged away from the Station. I didn't think much of it at the time. A sudden hush followed.

"Strange," Chase said.

Lulu was cool. "*Research Space Center Five*, please copy," she said with no emotion. There was no reply.

"Command, please copy," she repeated with slightly more urgency. Lulu looked over at a stone-faced Trenton. I heard frantic voices in Mandarin gradually emerge over the intercom. Lulu quickly switched the cabin speaker off so only she could hear. I was soon lost as she spoke in rapid Mandarin. Lulu barked something at Kang and he immediately turned to an instrument cluster nearby.

"It appears something has happened at the Space Center. Likely a communications problem," Lulu said calmly as she searched the monitor in front of her.

"What do you think has happened?" McManiss asked. "The lighter shook."

"Likely we brushed against some object nearby that we had not accounted for," Lulu said. "Or some additional air pressure release from the bay.

"Fifteen seconds, Jiuquan please stand by," Lulu said, repeating it in Mandarin. A loud hum began to fill the cabin.

"*Jiuquan zhichi*," I could faintly hear from Lulu's headphones. Then, Command said something to Lulu that caused her face to turn ashen, something I couldn't make out.

The iris closed on the porthole. Suddenly, I felt trapped.

"*Lǐ jiě*," was all she said, which means *understand*.

"Stand by for primary activation," Trenton called out.

"Ten, nine, eight," Trenton counted, as he glanced at Lulu, then back at the screen in front of him, "seven, six, five, four, three, two, one." The sound and feel of the lighter reached a crescendo.

The most unexpected thing happened: I didn't feel a thing.

Kevin M. Faulkner

* * *

I mostly grew up in a suburb outside of Seattle, Washington. When I was young my mother would come to my room on stormy nights. She knew that the thunder and lightning scared me, but I was always too sleepy to go to her, so she came to me.

My mother was a beautiful woman, with creamy skin and wavy brunette hair. She was practical, but kind and compassionate. I could tell that my father worshipped her. Everyone who knew her loved her. I loved her.

"Hey muffin," she'd say to me in her sweet voice, "I was looking for my lost sheep."

"She's here mommy, your little sheep is here," I'd say. I would hold up my favorite stuffed animal, a bunny named *Chance*.

"Oh my, that's not my little sheep, that's a bunny," she'd reply in a gentle exclamation. She'd take it in her arms and kiss it. She'd ask the bunny, "Do you know where my sheep is?"

I'd giggle, and she would smile and wiggle her nose at me. I would say, "Chance lives with the sheep in the forest."

Mom would kiss my forehead, and say, "I know you'll take good care of my sheep when she comes home because you are such a good girl."

Somehow my fear would subside and I could fall back to sleep. That memory of my mother has stayed with me all this time. So has the hopelessness she left behind. She was with me, and then she was gone in a rage.

I couldn't really process what had happened, I was only twelve. She'd left my father drunk, my little brother lost, and my soul on fire. I took it all and made it my own, and by the time I was sixteen, I was alone, dissipated, my being spent of all purpose.

It dawned on me that I never told my friend, Kepler.

The Sixth Traveler

TWENTY

Implant Record Date 25 January 2099
Research Space Center Five

A light was flashing in time with a *ding* sound on the console. It seemed out of place.

"Our coordinates are confirmed, we are 1.2 astronomical units from Alpha Centauri A," Lulu said, ignoring the flashing light and pressing an icon to silence the sound that accompanied it.

For a few moments there was complete silence. Lulu turned to her computer console, frantically reading information in Chinese and English streaming in blue and red letters on a black background. Trenton continued to work, silent, even stoic, at his station. He was oddly intense while the rest of us looked toward the open porthole at the stars, and at Beta Centauri, bright but not overwhelming.

It was moments after the jump that I noticed that I felt different.

"Let me take your pulse," McManiss said. Though we each had sensors beneath the skin of our forearms, he wanted to make direct assessments of our condition.

"What is your full name," he asked.

"Jenny Celeste Hsu," I replied.

"Where were you born?"

"Regal, Washington, United States."

"Good. How are you feeling?"

I hesitated, confused, not knowing how to answer his question.

"Jenny?"

"I don't feel right. I feel . . .." I couldn't finish.

"What do you mean?" McManiss asked.

Chase turned to me as the clock above him counted time: 27:00, 26:59, 26:58 minutes, and down. We were programmed to spend thirty minutes at our destination, the Alpha Centauri star system, and we had already been there less than five minutes.

"Chase, are you alright?" I asked. Though the cabin was cool, sweat beaded on his face.

"No, actually," he replied, "I can't imagine . . .." he trailed off. McManiss went over to him.

"Everyone," Lulu said. "Let's focus."

In spite of Lulu's command, it was obvious something was wrong. I looked over at Kang, who was rocking back and forth, in apparent pain as he held his head.

I thought of the craft's shudder minutes ago, and the panicked look on Lulu's face prior to the jump. My mind went to the worst.

"Something happened when the ship rocked," I said, somewhat to myself.

"An air release? An explosion somewhere in the *Space Center*?" Chase questioned.

"That is not confirmed," Lulu replied sternly.

The silence grew uneasy.

I looked over at Kang, increasingly in distress. "Zach," I called out, pointing to Kang, feeling the weight of an ever-sinking abyss inside of me. Thoughts flashed through my mind: surfing La Push with Katerina and Trinity, my father's face after my mother had left, Aravinda giving his presentation to a darkened room, John's hand reaching out to me, Erissa's commanding presence, the night Chase and I kissed, Kepler's flowers . . . the day in Bali with Branton. Laying there on the beach, staring up and wondering how on Earth I could be loved. I recognized something as if in a dream and tried to voice it to my friend an arm's length away.

"Chase, one of the men in the Command, I think I recognized him from somewhere. How could I know somebody like that?"

"What made you think of him?" he asked, wiping the sweat from his forehead.

The Sixth Traveler

"Somehow I had a bad feeling about that guy . . . ." I was beginning to realize who he reminded me of. "Sneshia, that guy who hit me." I was in disbelief. At first glance, the guy in the Command Center looked Chinese. Faces flipped through my mind like images on a deck of cards. Sneshia could easily have had surgery to change his appearance.

"Chase, I think it was him. I think Sneshia found his way into the system . . . or did something?" I asked, panicked.

"Chase, why are you sweating?" McManiss interrupted.

"I don't know. I don't feel right," Chase replied. "I feel nauseous, and dizzy."

Lulu turned to us, sweat pouring from her face. "All of you, focus on your tasks, if there was sabotage, there is nothing we can do about it now."

It was apparent that all six of us were affected. I could see that Trenton was agitated, and Kang was staring into space, holding his head.

"Kang, what's the matter?" McManiss asked.

"Headache."

"Trenton?" McManiss asked.

"I'm fine," Trenton said, with unmistakable anger in his voice.

"Something is wrong with the shell," Lulu said, forcing out the words as if she were in pain.

"Is that the light flashing?" I pointed. Lulu didn't answer. I could see sweat streaming from her forehead. I didn't understand why she hadn't said something before. Lulu looked over at Trenton, only to find him increasingly agitated.

Seeing Lulu distressed, McManiss rushed over, but she brushed him aside. "We have to evaluate the system before the return sequence initiates. Adeane, Kang, run a diagnostic. I'll go through the drive and external shell to see if there is anything physical. Could be that whatever happened at the *Space Center* before we left damaged the shinbo." Lulu seemed to acknowledge everyone's growing suspicion.

Kevin M. Faulkner

"Kang, can you help?" Lulu asked, her voice gentler. Kang was almost catatonic, but McManiss helped him toward the front. We were all disoriented, so much so that little of our intended schedule of observations within the Alpha Centauri system, and the lighter itself, would get done. It was a mess.

"Do what you can. We have less than twenty-five minutes," Lulu said. "If we can't figure it out in time, we need to consider shutting down the plates."

The tympani plates could become irreversibly damaged if we shut down. They were built to be sacrificial. Once lit, the tympani essentially burned and would be ruined once quenched. There was a backup system dedicated to keeping the plates from quenching until the whole event status, both the jump to the destination and secondary jump back home, had run their course.

"Well, we can't do that—" Chase started but was cut off by Lulu's scowl.

Whatever had happened was affecting me. I felt myself sinking, searching for a way out of something that had no visible outlet. Time passed slowly as I watched the clock above Chase's head count the time down to our return, now at 22:30 minutes. I wondered why I was here and not back home with my father, my mother, and Brae.

"Damn," Chase said under his breath while staring at code in his computer screen, "twenty minutes left. Kang, can you find anything?"

"No," Kang forced himself to speak. Chase was clearly anxious, while Kang was in pain, and like me, seemed to be in a chasm.

"Shut up, both of you," Trenton said. McManiss and I looked at one another, surprised at Trenton's growing anger. Trenton rose from his chair, hitting his console as he rose. His face contorted in an anguished rage.

"Get out of my way," Trenton grunted as he pushed past Kang and Chase toward Lulu, who was in the back of the cabin checking behind panels.

The Sixth Traveler

"Trenton, what are you doing?" McManiss asked.

"Trenton, sit down," Lulu ordered.

"Fuck you, bitch!" Trenton roared as he continued toward Lulu. Unfazed, Lulu grabbed him as McManiss pushed toward the two of them, floating over to help hold him down.

"What is going on?" Lulu asked.

"I think he's reacting," McManiss said. Trenton struggled against the two of them. He was clearly a powerful man, and in the weightlessness of the cabin, they began to flail around, hitting against the cabin walls.

"You think I'm reacting," Trenton yelled, still struggling to punch Lulu, and now McManiss.

"Michael, get a hold of yourself," McManiss ordered. Trenton only heightened his struggle, lashing out at McManiss.

"Go to hell!" Trenton yelled, pushing Lulu and McManiss away.

"Lulu, hold him down," McManiss said.

"Chase!" Lulu called out. Chase sprang into action, pushing off against the wall and shooting through the cabin and tackled Trenton, and with Lulu, pinned him against a wall while McManiss grabbed a syringe injector, filled it with a tranquilizer, and propelled himself back over. McManiss injected its contents into Trenton's arm.

"God damn it!" Trenton yelled, "I'll fucking kill both of you!"

As the tranquilizer took hold, Trenton's agitation subsided, and within moments he slumped against an exhausted Chase. We all breathed a collective sigh of relief. The excitement past us, I started to sob. Kang looked on with desperation.

Out of breath, Lulu calmed herself down. She and Chase pulled Trenton's floating body to Chase's original seat and strapped him in, tying his wrists.

"Thanks," Lulu said to Chase and McManiss.

They all resumed their places as Lulu brushed the hair from her face and surveyed the situation, thinking.

"What happened?" Lulu asked McManiss.

"I don't know, a reaction to the damaged shell?" he replied. "This is all so new, everyone reacts differently to trauma."

"But . . .." Lulu started, but changed direction, "How long will that tranquilizer hold?"

"At least an hour. I have more if needed."

"And what effect would the partially functioning shell have on us if we go ahead with the return?"

"It could make things worse. I just don't know," McManiss said. Of everyone, he appeared the least affected by the loss of the V-Shell. He was intense, but that could be from trying to manage everyone else on board. Lulu silently continued her search for signs of sabotage on the control boards.

McManiss turned to me, "Why would someone have done this?"

"I don't know," I said. "There was a faction of the VK, the military arm of the Federatsiya, that didn't like the deals being made to settle their border disputes and form the government."

"I'm guessing the settlement with the Chinese was the last straw," Chase said.

As the moments passed, Lulu regained her composure. Whatever had happened during the departure, she either had the psyche to recover quickly, or she was not as susceptible to begin with. I watched the transformation in her; she became more purposeful in her actions, decisive. She looked about the cabin to assess the situation.

"I can't find anything obvious. We have less than twelve minutes to act," she said aloud. "Chase, Kang, have you found anything?"

"Nothing obvious. If it was sabotage, it doesn't appear software related. That makes sense given how guarded we were," Chase said.

"McManiss, what is everyone's condition?" Lulu asked, glancing at the time, 11:13 minutes.

"It's difficult to evaluate. Chase is highly anxious, Kang may have mild psychosis. Trenton is exhibiting psychosis, but is out and stable, Jenny is struggling, but stable."

The Sixth Traveler

"Is this all reversible?" Lulu asked.

"Likely."

There was silence as Lulu looked at her console, going through screens and triggering data streams.

"Lulu," Chase said, "If we shut down there is no guarantee we can fix the problem, and shutting down could ruin the tympani plates. In any case, the V-Shell looks to be at least partially working."

"We only have enough food and water for about four days," I said, losing hope. I wanted to go home.

"It's complicated . . . it's hard to know," Chase said.

"Yes," Lulu said, taking a breath, "Whatever is wrong it's likely external of the ship, and we have no way of fixing that."

There were eight minutes left until our programmed return. Lulu turned again to her consol. I could see that she was weighing our options. McManiss was examining Kang and Chase. Trenton was buckled into his seat, with his hands tied, still out.

With five minutes left, Lulu calmly said, "Chase, let the return status go forward, let's go home."

There was movement after that, but no words. The cabin was heavy with silence, everyone quietly floated back to their seats and fastened themselves in. Chase took over the co-commander seat. Kang held his head in his hands, and Chase managed to calm himself. McManiss comforted Kang and me as best he could. He reached into his bag and gave Kang an injection that nearly knocked him out.

Four minutes left on the clock.

Lulu checked all the systems and made one last attempt to correct whatever problem was in the V-Shell, adjusting the system from her control console to no avail as far as we could tell.

One minute.

Strapped back into my chair, I felt isolated as I turned and looked helplessly out the porthole for something familiar. The stars became more visible as the light inside the cabin dimmed. Only moments ago I saw them with these eyes that had been capable of taking in their beauty. Now all I could see was darkness. I knew in some part of my mind that it had only been an hour ago when I saw the world, unafraid. It only took moments and I was broken.

Would it always be like this? I felt as if I were a child in the storm. Vulnerable and alone.

The iris closed over the porthole as the final seconds of our stay ticked away: five, four, three, two, one second. Tears ran down my face, and McManiss looked toward me sympathetically. There was little he could do, but his presence helped.

As with the departure Event, our jump back to some celestial *terra firma* was met with an eerie silence, as if vibrations from the air had been sucked into the vacuum of space. There was nothing.

"Chase, send the distress signal," Lulu broke the silence.

It took a moment, but over the radio chatter slowly drifted throughout the cabin from the *Space Center*. Then a call to the *Second Surfer*. Nothing sounded so good.

"*Second Surfer*, please copy," said a female voice, different from the voice we had heard when we left. I wondered if that voice existed any longer.

"*Er Chōng Làng zài, Second Surfer* here," Lulu said. I could see relief on her face.

"We copy your distress."

And like that it was over.

It took four hours for us to be rescued. As a towing drone pushed the *Second Surfer* back to the *Space Center*, we could see the charred veins and twisted metal around what had been the Command Center and docking bay. We were taken to another part of the *Center* where more conventional spacecraft would dock. We were all silent. The glow of the Earth below us was all the comfort we could hope for.

Lulu and McManiss relayed our conditions to what had become our new Command, and as the voices from the *Space Center* began to relay the tragedy, Lulu and McManiss both thought it best to turn off the cabin speaker and don their headphones.

The Sixth Traveler

I could hear bits and pieces, and later, learned that my suspicions were correct. There had been an explosion in the Command Center moments after we pushed off from the *Space Center*. It was a bomb, planted by someone who was there, an insider. While the damage was serious, most everyone in the Command Center survived, including Venka. Kepler had identified the saboteur before the bomb went off, took the explosive device from where it was placed and sacrificed himself by throwing it, along with himself, through the airlock leading to the bay.

Kepler's act was not only selfless, he acted quickly enough to go into the airlock with the explosive device, likely understanding that it was highly reinforced and thus the best place to absorb an explosion. If not for that act, whether programmed or an act of bravery and love, it would have caused even more damage to the *Second Surfer*, and most everyone in the Command Center would have been killed.

Having identified Sneshia, and with nowhere to run, he was taken into custody. I never saw him again.

Chase and I looked at one another. Before we knew the full story, we worried. It could not be good for Venka, since he would have been in the Command Center. I was also thinking about Brae, though he was not in the Command Center and likely not in danger. I suddenly wished I had my phone with me so I could contact him directly.

As we were led away from our damaged lighter, I was only partially aware of what was going on around me. Tears ran down my face; I remember a feeling of drowning, wanting to tear myself from my own skin and run away. Nothing mattered until I felt Lulu's arm around me, and the surprise of her embrace. Her severity gave way to empathy as she led me up the increasingly gravitized gangway to the waiting technicians in white coveralls and masks.

"*Tiān wú jué rén zhī lù* (Heaven never bars one's way)," she said, softly.

We looked backwards to see that a small portion of the tympani plates on the exterior of the craft were charged and damaged.

Kevin M. Faulkner

In turn, each traveler was led to a decontamination chamber. We shed all of our clothing, taking turns entering a beamed chamber that bathed our naked bodies, killing any virus or bacteria that could otherwise contaminate the *Space Center*, and the human race. I remember being grateful for the warmth of the red lamps in the secondary chamber before donning soft blue coveralls. I wiped my face as I tried to pull myself together.

Branton Ma'hai and John Mar were waiting for me on the other side of the glass barrier as I and the others were escorted from the transition room. There was a throng of media and observers present at the *Space Center* for the Event. I imagined there had been expectations of exuberance, replaced with relief that we had made it back alive. Those that came to rejoice now stood in solemn silence.

"Venka was hurt, Jenny," John said though the window microphone before I could ask. "He'll be fine, but Kepler is gone." I was too numb at the time to take in that last part. I simply imagined seeing my friend soon.

McManiss continued to care for Kang, Trenton, Chase, and me for the next several days as we remained in the medical center of the *Space Center*, waiting to be stabilized and transported back to Earth. Lulu also stayed with us, but it was apparent that she had quickly recovered.

Brae was with me, but we were kept isolated from the press and most other people. I wanted to see Venka but was told I had to wait. On the day that I was allowed out of the hospital, I learned that Venka had been transported back to Earth several days earlier.

"Let's go home," Brae said to me as we left the medical center. I was relieved to be heading home, but empty without Kepler.

* * *

I wept less, but still found little to my existence. I watched Brae as he surfed on the cold March waters of the Trestles, his good nature apparent even from a distance. I dug my feet further into the cool sand along the shoreline. I missed Kepler. *He felt, even though no one bothered to tell him.* I felt guilty but could not pinpoint why.

The *separation* was what Venka called his time after the First Event. I knew where his pain came from. I could understand it, but empathy and self-awareness only go so far unless you can believe in the alternative, that there is hope. I wasn't so sure I did.

The sun was high, lighting up the middles in waves of light over the translucent green waters as I watched Brae surf. I thought of our days in El Segundo, a much simpler time I wanted to suspend myself in forever. Finishing a wave, he walked toward me from the shoreline. A familiar smile shone on his face. As he approached me, concern filled his eyes. I loved him for that.

Branton knelt in the sand before me, and said, "It'll get better, Juju. Look at the waves."

It was something to hold on to.

PART THREE

THE FIRST WAVE

TWENTY-ONE

Implant Record Date 6 April 2104
San Diego

"Jenny, our government is only as credible as the trust of those who make it up." Amanta Kokotova said this to me with an earnestness that left me flustered, as she was no ordinary person.

Amanta, now the Foreign Minister of the Republic of Caucasus States, the fledgling country formed from the Caucasus Federatsiya, was incredulous at the suggestion of counsel that she would allow someone else to decide who should control an entire planet. It was true that the lighter expeditions of the Republic had found and mapped this new celestial body, dubbed the New World.

But still.

"We took the risks," Amanta said. "Our people fought for this, they trust only our government. They trust me."

Though she had a point, I was trying to avoid a fight between the new government and the rest of the world in her quest to exclusively colonize this New World. I don't think she understood the seriousness of the moment.

"Amanta," I said, "Perhaps it is best to bring this before the United Nations. Remember what we talked about? To build a nation you have to have the recognition and trust of other nations, not only the people of your own nation." I knew she would not like that idea.

"Why bother, Jenny? They are behind the times." I admired that woman, but Amanta wore her biases on her sleeve. With Amanta, my work was always cut out for me. My firm still advised Amanta and other upper-level officials with the Republic, and Amanta and I had grown particularly close. She wasn't one for "Thank you" but her gratitude toward me showed as an interest and warmth in me that she rarely displayed with others. I was grateful back to her, if for nothing else than for listening to me.

"Because leaders listen; you are a leader."

Amanta turned away from me as I sat at my desk in my new office in the highest section of the skyscraper in which my law firm, Lackley, Bei and Chavez, had established our new offices in San Diego. I was now a partner of the firm, my office at least three times the size of the one where I had drafted the first patent applications for Dr. Venkalaswaran's quantum mass-transfer technology six years ago.

"You took a risk yourself in the second lighter," Amanta said. "You still pay the price."

Also true. She was referring to my place in the *Second Surfer* and the lasting effects on my mind and body after having traversed the distance to the Alpha Centauri system and back with a partially functioning V-Shell. I was not the same. Though my depression lifted, I was left with seizure-like symptoms I referred to as lapses that occurred with increasing frequency.

"My mind is not what it used to be."

"You clearly think well. Perhaps your memory is off."

"They say that thirty-six is the new ninety for us Americans."

"You make light, but it is true."

Another result of my injuries from the Second Event was a slowly dwindling memory. My reasoning was sound, but my retention was slowly fading. Truthfully, I was scared, uncertain where it was all going and how incapacitated I would become. I did my best to hide my malady.

"Possibly," I said, "but you should think carefully about going this alone without at least approaching other governments, even if on an individual basis." We both knew that while India, China, the US, and the Republic had a head start in intergalactic exploration, other countries were on the hunt. "You want to avoid conflicts over who owns what. Talking can prevent that."

Amanta dismissively shook her head.

The Republic had yet to allow Russia to access the lighter technology, which did not sit well with them. Though it is likely that they were already trying to replicate and build their own star jumping craft from what was taught in the published patents, our firm's analysts concluded (and I agreed) that they were reluctant to carry it forward for fear of upsetting the Chinese, who took such intellectual property matters seriously. The Republic had decided to boycott Russia, and in retaliation there was growing evidence that Russia was supporting resurgent Vainakh forces, both of which were not happy with the direction the Republic was taking. Keeping Russia in the dark was a risk on the part of the fledgling Republic, as relations with Russia had been stable. Amanta and the Republic leadership were committed to complete evacuation of their government and people from planet Earth. With nothing to prove at this point, the need was to buy time.

"I don't think we'll avoid a confrontation with Russia," Amanta said. "Moscow is still not happy with the Republic, or with our control of the lighter technology. In any case, I like your one-off approach with the New World."

The New World that Amanta was so eager to enthrone herself upon was one of the newly discovered habitable planets found within what was called the *Perimeter*, a spherical area around our solar system about a thousand light-years in diameter. Since the Second Event took place, quantum mass-transfer had become more robust and predictable. The V-Shell was reliable and the tympani longer lasting as they were now encased in carbon alloy ruggrs (covered extenders) that made them a part of the exterior of the vessel, as well as extending their life.

In spite of the technological improvements to QMT travel, the Perimeter was deemed the safest distance that the current lighters could reliably navigate. Where pulsar navigation was once a theoretical possibility for interstellar travel, now it was a necessity, and apparently not as simple as once thought. For over a hundred years, humans have been using various techniques to locate habitable planets in the galaxy, but now that there was a means of getting to those places, the path was not so apparent. No one dared to venture near the center of the Milky Way galaxy, not knowing what the intense gravity of the black hole would do to navigation. Further, there were no detailed maps of the Milky Way galaxy in which we lived, no roadmap of the unseen obstacles: dark stars, planets, and asteroids, even dust and other matter. There was no real understanding of how physical objects being within the pathway from point A to point B would impact QMT travel. It was indeed the case that several lighters had been lost, with no clue as to their condition or status. Yet, even with these limitations, within that Perimeter there had been the discovery of a dozen or more planets with varying degrees of habitability for humans.

"You will have to deal with the Russians at some point," I said. "I understand your wanting to hold them off long enough to avoid competing with them. But it is a risk." The discovery of new, livable planets was so fresh, space-faring countries had yet to formally consider how to regulate or control matters of colonization, or if it should be regulated at all. Space had become the American wild west.

"Yes, it is a game of chess; likely a dangerous one," Amanta said. "The Republic is vulnerable, and the Russians will demand access to the lighter technology eventually. Though I think direct military action is unlikely, I'm betting the Russians manipulate Vainakh forces to their advantage."

The suspicion was that Russia was leveraging the discontent among the Vainakh to split them between forces that remained loyal to the Republic, and forces that wanted to go back to controlling things themselves. If it was the latter, they were being naïve, as it was too late to go back to the way things were.

"I think the more favor you carry with the rest of the world, and they see that your intentions with the technology are peaceful, it will make it difficult for the Vainakh, backed by the Russians or not, to act too aggressively."

"Mmmm, maybe, but not impossible. I don't think they care about what the world thinks."

"You're probably right." I didn't want to think of the consequences of that, so I poured each of us some more coffee instead.

"The next thing you are going to have to think about is the corporation itself," I ventured. "I know you don't want to talk about that."

"That the Vainakh will take over the country and nationalize? No, you are right; I don't like to think about that."

I could see the disquiet in her face at the possibility. I had suggested to her that it might be best to form a joint corporation, or merge, with a more established American or European company. This would allow a legal transfer of technology and prevent it from being monopolized by the Vainakh should they take the Republic over by force. Though the patents and the international agreements were in place, there was always technological know-how that remained secret, the little nuts and bolts of building a lighter. That was worth untold amounts of money, and I had to get Amanta to consider her options.

"I'm going next week to Chechnya to talk to Chase and Zévic about that, among other things," I said. Zévic Toreli was Svoboda Corporation's chief counsel, with a background in engineering and politics, a little of everything. He happened to go to law school in Europe and worked his way into the most important company on the planet.

"That might save the lighters, but how to save the Republic?" Amanta asked.

Amanta stood at the window of my office, stoic in her resolve.

"I remember when this all started, only several years out of college," Amanta started. "I was somewhat idealistic, but I also was determined. I wasn't afraid of anything."

Kevin M. Faulkner

"How did it start?" I tried to temper my eagerness, as Amanta rarely shared her past.

"Like most things, with my first job out of school."

I rose from my desk and walked over to where Amanta stood, taking my coffee with me.

"I took a job in the diplomatic corps of the prior Chechen government, in Grozny," Amanta continued. "I had a little apartment there, all alone. I shunned men, but I went to every social event I could. Diplomats rub elbows with diplomats."

"I'm terrible at that."

"It's a skill you learn, like anything. I learned it to get where I wanted. After several years, I had become friends with people in high places, and looked for more responsibility. Do you remember Canstaczt Noori?"

"The former Prime Minister of Caucasus Republic, wasn't he the first to open negotiations with the Vainakh?"

"That's right, though they were not called that in those days; they were referred to as the *Tukkhum*. I was his executive assistant before he was ousted. There was so much turmoil over the idea of forming an alliance with the Tukkhum. I was sure that it was the only way, and I told him as much."

She was silent for a while before she continued.

"But something happened."

"Yes?"

"The Prime Minister and I . . . .. As I said, I shunned men."

"What happened?"

"We were together in Paris for a conference. We were negotiating with the Russians. Paris has a presence; it can be romantic and tragic at once."

I nodded as she continued.

"After the second day of talks, our team went out with other officials for drinks and dinner. I could see the Prime Minister looking at me, just glances. I felt flattered but didn't think anything at the time.

"So, the night wore on and our group seemed to become diluted, part of the late-night revelry of young people coming from the clubs. I ended up nearly alone with the Prime Minister. Looking back, I think he orchestrated this. He said he wanted to talk to me, somewhere quiet.

"I followed him out onto the busy walk on the Seine in the district of La Salpêtrière. As we walked away from the clubs and tourist areas, we fell into a quaint and secluded quarter. I remember the lights reflecting in the river as the sounds of people grew fainter. We found a little café and sat at an empty table, watching people walk by, talking.

"The Prime Minister became more familiar with me than I had ever known. It was nice. I remember something he told me: 'Amanta, I have learned that once you get past having a certain amount of money, the way you spend your time is a direct reflection of your values, what is most important to you.'

"Then he continued: 'I see some men who have beautiful wives, children, a nice home, and enough money that they could work part time, even quit their jobs. They say they love their families, but they spend little time with them.'

"Canstaczt poured me another glass of wine, and asked me: 'Amanta, how do you spend your time? I only see you working, is that what you value?'

"We had a few drinks, too much." Amanta looked at the coffee in her hand. "I think he was old fashioned, maybe he felt like I should marry and settle down."

I stood next to Amanta, mesmerized.

"You didn't exactly do that."

"No, and I told him so. I was only thirty-two years old, about your age, still young. He was of course a distinguished man, and powerful. He was the Prime Minister, in talks with his Russian counterpart, and those of the rest of Europe. Yet he talked to me as an equal, a relief from the confrontations during the day.

"He talked to me about his plans for the Caucasus Republic, about prosperity. He talked about the uranium and how we held something precious, something the world was starving for."

"So, what happened?"

"Nothing happened that night. He walked me back to our hotel and we went to our separate rooms.

"I remember sitting behind him during the third day of talks, hearing his voice, and that of the translator. I rarely needed the translator; I could understand English then, and Russian, French, and German, as well as my own tongue, so at times I would tune it out so I could hear his voice."

"It must have all been exciting."

"I remember thinking: *Finally, this was where I wanted to be*. And it *was* where I wanted to be, how I wanted to spend my time."

She looked whimsically out the window as she continued, though I noticed the tone of her voice changed, bearing an edge I was more familiar with.

"That night, after the third day of talks, our delegation went out with the Prime Ministers of France and Germany, at the private residence of the French Prime Minister, Jean Michel Paquet. I remember the Prime Minister, Canstaczt, was with his wife, Megania. She was beautiful, an elegant woman.

"But that night, just once during dinner, he looked at me, a glance, and I knew what he wanted.

"After the meeting, he told his wife he had to meet with his staff. It was true in part, but the meeting was only the two of us. He took my hand, kissed it in a café late that night, a place along the Quai de la Tournelle, in front of strangers. He had just had dinner with his wife, but he didn't care, it was if she did not exist."

"Maybe she didn't," I ventured. "So, what did you think?"

"I wasn't sure what to do."

The Sixth Traveler

Amanta looked at me, and said, "Most women face this at one time or another. You are drawn to a man, and you think you know how you would handle it, a man you know you should not be drawn to, and yet, there you are."

"There you were."

"Yes. We were together that night. I wanted him." She thought for a moment, then followed, "I wanted him, but I didn't want the *implications* of being with him. I didn't fully understand that until much later.

"We went to a room nearby. He must have already known about this little place. Plush but out of the way. I spent the night with him."

I was anxious to hear what happened next as Amanta went silent while she walked over to a chair in front of my desk to sit. I followed her, sitting across from her but leaning forward, wanting to hear more.

"Did you see him again?"

"Yes, I did, we grew close. He would always talk to me about his vision for our country, which we shared. Tired of the fighting, tired of the poverty. The complications."

"The complications?"

"The Tukkhum, the alliances forming among the Nakh, the highland people. They were organizing to recover, refine and control the uranium. They found a network to sell it, illegally, and purchased the refining equipment to make it even more valuable.

"The Prime Minister saw potential in this, but at the time, the Tukkhum were resistant to the government. They weren't against us, only separate. They wanted to be left alone."

"The West saw them as an organized crime syndicate."

"I know, and still do. And they were growing rich, and powerful. We couldn't unify our country without them, and the Prime Minister wanted me to talk with them. We wanted to bring them into the fold of the government, legitimize their operations.

"So, I was assigned a position with a government agency that managed the resources, an interior department. We worked with the criminal enforcement agency. We would go to the locations of the Nakh in the mountains. At first, just to talk, establish some trust, at least some familiarity.

"We found that they were becoming sophisticated, selling highly refined uranium. They did not fight us, but they did not want us there. They resisted any real relations. I was good with them, playing the dumb girl lazily doing her job. Perhaps they felt sorry for me. I eventually became friendly with some of the higher-level men, and felt they trusted me. At least I thought they did."

I realized my mouth was dry, as I had not swallowed for some time.

"I finally convinced one of the Tukkhum leaders. I convinced him to have the interior department inspect a major shipment of uranium, to accompany the shipment to a destination where we could inspect and certify the ore, and have it properly registered and sold to energy companies. We even arranged a legitimate buyer.

"I rode along with the first shipment in a convoy with the carrier. We took precautions, having armed guards with us. I wore a plasma absorbing vest, very heavy. I felt confident, excited that I was doing something for my country, something to move us forward."

She looked down.

"I was bitterly disappointed."

"How?"

"Only one hour into our journey out of the mountains, in an isolated area near Beloti, we were ambushed. It happened so fast, I had a hard time comprehending what was going on.

"Armed men surrounded the caravan. They dragged me out of my van and held a gun to my head. I lay there in the dirt on the side of the road. They were shouting something I couldn't understand, and some distance away from me one of the men was talking to another as if they were discussing a deal. I couldn't make out what they were saying. I was afraid to even look, I dare not move.

The Sixth Traveler

"The young man who dragged me out of the van stood over me with a gun to my head and told me, 'Just keep quiet; don't say anything.' I don't think he wanted to be there, we were both frightened.

"I have never been so frightened, Jenny. I remember being disappointed. I wanted to cry but didn't let myself."

"I can't believe . . . ." I started.

"A few of us were allowed to leave in an empty van. The armed Nakh took the shipment and drove off. One of the men in our interior agency rode with them. I remember he was not at gun point."

"There was an insider."

"Yes, the whole thing was a setup."

There was some silence. Amanta took a sip of her coffee.

"Who?"

"Someone connected to the Prime Minister." Amanta looked at me, hardened but not angry.

"I remember thinking as we drove back to Grozny: *This is never going to end*. I repeated that in my mind, *This is never going to end*. I felt hopeless. For a long time I didn't know what to do.

"I was bitter toward Noori after that. I never spoke to him again, but I did not feel a loss there. I felt a loss for my people.

"I decided to stay on with the foreign ministry, and I kept quiet. The Prime Minister said nothing. But I searched from that day on for a way out of all of this.

"The rest you know. There was fighting within the government, and the forming Vainakh, who were already quite powerful, were forced to transfer even more of it, mostly to them. They placed their own people in power but kept the structure. I stayed on.

"Over time, I saw the riches, and wanted to use it. I didn't see any other way. I wasn't going to fight or ask anyone else to do it. I had to use what I had."

"The uranium."

"Yes. I convinced our department to sponsor research projects to find safer ways to build power plants, and ways to dispose of the waste, the two things that made nuclear power unattractive. Though, as you know, few nations had a choice as gas and oil were going out of use, the Wellington Convention having been implemented years before that.

"But I knew the Vainakh couldn't continue the way they were, the rest of the world would not stand for it. I convinced them of that, and as I pushed for alliances with our diplomatic neighbors in the Caucasus and Caspian region, further putting the Vainakh in a position where they had less choice. I did what Canstaczt Noori could not. I did it by giving up some power in one place to gain leverage in another."

She was silent, then she smiled and said, "It's okay, that is always how it works."

"Unless you take something by force," I said.

"Someone loses then as well. Usually young men."

Amanta looked at me, the anger of her past on her face, "I kept in my mind that day in the mountains, the thought that, *This is never going to end*. I was determined to end it, but I gave up changing things in the Caucasus. I dreamt of simply leaving, taking the people of Mountains with me, those that wanted peace, and starting a new life."

Amanta relaxed, and followed, "A silly, simplistic fantasy."

"I can see it."

"So can I."

In her silence, I ventured, "Do you regret any of it?"

She wasted no time in her answer. "No. I don't regret it. I did what I felt I had to do for my people, with the least amount of harm."

I marveled at it all, though I was always skeptical when someone said they had no regrets.

"What I have come to learn is that people, no matter how advanced in technology, even when we learn how to jump from one star to another, we are still very primitive, Jenny. We have hardly left the cave. We're all afraid. No amount of technological progress can change that."

The Sixth Traveler

I wondered if that was what Venka was mumbling about when I found him in his private library.

"I wanted love. I found it with Canstaczt Noori. I wanted peace for my people, I believe I have found that in the New World."

Hearing Amanta's story, it occurred to me what it means to have no regrets. It wasn't a lack of remorse so much as the ability to manage it or morph it into something productive. Seeing how Amanta had moved on, I felt a sense of relief.

"It was one of many steps toward my goal."

"You've lived an amazing life."

Amanta looked at me and said, "We all do."

I don't know about that, yet I felt somehow elated, and in that elation. I had so many more questions about her past but thought better of it.

"So, what do you want to call this New World?" I asked her. The Federatsiya, in conjunction with the Chinese, Indian and US governments, had discovered most of these planets. But the Republic found this planet that Amanta had her sights on and was quick to lay claim to it.

"When I was a little girl," Amanta started, "my father once took my mother and me to a small village in the mountains of Georgia. I remember that it was an ancient village, one of the oldest villages in Europe or Russia. Ushguli. It was a beautiful place. I remember thinking how delicate it was, such a small town nestled between the large mountains, yet it endures."

"Ushguli," I repeated.

"Yes. A sanctuary, far away from this world."

"A fitting namesake."

"The Republic is anxious to colonize Ushguli," Amanta said. "We are already doing it without anyone's consent, but we would like for you to facilitate, diplomatically and technically. You are skilled at both."

Amanta stopped to look at me, and replied, "You are free to contact my assistant for whatever you need. You know Nikhil Lecha, my deputy and advisor, away on travel now, but always reachable. We are both at your service."

"Thank you," I replied, grateful for her assurance. Amanta nodded, turning to gaze out the window again. I could tell something was on her mind.

"Jenny, will you be able to handle this alone?"

"Wen Lu commands a Special Forces unit with the Sino-American Joint Forces, and a small unit accompanies us on diplomatic missions," I replied.

"That's not what I meant."

I knew what she meant.

"I was referring to the work itself. The pace of the work. Travel."

"Oh."

"Why don't you get another android, Jenny?"

I pushed myself up from my chair and went to the window, looking out into the bay on that warm June evening of 2104. I had managed to muddle my way through since my better half had sacrificed himself for my world. I somehow felt unfaithful at the thought.

"Don't want another android."

"I know," Amanta said quietly. "Think about it, Jenny."

"I'll be fine, but thank you for your concern, Minister." I started to call her by her given name but thought the honor of a title was better placed on her.

* * *

Two years ago my health was much better, though even then my surfing days were numbered. It was plain on its face: the love I had surrendered would go the way of all others. At least, that was one of the little lies I abided by that day I sat in the stands. I wore sunglasses and a broad hat to hide my face. I wanted to see Branton Ma'hai but did not want him to see me.

O'ahu was beautiful at that time of year, outside the rainy season and plentiful sun. The waves at Sunset Beach were perfect. This was the 122nd annual Eddie Tournament, and Brae had surfed many of them. He still competed and looked amazing.

It had been three years since Brae and I went our separate ways. After the Second Event the fog of depression that had engulfed me eventually lifted, but it left a residue. I managed it, yet I simply wanted to be left alone. Though part of me wanted his love resurrected, I could see he had moved on and I didn't blame him. It wasn't the game I thought it was going to be, and I think he felt the same.

My mind was not the same. I could hardly remember what had happened during those days when we were together. My short-term memory was rapidly fading, and old ones were seeking shelter elsewhere. Maybe I had left them at Alpha Centauri.

"This place is so beautiful," the woman next to me volunteered. She was very sweet, but I tried nonetheless to avoid talking to her.

"Yes, he is."

TWENTY-TWO

Implant Record Date 16 May 2104
Chechnya, Caucasus Republic

I walked into Chase Adeane's office in his state-of-the-art corporate campus just outside of Chechnya having arrived only an hour ago from San Diego. That was my first time at this location to consult on the affairs of the newly formed corporation that was building the star traveling lighters, after which I was to meet with government officials handling the Republic's extra-terrestrial colonization plans. The former technical and the latter political, but both with issues, legal and otherwise.

Then there was my own fugue state. As much as I was afflicted with a sort of disorientation, I managed to otherwise function effectively. I avoided thinking about it, and was largely successful, but seeing Chase that day in Chechnya reminded me. I suddenly became highly aware of the lapses of memory, the occasional seizures, and on that day my heightened fatigue.

And when I thought of those things, I thought of John Mar.

"It's time you ease up, Jen," John had said only a month ago, leaving me feeling warm, but unsure of how to respond.

"I'm fine."

He offered his help in taking on some of the travel, but I declined. I could sense his concern, genuine and with no strings. Still, it stung. My feelings towards John were growing. For this reason I hated to accept his help. It wasn't for the usual reasons—it wasn't pride, or fear of being labeled a victim. I am much too lazy for the former, and don't really understand the latter. In most situations I declined help for the same reason I avoided friendships, memberships, and cocktail parties: I hated being on the hook.

With John Mar I wasn't sure it was even that. I think it was the depth I felt for him and wanted him to feel for me. The love Kepler calculated was inevitable.

I liked the idea that two people would chance upon one another, exchange glances, and a primitive kind of chemistry would ensue before physics would take over, gravity making a collision inevitable. I wanted John's love for me to be pure and unadulterated. I worried that the change in my physical and mental condition would smelt his affection away, or at least transform it into an undesirable state. That was something I couldn't stand. I was unmistakably drawn to John, falling into his inexorable pull.

"But thank you, John," I said to him. He smiled at me.

"I'm always here, Jen," he replied. I held back tears. *Damn it*, I remember thinking. Without Kepler's confirmation, how could I know? I hated that John's love might not be real, but I was intoxicated by its possibility.

In that moment, standing in the Chechen offices of this futuristic corporation, I lifted my arms and voice as I glossed over these imperfections in my life to give my brother Chastain Quentin Adeane his due.

"Hey there!"

"Jen, good to see you," Chase said, rising to meet my open arms, kissing my cheek. Chase had long since shaved his beard and put his jeans aside for a suit and tie. I had seen the changes in him over the last few years, shedding his lab rat look for the boardroom, but he was still the same Chase underneath, good natured and warm.

"You know Zévic Toreli."

"Yes, Zévic, it's good to see you," I said, holding out my hand to him.

"Good to see you Ms. Hsu."

"This is Charlie," Chase said, motioning to a slender female form across the room. She smiled and nodded. I could see from her hand that she was an android.

"I was telling Zévic that it is fitting the corporation has a Russian name," Chase Adeane said. He was the new Chief of Operations of the corporation that made the lighters, the Chinese and US governments being the only other licensees. I served as an advisor to his company, Svoboda Corporation, and represented the new government. Svoboda Corporation also sold some lighters to the US and China (until they could build their own), as well as the governments of India, Japan, Brazil, Europe and Korea, more or less as black boxes for now.

"The ancient Islamic and Christian states," Zévic Toreli explained, "fighting for so long, the people forgot what it was all about. Our neighbors to the north and south reminded us. Some of those neighbors became part of it all, especially Russia. Look at the Foreign Minister, she is both Russian and Chechen."

"True," Chase said. "That's what I like about the Russian name. Kind of ironic."

"It's an ideal," Zévic continued. Zévic was the Chief Counsel of Svoboda Corporation. The four of us sat in Chase's office on the twentieth floor of the corporate headquarters of the company.

"Ideals are the start of many things," Charlie said. Charlie had the form of a woman, slender and feminine in her formal business attire, and as I understood was an assistant to Zévic for legal and administrative matters. She stood behind a rolling breakfast table that had just been brought into the room as Chase, Zévic and I sat in an area in front of Chase's desk furnished with several cushioned chairs and a couch.

"For hundreds of years we have been desperate for peace and a bit of prosperity we see in the rest of the world. Now we have some control of our destiny."

"Yes," I replied. I was tired from my flight, not having slept on the liner, and fought an urge to lie down. "At the rate you are building the lighters and selling them, the company and the Republic will become very wealthy." Even though they had formed a separate corporation, the government had a hand in how it was run and in the funds earned in making and selling them. I would have to convince them to fully privatize the venture, or in my estimation, risk losing it.

"We are increasing production of the four to ten-seated lighters," Chase said. "We can't make those fast enough for governments who want them. We are backlogged with orders for the next five years."

"I know you are also building much larger lighters, capable of sub-light travel to get from the ground to orbit on their own," I said. "I'm anxious to see them."

"Yes, certainly," Zévic replied. "We may sell some of these, but at first we plan to keep them for the Caucasus Republic only."

"I take it your plan with these is colonization," I said bluntly.

"The Foreign Minister has told you about Ushguli," Zévic said. "You have known our situation long enough to know what the Republic is after."

"Freedom," I said.

"Correct."

"That is partly why I am here," I said. "I just came from meetings with Republic officials, and the Foreign Minister, Amanta, and wanted to talk about how best to go about that."

"Good." Chase replied. "Before we get too heavy into business, we should start breakfast. Jenny, you must still be a little jet lagged. Let's move over to the table. We can see the morning sun from there." I welcomed the scent of fresh coffee, looking eagerly at Charlie as she carried a carafe and tray of cups toward us.

As Charlie approached she hesitated, looking directly at me. Without turning away, she sat the tray down on a table and moved toward me. I was confused by her actions because she appeared to want something from me and I couldn't imagine what.

Rising from the couch, I felt it. The sensation I had come to know and dread over the last year or so. A sort of sick feeling, dizzy, disoriented, like I was forgetting where I was. By then Charlie was firmly supporting me by my arm.

Kevin M. Faulkner

"Jenny, are you alright?" Zévic asked. I didn't answer, but stood there blankly, apparently looking around for something I had lost, at least that was what everyone said I was doing when this happened.

"Jenny, let's sit," Charlie said, with an understanding of what was happening.

Charlie helped me back onto the couch. I later played back that day as it was recorded on my implant: the two men sat next to me with concern while Charlie stroked my arm. She placed her left, exposed hand on my forehead. Zévic asked Chase, "Is she the only one from the Second Event affected in this way?" Chase replied, "No, one of the Chinese on the mission was hospitalized for nearly a year, and one of the American astronauts has problems to this day." Chase talked in a soft tone, as if he were speaking in private.

The doctors called these *seizures* though they were a little different. In a classic seizure one can rarely remember anything at all. Yet I could often remember images and scenes, extensions of some struggle already on my mind. They were often real enough that they lingered for days as apparitions over my otherwise lucid moments.

I could predict this one, I thought in a little used part of my gray matter, as I watched Branton Ma'hai approach me. At first I felt the soft fabric of the couch beneath me, only to give way to warm sand, a small wave washing toward me. I reached for him while my body sank deeper. I welcomed the sinking feeling as it enveloped me in its warmth. He knelt and held my hand while I tried to kiss his lips, but his face remained out of reach. I wept, though I felt ensnared in his spell. The waves consumed me and the warmth was gone. I could swear I told him I loved him, though my implant recorded nothing.

After what felt like days, I grew tired. Brae's image was gone, and I lay in nothingness. I ached but I could not pinpoint if it was the muscles in my legs or in my chest.

Like the chilled shadow of an eclipse across a sunny landscape, these seizures darkened my world with greater frequency. I always hoped they would come about when I was alone, but that was rarely the case. According to my implant, this one lasted ten minutes or so before the fog gradually lifted. As this lapse subsided, I slowly sat up in a daze. Charlie's hand supported me, and Chase and Zévic nearby looking on.

"Oh," I said, brushing my pants as I sat up with Charlie's help. "I could use some coffee." I rubbed my face to bring myself to life.

"Are you okay?" Chase asked. "Why don't you lie down some more?"

"I'm fine," I lied. "Thanks."

"Sit a moment," Charlie said, quietly. "Here, drink some water." She had already gotten it from somewhere. It was exactly what I needed.

"Must be all the traveling. I get these episodes when I am over-tired." I reflexively brushed my legs as if to remove the sand of a beach and felt embarrassed by my confusion. In the last sixteen months I had nearly given up on surfing, too fatigued from my work and my worsening condition. I couldn't remember the last time I dug my feet into the surf.

"Jen, can I get you anything?" Chase was on one knee before me, holding my hand. During the second jump to Alpha Centauri, Chase exhibited some neurological problems, and they lingered for several months. His problems, somehow, were less severe and permanent than mine. Doctors monitored all six of the star travelers and have made careers out of researching us, trying to determine what happened and why each of us responded differently. They concluded that it is most likely we each had unique genetic strengths and vulnerabilities that led to the outcomes.

"I'll be fine, thanks Chase." I squeezed his hand. I remembered flirting with him a long time ago and wondered if he would want to flirt with me now, even if he weren't married.

Those thoughts made me eager to shake off my lapse. I pushed myself up from the couch, prompting everyone to stand. Charlie, kneeling next to me, helped support me as I rose from the couch. For such a slight figure, she was as solid as a rock.

As Charlie escorted me to the breakfast table, Chase motioned us all to the table where a catering service had finished setting up a light breakfast. Charlie seemed to know instinctively (if that was the right word to describe an android's programming) what to do. Charlie's presence reminded me how much I had leaned on Kepler in those early days after the First Event. My current challenges, however, were even greater.

I saw the concern in Chase's face, and said, "I'll be alright. I bounce back pretty quickly." After I sat down, Charlie went back to get the coffee.

"I just pressed it," she said. "And though I don't drink it, I know the difference between good Colombian brew and cheap American swill." Charlie's little jest lightened the air, and we all relaxed a little.

I took a sip of coffee and a few bites of food as Chase and Zévic also started to eat the scrambled eggs (likely artificial), yogurt and bread set before each of us. I tried to get past these lapses with as much grace as possible, but I was still a little dizzy.

"Chase, tell us about your wife, and little Chase Junior," Charlie said, deftly diverting everyone's attention away from me.

It didn't take any convincing to get Chase started. "Michael is all of two now," he beamed. "His favorite thing besides the toy lighter is earth movers and dump trucks."

"And the boxes they come in," I added.

I tried to look cheerful as Chase talked, hiding the fact that I was still struggling. Though I had become skilled at hiding my slight disability, it was a burden that only grew each time I had a lapse. I saw a doctor regularly who counseled me, and at times prescribed different medications or qualified new apps for my implant, but the problem only got worse with time. I knew that surgery was the only option to stop its progression, but I put it off. I'm not sure it if was fear or self-flagellation, punishing myself for my own hubris.

We chatted a while longer before I gathered myself to continue our earlier discussion. "Well, as I told Amanta . . . the Foreign

Minister, I believe the best approach is to be mostly open about what you want with the other major powers. But at the same time, you want to move swiftly to put your stake in the ground."

"But that's not what you told Amanta," Chase chided me.

"Well, she's a little eager," I said. "I'm an attorney. I didn't lie, but I had to cool the Minister down some." I winked at Zévic.

"Why do you think that? Why not have the Caucasus government propose a motion at the United Nations?" Zévic asked. "I think they would be receptive, and it could improve our standing in the world."

"I think it will be more effective to talk to the space-faring powers directly, since there are only several of those. In any case, the United States, next to China, is the most likely candidate for independently achieving a faster-than-light spacecraft, and in their own unique way, each distrusts the UN."

"I see," Zévic said.

"I agree with Jenny," Chase said. "The galaxy is a big place, even inside the Perimeter. There is enough space for everyone to move without the other nations following us. Making a fuss at the UN would only draw attention and beg rules."

"That is what I am thinking," I said. "We want to avoid rules. Better to talk to those most likely to cause a fuss, and otherwise, act now and ask forgiveness later."

"Makes sense," Charlie said, "though I am not an attorney."

"Charlie," Zévic asked the android, "Do you have something to say?" Charlie was slender and adorned with delicate facial features framed in closely cropped black hair. At the back of her neck her mechanical features could be seen, as well as on her left hand. I felt that the mechanical forms in her body were even less pronounced on her than they were on Kepler. From her actions, it was apparent that she was programmed to be extremely sensitive to humans, something most androids continued to refine as they interfaced with people, or a particular person.

"Since you asked, yes," Charlie said in her flawless French accented English. "I agree with Jenny, but would add—"

"What?"

"You should get Dr. Venkalaswaran's approval of your plan to have the Republic exclusively colonize the New World," Charlie said. "And in particular, the Indian government should be approached first."

"I don't think we—" Zévic started.

"Yes, you're right," Chase broke in.

"Yes, Charlie. I will talk to Venka," I said. Apparently, Charlie understood the sensitivities quite well. Venka, though he was a paid consultant for Svoboda Corporation, was still a professor at the Indian Institute of Science. India had a vested interest in what happened with the lighter technology, and the Indian Federation was a strong proponent of the United Nations, one of its staunchest members. So that might help appease the UN independent of a formal meeting before representatives or an assembly.

"Ultimately, I would suggest that we speak to the Indian Federation before any of the other space-faring powers," I said.

Zévic glanced at Chase. "I trust your judgment."

I was still reflecting on my earlier lapse and wondered what Zévic thought of it. He might trust my judgment, but I wondered if he trusted that I was up to all of this. I wondered too.

"I may need some help," I said, surprising myself as just days ago I declined help from Amanta. I looked over at Charlie, admiring such a marvel of engineering, even more advanced than Kepler.

Yet she was more than engineering. Charlie was highly intelligent and extremely perceptive. I guessed she was a fourth tranche Japanese android, a new generation of androids that were semi-autonomous, like Kepler, but self-enhancing. That was a fancy way of saying that her brain (or memory/control center) was built to mimic a mammal's brain. They comprised a ceramic hybrid matrix that had a high latent enthalpy, or a high potential energy. A network of carbon atoms bound together, all in an energy state poised to gently react. Isolated from one another, they roll down the potential energy hill when pushed by some external stimulus—self-programming ones and zeros. Advanced micromechanical circuits driven by ptesinochondria provided the energy for the push downhill and allowed the carbon to crosslink whenever the android took in data from its ears, nose, eyes and so on, creating memories, or the equivalent of those human qualities.

"Zévic, I wonder, would you mind if Charlie accompanied me, at least to India?"

"Not a bad idea, Zévic," Chase said.

"Certainly, Ms. Hsu." Zévic said. He was much older than me, and in a reversal of hierarchy, he often addressed younger people as "Mister" or "Miss." "I believe it would be productive for Charlie to go with you. Charlie, does it suit you?"

"Yes, it does in fact. I would like to assist Jenny in legal and other matters. It will give me the chance to meet Dr. Venkalaswaran."

"Excellent. My security team includes General Wen Lu as part of the Joint Forces, so she will also be with us," I added.

Likely anticipating what Zévic and Chase were thinking, Charlie added, "No need to worry about Jenny Hsu, she'll be in good hands."

* * *

"Why are you complaining, this is so nice," Lulu said, two years ago on one of our first of what would become many outings. She lay on a blanket we'd brought with us, sunning in her surprisingly little bikini, in her not so surprisingly hot forty-year-old figure.

Waikiki beach was not what a surfer would consider a beach; it is more of a tourist hell. I wanted to go to the other side of the island as the North Shore of O'ahu was famous for its waves. The Eddie was going on that week as a matter of fact. I had planned to take part a long time ago and had that time blocked out for it. Things change and I wanted to cancel it all. Lulu insisted we go on a trip; on the touristy, beachy vacation of tanning oil, sugary sodas, and rich Japanese in big, floppy hats.

"As you say, I like to complain."

She'd won a bet from over four months ago, at least as she tells it. We were together in Beijing after John Mar and I had finished negotiating a rider to the license agreement between the Chinese entities that settled with the Republic, and the Republic government, adding the newly forming Svoboda Corporation. Since the Second Event, Lulu retained her military status but also became an active advisor to the CNSA, so she was almost always at the same meetings I was at. We saw each other a few times a year, she flying to California to shop in San Francisco, and me flying to Asia for business or tournaments, the few I went to those days when my lapses were a rare event.

She always said she was coming to California because she couldn't find her favorite shoes anywhere else, the ones she couldn't live without (they strangely changed each year). I suspected that she would come to check up on me. She knew after the Second Event that I had struggled with the loss of Kepler, and that Branton and I were having problems. She sweetly wanted to fill the void. I think I also gave her an excuse to let her hair out in a way she hadn't before.

On this trip to Beijing, we stopped by a pastry shop along the main street in the Chaoyang District after our meetings were finished. We had already become pretty good friends by then. We seemed to find a connection, a common bond the six Travelers seemed to share. With treatment, Kang Hongbo made a complete recovery. Even Michael Trenton, whose reaction to the partially failed V-shell was the most extreme, was a brother to us all. We never held it against him.

"I bet you," she had said, "That the girl back there in the red top with the little Shih Tzu will get up and walk away from that guy. The couple back in the back."

"I know who you are talking about. Why do you think that? Look at them, they are talking together, she is smiling, isn't she?" I wondered if Lulu was serious or not.

"I'm telling you, I know Chinese women. I'm a Chinese woman. Look at her, look at her eyes."

"You're crazy."

"What? I'm good at this."

"You? Miss 'I don't care what people think' crouching tiger hidden dragon woman?"

"True, the crouching tiger observes. See, watch how she looks away. She's laughing, but looking at the door," Lulu insisted.

"You're imagining things; she's not looking at the door." Actually, I think she was.

Lulu often comes out of nowhere with these little observations, it's one of the things I liked about her. The harshness from the Second Event had worn off, and the camera's gaze was less focused on us as time went on, leaving a friendship in its wake. I was also close to Chase Adeane, in a brotherly way, but there was always a little something between us that I wasn't ready for, and likely missed anyway, so I kept that part of myself away, as I did with Branton Ma'hai. Turns out, men don't like that.

I wondered if that was what Lulu observed in the pastry shop we found ourselves in the Chaoyang District.

"Watch," Lulu said, nudging me. Indeed, the young woman brushed back her hair as she stood smiling at the guy she was sitting next to, a handsome guy, but a hapless victim, nonetheless. She said something we couldn't hear then walked away.

Lulu pretended to be busy as the woman approached, dog in hand. I watched in some disbelief, thinking at first that she was going to the counter to get a pastry or a coffee. But, no, the young woman turned back to look at the guy, making sure he was not looking. Then she turned the other way to push open the door and leave without looking back.

"Well, missy, looks like you were right," I said, in disbelief. "I'm impressed."

"You should be. I won the bet."

"What bet?"

So, there I was several months later, slathered in a mixture of oil and SPF, on the beach in Waikiki, a place only several years before I would not have been caught dead at. But I hung up my surfing suit and donned the latest little thing from a shop I found in San Diego. Though not as athletic as I was a few years ago, I didn't look bad in a bikini either.

"Lighten up, Juju."

We spent several hours like that, alternately going into the water and fending off the sharks and men. By three o'clock we headed back to our room on the other side of Kalakaua Avenue, closer to Ala Wai, in a cheap little place she'd found. We could do better, but she insisted. "Why spend the money?"

In spite of my solitary, surfer girl self, I had fun with Lulu in Waikiki, doing all the chintzy things that tourists do in paradise, each of us donning a flower behind our left ear and going through all the shops, some of which were quite pricey, not for the average tourist. We ended up in a bar at midnight surrounded mostly by men. The sounds of laughter and conversation were indicative of various levels of inebriation. I imagined I was somewhere in the middle. Thankfully, the music was low enough to allow the sound of the waves and the salty breeze to encompass us unabated.

"What's your drink?" I asked Lulu, as the waitress waited to take our order. Lulu had already become distracted by a little hula doll. There was one at each table, a little grass-skirted Polynesian girl playing her plastic ukulele for the patrons to enjoy.

"Mmmm," she thought, looking into the menu. I'd been around her enough to know she wasn't much of a drinker.

The Sixth Traveler

"I'll have a martini," I told the waitress. "So will she."

"Wait," she said, hitting me. "Okay, make mine an apple."

As the waitress walked away, Lulu asked, "What were you doing yesterday when I was at the gym?"

I didn't tell her I dropped in on the surfing tournament, the Eddie, on the North Shore, but she could probably track me. "Just wanted to see some real waves," I said, being at least partially truthful.

She gave me a suspicious look. "Mmmm, nice. I bet you used to surf there."

"Yeah, once upon a time."

As we got our drinks, I followed with, "A lot of things have changed."

"They do, but not all bad. You've told me more than once that when you started your job at the law firm in San Diego that you didn't care about it. That you avoided work."

"Yes."

"That changed. You don't think that way now. You care about Dr. Venkalaswaran, and I know you do a good job at work."

"True, thanks."

"So, what made you change?" Before I could answer, Lulu followed with: "I know I ask personal questions, but I'm always interested to know what motivates my crew."

"Yeah, right." I couldn't answer right away except to say, "I grew up I suppose." There was truth in that.

"And you have rent to pay," Lulu said.

"Indeed, San Diego isn't cheap." I looked toward the beach and noticed a light under the water, a green pool of luminescence where two snorkelers were looking for turtles.

Lulu was looking too. I wasn't about to disclose any nuggets of shame, but I had a whopper that always came to my mind. I was around ten or eleven years old when my parents started fighting, serious fighting. Something snapped in my mother, a psychiatric problem, and she refused to get help. I didn't understand it at the time, so I just lashed out at her, mostly through rejection. The day she left to check into a hospital I refused to say anything to her, even turning my back. She vanished weeks later. I didn't even feel it at first, but as I got older and processed it all I certainly did. I felt guilty as hell, and still do. The school's counselor told me that it wasn't my fault, that she had a problem beyond my control. I didn't buy it.

We moved from Seattle and my father eventually got himself together. My brother was young, and was an easy soul, so he quickly turned around. But I never got over it. I was angry, holding it in for a while before I acted out in my teenage years. When that didn't go over well, my response was to hide. School was easy for me so I could please my dad with good grades in high school and college, and even fake my way into a decent job, but I hated it like I hated everything. It wasn't until I was pushed into a corner by John Mar and Erissa Chavez that I realized I had to change.

I looked over at Lulu and was glad she was with me. But I didn't want to say anything to her; I didn't want to burden our friendship. We all have our crosses to bear, but just letting her in—that was enough.

"I'm just an uptight Betty finding my wave," I said, winking.

"Just like the rest of us." I think Lulu suspected I was on the North Shore to see Branton. We looked at one another as she rose to hug me. Lulu held her glass up in a toast, "Here's to being messed up."

She handed me the hula doll.

"I don't think we're supposed to take these."

"Sure we are! You worry too much."

"Then why are you whispering?" I rolled my eyes and stuck it in my bag.

The Sixth Traveler

TWENTY-THREE

Implant Record Date 19 June 2104
New York

The stakes are high, I thought, allowing my implant to silently communicate my thoughts to the only one that I would reluctantly allow a temporary pass, Charlie. It took some sophistication to understand the noisy chatter that goes on inside a person's head. One can't simply listen. There was filtering and interpretation, functions an android like Charlie was designed for.

"Our advice to the deputy is the same nonetheless," Charlie replied in my earpiece, above the continuous din of negotiations in the room with simultaneous translations of the delegates. I was on what you would call the floor of the negotiating room, sitting behind my client, while Charlie sat behind an observation window above the molded metal and plastiwood room at an office facility of the United Nations, near the financial district.

Nikhil is holding his own, I remarked on the deputy minister and delegate of the Republic that I represented. Charlie was my legal assistant and translator, replacing the *ad hoc* computer translations I had been relying upon. Seeing Nikhil Lecha negotiate for the first time was a shock. Behind his smiling demeanor was a determination that was both inspiring and unsettling.

"Holding a hearing at each discovery, at least at this level, simply does not make sense. These new worlds are discovered separately by the party—"

"That is exactly the problem, they are discovered by the party that owns the technology," the Russian delegate cut in. "And not everyone has access to it."

"Access to the minerals in the Caucasus is as much a problem for Russia as access to the QMT," I whispered into my commlink to Nikhil. "Remember, that's what's behind much of this."

"Yes, but other parties have the right to negotiate terms," Nikhil replied.

"But only on your terms, and the Chinese," the Korean delegate responded. "Even the US doesn't have full rights."

"We cannot allow rights to reside only with those that settled some litigation," the Brazilian delegate followed.

"It was never even decided if those patents were valid," the Indonesian delegate grumbled. They were referring to the original ICIP litigation that never reached a decision on the validity of the QMT patents (from all patentees involved) because the parties settled out of court.

Brazil and Korea were clearly on Russia's side of the debate. In the world of international patent law, the legal doctrine of *Verum est* (real thing) was increasingly argued to take precedence over simply first to file in questions of who invented what. This was in part what was litigated when China sued the US and the Federatsiya over what Dr. Venkalaswaran and Dr. Hu had invented (or, reduced to practice). Some would say that the first to file system favors those who have some preliminary data and clever patent drafting by an imaginative patent attorney and is thus unfair to those who have used their own resources to make what was only an idea operable. As these delegates pointed out, it was never decided if the US and the Federatsiya deserved their patent rights under *Verum est* because the parties settled.

As is the case with most burgeoning technology, other nations and corporations were also pursuing some form of quantum mass transfer. Russia claims they had extensively developed their own version of QMT technology and had invested a large amount of money in their endeavor. Russia claims they were on the verge of making a working spacecraft, only to be blocked by China's earlier patent filings. They contend that many of China's patents were based on early and speculative laboratory research. That may be true, but they got to the international patent office first. The problem with *Verum est* was proof, harder to come by than a filing receipt from a national patent office.

"Why not? The Republic took the risk, along with the Indian Federation and the US It was our right to negotiate terms to interstellar travel," Nikhil said to the room. "That is why we have an international court system."

"Governed by powerful countries."

"And repeating the wrongs of the past!" Several delegates nodded in agreement.

"What wrongs? We are proposing to inhabit worlds that are uninhabited."

"By humans," the Swedish delegate said.

"Yes, by humans or any other sentients. It is clearly not the same as the moon, or even Mars," the US delegate chimed in. At times I felt guilty representing the Republic, given that I am American. Luckily, our positions were largely aligned.

"Indeed," Nikhil happily added. "Those bodies are hardly *discovered* in any sense, and it is right that they belong to all countries, equally. But these new planets are different."

"But what if someone finds a world with sentient life?"

No one had an answer for that. There was endless talk of it in the media, but most scientists at the time did not really believe that there would be anything approaching humans in the universe. In fact, this had become the politically correct impasse of the early twenty-second century. Are humans the only sentient creatures out there?

"Surely not," Charlie said in gentle sarcasm. By then I already knew her well and trusted her. She was very thoughtful, rarely sarcastic (which is why her comment reminded me of Kepler) and eager to please and look after me. She was no sycophant; she simply had what you would attribute to a human as having a big heart.

"Good point, but those situations can be dealt with separately," I whispered to Nikhil. "We can agree not to interfere."

"In any case, I agree that humans should not interfere with sentient beings," Nikhil said to the room. "That situation should be addressed separately."

The delegates from a dozen countries in this subcommittee of the United Nations had been sparring for the last few days and were supposed to come to some conclusion by tomorrow. The goal was a resolution that would be voted on by the whole UN assembly later in the year. They were to address the issue of interplanetary exploration and settlements. The former had been going on for the last two years, the latter in the last nine months or so. I think everyone could see that this was only going to become more of an issue in the coming years and there were some bad sentiments developing around the world. Could explorers claim an extra-solar planet as their own property? If so, what rights do they have there? Does anyone on Earth even have a say in the matter? And what about the countries that don't have a license or the resources to the lighter technology, would they have any say? This latter question was an especially difficult one for Russia, Korea, Brazil and Japan, major powers that were not part of the original development, legal settlement, and license of the technology.

Though often heated, there was some agreement, mostly in the form of firm boundaries and timetables for claiming and receiving rights. It was all just words until reduced to formal legislation, which was the next step. As formal negotiations ended at four that afternoon, the delegates went their separate ways while those in the seats around the edge of the room, the undersecretaries, assistants, and lawyers (including me), left to gather in a separate room to hash out the actual language that had been negotiated. There was a basic framework in place, but every word mattered and it seems every word was fought over.

The Sixth Traveler

Knowing my biggest adversary would be my Russian counterpart, I befriended him.

"Maybe we can make some sense of this and go out for drinks before the bars close," I said to Leonid Petrova. I was close enough to him now to call him Leo and he referred to me as *the lawyer* or sometimes just by my name.

"Maybe if you agree with me we can start drinking now," Leo said. He was older than me, handsome and forward. I didn't take much offense at him talking down a little. He was good natured, just overly traditional.

"Ha, I can't do that. I'm too American." He laughed at that.

"We'll drink Kentucky whiskey then."

I looked over at Charlie as Leo walked ahead of me and led us into what was hastily christened by our hosts as The United Federation of Planets room. I couldn't tell if that was an inside joke or an attempt to capture the gravity of the situation.

"I just want to win a friend." I winked at Charlie. I knew that I had to be careful these days about how much I drank. It seemed that even a little alcohol could trigger a seizure. Yet, I wanted a good rapport with my Russian counterpart. And he was no slouch with a bottle as I had seen earlier in the week.

The drafters gathered around a table as attendants delivered coffee, tea, and snacks to a table in the back. About two dozen of us talked across and over one another while a designated stipulator recorded our shouting, laughing, and groaning and massaged it all into a form that was comprehensible in at least English, Chinese, and French. Dinner was served around seven and we continued to work as we ate. I remember that time fondly, and as all good times go, it went fast. In no time we were instructed to end the session.

"Are you up for that whiskey," Leo asked me as I got up to leave the room well after eleven.

"Sure, I'll meet you at *Canter's Way* down the street." I pressed my finger against the stipulator's stylus to confirm my approval of the night's work before Charlie and I walked out. Once the first

Kevin M. Faulkner

person gave such approval, the wording was locked once two other negotiators did the same.

"I won't keep you waiting too long," Leo replied.

"Ha, tell that to the stipulator." Leo was the second to approve but stayed behind to talk to others. With this informal final draft in place, the primary delegates would vote tomorrow for final passage of the language and formal resolution to the UN.

Charlie and I stopped by our hotel room before going to the bar. I just needed to splash water on my face to come alive. "I can tell you enjoy this part of your work," Charlie said to me. "At your level, you could have assigned this to a junior counsel."

"Yeah, I suppose I do. When I was a kid, I never thought arguing over words would be so much fun." I washed up in the bathroom while Charlie stood by and waited for me.

"I hope you are coming with me," I said, glancing at the medicine on the bathroom countertop that I knew I should probably take. Charlie had gently reminded me, but it was that or the whiskey, and I had already made a promise.

"Of course," Charlie brightly replied.

"You can keep me out of trouble."

"I don't know if I am capable of that."

Charlie reminded me of the unique bond I had had with Kepler. The kinship with his kind was unmistakable. There was a different kind of bond with an android. The Japanese knew what they were doing when they created those creatures; they went well beyond humans in terms of how they latched onto our behavior, internal dialogue, and personal identity. Combined with their appearance, it could either be comforting or disturbing. From Charlie familiarity was a comfort to me.

We chatted as we walked to the elevator and down to the street. It was surprisingly cool, and still wet from having rained all day. The streets were empty enough to see the reflective glow of the city lights in the wet pavement, and the faux gas lamps along the way created a warm path. We passed a statue of Alexander Hamilton while I told Charlie of my childhood days.

"Our early days are important," she said. "Once imprinted at a tender age, the good tends to stay, the bad difficult to get out. Depending on your genes."

"I suppose so," I replied, surprised at how sad I sounded. I shook my head and joked, "That's why we drink."

"Ahhh. Mystery solved."

Once in the bar, we settled at a table large enough for four, and I allowed Leo to access my locator so he could easily find me once he arrived.

Canter's Way was where many of us gathered after our negotiations, and though it was more laid back at midnight than it was during the day there were still plenty of people sitting around tables and benches, some at the bar. It had an old American Colonial look, with pictures of our founding Fathers along the wall in a modern take of this Nation's glories and its sins.

Just above us was a famous unfinished painting of George Washington, reminding me of the ideological revolution he and others of that time started. Though I was representing America in negotiations as part of a United Nations initiative, that organization had become less relevant in the world, with countries ideologically divided between the restricted order of Russia and China and the chaotic freedom of the US and India. Some played one off the other, while others chose sides, creating the real tensions I was observing in these negotiations. I wondered if Washington could have foreseen all of this.

"Jenny, do you miss your childhood?" Charlie asked.

"Mmmm. Some. My very young days were the best, running around like a gypsy around Seattle, catching a ride on the ferry to Bainbridge to run along the beach there. My parents would have killed me if they knew."

"They probably knew."

"It was exciting to feel like I was getting away with something."

Kevin M. Faulkner

"Maybe you miss that."

I nibbled on some bread and sipped water while we looked at the people walking by on the street, wondering why they would be out so late.

"I remind you of Kepler." I knew right away why she said that. Thoughts of him flashed through my mind when I heard her voice his name, and I somehow translated her words as his.

"You aren't as sassy as him," I replied.

"Maybe I should be, missy."

"Ha, you don't have it in you. It's okay." There was some silence before either of us spoke again.

"Jenny, did Kepler leave an MDM?"

"A what?" I knew what she meant, but somehow wanted to be coy. I wasn't sure I wanted to really know the answer to her question.

"A key stone." A *mémoirs de masse* or key stone was like a computer memory chip only it was designed specifically to store the electronic inner workings, some would say memories and thoughts, of a higher-level android. Androids in most jurisdictions were required to download to an MDM at least weekly, the readable device then kept separately from the android itself. This was a failsafe for a feared uprising or takeover, or in the least, malfunction.

"I don't know." I didn't. I purposefully didn't want to know. I assume, however, that he did.

"It's okay." I'm not sure why she said that, except that she was a highly perceptive android who had already been outwardly reading me, and for the past several days literally reading my mind. She must know.

"I'm sorry, Jenny."

"I know, thanks Charlie." I marveled at the symbiosis the two of us seem to have already formed.

"Kep probably did have a key stone, and I'm sure he'd want me to know what he was thinking. He never held back when he was alive," I said, joking but holding back my emotions.

The Sixth Traveler

"What are two women like you doing in a place like this?" A male voice shouted from a distance. Looking up, I could see Leonid walk towards us.

"I can leave if you want."

"What?" I held Charlie's arm. "I need you here more than ever," I said quietly as I stood to greet my Russian counterpart.

"I didn't think you would show up, I was just about to order a drink on my own."

"I would never let an American get the upper hand on me, but I might make an exception for a beautiful woman."

"Yeah, you just watch yourself." I turned to Charlie, "See, this is why I need you here."

"She's beautiful too!" Leo replied.

"Oh," Charlie said in mocking disapproval. "You're not my type, but we'll see."

Leo laughed as he told the waitress to bring a bottle of her best Kentucky sour mash and two glasses. He turned to me and winked, "When in America." Leo was quick to tell stories of his life back home in Russia, his work as a consultant and lawyer-like dealings that I probably shouldn't have heard about. Through it all, Charlie's sweetness matched Leonid's good nature, making fun of things he would say and making us all laugh.

I touched on some issues with Leonid, especially the Republic's desire for peaceful coexistence. He would counter that Russia wanted the same, but felt they had a right to the lighter technology on special terms given that the Republic occupied what they believed to be Russian territory, at least in part.

"Jenny, I know a thing or two about patents," Leonid started. "I know your people have this pretty well covered. Russia and Korea and other countries are behind. But you and I both know that many of those patents are worthless."

"Do we?" Again, depending on first to file or *Verum est*, the conclusions could be different. "I don't think we do."

"Lawyer!"

"Well . . . yes. In any case, I have a feeling that patents are not going to get in Russia's way for long." I think that was true. The Chinese would quickly file suit, but Russia and China were long-time allies and they would likely reach some agreement that would ultimately pull Russia along. I just hope they were patient enough to leave the new Republic alone.

"I suppose we have made some steps forward the last few days here in New York." He held up his shot glass in toast.

"Here's to another day of peace." I took a sip, pacing myself.

"Agreed," Charlie reached her finger up in toast, emitting a red glow as it touched our glasses.

As romantic as it sounds, we weren't going to solve the world's problems over drinks. Especially when we were well past the last call. Though I enjoyed the work of negotiating with people, it exhausted my mind and body and I was ready to call it a night.

"I'm done," I finally said.

"You're a good girl, Jenny, I can tell. You stick close to Charlie."

"Oh, I will."

"So, you don't object to androids?" Charlie asked.

"Object? No. Trust them more than humans."

"*Chto u trezvogo na ume, to u p'yanogo na yazyke* (what is sober on his mind, is drunk on his tongue)," Charlie said, making Leo laugh.

By then I was also drunk. Luckily, I had Charlie to hold *my* truth, wherever it could be found.

"Now I know why you brought me to this place."

"My pleasure," I replied as I rose from the booth. Drinking was no longer the pleasure it once was, especially in the last year as my health deteriorated. I steadied myself as best I could without Leo detecting anything. As discreetly as she could, Charlie steadied me.

The room started spinning. I was surprised because I hadn't thought I was so drunk, the warmth of the whiskey just a burn on my tongue until now. I turned once more to Leonid and said, "Cheers!" waving with one hand while holding onto Charlie with the other.

Leonid had a look of concern on his face when Leo said to Charlie, "Take care of our friend . . . I would offer to walk you back to your hotel, but I know you are safe," then he reluctantly turned to leave.

Once we made it to the hotel I openly clung to Charlie. "This'll have to be the last time I drink like that." Charlie helped me to the elevator and into our room. She nearly carried me as the bed was spinning and I could feel another lapse coming on. "Shit," I remember complaining, "I hate this."

"Let's get you to bed." Charlie carried me to the bed, pulled my shoes off and placed her left hand on my forehead. I don't know if she was simply reading what was going on in my mind or was able to influence it in some way, but I remember being grateful for Charlie's presence as I lay there, the ceiling of the room spinning. I felt a little sorry for myself, not being the girl up for a party the way I had been just four or five years ago.

"You really know how to push your limit," Charlie said.

I don't remember responding. The last thing I do remember was Charlie coming back into the dimly lit room from the blackness of the bathroom with a wet washcloth. I remember thinking that, of course, she did not need a light. She sat next to me and held the cool cloth to my face. Then I was out.

* * *

I was in my usual post-seizure haze when I remembered where I was and that Charlie was with me. "Let's keep this one between us," I said, looking over at the clock to see it was three in the morning. Charlie gave me a skeptical smile and patted my still paralyzed hand as it lay upon the white sheets of my bed.

Kevin M. Faulkner

TWENTY-FOUR

Implant Record Date 12 August 2104
San Diego to Bengaluru

"Sure, sweetie, I would love to sign your book," General Wen Lu said to the little boy who shyly stopped her as she walked from the galley back to where we were sitting on the liner. Though her exterior was tough, Lulu could be surprisingly gentle, especially with children. She was quite a hero to so many.

"What is your name?" Lulu asked.

"Lester, ma'am." The boy said. "Lester Minsk." Lulu took his book and signed it. I could see it was about space travel, *From Mars to Mystery*, was the title, likely the new book chronicling the Second Event.

Lulu smiled and handed the book back to the boy, then shook hands with his parents before continuing back to her seat next to me.

"Move over, *xiǎo mèimei* (little sister)," Lulu said as she pushed past me to sit in the middle of three seats. Our liner was one of the last of the rapidly vanishing airfoils since the recent commercialization of anti-gravity systems for passenger liners.

"Did I miss anything while I was gone?" Lulu asked.

"If you did, do you think I'd tell you?" I looked at Charlie. That robot must wonder.

Lulu noticed me fiddling around with an application on my phone that controlled my implant. Prior to my doctor's upgrade, my implant was only able to passively record my thoughts and some sensory input and interpret emotions. My new prescription, several applications that were controlled by any computer device I chose, could additionally manipulate the neural activity of my brain through the implant, such as to calm my nerves when I was anxious or give me a jolt when I was fatigued. I was setting it to *Sleep* to allow me to rest for the duration of the flight to Bengaluru. In the last year I had gotten to where I couldn't sleep much at all without using the sleep app.

"So, Juju, how are you?" Lulu asked, as we started our five-hour flight. We had not seen each other for a couple of weeks.

"I'm fine. I just need a little help sleeping these days."

"I heard about last month."

"Oh, that," I said, trying to play it down. I didn't like to talk about it. I realized that Lulu was feeling guilty, as if she were responsible for the bomb that went off four years ago and my neurological problems that ensued. She was in command, but I never blamed her. I knew she had some lingering problems herself, though less severe than mine. I wondered if her physical fitness made it less severe for her. Though she was no longer a pilot or taikonaut, she still trained with the Chinese Air Force and had earned the rank of Major General. At forty-two, she was still an excellent marksman, martial artist, and in all-around great physical fitness.

"Tell me."

I stopped for a moment as a flight attendant stopped in the isle: "Ms. Hsu, I'm sorry to interrupt, I'm checking papers for your friend," she said, glancing at Charlie.

"Oh, yes," I replied. It felt odd to me whenever this happened, having to prove ownership of Kepler, now Charlie. The world seemed a little nervous about androids running around on their own, unaccompanied as it were, so most countries required that they be accompanied by a human. I handed the flight attendant Charlie's passport, colored different from mine but issued by the US government, nonetheless.

"Thank you, enjoy your flight," the attendant said, handing back Charlie's passport.

"I had a lapse last month in Grozny. No big deal," I said in reply to Lulu's question.

"Really," Lulu said while looking down to adjust her seat. "Then you can tell me about it."

"Probably Charlie can tell you better than I can. She was there." I looked over at Charlie.

"I recorded the incident, I can play it—"

"No!" I said half laughing, half serious.

"So fussy." Lulu teased. "So, tell me, Charlie."

"Yes, Jenny had a seizure with some atonic character, losing muscle strength, lasting about ten minutes," Charlie said. "She was breathing throughout so there was no apparent loss of oxygen to her brain, but her body collapsed and there was memory loss, taking some time to regain control."

"Charlie could see it coming," I said.

"I heard," Lulu replied. "Charlie, I'm glad you were with her."

"Stop worrying, I'll be fine. And, by the way, where do you keep *hearing* things from?"

"Never mind. When will you get NPN like we talked about?" Lulu asked, referring to Noninvasive Particle Neuroplasty, a laser-particle neurological procedure that corrected most neurological and psychiatric disorders, everything from seizures and dementia to bipolar and schizophrenia. It was even used cosmetically for what was called *Corrective Personality Oblation* to alter behavioral issues such as anger or kleptomania, or making a person bolder, if you wanted to change such things.

"These days it's remarkably good. Your recovery time wouldn't be too bad," Charlie said.

Since the Second Event, Lulu and I had become almost constant companions. She has been somewhat of a big sister to me, protective and kind. Everyone who knew her was surprised at her attachment to me, but like with the little boy, I saw a different side of her.

"I don't know. I have my implant that records everything, and I can see what has happened, and review it when I have a lapse of memory," I told her.

The Sixth Traveler

"Not everything. Even with your implant you are losing memory," Charlie said. "I can tell in your speech patterns since I've been around you. The implant may tell you things, but those memories won't be recorded in your brain. It's not the same, and your brain knows it."

"Right," Lulu said. "The implant can't replace the real thing. Charlie, can you talk to her? She won't listen to me."

"Jenny, Lulu is right, there is a good chance that neuroplasty could relieve the problems that have developed as a result of your exposure to the quantum event," Charlie said. "I know the procedure myself, though I am not certified to carry out the procedure."

"Thank you, but it still sounds a little scary," I admitted. "I will get the surgery if things get bad enough."

"I understand," Charlie said. "Until then, I will help you."

Charlie's sweet nature was a gift: her preternatural ability to take my vulnerabilities and turn them around with a kind of love touched me like no human had before. I reached over to Charlie's arm. "Thanks, Charlie, I'll need it. From *both* of you."

* * *

Though it was dusk as Charlie and I drove to the hotel in Bengaluru, I was wide awake. Perhaps it was because I had slept on the plane, or the ammonia-like scent inside the auto taxi that I secretly enjoyed, awakening my senses. Outside the window the lights of the city were alighting as we approached from its outskirts, and they were dazzling to view. I could imagine its people moving about like millions of ants in a colony, all working together for their queen—Necessity.

I turned to Charlie, and she looked back in her usual sweet way. We had grown so close so quickly. Perhaps I saw her as an extension of Kepler. I think it had to do with her lack of defense. There simply was no wall there. Diving deep was never natural for me, fearing the closeness or distance that could possibly ensue. I didn't care about that now. So, I dove.

"Charlie."

"Yes," her eyes widened as she listened to me.

"Do you remember being born?"

For the first time since I have known her, Charlie hesitated in answering me. I could see she was being thoughtful, perhaps caught off guard by my randomness.

"You mean when I was first activated? Yes, I do remember."

"Were you given a personality?"

"Given? No, not really, not in the way that people think of it."

"How did you know how to treat people?"

"Treat people?"

"Yes. How did you know how to talk to people, what to say, how to respond to questions?"

Charlie smiled, seemingly delighted with my questions. Perhaps she sensed the change in me that I felt myself, one she had been looking for.

"The earliest androids, from the 2050's, were preprogrammed with some capacity for that, programming set in algorithms, coding, by the people who created them. For the later generation androids, such as myself, there is less of that. Our input of information is partly from programming, and partly from learning, much like humans."

"What did you learn?"

"There were five of us in the group I was educated with, almost two years ago. Androids like me are of course programmed to have all sorts of knowledge, including literary, but in addition to that we were taught, that is, we studied certain works of science and human arts with our Maker. We studied the earliest of human literary classics: Sophocles, Rumi, Lao Tzu, Pliny, basic Hebrew Scriptures, and the Brahmanas. Later we studied more modern poetry: Shakespeare, Antonov, Frost, Blake, Angelou, and the Song Dynasty love letters."

I was surprised. I had assumed that if androids learned anything it would have been more informational. "When did you . . . I mean, how did you learn math, chemistry, medicine, the law?"

"Much later. Much of that was programmed, but our Maker trained us as well. I can recite most any known information in human arts and sciences, but that is different from study."

"I see."

"You're surprised. We learn much like humans do; that is, not just taking in information, but reflecting, ruminating, reinterpretation from others. Children typically start with what would be considered the arts, simple literature."

"Dr. Seuss is not the same as Rumi."

"Really? They teach the same thing, on a different level."

I was stumped for a moment. "So, what did you learn from those early lessons?"

Charlie looked ahead as the auto taxi began to turn into a banked entrance ramp to a major highway, and looked back at me, her tone unvarnished. "There is oneness between people and its name is love. Though emptiness and pain exist, the oneness breaches all."

I was taken aback by her answer. I would not have thought that an android could be so spiritual. I was hopeful, yet skeptical. "What the hell happened?" I blurted out. She just smiled.

"Getting to love is not always easy, Jenny, or even possible. There are some among you for whom it comes naturally, but most have to find their way. It is not always self-evident, apparently."

"What do you mean 'apparently'?"

Charlie did not respond right away, being deliberate in her answers to my questions.

"To an android it is apparent. A shared comfort and security flows from basic needs of higher mammals. It is what creates security, but it doesn't always appear that way, superficially. While there is evil in the world, most conflict arises from a perception of incompatible needs, the superficial being what it is."

Kevin M. Faulkner

"You are programmed to see the commonality?" I wondered aloud.

"We are *educated* to see past the superficiality."

"Why is it so hard for humans?"

"Human-built androids have no real filter, or ego-equivalent. We are functionally aware of our weakness, and our ultimate need for external support, but do not fear it. It simply is."

"No man is an island," I said absentmindedly. I will never forget that moment. Her face framed by the city lights in the twilight of the Indian horizon. Charlie's eyes were those of a goddess, gazing upon me as one would their greatest creation: her child, her painting, a sculpture held lovingly in her hands. I felt that she wanted to consume me, my madness, and I could only yield and let her in.

"In my group's third month of formal education and programming, to test our response—reasoning you might say—we watched footage of the bombings and kidnappings that were occurring in Astrakhan: the massacre of innocents, the destruction of homes, the soulless look in the eyes of the children and the soldiers."

Charlie hesitated, looking inward before speaking. "We were asked to respond. Each of us was given a chance to speak or write in the language of our Maker. I created a poem."

"Do you remember it?"

Charlie gazed at me as she recited (in Japanese):

> *The fox is shy*
> *Speaking softly.*
> *What does she say?*
> *It is all too apparent*
> *when she moves.*
> *The ten thousand things*
> *run too deep*
> *sail too far*
> *for words to capture.*

The Sixth Traveler

> *Brush on paper*
> *coal beats stone*
> *so harsh*
> *you can only feel her glimmer*
> *when still in the woods*
> *quiet in the desert*
> *alone on the horse's back.*
> *There she is!*
> *Do not try*
> *she is alone*
> *and she will only run away.*

Perhaps due to the juxtaposition of the peace that consumed me, I felt an anger I did not know existed, one that I had become so accustomed to that its presence coincided with my breathing, eating, laughing, and drinking. In that moment I felt pure. "That's beautiful, Charlie." I looked away, though she continued to gaze upon me. "There were five of you. Did you each have the same poem?"

"No," Charlie answered. "One said nothing, one spoke movingly in sadness. Another created an essay expressing his views, one in anger."

"You were introspective."

"Yes, I suppose so," Charlie responded.

"Then you do have a personality."

Her eyebrows arched as she nodded in agreement.

We were interrupted by my phone. I looked down on my lap to see Lulu's face looking up at me from the screen. "Hello, my love," I said, laughing as I looked at Charlie.

"What? Hello to you too. Wake up, sleepy head, we'll be at the hotel soon."

"Why do you assume I'm asleep?" I winked at Charlie.

"I know you, you're always sleeping!" Lulu responded.

I turned to Charlie, continuing my thought. "I like yours."

Kevin M. Faulkner

TWENTY-FIVE

Implant Record Date 14 August 2104
San Diego to Bengaluru

In the morning, the three of us rode together in a security vehicle to the Institute. We had already discussed Venka and his condition, and Nithia filled in the gaps. In short, his mind was degenerating after what turned out to be years of interfacing in one way or another with powerful computers. Though you read about this sort of thing it wasn't real until you saw it happen to someone you were close to. Nithia said that he had moments where his memory would simply vanish, and he would be confused. He did his best to hide it, as did those around him. The Indian media completely ignored it.

I knew some of this already, having talked to him from time to time by phone or phaeton, but increasingly, according to his students and ever-present assistant, he was not available.

We drove past a marble statue of his likeness as we neared the Indian Institute of Modern Physics, adjacent to the experimental construction hangers hidden behind strategically planted vines over ornate fencing. Our vehicle stopped before the entrance to the research hall, named after the famous twentieth century Nobel Prize winning astrophysicist Subrahmanyan Chandrasekhar. There were tropical trees and flowers growing along the shaded sidewalk as we approached the entrance, almost hidden by the lushness. I had walked through its hallowed halls many times since its completion in 2078 and was always inspired by the layered meaning behind each section, representing stages of Indian civilization.

As we approached Venka's offices, we were welcomed by his staff.

"Jenny, it's so good to see you," Venka exclaimed, embracing me. "Hello, General Wen, so good to see you as well."

"Hello Dr. Venkalaswaran, it is my pleasure," Lulu said, as Venka held out his hands to her. A young woman, perhaps a post-doctoral associate or intern, was constantly at Venka's side when he was with us, but she never spoke. Venka introduced her as his assistant, Libra.

"I see you brought a friend."

"Yes," I said, looking at Charlie. Before I could answer, Charlie made her own introduction.

"I'm so glad you could all come," Venka said. "Please, join me outside while the weather is still nice. Storms are coming later, they say. I've gathered some of my students and staff to join us. We'll have some tea and a bite before our meeting and tour of the construction hangars."

We walked through the open doors in the back of his office into an open graveled courtyard where two tables were already set for us, eager young students and the engineering team filtering in around them. They all turned to greet us as we approached.

"Everyone, please, have a seat and enjoy," Venka said. Libra whispered into a headset and a team of people in dapper outfits appeared.

The servers came around the tables waiting to bring us tea, and our first course of a meal. It was early spring so the trees surrounding us were turning a darker green, and the air was fresh with a cool humidity before the heat of the day. Venka motioned for me to sit next to him as he held my arm. Charlie sat on my other side as Lulu took up residence somewhere at another table. A young researcher sat across from me, visibly excited to be near Venka.

"We try to do this at least once a month, your timing is excellent," Venka said to me. I could tell that Venka was doing well. Though he had a little more gray hair, his face was youthful, and his manner light. He came alive when he talked about his technology, beaming at the latest details.

Kevin M. Faulkner

"You're looking good," I said. "It's good to see. Tell us more about how the current lighter construction is going."

"Yes," Venka said. I noticed Venka hesitating, and Libra touched his arm. "Before I go too far, let me call Shamim over."

Libra spoke into her headset, mumbling. Shamim Ganju had been a close colleague of Venka's since after the First Event, when the commercial construction of the lighters was in its infancy. He was a former student of his, and had stayed on to post-doc, then worked for Svoboda Corporation as Venka's assistant.

"Dr. Ganju is coming up from the student lecture hall and will be here shortly. Please, everyone, enjoy the tea," Libra said in a delicate voice I imagined from her slight appearance was normal for her. Venka nodded, as Libra, standing behind us, leaned into him and whispered. She continued, I suspected as a diversion to Venka's dementia-induced confusion. I soon learned that everyone around him, the whole country, did it's best to hide his condition.

The young man across from me started a conversation with Charlie and me.

"Ah, here he is," Venka said. Shamim introduced himself as he approached. It was just in time, as I could tell Venka was fading.

Libra made a motion as if conducting a symphony and the young man across from me rose to move down the table as Shamim took his place.

"So Shamim, Jenny asked how the newest lighters are coming." Libra said. Venka looked on, and somehow it seemed that the words came directly from Venka himself.

"Yes. We have at least a dozen smaller, six to ten-seat lighters in progress. We call them *explorer class* lighters, and at least ten of them are nearly complete and ready for delivery," Shamim said. "Then there are the mid-range lighters that carry up to fifty or sixty people. Most of the lighters sold to date have been the explorer class, while the Republic, the US and China have kept the mid-range lighters. We have two much larger lighters that are nearly complete. They can hold up to three hundred people each, and equipment and provisions for two months stay at their destination. Those are for the Caucasus Republic."

"Jenny," Venka started, his composure coming back, "as with the smaller and mid-range lighters, these larger lighters are capable of flight, launching from the ground to Earth's orbit. Their primary mode is driven-field propulsion, a combination of AG and semi-combustion. They are very advanced. We are calling them transport-class lighters, and the intent is to use them for forming permanent settlements on other planets."

The anti-gravity (AG) technology Venka referred to was concurrently being developed throughout the world, though it started back in the 2060's. Unlike QMT, however, anti-gravity technology developed from many sources and from many places so no one government or entity had independent control over it, at least not anymore. It allowed objects to use a planet's naturally occurring gravity field to push and steer against. I didn't understand the details, but it sounded as though there was some overlap in how power was generated in anti-gravity devices and Venka's lighters that had made them function. The semi-combustion technology was an ancillary result of the fusion systems used to power most AG systems and thus had a dual purpose of directionally driving the craft as the AG provided lift.

"We already have much larger lighters in the beginning stages of construction," Venka added.

"So, with the transport-class lighters, will they have any separate propulsion to maneuver?" I asked.

"Yes," Shamim said. "They will have basic thrusters for guidance but will be mostly driven by anti-gravity before quantum mass-transfer will take place outside of Earth's gravity."

"Pretty amazing stuff," I said. "I look forward to seeing it."

"Indeed," Shamim said, excitedly. "What we are witnessing is the largest human migration ever to take place since Europeans ventured to the Americas. The Republic will lead the first human migration to another world. I don't believe its significance can even be calculated at this moment, or in what's left of our lifetimes. These days will be remembered throughout human history, even two thousand years from now, as the first wave of migration of humans off our planet."

"And Dr. Venkalaswaran will be remembered as its father," Charlie said.

"Goodness, thank you, Charlie," Venka said, "but I don't know. I still worry about all of this. I am cautious of human nature. I wonder if we have evolved enough to handle such changes."

"I wonder too," Charlie said.

"And thank you for looking after my dear friend," Venka said to Charlie.

"It's true," I said, taking a sip of my tea. "She does."

Venka looked at me, then at Charlie, "Jenny has changed since I first met her eight years ago."

"Really, how?" Charlie asked.

"Yes, tell us," Lulu chided, coming over to join our conversation.

"I thought you were somewhere else." I said.

"Jenny has always been a free spirit" Venka laughed. "When we first met, she had a tattoo running up her arm (he pointed to his arm). Quite unusual for an attorney in a big law firm."

"I was a little drunk when I did that," which was the truth.

"She was filled with energy, but selective with those she gave it to."

"Yes, I noticed that too," Charlie said.

"She's a loner," Lulu said.

"Yes," Venka laughed. "There's nothing wrong with that, but I'm glad that I was someone she let in."

"Me too," Charlie said. "And how has she changed?"

"No more tattoo," Lulu blurted out.

The Sixth Traveler

"True," Venka replied. He looked at me as he continued, "She's a corporate woman now." Everyone laughed.

"No way!"

As he continued, I noticed my friend had changed himself. As far as I could tell, he was no longer hooking up to a computer, but his manner was different. His speech was slightly slurred, and his mind seemed to wander. At the same time, he has become more reflective, even philosophical. I'm no expert on the *Bhagavad Gita*, but I think he was quoting quite a bit from it. I saw a well-worn copy on his desk. His transformation was fascinating to me because I had seen it before my eyes and felt a part of it. Yet his connection with me, his family, and his work was unfazed by it all.

"It's time," Libra said after some time, motioning for the tables to be cleared and for us to leave. Shamim led us from the courtyard, through a maze of buildings, finally ending at a conference room above the hangar that held one of the two partially completed transport-class lighters. We were taking part in a working group meeting, where some of the scientists, engineers, and businesspeople of Svoboda and the Institute met to discuss the progress of the lighters and where it all fit into the clients' needs. There must have been thirty men and women in the room, some of the best and brightest people from around the world.

Lulu turned to me, "Those lighters look pretty amazing," she said. "They are beginning to look like spacecraft and not some fat chinchilla."

Most of the heavy construction of the lighters took place here in Bengaluru in a joint effort with NASA. Major components, and the smaller lighters, were also built in Pasadena, California at JPL, and other components in Chechnya. These meetings switched between Bengaluru and Pasadena, but Venka was increasingly absent from the meetings at JPL. The lecture room overlooking the construction hanger was about as far as he went these days.

The chatter in the room died down as Venka stood before the working group, next to a lectern and in front of an old (but working)

Kevin M. Faulkner

chalk board, with windows on each side overlooking the hangar below as everyone became silent. As I know was a tradition here, Venka always opened the meeting by asking, "Where are we today?"

Apparently, before each of these meetings the senior researchers would agree among themselves who would speak first.

"We've achieved an external wobble in the tympani that will encompass the sphere of the entire craft, as calculations predicted," a young engineer spoke up. "We fired them last night and the test showed reversible coupling and decoupling." *Funny, the terms physicists came up with.* The tympani plates were still an integral part of the lighter that created the quantum effect that drove the craft to interstellar distances. A *wobble* was what the research scientists referred to as the extent of the quantum mass-transfer effect such that everything within its charge would behave as a sub-atomic particle. It had been believed at one time that there was a low-frequency vibration in such matter, so the term was somewhat of a joke.

"How reversible?" Venka asked. "Can it go for two, three, or more events before being replaced? For a month?" The tympani plates had been sacrificial in the earliest lighters, lasting only as long as they were energized, so for two short jump sequences, spaced only minutes apart.

"Based on the tests and modeling, the tympani plates on the two new transport lighters can last for up to a hundred events, non-sequential, and not necessarily continuously energized," the engineer replied. The materials to make the tympani have also evolved from the heavy and expensive silver alloys to a carbon-titanium supercomposite, where the structure of the carbon-carbon bonds allowed for electrons to flow freely as if a conductor. In fact, it was not a conductor, but a tunnel-facilitating system that allowed quantum tunneling of the electrons through the material.

This line of discussion became more technical, losing me. Venka grew quiet but leaned forward and listened in earnest. I followed pieces of the conversation as my mind drifted to my days before college, back in Washington. It was so far away, high school, weekend skiing in the winter, hiking in the Olympics in the summer. Canoeing on Crescent Lake on a sunny afternoon, running back to the tents when the wind picked up, holding hands with someone I no longer remember. *I'll do all of those things again, soon.*

"So exactly where is the large lighter behind us going?" This question brought me back into the room.

"So, the current transport lighters behind us in the hangar are due to be delivered to the Republic," one of the planners, an American from his accent, chimed in. "They will have space for large expeditions, including food and water for at least two months. In addition, there will be room for heavy equipment."

"Dr. Otieno, when do you think the two transport lighters will be ready for delivery to the Republic?" a business member of the team asked.

"Very soon; in another month."

"I take it that this is a one-way trip for the cargo and passengers?" I asked the group.

"Yes. And there will be multiple trips just the same. Naturally, people are free to come back to Earth."

"But almost no one takes them up on it," a voice from the back of the room chimed in.

"How will these people be selected? Will there be the same number of people on each lighter?" someone asked.

"Yes, nearly the same number of people," Shamim said. "As for choosing the travelers that is up to the client."

"We thought you might know how the Republic is choosing its passengers, Jenny," Venka said.

"Not exactly, but I have some ideas. I know they are being selective," I said. "They have to be, this planet is unknown and conditions are primitive." I hedged. I didn't want to be specific as this was attorney-client information. The criteria the Republic government used was a desire to do no harm; they wanted to start a new life, and they wanted peace more than anything else. The leadership was enlightened enough to have gotten past religious, racial, and ideological differences so that they could form a blended society. The goal was peace and prosperity: a high Gross National Happiness. They wanted to make sure it stayed that way in the New World.

"Though the New World is relatively lush with photosynthetic plant life, high in oxygen, water, and temperate, it is new and there are many unknowns," I added. "So, as you could imagine, their initial selection process is not much different than that of the process NASA uses to select its astronauts." True statement, the key being *initial*. The current selection process is already changing to be more akin to an immigration process than a selection process.

"Are there any xenocreatura?" someone asked. "Anything dangerous?"

"No monsters yet," one of the scientists replied, making everyone laugh. "There are oceans, with tides," she continued. "So, likely there will at least be some amphibious life. You could bring your surfboard, Jenny." More laughter. I thought it was funny too, but I felt a drop in the pit of my stomach as I was reminded of my past.

"As long as there are no monsters in the oceans!"

Everyone laughed.

"However, there are xenophage present," Charlie said amid the din of voices. "And humans will need numerous inoculations to survive." There was silence as all eyes turned to Charlie. "I have footage from an expedition of the planet," Charlie continued.

"Excellent" Shamim asked. "May we see it?"

"Of course." Charlie went to the monitor control panel and placed her left hand on the input plate. I had seen it already but could watch it a hundred times and still get goose bumps. As she settled her hand on the panel, an image was projected on the screen behind her as the room partially darkened. There was small Chinese script and Chechen writing in the upper corner of the video, and Charlie narrated what we were seeing.

"This is footage from the second expedition, July 28, 2103, of the New World in the Cygnus quadrant, currently referred to as system *CYG120945697*. The New World Number Five is 634.288 light years from our sun and is the fourth of eleven planets that orbit a class G5V star. The New World has 1.873 times the Earth's radius and is in the habitable Goldilocks zone of the system. I have authenticated the source of the video you are watching as the RCS Expedition Twelve, on a small lighter owned by the Republic of Caucasus States," Charlie said. The room was in awe with muted chatter in a dozen languages.

"The gravity on the New World is nearly the same as that on Earth, slightly more as the density is higher at the core. There is a strong magnetic field, thus persistent and extended Van Allen belts protecting the planet's surface from radiation. The planet rotates every 20.5 hours, and revolves around its sun every eighteen months, as measured by our time. The atmosphere is breathable, having an even higher concentration of oxygen than Earth," Charlie narrated, stating the exact content of atmospheric components.

"With such a fast rotation, no large animals, and the composition of the atmosphere, it seems the planet is very young," someone commented.

Some in the room might have seen this video, but it was obvious many had not. I had not watched all of it myself and have not had time to look at all the different videos pouring onto the internet from various explorations. In the last year there must have been a hundred overall, originating from lighters made by Svoboda Corporation.

My mind faded in and out as the audience reacted. Some were silent, others chatted in disbelief. Yet others simply made scientific observations and speculations. It still felt so strange, even surreal. *How could this be? How could we be seeing the surface of a planet light years away?*

Kevin M. Faulkner

Once the video ended, the room came alight with conversation. It had been two hours since the working group gathered so attendants brought in tea, coffee, and light finger food for everyone. As was the tradition in closing, Venka stood up to indicate a close to the meeting, and said, "My friends, let us adjourn for the day."

As people filtered out of the room, Venka pulled me aside. "Charlie, Lulu, can I speak with Jenny for a moment?" Venka asked.

"Of course," Lulu replied.

"I'll take them down to inspect the lighter," Shamim said.

"I'll meet you," I replied as they walked out the door. I watched Charlie as she walked out with Lulu.

"Libra, I'll be fine, why don't you wait outside," Venka said. She looked at me, and I knowingly smiled.

"Call me if you need," she said, quietly, obviously reluctant to leave him.

"Come, sit down with me," Venka said, motioning to several chairs near the lectern in the front of the room.

I held onto his arm, in part to guide him, and partly because I wanted to hold him, feeling for him as he struggled against the phantom that may have given him the gift of enlightenment while taking away his strength.

"Jenny, how are you?"

"I'm okay, losing my mind, but other than that, fine," I said, trying to be honest and light, noting the irony of both of us. I immediately regretted saying that as I saw him wince.

"I heard you had another seizure." Venka shook his head and took my hand in his. "Jenny, have you thought about particle surgery? This is a medical condition that most likely can be corrected with the right treatment."

"I have looked into it," I replied. "The doctors say that because it was caused by a new phenomenon they are not sure how to treat it. They could zap parts of my brain, but the damage from the Event is in various places, some that control crucial functions. I'm afraid it is hard to get at. To tell the truth, it's all a risk so I'm a little nervous about it."

"I can understand."

"I promise I will get treated if it gets any worse, I've already told my doctor that."

Venka was silent for a moment, as he took a seat.

"I feel bad," Venka said. "After all, it's at least partly my fault, it was my invention."

I sat down next to him and held his hand. "Please don't," I said. "I'm glad you invented it, and I'm glad I was on that mission. I wanted to do it." Venka and I had been through this many times these last four years. All I could do was assure him by continuing to move forward with my life and change the subject.

"Well, whatever the case, I am so happy to see you have some help."

"Yes, Charlie is great. I . . . ." I hesitated, feeling vaguely ashamed.

"I know you miss Kepler."

"Yes, both of them are amazing. Kepler had this honesty that was exhausting but comforting at the same time. I never had to guess with him. Charlie is the same, but she has her own personality. Kepler's delivery was his comedy."

"And with Charlie?"

"Love. That, and the cool French accent."

Venka laughed.

"She tells me her name, Charlie, comes from an old movie actor, Charlie Chaplin. Apparently, he was loved by the French. Charlie's Maker had a sense of humor."

"I hope she gets to stay with you."

"Me too." Charlie and I had grown close and when you spend so much time with an android, you forget they are not human. Sometimes I thought I favored her company. I'm not sure if that was a good thing or not.

Kevin M. Faulkner

"There was a time when I would have thought that Charlie was too precious. On the way here she recited a poem she had written. She can be so overtly existential."

"And she doesn't hide it, does she? That is how androids are; she has no real social inhibitions because she does not worry about what people think of her. She is as poetic and flighty as she wants to be," Venka said.

"Yes. I know there is a lesson there."

Venka simply smiled at me and nodded. "Speaking of that, I hope you don't judge me too harshly," Venka pointed to the dark spot on his neck where his implanted conductor plate had healed over. "I . . .." It was the first time I had seen Venka near tears. I was touched that he even cared what I thought.

"Of course not. But I am glad you stopped." I rubbed his arm, somewhat alarmed at seeing him upset. "Besides, who am I to judge?" I followed, thinking about my growing dependence on similar technology. I heard a throat clear as Libra walked in. We rose as I spoke, "So, how are those kids of yours?"

"My students, or the ones my wife also claims?"

I thought of his three children and how they would call me "Auntie" and, when very young, would run into my arms and hug me, enticing me to "See this!" and "Come play with me!" Though they didn't know it, Mika, Prashid, and Yhama took me to a place I avoided, a time when I was their age and my world was shaken. That may now be happening to them as their father was slowly and painfully torn away from them.

Later that night, at Venka's home, I sat with Nithia at her dinner table. Lulu had already left for her duties and Charlie was resting. Each of us with a cup of tea in our hands, Nithia shared her struggles with her husband's growing incapacity. It was clear that he was getting worse; in fits and starts, but worse all the same. And I could see that it was breaking her heart.

TWENTY-SIX

Implant Record Date 24 September 2104
Delhi

With just the barest attention to my phone, I discreetly adjusted the app that controls my implant for the third time since waking that morning. I asked myself if it was too much, or why I would need such a thing at all. I looked around ruefully, afraid someone might witness and judge a disgraceful act of weakness, or simply the truth of my disintegration.

After my time with Venka last month, the weeks that followed moved in rapid succession. My mind was failing, and I struggled against a nearly constant fog, trying my best to keep it hidden. I barely remembered traveling back to Chechnya in early June, before coming here to Delhi with Amanta Kokotova. To make matters worse, on a diplomatic level, things were happening beyond my ability to really keep up.

I sat in the back of the large conference room, several stories above the large indoor plaza below, Amanta and the other Chechen diplomats sitting around a shiny black conference table with their Indian counterparts. The dark carpet absorbed the light reflecting from the bright, undulating curtains and artfully washed-out world flags along the walls, accentuating the three-dimensional graphs and images around us. Amanta would often turn to me to ask a question in her discreet commlink, while I would answer as best I could.

"Should we agree on port rights along with orbital rights, or keep them separate? Will this push Moscow into a corner?" I remember her asking at one point. I shook my head at first, forgetting that I could speak back to her; perhaps I even wanted to avoid it. To be honest, during this time I felt like I did not really understand what was going on or what I was doing. I was insecure, and I couldn't help but bounce repeated *help* signals at Charlie while searching within myself for answers. As my mental state declined, so did my confidence.

"I think we need to consider Moscow's port rights, but I would be careful about agreeing to orbital rights along with that, especially anything within a half radius of the planet," I had replied. "So much can happen. Keep sub-orbital rights separate. It would be best to be consistent, at least for now."

Once the meeting was over I went to Amanta, wanting to leave the room as soon as was practical. I knew that Lulu and her security team were just outside. We did not speak during these events, but I liked being able to see her.

"I think your meeting with Gupta went well." I said to Amanta once we were alone. This was no surprise, but I did not want the moment to go unnoticed. "I thought the conservative factions of the government would cause more of an issue than they did."

"Oh, I still think they will," Amanta said.

"Right. Having India on our side will help you, but also polarize things."

"What do you mean?" I was surprised at her question. We continued to walk down the hallway of the South Block building in Delhi to the press room. They were to give statements to the press, and field questions.

"We're taking sides, they're taking sides. It's unavoidable, but there it is."

"You mean within the Indian government, or with the rest of the world? With Russia," Amanta replied as more of a statement than a question, smiling to the diplomats and reporters lining the hallways as we walked past them.

"Mmmm. Maybe all of it," I replied with a sudden burst of insight. I was still her counselor, and I had to trust that my instincts would take over where my reasoning fell behind.

The Sixth Traveler

"Yes, well, conflict is unavoidable. In any case, that is what press conferences are for. Telling the world where you stand, forcing others to make their move. I prefer that to secret meetings and backroom deals," Amanta said.

"I think the peoples' regard for Dr. Venkalaswaran will weight in our favor."

"Of course." I wasn't sure she even remembered Venkalaswaran.

We were followed by Charlie, and in the distance, Lulu. I had worked with Amanta for weeks leading up to this meeting, which was to be followed by a blazing schedule that included Munich, London, Washington, Brasilia, Tokyo, Seoul, Beijing, and ending in Moscow (the hard part). The advent of anti-gravity transport made jumping from city to city simple and efficient, but I nonetheless planned the meetings based on the shortest route. It was a convenient excuse to put the visits in the most diplomatic order.

Moscow was the rub. The Russians would likely balk at the Republic's galactic ambitions, and there were worries that Russian-backed Vainakh troops were preparing to invade the Republic, amassing troops in the north. Nationalism was high in Russia, with posters of the face of Yuri Gagarin, the first human in space, adorning screenshots to promote an invigorated space program. The Russians felt it was their destiny to discover and colonize a planet of their own, and in any case, they challenged the legitimacy of the Republic. Factions of the Russian government were not content to let it slip away.

We approached the media area and entered from the rear standing behind a press stage. There was a podium for each of Secretary Gupta and for Foreign Minister Kokotova. I stood back as Amanta and Secretary Gupta walked up to their podiums, the green and red flag emblazoned with the pinwheel emblem of the unified States of the Caucasus Republic behind Amanta, the Indian flag behind Gupta.

"Madam Prime Minister," the reporters shouted. Amanta pointed to a young man in front. I could see from my vantage point the two diplomats, but only the heads of the reporters crowded below the stage.

"Madam Prime Minster, Nisk Elba of the Delhi Raajaneta," the reporter said. "Can you tell us what your intentions are for the New World? There is a word that you already have a name for it, Ushguli. Can you confirm?"

"Thank you, Mr. Elba, for your question," Amanta replied. "As you may know, the Republic started with a dream of uniting the peoples of the Caucasus, after fighting among one another for so many years, and often defending ourselves against outside forces. Though we have had our differences, the people of Chechnya and surrounding areas could see that the only way to mutual prosperity was through unity and peace." She went on, not really answering his original question any longer. Eventually, she picked back up, "Yet, even as I speak, we may still not have achieved that. We fear our peace may be short lived as Vainakh forces turn against the Republic and gather in the north and south, surrounding Grozny. We feel the only recourse for our people is off world, a new home, away from the old hatreds and border disputes." Her goal was to garner sympathy, and as I suggested, she was careful not to publicly implicate the Russians, though we highly suspected their backing, or at least, encouragement.

She continued, reiterating the points we agreed to: If she was serious about colonizing the New World, best use current circumstances as a motivator. War from the outside was pushing the Republic to go forward on its own. Though other space-faring powers might argue that rights to newly discovered and uninhabited planets should be negotiated, the Federatsiya had pushed for this technology, had mostly paid for it, and thus deserved some priority. Through their funding of Dr. Venkalaswaran and the Institute, they made it all happen. In any case, there would be no shortage of planets that were habitable. We didn't have to squabble over this one world.

I looked back at Charlie and whispered, "I wonder if we aren't going to create a galaxy of balkanized worlds."

I could see Lulu standing back, dressed in a plain suit, her weapons hidden beneath her jacket, watching the crowd. She glanced at me, then back at one of her team members. I turned back to the podium to listen to what was going on when I felt a little dizzy. Charlie turned to me, focusing in on my face as she reached out and gently took my arm.

"Jenny, let's go to the dressing room," she said.

"What?"

The tone in her voice said it all. I let her guide me away from the conference, Amanta's voice growing dimmer. As we entered the room I could feel myself losing balance, and a sense of where I was.

I leaned on Charlie as we turned to leave, amazed again at her strength, so well hidden in her slender frame. My legs collapsed once we reached the dressing room, Charlie caught my fall. The last thing I remembered saying was: "Lulu." After that, it was as if I were in a terrible dream, calling out for help but finding myself mute and moving in slow motion.

"Jenny," I seemed to hear Charlie say, "This is a severe episode." She placed her left hand on my head. As my memory of events became spotty my implant captured the rest.

"Lulu, Jenny needs intervention, she's not breathing."

"Medic, now, dressing room," Lulu said into her commlink while Charlie bent over to ventilate me. This lapse was much longer than the last few I had, and deeper. My implant could take in most of the information as long as my eyes were open and ears alert. The visuals were confusing, out of focus, and chaotic, but the audio was essentially a word-by-word account of what was happening, without being garbled by my brain.

Several minutes passed as the people around me moved in and out of my fuzzy visual frame. The only constant was Charlie, who stayed with me, bending over to push air in and out of my lungs, the messages from my brain no longer able to keep pace. The implant recorded: "Lulu, bring the medics in." Charlie continued to breathe life into my lungs.

There was determination in Charlie's motions, as if she had suddenly discovered a treasure she could not live without. There was pain in Lulu's face. It saddened me, as much as I could label an emotion in the transient state I was in. I loved them both, and wondered why I hadn't acknowledged that fact until now.

Later, the implant recorded Charlie talking to a doctor: "She needs surgical intervention, I detect sustained frontal lobe discharges on OSI 12, and left parietal at QMP 1283; her ANS erratic through her medulla," followed by more technical details. I was amazed she could determine all of this from the sensors in her hand. "I have her Power of Attorney to confirm her wishes if she were to stay in a catatonic state for longer than thirty minutes. She is fully aware of the possible consequences of surgery."

Some time passed, at least thirty minutes. I stayed in the state I was in. I remember from the implant that Amanta came in and hovered around me. I was transported to a hospital in Delhi, the best hospital in the Indian Federation. I was placed in a bed with an oxygen mask for air and an intravenous drip of fluids in my arm.

Later that night I was aware that John Mar was standing over me. *Must be serious*, I thought in some cogent neuron of my noodle.

* * *

My implant performed two separate functions. First, it acted as a simple audio recorder, recording the words spoken by myself and others near me, as well as other sounds external to me. In this mode, the recording was direct, that is, not filtered by my own senses. The second function was to record and translate internal thoughts, sights, sounds and tactile sensations that were first recorded by my eyes, ears, and fingertips, then translated within my brain.

At some point, I believe after I had arrived at the hospital in Delhi, the doctors shut down the first function of my implant, leaving only the portion that recorded memories, feelings, and sensory input filtered through my brain. Playing back the record from that day haunts me.

"Jenny, I'm sorry," Lulu seemed to say. I couldn't tell if it was all a dream, reality, or simply neural confusion from a misfiring brain. The implant interpreted the signals, whatever their source. Reading the raw feed from the implant, which was usually fairly lucid for a typical state dream, did not lend itself to dream or reality. The raw processor feed from my brain during the seizure converted my feelings and auditory nerve signals into an initial machine language, reading in part:

> ##nine/eighteenjuju##anx.anx.SORRY//bptt.stop/#sequence/momentlos.two##Spacenter//mknlt##oceanman##camus/plane/dethtwelv#elTOD/etwelve#hert#nnqibi#nobilitacboa;tabclicao//NO#tmalesoftBRA##hrtlst/rrem/.

It went on like that for some time. The Lambert-Troch translation recalled words coming externally, the # indicating auditory information and the / some type of emotion. The implant recorded some dialogue from its programmed store of human language, while some words were pieced together through a processor. The emotions are even more difficult to process unless the implant is familiar with the voice and inflection of the person talking. My implant was familiar with Lulu but was picking these things up in a sea of electronic noise created by my seizure.

After a rough translation, the implant output read, in part:

Kevin M. Faulkner

I'm so sorry. I should stop the event. I knew an act terrible on station. I knew it, damn it. I am sorry. You should be on your ocean, love, surfing on some wave with man yours.

I feel I had imagined those waves before they put me out, a sort of *déjà vu*. Were they Lulu's words, or my own dreams? Both functions of my implant were shut down by the nurse before the operation began. Such devices were not allowed to stay on during surgery, lest the patient recall the pain.

It didn't matter, I could recall the pain. I decided to never ask Lulu about it. I think there are just some things that I am not meant to know, private thoughts and feelings shared by accident, owned only by its giver.

The Sixth Traveler

TWENTY-SEVEN

Implant Record Date 30 September 2104
Delhi

The first voices I remembered hearing after my surgery were those of John Mar and my father.

"All hell is going to break loose," I could hear John saying in a hushed tone, my father agreeing with him. Nauseous and groggy, I opened my eyes, wondering where I was. I saw Charlie sitting next to me and I remembered.

"The Vainakh troops are advancing toward Grozny," Amanta said to John. "Iran is not fighting, but they block the south." I turned in the bed and looked to see John and Amanta Kokotova, watching the television. Charlie gently called for everyone.

"Hey, Jenny," John said in a quiet tone. My father simply smiled, a look of relief lifting his face. They both walked over to me. John took my hand, his warmth coalescing with mine.

"Thisss . . .." I trailed off, my voice not able to articulate what I wanted to say. *This is the second time I've dragged you across the world to see me laid up in a hospital bed*, I thought. "Sorry."

"Jenny, relax," Charlie said. "You won't be able to talk right away, don't try to force it."

"How are you?" John asked. I felt excitement in seeing him and knew with clarity then how I felt.

"Good," I said with effort. *Where is Lulu?* I wondered, looking over to Charlie.

"Lulu is here, she's gone for some food," Charlie replied. "You are just waking. Let me call the doctors."

"Sorry, I shouldn't ask you any questions," John said. He continued to hold my hand, reminding me of the day I held his outstretched arm on the *Indira II*.

I looked up at the television monitor, probably with worry on my face.

"Don't worry about that now, relax," Charlie said, turning the monitor off.

"You gave me quite a scare," Amanta said. I turned and saw she was standing there with John. "Right in the middle of my important press conference that I love so much."

Glad I could help.

The doctor came in and took up my chart, sitting down next to me. "Ms. Hsu, I am Dr. Amiz, your primary doctor. I see you've decided to join us. Let me take a look at you." He leaned in to look into my eyes, then checking the instruments around me. "You had a major seizure and we operated on you. Your friend Dr. Amelia Prasad and I oversaw the android performing your surgery."

I tried to sit up, wanting to see Amelia. Dr. Prasad was one of the training astronauts with Venka on standby at the First Event.

"Take it easy," the doctor said. You need to lay back and rest."

I sat back in some pain. I felt my feet move, but I was terribly sluggish.

"How did it come out?" Amanta asked the doctor.

"We are pleased, the surgery went exceedingly well. We expect your counsel will make a full recovery. Just give her some time."

I gathered my thoughts. *Will I have any more episodes? How long will my recovery be?* I wanted desperately to speak but could not get the words out.

"Doctor Amiz, will Jenny have any more seizures?" Charlie asked, placing her hand gently against my forehead, part soothing, and partly to read me. Her clairvoyance no longer surprised me.

"We can't guarantee yet, but we feel fairly confident they are gone for good," the doctor responded. "It will take some time to tell for sure."

I lay there, resigned to having my mind read by Charlie. It was amazing, and strange, to be so transparent. Charlie continued to ask more highly technical questions, well beyond what I can describe. My father silently listened to the back-and-forth, at times nodding in approval. I remember Dr. Amiz said the android that performed the surgery was an American made system, very advanced, but mostly just made for performing specific medical tasks, not as sentient as Charlie.

Lulu came into the room. I could see the relief on her face as she saw me, though she tried hard not to show it.

"Hey there, *xiǎo mèimei*."

"She can't speak yet," Charlie said.

"Ah, good. Some quiet."

Haha. Very funny.

"Amanta, you should continue on with your meetings," John said. "I believe you head to Munich next."

"Yes, soon," Amanta replied.

"You, young lady, get some rest," Amanta said. "You've been invaluable, Jenny, but for now, rest. When you are feeling better, you can join me. Let Charlie and Wen Lu take care of you."

I looked over at John.

"I'll be ready to accompany Amanta if needed," John said.

I was restless, but when I tried to move I realized I was down for the count. My mind was clearing, but my mouth and legs were nearly immobile, not responding to what my brain was telling them to do.

"I hate to leave you, Jenny."

"Issssss okay," I said. I knew at that moment I loved John Bradford Mar, whether he loved me back or not. It may have been just as well that I could not tell him in that moment. Knowing its truth was elation enough.

Kevin M. Faulkner

I fell back to sleep as Amanta slipped away, accompanied by Lulu and John. After another day or two, John left with Amanta for Munich, then London and Washington. Lulu came and went as her military duties called, but Charlie and my father stayed by my side.

While I recovered, two transport-class lighters were flown from Bengaluru to a launch facility in Chechnya, now a state of the Republic. The ships were quickly being outfitted for the trip they were about to take. It looked as though these would be lifeboats for the unfortunate people caught in a world that would not leave them alone.

My strength grew, gradually. While Lulu stayed in a nearby hotel during the times she could come, Charlie stayed in the hospital, helping me re-learn to speak, and use my arms and hands. My father stayed with me until he could see that I was in the clear. He was a quiet man, content to be in the background, yet always there for me.

"I promise I will let you know if there is a problem, Mr. Hsu," Charlie said to him, tapping her head to indicate that she could call him anytime, and he could call on her.

As the days passed the fog lifted and my mind became increasingly clear. The most recent events were especially sharp, and more distant memories somehow in better focus: My childhood, skiing on Mount Rainier in the summer, out late with friends at Caltech, surfing the Trestles in San Diego.

* * *

Every morning, a nurse would bring a breakfast of scrambled eggs, milk, and a bread-like mash to me for breakfast. They would have honey and jam on the side, most of it real as far as I could tell. They told me it was provided by the firm, requested by John Mar. It must have been expensive, as real eggs and honey were uncommon.

Right after my surgery, when I could not use my hands and arms with much dexterity, Charlie helped me eat, spoon feeding me until I could feed myself. I was thankful for Charlie and surprised myself at my lack of self-consciousness with her. My muscle control, especially in the upper part of my body, came back gradually, especially with her help. Charlie's sweet and direct nature made her a pleasure, though often bracing, to talk to. Nothing was off limits, but she had a way of approaching things at the right time. This morning in September I must have looked ready for a whopper.

"Jenny," Charlie started.

"Yes?"

"John Mar loves you, and I know you love him."

Of course she knows. I thought of Kepler.

"We are open books to you, aren't we?" It wasn't much of a question.

"Of all the human emotions to read, passion is one of the easiest. Evolution has placed a priority on it."

"Yes, I suppose that's true. The last android I . . ." I had trouble talking about Kepler.

"Kepler would have known too," Charlie said, taking my hand. She knew I missed him. "Androids can't always predict all that humans do. Your behavior is highly individualized, and there is free will. But one person's behavior can be accurately predicted once we have some specific data, and Kepler certainly had that."

What could I say. We talked about what I was going to do about it. I didn't know, but I knew I would tell him, soon.

* * *

Lulu was in and out, a week at a time, and would help with my physical therapy, mostly by trying to annoy me to the point that I didn't want to stay in bed any longer.

Kevin M. Faulkner

"Hey Juju," Lulu said one morning, after having been gone for a week. "I'm just in time for you to get your lazy butt up."

"Good morning to you too."

She walked over to my bed, grabbing my hand and pulling me up. I resisted, but it was no use.

"Okay. Can you help me up?" I tried to stand. It was already Tuesday morning, when my physical therapy normally started.

"Do you want the walker?" Charlie asked.

"She doesn't need that," Lulu said.

"Okay," Charlie said, putting her hands up. I winked at her and said, "Why don't you take a break and let me deal with Lulu for both of us."

"Ha! I'm the one giving poor Charlie a break."

I didn't feel that I needed the walker at first, but after trying to stand on my own, I lost my balance and grabbed onto Lulu. She helped me stand, and walked me down the hallway, as much as I could tolerate. As I struggled to take steps, I looked back to see if we were alone. I had been waiting for a chance to talk to Lulu. It was hard for me to even articulate where it came from, what I wanted to say. Something about the beach; something about Branton Ma'hai. A dream I must have had but was not sure. I had not had time yet to download my implant files.

"Lulu," I said, grunting through the pain in my legs. I looked over at her, "*Dàjiě* (big sister)."

"What?"

"You know I was the one who ended things with Branton Ma'hai, right?" She didn't respond right away, I think the question threw her off a little.

"Oh, yes, I know," Lulu replied. "Not good enough for you."

We turned and walked back in the other direction. Then I remembered that I wasn't going to say anything about all of this. *What to do now?*

The Sixth Traveler

"I don't know about that," I said. "I ended it. He told me he loved me. You'd think that would have made me happy, but it scared me. I just didn't feel it." I took another step, feeling more balanced.

"If I had been younger. We probably would have been a better fit, but I was different from when we were kids in college." I stopped myself, and wished I hadn't said as much as I had. I didn't want to make her worry. I knew she blamed herself for what happened to the six of us on the *Second Surfer*.

"It's okay, *xiǎo mèimei*. Underneath the wet suit and attitude, you're an old soul. It's like Dr. Venkalaswaran said, you're a free spirit, *wú jū wú shù* (unconstrained); you don't want to have to take care of somebody, especially a grown man. He was fun, but he was a kid."

Pretty insightful. We walked a little further in silence, before she asked, "Why do you bring it up now? That was so long ago."

"I felt like I needed to tell you. I know you are not a worrier, but . . . I thought you might."

"No worries," Lulu said. "Look at me, I'm still single. All that time on Mars. There were only a few men and no sex allowed anyway." She guided me back to my room and helped me lie down in my bed.

"I'm getting better," I said to myself, exhausted. Lulu went over to turn the television on and open the curtains to let the light in. Charlie, having just turned the monitor off, was annoyed. "Mars can't be that bad," I chided.

"Oh, let me tell you about Mars," Lulu said. "Mars sucks."

"What?" I laughed.

"Mars sucks," Lulu exclaimed. "There's no water, there's dust everywhere, the light is always dim and a crappy shade of orange, in my day it took *forever* to get there, puny gravity, no oxygen, no magsphere so you are always getting zapped with radiation." She sat down on the bed next to me and leaned in. "See this line in my face," she pointed to a crease in her forehead. "That's from Mars." I think she exaggerated the wrinkle.

"People do romanticize that place," I said.

"I know because they've never been there. I have, and it sucks."

"Interesting," Charlie said, listening to the two of us. "I'll record that as an official summary of life on the fourth planet from our star. No sex, crappy light."

"Maybe they're related."

I have heard variants of the same rant from Lulu before and she always made me laugh. She jokingly blames most everything on her time on the red planet, which was around the year 2087. It was sweet of her to make me laugh, and to so deftly change the subject.

Not long after the Mars stories, Lulu left for her official duties, while I stayed in rehabilitation at the hospital with Charlie. As I grew stronger, I spent more time working. The Republic had just launched two transport lighters from Chechnya while light fighting had begun in the north. I would no longer have the luxury of a hospital bed or flying commercial aircraft. But I was ready.

TWENTY-EIGHT

Implant Record Date 19 November 2104
Grozny

Charlie and I flew with Lulu on a military craft to the Caucasus. On the flight, Lulu's mood had become more serious. "What's wrong?" I asked, Charlie looking on as we sat along the wall of the cabin of the mid-range military transport, a lighter fitted for long, continued flights but no armaments.

Lulu was silent for a long time before responding. "It's been too long since I've visited my mama and baba."

I wondered if there wasn't something more, but I left Lulu alone as we sat in silence most of the flight to Grozny to take up where John Mar left Amanta Kokotova, at the capital of the Republic.

I was able to keep pace with the others through the Parliamentary Hall in Grozny, but only because Amanta and Charlie slowed down for me, Lulu following behind with our security spread around the Hall. The surgery improved my memory, but I had some damage to my motor control, especially in my legs. While I had been recuperating, Amanta made her international rounds as the Minister of Foreign Affairs but had yet to go to Moscow. Tensions in the weeks since my procedure had grown, and the opinion of counsel was for her to delay.

"Hey, Cali girl, you look good," Chase hugged me as he and Zévic Toreli joined us from a conference hall where people were leaving. Chase and Zévic were here for meetings with government officials on contingency plans for Svoboda Corporation in the event the Vainakh forces invaded.

"Thanks, I'm feeling pretty good," I replied, glancing at Lulu. I thought she was worried about me, and I wanted her to know I was okay.

"Jenny Hsu is tough," Amanta said as she stopped and turned to us. I looked down at my cane, which was supporting me as I walked.

"I know, but I still worry," Chase said.

"I will need to discuss our position with Prime Minister Mdivani," Amanta said, referring to the head of state of the Republic. The position she referred to was the growing crisis with renegade Vainakh forces, and the potential for Russian intervention. The Republic was already looking for help from NATO and the United Nations, but that was never a sure thing.

"If you would, please wait for me in the reception room." She pointed. "Feel free to order whatever you like. This should only take an hour or so, but I will call you if I need you, Jenny." With that she turned and entered the office of the Prime Minister where he was waiting for her.

"Jenny, Charlie, why don't you go in," Chase said. "Zévic and I need to speak to the Commerce Secretary before they leave. We'll be right back."

Charlie and I went with Lulu to the reception room, where we found plastiwood replicas nineteenth century furniture, of upholstered chairs, sofas, and bookshelves. Cleverly hidden were the comforts of modern life: monitors, computer terminals, and other amenities well blended into a nice wooden façade of oak, windows facing the large courtyard and landing area outside. What were once gravel paths and grassy retreats was filled with troops retreating from the north where the Vainakh were advancing. Some NATO supported Republic troops were setting up a perimeter in the event the Vainakh got this far.

"Well, I need a cup of coffee. Lulu, do you need anything?" I asked.

The Sixth Traveler

"No, I'm fine."

I went over to the barista, somewhat gingerly as I left my cane behind. I could see Lulu watching me and I knew it pained her. I put a green ceramic coffee cup underneath the nozzle of the dispenser, enjoying the hissing sounds of the steam as a frothy dark liquid extruded from the filter basket.

"Well, I will need to use this time to report to John," I said. "Things appear stable for now, but I have a feeling that could change." I wanted to shake Lulu from whatever funk she was in. I glanced at the Special Forces team Lulu commanded and said, "Lucky we have you here."

I turned and went over to Lulu, cup in one hand. I placed my coffee on the table before us and sat next to her. I cautiously looked over at her. It was the first time I had seen anything close to tears in her eyes. I started to say something before she spoke.

"That day, four years ago," Lulu started.

"Stop, Lulu."

"No, let me finish. That day on the *Second Surfer*, when I first knew something had happened. I only had a few seconds to make a decision. It wasn't clear what was going on, but I knew it wasn't good. I didn't think it had impacted us."

"I know, Lulu."

"I didn't get to where I am by not taking risks. It's a reflex."

"We all knew the risks."

"Really?" She turned to me.

"Yes." I could see the pain in her face.

"I don't want you to feel bad, Lu."

She took a deep breath, then looked away, saying under her breath, "I do anyway."

"It's all right," I said, putting my hand on her arm. "I'm feeling stronger every day. It inspired me. Heck, in a few months I might go for an op to get rid of some of my bitchy sarcasm."

Lulu started laughing through her tears. "I doubt it will work."

Kevin M. Faulkner

I was glad to see a Lulu smile. "In any case, we need to make it through whatever happens next," I said, looking up at the monitor. The news was reporting that Vainakh troops closing in on the Chechen border. There was no fighting, for now. Amanta convinced the Republic's Prime Minister to take a defensive stance with the troops remaining loyal to the Republic; try to move as many people as possible to the mountains and stay there.

"We have lifters in the courtyard waiting for us," Lulu said, referring to the anti-gravity driven craft gradually taking the place of helicopters in most military units throughout the world. She must have seen that I was nervous. "I need to check in with my team," Lulu said as she rose to leave.

I made my report to John as we watched the news monitors as the hour passed and darkness fell outside. He was in San Diego, but making plans to find his way here, likely through Turkey. I imagined seeing him here and rebuked myself for such notions. I distracted myself on my computer as I wrote my report and took in the news. We sat quietly in the reception room. Chase and Zévic joined us, but Amanta still had not. I grew concerned.

"Where is that woman? She hasn't called," I said. I looked over at our security, eight men and women, part of a combined Chinese and American Special Forces team, standing guard outside our door. Lulu commanded the team, and she personally knew its members. Given the proximity of hostile forces, Russian or Vainakh, the team carried heavy weapons and wore their military armor. I was concerned when I saw one of the men talking into his headset, and Lulu into hers while the others grew alert. Lulu came over to me.

"Please lie down and rest," Lulu said, addressing us all. "I'll send someone to ask about Amanta." She returned to one of her men and they went off together, as others positioned themselves. I was truly exhausted and managed to fall asleep on the couch (without the aid of my app), as did Chase and Zévic.

The Sixth Traveler

I was somewhat resigned to the situation, having grown close to Amanta Kokotova and the cause of her and her people. I feared military conflict was inevitable but was more worried about the longer-term future of the Republic. *Was this all a waste of time?*

The room had darkened as night fell. I dozed off for a couple of hours, and I was half asleep when I woke to the sound of chatter in the hallway. I looked up and could see the news on the monitor above. *Was that VK troop movement the arrow was pointing at?*

I heard a thud. Still groggy, I rose, grabbing Charlie who sat alert next to me. "What was that?" I asked, looking for Lulu, who was already at the door talking to her team.

There were more thuds on the roof then plasma fire. Immediately, three members of our security came into the room. Lulu approached one of them, talking quietly, then left the room, only turning to say, "Stay put." I turned to look for calm in Charlie and Chase.

"Don't worry, we are well guarded," Zévic said.

Lulu came back, this time carrying a heavy-caliber weapon: a plasma rifle and grenade launcher. She wasted no time getting down to business. "All of you, go to the back of the room," she said in a calm but commanding voice. "We need to secure the room and prepare to evacuate."

"What about the Prime Minister, and Amanta?" I asked. Lulu didn't answer. Events unfolded rapidly and I remember certain moments like scenes in a movie, but I mostly remember the utter chaos.

I turned to Chase for answers but of course he had no more idea of where Amanta could be than the rest of us. I could see through the open doorway some quiet movement, men running across the Hall among commlink chatter and hand signals. Ghoulish androids with the sword-on-shield Vainakh markings were filtering into the building, their presence unmistakable in the chilling electronic chirps they would make as they homed onto a target.

I glanced at Charlie. She knowingly whispered, "I can't pick anything up, signals are scrambled." The relative silence ended as a blast of plasma shot across our line of sight in the corridor and I could hear shouting.

Lulu gave orders to our Special Forces guard, some in battle language I failed to understand. But I could see Charlie reacting.

Three of the men fell back to stand directly in front of us. The others took positions at the entrance to our chamber. I could hear the sickening *thump-thump-thump* of plasma discharges in the distance but growing closer.

"There is an exit in the back of this room that goes to the courtyard. Be prepared to leave when I order," Lulu said. I looked out the window toward the lifters and helicopters in the courtyard. Their engines were starting as people ran, soldiers taking position. From above, I could see a man drifting down, his black parachute blotting out the stars in a moonless sky as he fell.

"What the hell," I said, open-mouthed. I didn't know much about warfare, but I had thought parachuting into combat areas was a thing of the past.

"Paratroopers," Charlie replied. We watched as men and battle androids fell slowly and rhythmically from the sky, creating an unreal scene outside of another world, a world where ghosts of war overwhelmed us. My mind flailed, and my heart raced. I had completely forgotten the weakness in my legs as I tried to stand and move. Charlie steadied me.

"Hold your positions," Lulu ordered, quietly. She looked back at us, "Get behind the sofa."

Lulu transformed in those moments. She brandished her plasma rifle as if it were weightless and took command of the worsening situation while hastening the escape of our small, vulnerable group. I looked on helplessly, not able to focus my mind on any one thing but the screech of terror running through my nerves.

The Sixth Traveler

"Shit," I said under my breath. You never know how you are going to react when you are in this situation, with plasma fire nearby and the sounds of men suffering. I was petrified, frozen with fear, and was thankful for Charlie's outstretched hand. I clutched it as if I were drowning.

"Don't worry, we'll be alright," Charlie said.

The reception room was quickly losing ground to an overwhelming Vainakh force. I could hear shouting from Republic forces, but a sickening silence from the hostiles. The nature of the fighting made one thing clear: this was no hostage situation. There would be no prisoners. The Vainakh meant to demonstrate a hardline stance.

I heard voices in the main hall, a mix of man and machine, and plasma fire. Our guards returned fire as one man fell, severely wounded. Lulu ran out and grabbed him from the floor and pulled him back into the room. She laid him down, and turned to return fire, not even bothering to take cover. I could see that she hit several men and androids in the distance. But she had also been hit, blood running down her side.

Lulu turned to us. "You need to evacuate, now."

"Where?" I had never been more frantic. "What about you? You're bleeding."

Lulu barked an order at her Special Forces team who were returning hostile fire, before looking back at me.

"*Qǐng yuánliàng wǒ* (Please forgive me)." Lulu turned to the corridor where the fighting was intensifying, her plasma rifle raised.

What was she doing?

Lulu yelled, "*Chung, Chung,*" in battle language, signaling with her rifle-free arm. Without hesitation, our Special Forces team reacted, one of them grabbing me around the waist to carry me through the back door to a waiting lifter in the courtyard. Another man carried the wounded soldier Lulu had brought in from the corridor. They guided Chase, Zévic, Charlie and me out as the last two soldiers covered us.

I had no time to react. All I could do was yell back to Lulu: "*Jiěmèi zhī jiān méiyǒu shé me kě yuánliàng de* (There is nothing to forgive among sisters)."

As I was carried away, I looked next to me to make sure Charlie and Chase were with me, and back for Lulu. The last image I had of our escape was of Lulu turning into the room one last time, aiming her rifle and returning fire in blazes of intense light as Vainakh androids poured into the room. As smoke filled the air all I could see were the streaks of red plasma. It was the last time I saw Wen Lu.

We ran toward the open hatch of a lifter, a small ten-seater. I was shoved inside as others followed behind, mostly soldiers. Fighting an overwhelming nausea, I focused my mind on the feeling in my hands, one hand holding on to the straps across my chest, the other on Charlie's hand.

"It will be alright," Charlie said. I don't remember responding, but I noticed that Charlie was focused, rendering aid to the soldiers around her. The lighter was quickly over-packed with the four of us and almost a dozen soldiers, some wounded. I thought that surely Lulu would be running toward us. I looked back to see the building where we had been exploding in a brilliant white light. I thought *she'll be in another lighter*. My heart sank as the hatch to our lifter closed, and our overloaded craft rocked and set alight without my friend.

Soldiers shouted orders as we lifted from the ground, gaining altitude. One brave soldier took control of a mounted gun and fired back at ground troops firing at us. We rapidly gained altitude, banking sharply, I guessed to avoid some weapon whose purpose was to block our escape. The lighter shook from repeated ground fire, but I hardly noticed. Someone yelled "countermeasures," and there was an explosion outside our craft. I could only see glowing, red-streaked clouds. Charlie assured the pilot as she took command of the lifter. Our craft shuddered then suddenly accelerated, adding to my terror. The bodies the human occupants were pushed back into our seats or into our harnesses, our faces contorted from g-forces only Charlie

The Sixth Traveler

could bear. I remember little else from that point on—the humans must have passed out.

I discovered later that Lulu had stayed behind, ordering her security team to escape. She acted as the final barrier to a storm of androids pouring through the parliament building, holding them off until she was overwhelmed. Her last act was to detonate her rifle to buy us all a little more time. It was a slight edge on life, a gift given to me by my friend. I wished I had told her I loved her.

I remember seeing Vainakh forces closing in around the Parliament as we left, those ghosts in the night. I thought I could see the State room where Amanta might have been. The house that Amanta Kokotova built on this world was ablaze. Her dream had been to find a new world where finally the fighting would stop. Amanta was at peace that night.

Kevin M. Faulkner

TWENTY-NINE

Implant Record Date 22 November 2104
Tsodoreti, Georgia

It had been only a few days since Chase, Zévic, Charlie and I escaped Grozny. I knew John Mar was on his way but was not sure when he would arrive. My mind was still overwhelmed by what had happened to us, and I was in a daze for the first couple of days in the Georgian town of Tsodoreti where we and many others from Chechnya were seeking refuge. Trying to regain my balance, I looked for Chase, who was seeing to a transport lighter that had been moved here to avoid capture by the VK.

"Who was taking delivery of this transport lighter?" Chase asked the supply chain captain as I walked up to them. We stood on the edge of the woods outside Tsodoreti, further into the hills away from town. The government had opened its border to refugees, considering it might be a target of fighting itself. The old hanger next to where the lighter was docked belied the wealth of hastily arranged technology inside. This lighter could carry over three hundred souls and six months of supplies. I was in awe of its size and sophistication. No longer the pincushion of the first lighters, its surface was smooth, with layered levels, in a matt black finish. Painted on its side was the colorful Republic pinwheel with the ships name, *Les Fidèle*, emblazoned on one side.

"It was bound for Grozny from India, but diverted here in the fighting," the captain said, still working on his lytfascia. I imagined it wasn't the first time he'd seen conflict.

I wondered if the captain would be making the trip to Ushguli. This same lighter would make many trips back and forth between Earth and Ushguli, bringing an ever-increasing number of people, now refugees. Amanta Kokotova had convinced the world's powers, except for Russia, to allow the Caucasus Republic the exclusive right to colonize Ushguli, her crowning achievement. It was sad that she would never see the fruit of her sacrifice.

Nor would Lulu. Little else was on my mind, and there were many moments when I drifted into a darker space. I couldn't shake the final images I had of her, bravely fending off VK fighters as blood covered one side of her face and body. There was no real way to deal with such losses. I did my best to honor Lulu; she was a woman who was full of life, and in a real sense she had given it to me. I found strength in focusing on hers.

"Do we have a flight manifest for its next voyage?" I asked Chase.

"Yes, we do, but not a complete one," Chase said. "Everything has been disrupted since the VK forces invaded the Parliament a week ago."

"Are you and Zévic part of the voyage?" I asked.

"No, we plan to go back to JPL for the time being to set up headquarters for the Corporation, and re-establish construction in Huntsville and Gothenburg," Chase said. "It no longer makes sense to stay here. Luckily, the venture with Galactina Aerospace is a papered deal, so that puts Svoboda Corporation in a better position to avoid nationalizing by the VK."

"The VK can have the scraps we left behind in Grozny," Zévic said with some venom in his voice, "we managed to get the computers, storage, plans and machine formers out and in route to Gothenburg and California."

"Can you still maintain flights off-world?"

"We estimate there are from eight to ten thousand people on Ushguli," Chase said, "the numbers are still increasing, but will obviously plateau soon. The population is limited only by how fast we can empty one lighter and fill another . . . and for as long as we can repeat that cycle."

Kevin M. Faulkner

I wondered at it all. Getting on board a still relatively unknown spacecraft to go to a world you had never seen. Most of the people of the Republic had no interest in going off-planet, either taking their chances in place or migrating elsewhere on foot. The most adventurous travelers were already on the Ushguli. Growing numbers of people were leaving now out of desperation. Older people, young families, poor, and others with nowhere else to go but with enough courage to make the journey. The Western media likened the situation to the earliest immigrants to North America from Europe, sailing uncertain waters for a fresh start. No matter how advanced we humans were, we were still willing to traverse a rugged, unknown passage to some promise land.

"Here comes John Mar," Chase said, waving and looking behind me into the path leading from the town through the woods.

"The question is: do *you* want to be a part of it?" John asked, coming up to us in a black armor vest that Chase and I also wore. Accompanying him was the assistant Foreign Minister Min Jaqeli, along with Nikhil Lecha, who took over as the acting Foreign Minister. His trademark smile was gone.

"John." We looked at each other for a moment before we embraced.

"It's good to see you," he said quietly.

"You must be Minister Jaqeli," I said, reaching out my hand, still holding John's hand with the other.

"Yes, it is good to meet you, Jenny."

"Jenny, I'm sorry about Wen Lu, and Amanta Kokotova. I know you were close to both of them."

"Thanks John." I let out a breath, not wanting to talk or think about it. "There's so much going on."

"Yes," John said. "The initial stage of migration looks like it will end soon. Things are developing." John looked back at the makeshift tent city in the distance, where caravans of refugees from the north were streaming in, hoping for a ride off-world or passage out of the region.

"Jenny, I hate to press at such short notice, but the Republic is in disarray," Jaqeli said, "We need to re-form what is left of the government, and that on a new planet. We need your help. I hope you will consider coming on this flight on what could be one of the last for some time."

"At least until we can get operations re-established in Sweden and the States, and refugees sorted out," Nikhil said.

"Yes, this and the several other lighters on the ground may be the last to leave for a while," Jaqeli said. "They will soon be vulnerable to the Vainakh advance."

"Jenny, it is of course your decision, but the firm will back whichever you choose," John said.

"Nikhil, Minister Jaqeli, I'm honored by your offer," I replied. John had already texted me their request, so I was expecting this, but wasn't sure I was ready to leave so much behind. "I will consider it."

Thinking of Lulu, I found myself wanting to be of service, to help in some way. I was overwhelmed by what was happening around me. There was a growing sense of urgency, as fighting could be heard in the background, the reverberations of war were growing louder by the hour, the terror on people's faces distinct. The confidence I felt before the Second Event had transformed to fear, but also empathy.

"Don't take too much time. We plan on launching as soon as possible, within the week," Chase said. "We are only delayed by the time it is taking to load supplies and equipment. Right now, earth moving equipment is at a premium, as are medical supplies."

"Minister," John said to Jaqeli and Nikhil, "I served in the US armed forces. I would like to assist with the evacuation." John was in a unique position to help those around him, inspiring me all the more to find some way to be of service.

"Thank you, John," Jaqeli said. Then he turned to me, "There is an inn near our temporary control center in town, I suggest you go there and stay until we are ready."

Kevin M. Faulkner

"Thanks, Minister."

"I'll find you soon," John said.

God, it's the Mayflower, I thought as we walked away toward the hamlet where we were staying. Charlie and I parted as John stayed behind. I was surprised at the difficulty I had in pulling away.

As soon as we had arrived in Tbilisi from Grozny, Jaqeli had found a room for us in a small hotel. It was in a small hamlet of older buildings with a street running down the center. There was a five-story building across from the inn that would serve as an administrative center. Its surface was patterned concrete with modern windows made to blend in with the rest of the building. As we approached, we became part of the flux of refugees moving from the north to the mountains deeper south of us. I had my few possessions with me in a backpack, and Charlie had only the clothing she wore and a small satchel.

The inn itself was in the middle of the town, with buildings mostly made from stone with black iron fittings around the windows and doorways. We entered from the street into the main lobby, an area that at one time must have been quiet and cozy, but now bustled with refugees. The two of us sat by a rustic stone fireplace, keeping warm with others who were seeking shelter. A woman went around with a carafe of coffee. A man sat across from us, and near the fire was a young girl who was with her mother, sitting next to Charlie and me. The woman held her youngest, an infant.

"What is it like on Ushguli?" the girl asked. Before I could formulate a response, Charlie answered.

"Well, life is simpler on the New World than on Earth," I could see that the adults were listening, so Charlie answered for everyone. "But improving all the time as more people and supplies arrive. They are all living in a small town they call Kokotova."

"There is plenty of fresh water on the planet already, though it must be boiled or filtered as a precaution, and the settlement is temperate, so there is not much need for heat, except for the night.

They are setting up reactors now and probing for geothermal sources of energy.

"They have a small hospital," Charlie continued, "it's simple, and they will need supplies from Earth for quite some time. It looks like farming will be possible there, they've just started growing crops. They even have some livestock brought from Earth, goats, and cattle. The native animals there are too small to pull a wagon," Charlie smiled at the girl, "like mice and squirrels. The settlement should be sustainable in a year or two. Even then, life on Ushguli will be simple."

"That could be a good thing," the girl's mother said.

I doubt the girl could relate to much of this, she looked worried. I looked at her mother and she smiled at me. I wanted to encourage the girl, so I searched for words she could understand. "It will be different from our life here, an adventure." I pointed to the stuffed animal she held in her lap. "What's his name?"

"Netta," the girl said, barely audible.

"Netta will like it there and the two of you will have fun on the New World, Ushguli. He'll have more room to play." She seemed to like that.

The man who had been sitting across from us wanted to speak. I noticed that he was wearing a nice leather jacket and was well-groomed. His shoes were clean and polished. Unusual in these circumstances, since most people here had to walk some distance.

"I hear it's paradise," the man said, "and if it is the last thing I do, I will put my children and their mother with me on board that ship so we can all leave this place." I wondered where his children might be.

"I came from Grozny," I said. "I can understand how you feel. I'm considering it myself."

"It is never going to change here, for hundreds of years it has been this way," The man continued, "And the gods are determined to make it a hundred more years."

Kevin M. Faulkner

"I hope not," I replied. I could see the girl next to us was restless, her mother consumed with her smallest child. I smiled at her and held her hand, bringing her next to me near the fire as we talked about our lives.

The room seemed to open after that, and questions and concerns filled the air.

"I hear there are new diseases on Ushguli," one person said.

"I don't have any information about that," Charlie calmly replied. "I have the latest news downloaded from the last returning vessel, and all is well. There are some problems adjusting to the atmosphere, but there are treatments for that, or bariatric masks to help adjust."

"What about the creatures there?" Someone asked out loud. Then there was a wave of questions. Mindful not to alarm the children, Charlie tried to address each, explaining how there would be an adjustment, but there were no dangers found after a search of the surface of the planet. The oceans were still a mystery, but after months of exploration there had been no reports of deaths or injuries due to any life on Ushguli. We would need inoculations, but that is all. As she said three months ago in Bengaluru to a room full of scientists and businesspeople, no monsters.

We continued to rest in the lobby of the hotel for an hour or more as the day passed. I kept in constant contact with John via text. Without a formal declaration of our feelings towards one another we suddenly seemed bound as if it were the most natural state of things. I wanted to know his every move, and he did the same.

As night fell we eventually made our way to a small room upstairs that we shared with the same women and two children. The girl was holding my hand now as we got ready for bed. The face of the man in the leather jacket was on my mind as I fell asleep in the tiny room we shared, Charlie lie on the floor next to me while the women from the fireplace and her two kids took the other two beds. The sounds of war continued into the night, making it difficult to

The Sixth Traveler

settle down. *If I went on board that lighter would I be taking her place?* I wondered, as I drifted off to a fitful sleep.

Kevin M. Faulkner

THIRTY

Implant Record Date 23 November 2104
Tsodoreti

I thought I heard an explosion and the rumble of fighter jets. It was only five am. I wondered briefly where Charlie was then realized it was not a dream that she had quietly left the dark room over an hour ago. I was still waking when the door opened and she appeared.

"Jenny," she whispered, trying not to disturb the children. The mother briefly opened her eyes then fell back asleep.

"What is it?"

"The VK have advanced overnight. They are sending fighter jets north of us and say they will block further flights in and out of our area after a forty-eight-hour window."

"What? How so fast?" I was still groggy, trying to think. It dawned on me that much of the Vainakh's rapid advance could be attributed to the mechanization of armies and air forces. Today, much of that can be purchased as androids and drones. It's no wonder why Amanta didn't trust androids. No training, just programming and a remote control. "Damn." I went back into the room and dressed.

I texted John saying we were on our way. Leaving the inn, we walked down the street until the military vehicle John sent stopped to pick Charlie and me up. It was still dark as we traveled several miles away to government buildings where Nikhil and Jaqeli had organized with other diplomats and military leaders, the few that were left.

We pulled up to a drab, white brick building, at least as close as we could. There were military vehicles blocking the way, and we had to pass through a guard gate of barbed wire before getting in. The guards were suspicious of Charlie, but a call inside to John eased their concerns. To complete the trust, John suggested two guards join us as we were guided into the heart of the building where the command center was located. Later, we were formally joined by two members of Lulu's security team that safely got us out of Grozny.

"Jenny, I am glad you are here," Nikhil said. He was there with John, Jaqeli, Chase, and Zévic. "I am sure the android has filled you in on what has happened. We have asked for help from European officials and NATO, who have established a Protected Zone to hold off the Vainakh troops long enough to allow one more wave of lighters to leave and allow other Earth-bound flights out of this area, and more refugees in. But we don't have much time."

"Your government and the Chinese are negotiating with the Russians," Jaqeli said. "It is clear that Moscow has some influence over the Vainakh. We are hoping for a cease fire, but—"

"Hell, cease fire against what? There isn't much left," I said, exasperated. I could hear shelling in the distance, louder than yesterday.

"I know," Nikhil said. "The Protected Zone extends across the border with Turkey and Iran, but the Vainakh appear intent on occupying the space in between and halting all traffic in and out."

My mind raced.

"Nikhil, have you tried to contact the Russian Foreign Minister, Sokolov?" I asked.

"Yes, but he won't acknowledge me."

"I suggest we complete this last mission to Ushguli soon, by tomorrow," Chase declared. "I don't trust this window they say we have. Jenny, the time is now if you plan to leave. Zévic and I will be leaving soon ourselves."

"I agree," John said. I could see that he was tired, likely not having slept much, if at all.

I looked over at Charlie. She probably knew what I was about to do.

Kevin M. Faulkner

"Jenny," Nikhil started, "there is a negotiated corridor between here and Turkey through the Protected Zone. If you want, I can call the assistant Minister in Istanbul and clear passage for you. We have diplomats in Istanbul who were waiting for passage here."

I thought: *The Republic did garner the trust of its people; they actually want to come back into a war zone for their country . . . or to escape with their country.*

John looked at me and said, "It's up to you of course."

I was filled with emotions, many at that point. Part of me wanted to jump into a new life of extraterrestrial attorney, influencing and making laws of first impression. With that excitement was also a level of hesitation; a feeling that I needed something to cover my losses, a sheath for the knife in my heart. I wanted its strength; it simply needed a place where it could do no harm.

"Okay . . . wait. I need to make a call first. Minister, may I use the office down the hall?"

"Of course," Nikhil said. "And if we may, we need the android to help link with the servers and set up our communications with the outside."

"Of course," Charlie said.

I walked down the hallway to an office I had passed on the way in, closing the door. The semi-dark room was lit only by a small window, and I left it that way. Pushing my hair back and gathering my thoughts, I sat before a phaeton on the table to the side. I paused for several moments, feeling an urge to weep but not sure of which sadness to shed tears for.

"I don't know what to do."

For most of my life I treated relationships as merely functional. Even the fickle threads I kept with surfing brahs easily lapsed at a whim. Like so many other things friendships were disposable. I saw them as too much work. Affirmation of my humanity was never my thing and the fear of loneliness never overcame my fear of someone's intrusion.

The Sixth Traveler

If anything, I feared commitment. What was expected? How much time would this take? Could I empathize with someone's failure? Could I cheer for their success? Would it matter? I always assumed that people needed something from me. That assumption was easily affirmed because it was often true. It never dawned on me that someone might simply need me. Expectations were indeed evil, and I avoided their necessity.

That started to change with Dr. Venkalaswaran. My defenses and indifference slowly melted with the man who wanted nothing but the thoughts in my head. The reason was simple: Venka didn't want things, or the performance of a task (at least, it didn't seem paramount), or even my recognition. What he did want was something that I never realized I needed so much to give: what was on my mind, how I felt, what motivated me, and why it mattered. With little judgment, and great empathy, he took it.

My thoughts at that moment were of Wen Lu, whose strength flowed through me. Losing her, I needed Venka more than ever, if only in the recombination of electrons on a phaeton screen. I had the phaeton dial the number I had long since memorized. It didn't take long to see that familiar face.

"Aravinda."

"Jenny," Venka's voice was sympathetic. He knew that Wen Lu had died. Speaking to Venka was not enough: I needed to be seen, and to see his face so I could know what to feel. Once I knew, I could grieve.

We talked for almost an hour through static filled signals before Libra pulled Venka away. After the phaeton went dark, I sat alone and wept. It was only when I heard people talking in the hallway that I woke from my thoughts and left the office to find Jaqeli. He was working with Charlie on the communication system, Charlie's hand on an archaic connector relaying information she received.

"Hey, are you okay?" John asked.

Kevin M. Faulkner

"Yes," I said, confidently. I looked at Charlie, who smiled back at me, nodding. I felt a purpose I had never known. I said for Nikhil and John to hear: "We would be honored to go."

* * *

Most of the day had passed when John and I left the command center while Charlie stayed behind to help with communications. Both of us were exhausted, yet I was hyperaware of John walking next to me. Thinking of Kepler, I looked at John and took his hand. Perhaps it was fatigue combined with Kepler's "estimation" (and Charlie's confirmation) that John was in love with me that lowered my defenses. I could feel John's energy reciprocated through me.

"There is a place I saw between the buildings down the street, a courtyard. Let's head there for a while," I said as I led the way. It was midday and sunny. The sounds of fighter jets screeched overhead but became more distant once in the overgrowth of an unkept garden in the courtyard. We found a shaded bench.

We were both tired and emotional. John was looking at me, waiting to say something. I spoke first: "I've lost a friend. I've just committed to leaving Earth and all that I know. But right now I just want to be with you."

His weary eyes softened as he said, "I've been thinking of you for a long time."

"We're in the tree together."

"But more than brother and sister," he replied as he leaned in to kiss me. We embraced as we fell together on the bench and slept in each other's arms. It was all we had the energy for.

* * *

The Sixth Traveler

I fell asleep that evening in my room at the inn reflecting on the past, the time just after my mother left. Though I used to hold bitterness of that time in my life, looking back, I can see it marked a turning point for me. It marked the period in which I became a young woman. My feelings of those days have transformed from anger and ambivalence, to what I can only describe as acceptance.

I remembered stepping into the living room of our home just outside Seattle. It was the middle of the day but the room was dead, the orange tinted drapes darkening the carpeted floor with a glow that left everything washed out, including my father. He was planted in front of the flickering glow of the television, his eyes glazed over, with a bottle of whiskey between his feet on the floor. It was his half-hearted attempt to hide his rapid disintegration from Patrick and me. I loved him for it.

Nonetheless, I decided things had to change.

"Dad, we need to take Patrick and get out of Seattle," I remember telling him. It had been about four months since the spring of 2080 when my mother left. In spite of dad's best efforts at the time, the kitchen smelled, the weeds were taking over the yard, the laundry was piling up, and Patrick was flailing, lost in his computer and phone, doing who knows what.

"Let's just move west, near Uncle Jack in Port Angeles. You can find a job there."

"It's not that easy," he replied, "and school is too important."

My father was a gentle soul, now a damaged one. He didn't want to disturb our studies, but we were clearly past that. What was happening to us permeated everything.

"They have schools in Angeles."

"You're too young, Juke. I'll be fine." He said this without looking at me.

"Patrick and I will be fine in another school."

There was some silence before I gathered my courage.

"I'm worried about you, Dad." I loved that old house, and I knew it was close to where dad worked, but he was worthless there now. I was guessing they were about to ask him to leave anyway. I think he wanted them to. The memories in this house were eating him alive, but he did not have the will to do anything about it.

My father sat motionless, and I was left wondering what to do next. I knew I had to do something. In a rare act of pluck, I pulled his arm until he rose from his drunken stupor from the couch and I guided him to the kitchen. I plopped him down (really, he plopped himself) on a chair and I started some coffee, as much as a twelve-year-old could do. I must have seen it in a movie.

I could see in my father's expression, and the way he held his body, the pain he was holding inside. We both suffered, but I had nothing to show for it, not even a tear. He couldn't bring himself to really talk to me. He tried his best to hide his pain, but we played cards while he drank coffee. He talked about work, I talked about school, and several hours passed by. It was after midnight when we called it quits.

"Let's call Uncle Jack in the morning."

Patrick was asleep, but on my way to bed I looked in on him, only nine years old. For me, it was the best I had slept in a while.

I was ready to leave that place.

In the following weeks I almost single-handedly did a month's worth of the laundry, then packed our possessions from boxes I scrounged up from the grocery store. I got dad to call his brother Jack, and from the tone of the call, it sounded good. We planned a moving date, just before school started. Uncle Jack and Aunt Nay arrived during the last two days of packing and helped with the big stuff. When dad wasn't looking, I dumped his whiskey. He probably knew, but never said a word. Uncle Jack was agreeable, he was a health nut, always into fitness and food, and never drank as far as I could tell. I was grateful for Uncle Jack and Aunt Nay's presence, and it seemed to bring my father and Patrick alive. Dad and Uncle Jack were not super close, and Jack and Nay didn't have any kids, but they all got along just fine.

"Let's just leave the rest," Uncle Jack said after we finished filling his borrowed moving van as much as we could. Patrick climbed in the back seat as I followed him. Patrick stayed buried in his computer games, which was just as well. It made it all easier at the time.

Except for some things I found in my mother's dresser and kept for myself, we left behind all the things that she had not already taken with her. From that day on my brother and I heard little about her. We lived with Jack and Nay for several months in Port Angeles before we found a little house of our own nearby. Occasionally, I would hear hushed discussions between my dad, aunt, and uncle about my mother, but even that faded with time.

Over the next couple of years my father found another job and settled down. It seemed to be consulting type of work, mostly out of our home. The place we stayed in was smaller than our home in Seattle, but we didn't care. My brother seemed content, making friends and moving on, apparently oblivious to our mother as Aunt Nay took her place.

I, on the other hand, was not the same. I was content, but my world was different, less colorful, less alive. It didn't dawn on me at the time that I could drop it. I felt I had to carry the family burden, to own it. As I grew older, it simply became a part of me and I took it for granted.

I remember the last day in Uncle Jack's house, the white clapboard exterior and patches of green grass in the front, a single hemlock standing sentinel. The details of that day have become vague, but with each passing year the feelings were warmer, acquiring a significance I didn't see until I was much older.

"Jen, you did the right thing calling us," my uncle said to me as we sat in his little garage, too full to hold his vehicle. It was old and dingy, with tools hanging from the walls in a random fashion, and dust from years of woodworking caked on the items most unused. There was a smell of linseed oil and lacquer that appealed to me,

Kevin M. Faulkner

somehow relaxing as I imagined the vapors permeating my mind and dissolving my burdens. It was his retreat and had become mine while I lived with him.

"I like it here," I said, watching him sand the upside-down sailboat. Uncle Jack smiled as he worked, steam rising from his familiar dusky green coffee mug encircled with brown spindle whorls of Native American Salish designs. I would watch him take a sip and imagine myself doing the same one day.

"Your dad will be fine, and you can come here anytime."

As Uncle Jack spoke, something caught my eye that I had probably seen many times before but had never paid attention to. My mind simply filtered it away until that moment.

"Besides, it will give us time to go fishing," he said as I continued to look past him. Just over his shoulder, adjacent to the lumber stacked against the wall.

"Yeah, definitely." I stared past him, hypnotized. The image will never leave my mind, characterizing my life from that point forward.

Uncle Jack turned to look for whatever it was that I was so enthralled with.

"Or maybe . . ."

My line of sight ended at a seven-foot cream-colored tear drop whose surface was hidden in layers of old wax, its brand partially revealed in black lettering and bold neon streaks, ending in one black fin.

A surfboard.

THIRTY-ONE

Implant Record Date 24 November 2104
Tsodoreti to Kokotova, planet Ushguli

I woke from a dream in the dark room. Though the room was silent I felt I could hear my heart pounding and fading dreams of conversations still in my ears. They seemed important. I looked around to see the woman, her baby, and the little girls asleep, and Charlie's eyes open, looking at me. My phone said it was 2:36 a.m.

"It's okay," she whispered.

I opened my phone and looked at John Mar's stats. He was awake. I texted: "I need to see you."

Within seconds, he texted back: "Go downstairs, I will be there in ten minutes."

I dressed, biding my time, but found myself at the door in less than a minute. Glancing back at Charlie, I started to say something. She smiled at me, so I said nothing.

I stepped out of the door and walked down the dusty, wooden stairs of this ancient inn, likely built in the late twentieth century. It had only been moments since John texted me, but my mind was frantic. Several travelers were lying next to the flickering sparks of a fire in the stone fireplace of the lobby. I quietly placed a log on the dying embers and sat in an open spot on the brick landing within range of the growing fire's heat.

I tried to look away from the street entrance from the lobby, but eventually gave in. *Who was I kidding?* There was silence but for the crackling fire next to me and the sound of male voices outside in the falling snow, the light of a cigarette passing between them. The inn keeper, an older lady behind a counter, leaned against its wooden surface trying to stay awake, fighting heavy eyes, cycling from falling asleep to bouncing awake.

I was mesmerized by the snow fall, large flakes glancing gently against the fogged glass of the windows. "*Prikhodit kazhdyy god ran'she* (Comes earlier each year)," the inn keeper said (Her words were translated in my implant), eyes closed.

I listened to the flakes of frozen snow and ice, uncommon serenity for me and the sleeping guests. The log I had placed on the fire began to flame, making a crackling sound that was a visceral reflection of my emotions and created a dance of light in the dimly lit room.

When John stepped in the door, I turned to him and I was found. The older lady took notice and looked at the two of us with no expression on her face, placing her tired head back onto her hand. "*Poteryat' druga legche, chem nayti* (It's easier to lose a friend than to find one)," she said with her eyes closed. *I suppose she'd seen all this before*, I thought.

I ran to John, embracing him as if I would never see him again. He pushed me back, placing his hands around my face so that he could look into my eyes. Our lips pressed against one another and as soon as I was found, I closed my eyes and I was lost. I had waited years for this; our worlds coalescing as we both let ourselves come undone.

Without a word he took my hand and we went outside. I was wearing the coat I had purchased in town the day before. My boots were on, but the straps undone; the moments it would take to press the activator to tighten them around my calf were moments I no longer had to give. Their thick treads made tracks in the slush left from the snow falling on the warm ground but clung to the grass around us as we walked across the small yard in front of the inn. We passed the two men I had heard before and I could see they were soldiers. They glanced at us only briefly before turning back to one another. I imagined in a brief moment the things that must be

The Sixth Traveler

running through their minds: mothers, girlfriends, wives, lives they have somewhere else, passing the time with one another until they can rejoin that world again.

We hurried across the street and into a stone-faced building. John typed in an access code and held his hand to a sensor. There was a click and a rush of sudden warmth as the door opened. We walked into a darkened lobby of tiled floors and walls. A security guard looked up from his desk toward us. John simply said, "I am with the Republic," and flashed a badge. The guard waved his hand.

Before following John, I looked back through the window into the shivery dark outside at those men we had passed. *Who knows? They could be running. Scared. Who could blame them? Who is there to understand? Who is there to forgive?*

John led me through the darkened lobby, past a set of elevators, to a stairway. Two flights of stairs led us to an open hallway. Except for the hum of desk computers, and the occasional lamp, all was quiet and dark. We didn't speak a word; we didn't have to. My hand in John's, I was aware of every sensation, parsing each as if it were the first I had felt, and would never experience again.

Through a transparent wall to a darkened conference room I could see the snow silently fall outside, a gusty wind forming layered patterns. On instinct, I opened the door and pulled the man attached to me inside the darkness. At the center of the room was a black-topped table reflecting several soft night lights along the wall illuminating paintings of men from the past, and the glow of the night through the windows. John made the wall to the hallway opaque as I dropped my coat and any pretext of reason. John pushed aside a chair and lifted my body onto the table as we embraced one another.

I grabbed John's head, his hair in my hands, pressing my lips against his as his arms engulfed me. I could feel my tears on both of our faces as we consumed one another.

"I love you. I've always loved you."

Was it worth it?

Kevin M. Faulkner

Of course, it didn't matter; it never does in those moments. It was who we were—naked, scared humans in a cave hiding from the wild things outside. Drawing this man to my body was the most natural and ancient of acts, a passion that has played out a billion times. Yet somehow it all felt new.

* * *

I still wore the thick, wool coat we had found from the day before. It was a cold morning, snow on the ground from the night before, and starting to fall again. Underneath, I layered up with whatever else I had. Among other items, I had my phone, lytfascia, an extra battery, two changes of clothes, and a few small trinkets. The clothing I still had on was thermally adjusting, but everything else was ancient. My coat was made from old-fashioned cotton-wool material.

John met Charlie and me at the little inn, and traveled with us by bus to the place where the *Les Fidèle* was docked, sitting in a docking saddle, its landing gear like the legs of an insect extended against the earth. I was glad for his presence, and that of two soldiers, part of what was left of the security team that Lulu had led only days ago. I could hear the renewed sounds of fighting in the distance, muted by the snow but ever present. It is not something that I could ever get used to.

As we left the old electric bus John walked next to me as we made our way to the waiting lighter. The snow picked up its pace as we approached the parked spacecraft. The wind was light, allowing a sort of fog to form and hiding the spacecraft's unbelievable size, creating the illusion that we were entering a portal into an alien realm.

I took John's hand and looked up at him. He squeezed back. We walked that way until we got to the checkpoint. Several Republic guards were checking bags and papers, allowing some to pass, one or two at a time, some alone, some as a couple, and some families with small children. The snow continued to fall all around us.

"John, I want you to come to Ushguli. As soon as you can."

"I will." He bent down and kissed me, and we embraced in a long kiss for several moments, hugging one another.

"I love you, Jenny," he said, as he looked down into my eyes. I knew he meant it. Kepler knew it, now I do.

"I love you too," I said back to him. There was still a sense of urgency around us, as the enormous lighter came to life, its systems warming up. The guards guided people inside.

"I will see you soon, both of you," John said, looking at Charlie.

"Take care of one another."

"We will," Charlie said to the two of us. Before we parted, John embraced Charlie. I could hear John whisper to Charlie, "I won't be long."

As John Mar walked away he looked back, waving. We went through the check point then toward the open cabin door of the *Les Fidèle*. I kept looking back at John. He was a fading shadow among the other souls gathered to find passage on the same vessel or wishing a loved one well as they parted.

I dug around in the bottom of my bag to make sure I had everything as we approached the *Fidèle* and found that I still had the hula doll Lulu had given to me. My fingers ran over it as my emotions surged at the feeling of the plastic strings of a skirt and the girl's long, black hair. "This is for you, girl," I said to myself, finding the strength to move forward.

I remember as a small child learning about the English pilgrims sailing to America on the famous *Mayflower*. I was struck that these people would leave the relative comfort of their English homeland to sail upon what was an unknown and treacherous sea, possibly filled with monsters, pirates, disease, and if nothing else, boredom. I thought that they must have either had an unusually bright image of what was to come, or an unusually dark life where they were. How bad could it be? I wondered if we weren't at the same point in history now, as I stood in line with Charlie to board our own *Mayflower*.

"Popular place," I joked, hiding my nerves. I held my passport and travel voucher, a document giving me permission to travel to Ushguli with my property, an android. At this point it felt odd to ascribe ownership to Charlie. She had become a companion to me, a friend.

"Sure, you want to go with me? I can be a pain in the ass." Charlie pretended to consider my proposition.

"Nonetheless, I want to go."

I loved Charlie.

Most of the people in line with us had been given clearance to travel months ago, and at the time I would imagine there was no rush. That has all changed. The gravity of the situation hit me as the immediate window of opportunity for escape was rapidly closing. It was unclear when it would open again.

I reluctantly released my solitary bag of worldly possessions as a security team rummaged through it for bombs, weapons, and anything that could carry parasites, bugs, seeds, or other items disruptive of a fragile planet. I thought of what I was leaving behind: family, surfboards, my favorite coffee shops, and bars. John.

I was ushered onto the lighter, looking back to see that Charlie was with me. She wrapped her arm into mine. I could hear one of *Les Fidèle's* attendants say that the transport lighter was filled well over its capacity with almost four hundred people seeking sanctuary. Walking inside I felt conflicting pangs of good fortune and guilt to be on board. I took in the sleek look of the interior, no doubt the handiwork of Chase Adeane, the passenger compartment in the style of a futuristic commercial liner.

"Twenty minutes," a voice over the speaker called out, disturbing my train of thought. "Please take your seats."

Min Jaqeli was busy getting supplies loaded, people settled, and what leadership could fit in situated. He eventually made his way to

Charlie and me, both of us seated in a general boarding section of the spacecraft, but he was otherwise on the go. His concern for me was kind, as he placed a great deal of importance on my presence.

I had a view of the passenger door and could see people filing in, some fighting with guards to be let on, some walking away disappointed. Most showed a passport and documents as they passed through metal detectors and body sensors. An occasional loud alarm would signal the removal of someone from the line, while others passed into the lighter cabin. Some were excited, but most were weary. I saw a hand with a wad of cash, and another hand took it. The man in the leather jacket from yesterday sat down just meters from Charlie and me.

I turned to Charlie, and before I could ask, she said, "He's a criminal." I started to protest when she added, "Don't do anything."

What? I fumed, then relaxed. "Bad finds a way."

"Yes," Charlie replied. "I'm afraid humans are programmed for it. That's why you have a job." I hadn't exactly thought of it that way before.

The door to the lighter shut with a hiss and attendants began ushering people down the aisle, imploring them to sit or otherwise secure themselves. Not everyone could find a seat. It took some time to prepare the lighter for departure. I recalled when the doors to the *Second Surfer* shut four years ago.

"I guess there's no movie on this flight," I said to Charlie, again masking anxiety.

"Probably not." Then she followed in her usual clairvoyance, "Don't worry. We'll be fine. Things have changed quite a bit since the *Second Surfer*." She patted my forearm.

"Prepare for departure," A voice said over the cabin intercom. The attendants took their seats. Moments later, I could hear mechanical sounds outside the lighter, followed by a rocking sensation. The craft lifted slowly at first and as momentum built the lighter lifted directly upwards, creating an unusual feeling of being pressed down into my seat. The anti-gravity drive made a humming

Kevin M. Faulkner

sound, pushing the mass of the lighter against the gravity of the Earth. Over the time span of several minutes, the sky visible through the windows went from snow white to blue, then gradually dark as stars appeared. Amazingly, getting from the ground to the outer edges of the Earth's atmosphere, over 400 kilometers, sounded effortless with the anti-gravity drive and minor tugging of the guiding rockets.

Les Fidèle attained a stabilizing orbit around the Earth for thirty minutes or so while the lighter drive heated up. I tried to close my eyes to rest but could not get my mind off my companions, soon to be cohabitants of a new world: children of all ages, women and men holding hands, caring for young (and grabbing them down as they tried to float away in the zero gravity), clasping their possessions. Some passengers had excited expressions, some had frowns and wide, worried eyes. One woman cried and out of instinct Charlie rose—floating through the cabin under the protest of the flight attendant—to comfort her.

"We will depart Earth's orbit in five minutes," a woman's voice said over the intercom within the cabin. Attendants went down the aisles of seats to make sure everyone was fastened in. "Miss," the flight attendant said to Charlie, "You'll have to take your seat." I could see their point; if everyone started moving around in zero gravity it would be somewhat chaotic. The temptation was hard to resist.

Once the attendants were seated again, the iris of the windows near us closed. I was surprised at the effect that had on me.

"Charlie," I said, grabbing her harm. "I don't want to be alone."

"Nor do I." It was a statement, one that in the past I would have been embarrassed about. In her usual way, I knew Charlie understood.

Several moments passed and a soft hum filled the cabin as the lighter started its departure Event, beginning the jump to the Ushguli star system with little fanfare. The lights in the cabin dimmed, a low

The Sixth Traveler

hum deadened all other noise as the tympani plates (more a covering or arc now) prepared to light.

At the moment of the Departure Event the cabin went silent. Unconsciously, I held Charlie's hand and my body braced itself for the cataclysm it expected. I could see that Charlie was patting my hand, but I was detached from it all. I felt I was floating through the darkened cabin then accelerating through space. I could feel the accumulation of thousands of years of human existence coalesce into a blink of an eye, moving me to a state of terror. I wanted to look away, but there was nowhere to divert my gaze, and closing my eyes only brought vertigo.

I took Charlie's hand. *Help me.* My mind raced, and I closed my eyes, thoughts coming from all directions, but mostly, my deepest fears. I imagined my mother was there sitting across from me: "Why do you and your damn father do this to me," she shouted, drunken tears of rage in her eyes.

"I'm trying mom. I don't know what to do."

"You're not doing enough. It's not enough!"

"I'm sorry."

Suddenly, my mother became quiescent, but resolved.

"I'm leaving your father . . . you and your brother. I can't stay here any longer." My mother hesitated. Was it regret in her eyes? Surely, she couldn't have meant what she said. I waited, looking at her, with tears in my eyes, and the seeds of my own anger. *Why was she doing this? Why did my mother do this?* She stood, grabbed her bags, and left. She never looked back.

Charlie leaned into me, putting her forehead against mine.

"Charlie, I want to know."

"You do. Forgive her." Charlie said, gently. "What choice do you have?"

I took a deep breath as we held hands, awaiting our journey's end.

Kevin M. Faulkner

* * *

Another ten minutes passed—a total time of about twenty minutes in jump time—before we had completed the traversal of the sixty-four-light year distance to the Ushguli star system. A chime sounded over the cabin intercom followed by a static-filled voice calling out "Cross-check" and informing the cabin of the momentous event about to occur.

"To all weary travelers, may you come in peace," the captain said over the intercom.

The window irises promptly opened to reveal the crisp blackness of space, and in the distance, a blue planet dotted with white clouds, not unlike Earth. After several miscalculations in the event status of several missions, where lighters ended their journeys too close to a planet or star, lighters were programmed to exit their jump a safer distance from their intended destination. Thus, we had some time to travel at more Newtonian speeds, 80,000 kilometers per hour or so, slowing into a comfortable orbit around our new planet.

After several hours of travel, the light from Ushguli filled the portholes, eliciting excitement throughout the cabin. I could see landforms through the wispy white clouds, smaller and more evenly distributed around the planet than on Earth. About eighty percent of Ushguli was covered in water, where even the landforms were dotted with blue. There was some ice and snow at each pole. And, in the distance, on the other side of Ushguli, were two moons, *Execault* and *Renacault*, each about the size of Earth's moon. One of them had a purplish hue, the other was nearly black, creating an eerie scene through the porthole.

"There is more water on Ushguli than on Earth, and a variety of plant life on the land. Different from Earth, but a form of photosynthesis takes place just the same," Charlie said. "I will be interested in studying how it works. You can breathe the air fine, but it is denser than Earth's atmosphere, so it will take a while to get used to.

"Oh, and that large landform below us," she pointed out the window, "is where the first human encampment is. They are going to give it a permanent name: *Kokotova*."

After our pre-landing orbit was complete, we descended toward the planet's surface, gently gliding down through the clouds until we could see the details in the land gradually coming toward us. That was when Min Jaqeli approached me from behind and placed his hand on my shoulder. "Jenny, we are excited for you to be here," he said. "The Republic is indebted to you."

"I'm honored, Minister."

"We are counting on you to help us form the government, and to carve out justice for our new life on Ushguli. It's fitting to have an American. We could think of no better place to start."

Jaqeli stood in the isle and looked with us out the window in wonder. I could sense, however, his more immediate desire for my affirmation. I glanced back at the man in the leather jacket and sighed. As perceptive as Charlie was, I couldn't take her word for it. There were all sorts of due process problems in that. New law would have to address old problems.

I didn't need my implant to tell me what I was feeling: sadness and hope. I turned to Charlie, perhaps the purest embodiment of love, and felt sure. Seeing this fragile, virgin planet outside the window, I remembered my first encounter with Venkalaswaran in the darkened conference room years ago. *Of course, it's an Event, I am here and there. I never left one for the other.*

I turned to Jaqeli, who was patiently awaiting my elaboration. I didn't want to overpromise, so, like a good attorney, I equivocated: "Well, we'll see what we can do."

Nonetheless, I had great hopes.

Kevin M. Faulkner

Acknowledgments

I would like to thank Patrick LoBrutto from the Independent Editors Group for his initial encouragement and guidance as I tried to figure out the arc of my characters and direction of my story. I also appreciate Sally Arteseros of the Independent Editors Group who edited my early rough and confusingly verb-tensed drafts, as well as taking the time to point out the features of my story that might not be apparent to an audience unable to read my mind. As my story took shape into a novel, I am indebted to Erin Davis for encouraging me to give depth and dimension to the characters and settings, and for reminding me that even in fiction, perfect people are boring. I also must thank all the folks who took the time to read early drafts of my work and provide valuable feedback, allowing me to rethink and rework old and stubborn notions, and find impossible-to-catch hacks. Those closest to me were my greatest influence: my wife who encouraged me, patiently read my early drafts, and kept me grounded. And my daughter who at the tender age of eighteen gave me the sage advice to follow my heart and allow the reader to come to what I had to say, and not the other way around.

About the Author

Kevin M. Faulkner was writing stories and illustrations at an early age, especially science fiction. Interested in all things science, he obtained his undergraduate and graduate degrees in chemistry in his home state of North Carolina. While in graduate school he wooed a young woman with poetry and followed her to Texas where he eventually attended law school and married the girl. He has been an attorney for over twenty years and has authored numerous scientific papers, legal articles, and short stories.

Printed in Great Britain
by Amazon